Spooning

Spooning

a Novel

Darri Stephens
&
Megan DeSales

Broadway Books ∽ New York

PUBLISHED BY BROADWAY BOOKS

Copyright © 2006 by DARROW STEPHENS AND MEGAN DESALES

Published in the United States by Broadway Books, an imprint of
The Doubleday Broadway Publishing Group, a division of
Random House, Inc., New York
www.broadwaybooks.com

BROADWAY BOOKS and its logo, a letter B bisected on the diagonal,
are trademarks of Random House, Inc.

Book design by Fearn Cutler de Vicq

Cataloging-in-Publication Data is on file with the Library of Congress

ISBN-13: 978-0-7679-2139-8
ISBN-10: 0-7679-2139-9

PRINTED IN THE UNITED STATES OF AMERICA

1 3 5 7 9 10 8 6 4 2

FIRST EDITION

To our amazing families, the Stephens and the DeSales, we both thank you for all of your constant love and unwavering support.

And an extra spoonful of sugar to our inspirational mothers, Josie and Madge, who are still hoping that we'll find our true loves and our true cooking skills.

Spooning

August

Macie's Mojitos

Serves 1

1 tablespoon superfine sugar
Several sprigs fresh sweet mint
Juice of a whole lime (can add a little lemon juice too!)
1.5 shots white rum
Splash club soda
Ice cubes
1 lime wedge

Place sugar and mint in a tall glass and using the back of a spoon, mash the mint leaves into the sugar to release the wonderful mint flavor. Add the next four ingredients, mix, add lime wedge as garnish on side or top and serve.

These can be dangerous, so sip with caution! Enjoy with good friends or by yourself.

Gin and tonic, nine dollars. Way-too-tight Seven Jeans, one hundred and ninety dollars. New Nars lipstick, twenty-two dollars. First night out on the town with my girls, priceless. This was so exciting, our first real post-college bar experience. "Here's to our virginal glow, gals!" I shouted with glee, raising a shot of tequila. "We are independent women.

Watch us dance! We are not gatherers anymore. We don't sit at home drinking tea, gathering dust and fat asses. We are the hunters. Hunting is hard work. So we must quench our thirst as we work!"

Ahh, I'm finally here! My name is Charlie Brown (don't ask yet) and I am a New Yorker. It just took me about twenty-two years, five months, ten days, two hours, and five minutes to get here. But who's counting? I am a single goddess, a working girl, a creature like no other. I'm on my way to the top, moving on up. Yep, friends, brothers, ex-lovers, mothers and fathers, I am on my own in the big city and no one can stop me. Watch out New York, here I come! There, I said it. I said that cheesy cliché. You know you've all said it whether you said it out loud or kept it to yourself. It's the moment you know that you've finally arrived. Maybe it was your first kiss, the night you lost your virginity, or the day you got into college. For me, it was the day I moved into my first New York apartment. It might have taken me a few months, but boy, it was worth the wait.

Trying not to squirm as the tequila from the shot blazed down my throat, I thought about how far I had come in a mere twenty-four hours . . . Per the advice of Maria Von Trapp, aka Julie Andrews, "Let's start from the very beginning, a very good place to start." How much had I had to drink already?

&

First thing this morning, I was faced with a complex math dilemma. When a box frame which does not bend by design is 54 × 75 × 8 inches, how do you fit it up a stairwell that is 43 inches wide with corners that are 52 × 52 inches? As I squeezed my road trip–enhanced ass (yeah, McDonald's Big Mac with Super Sized Fries) between the banister and the box frame, my dad muttered, "All I had at age twenty-two was just a plain old AM/FM battery-operated radio. Boy, was that a classic." I rolled my eyes and jokingly threw two hat boxes, a box of picture frames, and a bag of hangers at him. He dodged the hangers artfully using the box frame as his wall of defense.

Gone are the college papers. Gone are the fraternity parties. Gone are the underage boys. Hello, Manhattan Men! Hello, Morning Meetings! Hello, Money (yes, with a capital "M"). I've been out for a couple of months now. No, not from some federal pen, but from college. You remember that warm cocoon of security? Sure, it didn't seem like that during the four years I was there. I could still remember complaining to my mother about how stressed I was over my upcoming exams and hearing her say calmly, "Remember, this is a free ride."

"What?" I'd responded with the indignation that I had perfected over the past ten years. "What do you mean *a free ride*? I'm working two jobs to pay for those overpriced textbooks I need for my senior thesis class, which I have to ace in order to receive the diploma that is necessary to succeed in the world. Never mind making you and Dad proud—you know a college dropout would not pass muster in our family."

"Darling, all I meant was that you're lucky to have these wonderful four years of no responsibility." My mother had a knack for digging herself in deeper and deeper under my skin. I liked to blame it on the fact that she was an only child and had never had to soothe a younger sibling's scraped knee or bruised ego. She could never quite come up with the right words in any sensitive situation. From countless miles away, she could, with the help of fiber optics, make my skin crawl and my defenses rise.

"Responsibility? Mom, I have two part-time jobs, six

classes—eighteen yes, that is eighteen—credits, plus a house to contribute to, and a boyfriend to appease when his lacrosse games fall a bit short!"

Of course, she'd just answered calmly, "I mean *real* responsibility. You do work hard, and we are proud of you, but you are not managing a household, supporting a family, working long days." As her argument started to peter out, I'd jumped in with my last defense: "Whatever, Mom! I need to go deal with my unburdened life." And I'd hang up on her.

But now here I am, on day one of my new life. And don't think I didn't have help on the big day. We had U-Hauled my prized possessions to New York on a Wednesday. My father drove, with my mother in the copilot seat, and me perched on an upturned laundry basket protecting a few plants. After spending the night in a Holiday Inn, we'd bumped along the rain soaked road to arrive at my new apartment building at 5:30 A.M. My dad is an early riser and he figured we'd be able to find a parking space if we were up before the birds. He was also math obsessed.

"With X amount of streets—and there are a lot of streets in Manhattan—you'd think there would be one parking space for us," he mumbled. "And there are two sides to every street," he went on. "Hence, multiply X by two, and don't forget the parking garages for those Sunday drivers." I sleepily tried to tune him out. Hell, did I still have to multiply? I had graduated.

"Dad!" I groaned. "Just double park, please. Mom can wait while we haul the loot." Round and round the block we go. Where is a parking space? Nobody knows!

"Ah, there it is," Dad said. "Home sweet home. 167 West Eighty-first Street." We both craned our necks to look up at the looming brown façade. There were four of us—three of us friends from college—moving in together on the Upper West Side. The realtor had pitched the building to us as one of the "few remaining true brownstones." When I questioned the fact that this brownstone had five floors (?), she said that if you took your fingernail to stonework, you would see that it would crumble into brown dust, hence "brown stone." Who knew if that was true. The important thing was that my friend Sydney's parents had wanted a doorman building, but the closest thing we found was a five-floor walk-up with a white-gloved doorman building next door.

"This building is on the historical registry!" my mom had marveled. I hoped that reason alone would excuse the crumbling cornerstones and dilapidated windowsills. As my father and I hauled up my box frame, he surveyed the interior.

"These hallways are pretty bare with just the doors," he commented. Yes, dear old dad, I thought, we are in an apartment building where no one has been assigned to hallway decor.

"And they're pink," he grimaced. "Makes me think of a seedy hotel."

Immediately my glamorized view of the halls in my grown-up apartment building had been reduced to those creepy hallways in *The Shining*. I turned my head fully expecting to see two sullen girls around the bend, then I looked the other way anticipating the dull roar of a Big Wheel. Red rum, red rum! Speaking of rum, I needed a shot of something strong, and it was only 6:20 A.M. Great. Thanks Mom and Dad. I was home.

❧

"What did you just say?" my mom asked casually as she put the last sock ball in my dresser drawer.

"Nothing. Um, so are you almost done?" I asked eagerly. It was almost 10:00 A.M. They'd been in my apartment for almost five hours. Mom and Dad had thought it would be cute to move their baby daughter into her first real apartment. And who was I to refuse? They'd let me lounge around the house for the past two months: free rent, free food, free money, free everything. So the least I could do was give them this final moment to feel like parents. But like all of us just getting started in this big, mean, exciting world, this was the day I was destined to sever the ties from the womb. Well, I'd like to think that this was the day.

"What? You don't need any more help?" my mother asked. You could see the frown forming. And with that impeccable timing of hers, those big blue eyes begin to fill with salty discharge. Yep, here came the tears. And let me tell you, I'm not talking about a few measly drops here and there. When Mom's floodgates opened, it was like the Red Sea, and this time, there was no Moses to come to the rescue. I sprung into sorry daughter mode.

"Mom, you know what I meant. Please stop crying."

"It's just . . ." she sputtered. She couldn't even get the words out.

"What, Mom?"

"You're just going to be so far away!" she cried. She had reverted to her "my baby's gone" routine. I'd been hearing this one since I first left for summer camp.

"Mom, it won't be so bad, I promise. How about this—why don't you take the train into the city next Saturday and meet me for a girls' lunch?" She actually stopped sobbing and cracked a minuscule smile. And there you had it ladies and gentlemen, the moment we'd all been waiting for.

"Oh, Charlie, I would love it. Are you sure?" Like I was going to say, *um, no I'm not quite sure, but my people will call your people and we'll figure something out.*

"Totally." I gave her my best smile. "I would love it."

Now I should stop here and say something in my mom's defense. She's the most hardworking, most dynamic, most selfless, intelligent woman I know. Today was just one of those traumatic moments for a parent. Saying good-bye to a child is a tough thing to do. The same thing had happened when they'd dropped me off at my dorm freshman year. Mom was a little emotional, as usual. Hugging and crying, crying and hugging. Fighting to be strong, even though she really wasn't. She was standing there sort of lifeless in the middle of my dorm room, lining the bottom of my underwear drawer with that smelly Laura Ashley paper. She loves doing that kind of stuff. Whether it is folding my socks in perfect little balls or making sure my panties and bras were color coordinated, she does things like this because they make her feel that I'm going to be all right, or at least well-organized.

I glanced over at my mother, who was smoothing a lacey bureau scarf across my dresser. She was muttering something about the insurmountable dust bunnies just as a NYC bus roared by sending a whiff of exhaust through my wide-open window.

"Okay Charlie, I think that's it." My dad, ever the voice of reason, emerged from the bathroom. In his hand he carried the toilet brush. Was our plumbing all set? Was his plumbing all set?

Suddenly, I felt myself turning into that little fourteen-year-old Charlie girl who'd been dropped off at soccer camp for the first time and spent her days feeling homesick and waiting for mail—that is, until she'd met Kent Schindele and had her first-ever summer romance.

"Don't go!" I wanted to scream. But then I remembered, I am an adult.

"Yeah, Dad, I think that does it." I gave him a false yet beaming grin. And with that, they were heading to the door. "So Mom, I'll give you a shout tomorrow about our girls' date. Cool?"

"Yes sweetie, I can't wait to hear from you." And there you had it. A few more kisses, a couple of bucks from my dad, and they were scurrying down the five flights of stairs.

꙳

*A*s if on cue, I could hear the soulful words of Mr. James Brown come blaring out from Syd's room. "Get up, get on up, get up, get on up . . ."

"So are they gone, Charlie-poo?" Sydney appeared sporting a wife beater, paint all over her face and a cigarette hanging off her lip. She was painting her room an unattractive shade of green. She'd been thinking of the green that you find in celebrities' hallways or kitchens, but she was getting the mossy color found in mental wards.

"Yes, I'd thought they'd never leave," I sighed. "Can I get one of those?" I reached out for a Marlboro Light and Sydney whipped out her hot pink lighter.

"I haven't touched a cigarette since graduation," I said.

"Are you kidding me?" Tara appeared in her bathrobe and went into the kitchen to grab a cup of coffee. "That's a long time to wait for some stick. You must almost be a born-again virg," she tossed out with a grin as she disappeared back into her room.

"Whatever," I sang. "I think you've had too much stick. You probably wouldn't know a good one even if it was in the palm of your little hand."

"Ha, ha! Very funny, Charlie," she called from her room. Before I could even take a drag though . . . *ring-ring*. I picked up the phone. A voice on the other end said, "I had a thought."

"Hey Mom, what's up?" I tried to sound as if I hadn't just talked to her in person about ten minutes ago.

"Well, you are in such a cultured mecca, I was thinking that you could probably find a cooking class somewhere in the city," she said.

"Cooking class?"

"Yes, there must be so many there."

"Mom, I can't cook. Why would I want to take a cooking class?" You could hear the annoyance building up in my voice.

"Precisely my point! You need to *learn* how to cook."

"Why?" I asked. "After all, I did just master boiling water!" This was a family joke. When I was thirteen, I'd been babysitting and had to make some mac and cheese for my charges. Due to my lack of cooking skills, I'd had to call my father to ask how to begin the process—that is, how to boil water. Needless to say, it had been hard to live that one down.

"But Mom, really, cooking is pure torture for me. I ruin everything. Everything!" I reminded her.

"Right, so you need to learn how to cook. How will you make sure you're eating properly otherwise? Now, I think you should find a class that focuses on the basics. You know cutting, slicing, dethawing—"

"Mom! I do know how to slice."

"Not frozen pizza, honey. I'm talking about being able

to make a decent dinner. Someday you may have a family to cook for."

"Wait, oh so I see. So this all goes back to the boyfriend issue." I heard my mother draw in her breath to begin making her case.

"No, no need, Mom. I see. You are worried that I will never get a boyfriend because I can't cook, thereby never having a boyfriend who will turn into a wonderful husband, thereby never procreating to give you several adorable grandchildren to spoil. Mom, we are in a new millennium! I have very talented digits that can flip open a cell phone to dial for takeout. It's one of the beauties of life in New York. Did you know that you can have McDonald's delivered here?"

"You can what? McDonald's? Don't the French fries get cold?"

"No, Mom, the fries are just fine. But back to my point—there are other ways to get a guy than by cooking him five-star meals. I have a well-manicured brain. Your four-year investment will pay off. Don't worry."

At times I swore that both of my parents had hidden agendas for my college years beyond my intellectual growth and fulfillment. My father saw it as a way for me to get a good job in order to help supplement their upcoming retirement. My mother saw it as a way to meet and marry an intelligent boy whose well-paying job would help supplement his in-laws' upcoming retirement.

"Anyway, I think you should consider it," Mom said. "I'll even pay for the classes."

I wasn't sure what to say. On the one hand, this was Mom's way of reaching out. On the other, I could tell that she thought of this charity as yet another financial investment for their future. "You are in a great city with ample opportunity to learn new skills," she went on, "And all I'm saying is that these new skills might . . . might attract a special friend."

"Come on, Mom," I said. "How old-fashioned can you be? Besides, you're no Julia Child. Remember—you used to hire babysitters just to make cookies with us."

"I'll admit my shortcomings," she retorted. "But I married your father because he loved hamburgers, and I am the queen of the backyard barbeque. I wish I knew more about cooking to this day, but you are young and have plenty of time to improve yourself. There are so many more opportunities for girls of your generation. And plain old hamburger men like your father are so hard to find nowadays."

"Okay, Mom!" Enough! Obviously she believed in the old adage, The way to a man's heart is through his stomach.

"I'll look into cooking lessons," I agreed. Who knows, maybe I'd get beyond the water-boiling stage. And maybe I'd even be able to gather enough cooking skills to whip up the recipe for the perfect man.

∽

Why was my mom more caught up in my love life than I was? Jesus. But deep down I wondered if she had a point. I now lived in a city where, I'd been told, your best friend was either a cab driver on a cold winter night or the local Chinese food delivery boy who put extra duck sauce in your bag because he knew you loved it. Couldn't kung po chicken be just as convincing to a man's heart as a homemade pot roast with garlic mashed potatoes? This was a question for the girls. They would set me straight. Cooking Classes vs. Delivery Boy? It was a straight-up question. The answer was either one or the other. Then again, there had to be some way to combine the two.

"Hey!" I called out from the middle of our empty living room.

"Who was that on the phone?" Tara shouted from the other side of the apartment.

"My mom just called—"

"Oh God, separation anxiety. It's the worst," Syd lamented.

"I just got a 'You're going to be single for the rest of your life' lecture."

"That woman is going to drive us all mad," Tara moaned. "But," she acquiesced, "I do love her!"

"You know she's right, C." Macie, my third roommate, appeared on the doorjamb wearing full workout gear and holding a glass of OJ.

"Mace, where did you just come from?" I said observing her spandex and sweaty ponytail.

"Oh, I went for a jog in the park and just did some abs and now I'm gonna hit the showers," she said.

Meet Macie, the queen of organization. The queen of time management. Always striving to be the best and look the best. She was absolutely perfect. Perfect, but in the sense that you couldn't hate her. Think petite, think perfectly put together. Voilà, Macie. She was our motivator. I often suspected that my mother wished that Macie was her child. Every time they saw one another, it was like I didn't exist.

"Oh Macie, you look so wonderful!" my mother would coo.

"Why hello, Mrs. Brown. You're looking just as marvelous as ever. Playing tons of tennis I can tell." Their encounters usually made me want to puke. Throughout college, Macie was the one who never melted a hotpot or mistakenly bleached her laundry. She went to all her classes during school, took perfect notes, and even put those little tabs in her notebooks to categorize the notes by subject matter and date. Around finals time, we would all swarm around her like bees on honey, just to get a quick glimpse of them. Not surprisingly, she made straight A's and, more important, now already had a job here in the city (we'll get to my situation later). She was Super Woman reincarnated—she could even pull off the slutty panty-slash-gold-belt ensemble, if she was into that kind of thing (it was more Tara's territory). But beyond her "Perfect Woman" stigma, Macie was our protector and our voice of reason. When in doubt, you always asked Macie and she'd give you the straight-up answer from her heart.

"You're the Energizer bunny," I said. "I didn't even know you were gone."

"So what's the problem with your dear sweet mother? God, I love that woman," she replied.

"My mom thinks that I ought to take cooking classes. She thinks that it will get me a man," I said.

"She's right," Macie said. "No man wants a girl who can't cook. It's simple fact. No cook, no guy. End of story."

"What? You think so? I mean, she does have a point, but you think that's still really important nowadays? The whole idea just sounds so 1950s-ish," I grumbled. From afar, I could hear Syd singing the Flintstone's theme song. I wasn't about to face the reality that I needed to go domestic on my first day in New York City alone. This was a conversation to have with all the girls and a little liquid libation.

"Is everyone around tonight?" I asked.

"Yes," all three replied in unison.

"Great! I'm going to invite the other girls over. How does that sound?" I asked. Our other old college housemates, Sage and Wade (who already scored a job as well), had also moved to New York City right after graduation.

"Sounds great."

"Perfect."

"Count me in!"

❧

"Y'all, we need a Cooking Club to solve this dilemma, not to mention to quell your mother's deepest fears!" Wade emphatically announced in that sweet southern accent of hers when we gathered that evening.

"A Cooking Club? What the hell is that?" we all scoffed.

Take the most undomesticated girls you could find, put them in the same neighborhood, and you'd have us six. But Wade was undeterred. A proper southern girl with a strong proclivity for sweater sets, thank-you notes, and separate monogrammed guest towels in the bathroom, she suggested that we "come together" once a month with a creative dish and recipe cards in hand. We'd "taste test" one another's dishes, then swap recipes.

"Then what do we do with the recipe cards?" we all wondered (though it was actually Sydney who said it out loud).

"My Latin teacher had us keep our index vocab cards in an old shoebox," I suggested.

"Or you could scrapbook them," suggested Wade.

"What kind of recipes? Oh, I'll make cheese and crackers!" yelled Tara.

"Cheese and crackers do not qualify as a recipe or a dish," Wade protested.

"Wouldn't it be a dish if you put it on a platter or something?" Sydney reasoned. Syd had a way of stating the obvious and interpreting everything far too literally. She also had a habit of redundantly stating things twice (we soon came to call it her "ADD," as in AdDendum Disorder—"I went to BC College!" she'd announce time and time again).

"You have not had my ensemble of exotic cheeses, like the triple-cream brie," Tara argued.

"Maybe my mother can ship me some of her cannolis?" Syd asked.

"No shipping and absolutely, I repeat, absolutely no delivery allowed, ladies," Wade ruled. "You must always make or bake. No exceptions." She was getting quite firm with these rules. She was a kindergarten teacher, and she was good at it. "Come on girls, let's make our mommas proud."

"I had a bad experience with a rule-ridden girls' club when I was little," I began.

"Oh and y'all, no photocopying of recipes," continued Wade. "Actually, you should handwrite the recipes on the cards. That way you can add your own little flair to each one. And y'all know how I love a little flair. I sure as hell don't want this big city to take away my little ole southern sense of style." Wade had that look on her face: the one she got when she dove into her ultracreative teacher mood zone. I could see flowered recipe cards of various colors adorned with stickers and glitter, and laminated in good firm plastic, floating above her head. I, for one, knew that my personal twists would probably be a bit scary for her. Boy, our little Scarlett O'Hara was in for a real treat with this crew.

Ten minutes later, Wade had declared this powwow our

first ever unofficial Cooking Club meeting. We might not all know how to cook, she proclaimed, but baby steps were just what the chef had ordered.

"I think in honor of tonight, we should whip up a Cooking Club specialty!" Sage sang.

"We already have a specialty? Damn, we're good!" Tara giggled. Sage swung open our fridge and stared, dismayed at the lack of contents. Then again, Skinny Sage always frowned and looked fraught with inner battles when she encountered visible signs of actual food.

Syd laughed, "We just moved in!" But like Vanna in front of the letters, Sage proceeded to highlight the bare necessities that had already made it into our humble icebox: a half-empty bottle of club soda, a jar of pickles (Tara's obsession—she was going to be a scary pregnant woman), a crisper drawer full of lemons and limes (courtesy of Mom, ever worried about the "dressings"), and a bottle of rum chilling in the freezer.

"How about some of Macie's Mojitos?" she threw out to us.

"Sage, you read our minds," Macie eagerly replied.

Now Macie knows her mojitos, hence the name. She introduced us to her dirty little secret during our senior year. A mere drop of her sneaky cocktail concoction will tingle your spine. The sweet and sour juice had a way of wrapping itself around every inch of your tongue and making it swell with glee. It was like going to Disneyland for the first time. You couldn't sleep before it happened and you wanted more after you'd experienced it. It was deadly—really easy to make and really good going down. What a kickoff! What a recipe!

"Hydration is important," rationalized Macie. The mojito actually tasted sophisticated—tangy yet minty with ice clinking ever so delicately. So there we were, embarking on the virgin voyage of our Cooking Club. How fitting we had chosen alcohol as the main dish.

✑

By eleven o'clock all us roomies were piled into our barely there bathroom, mojitos in hand, for some last-minute adjustments before heading out. Macie brushed her Bright Smile pearly whites. Tara was bent over, meticulously rubbing raspberry lotion onto her perfectly shaped legs. And Syd was sipping her mojito on the toilet.

"Mace, take off that top. You look like you're expecting!" Tara chided. Macie had put on an empire waist, peasant-looking top. It was a pretty green color and looked good with her eyes, but the free-flowing material was a little much.

"I'm not as trampy as you," Macie countered.

"I'm not telling you to be a ho, but I do think you should flaunt those abs you work so hard on." Backward encouragement, but encouragement no less coming from Tara.

"I work them so hard, because I don't have any. I am cursed with the McDougal middle," explained Macie. She lifted the green chiffony thing and grabbed at the white flesh covering her stomach. "Pinch an inch . . ." she quoted gleefully with her fist full of fat. Truthfully, she really wouldn't have had much to pinch if she stood up straight and wasn't grabbing as if she had to hold on for dear life.

"J. Lo wouldn't wear that top. J. Lo doesn't hide!" Tara had just recited one of our mantras. Macie nodded and turned back to her bedroom. If you ever wanted the last word among us all, you only had to somehow bring J. Lo into the mix. J. Lo. Those two simple words signified so much. Take a typical name like Jennifer, so American, so bland, so predictably the name you would find on a mug or a license plate key chain at a rest stop along Route 66. But now shorten it to a simple letter, and ta da! You have a superstar. Maybe my name could be shortened to C. C. Bro. But then again, I was no J. Lo. With her ample derriére and low-slung pants, J. Lo could shorten her name any way she damn well liked. And what a superstar—to have a big old bootie and never make one single excuse! Have you ever heard J. Lo complain that she missed the gym this week, or that she indulged in just a little too much Häagen-Dazs? As if! No, she swings that butt out there with pride. Every girl should take a lesson or two from her. Macie came back out in an adorable tube top.

"Notice the placement of the wide black stripe," she pointed to her midriff area, "Pure genius on the designer's part. Had to be a woman!" Ah, black—the essential color of New York City.

It was our first night out. No curfew, no homework, no worries, no nothing. It was our maiden voyage as single, soon-to-be professional ladies and we were on the prowl looking for love, drinks, and some Top 10 cheesy songs to ease our minds. Pink might say, "I'm coming out." Well, we were already out and ready to go . . . ready to get this party started right.

⟡

Part of me felt silly being so excited about all these "firsts." But you have to understand, for some of us, the only thing we had to get excited about back at school was the fact that "drink or drown" at the local bars started at 4:30 P.M. sharp on Fridays. For ten bucks, you could drink either really watered-down beer or imbibe on the themed shots of the evening (with such charming names as the Buttery Nipple or the Blow Job). Can you tell the oh-so-clever bartenders were of the male species? Overall, the whole "drink or drown" thing was pretty gross. The end result was that seven plastic beer cups later, you either felt really bloated or really tanked. Neither of which was really attractive. But we did it for four years and, by golly, we never missed a night.

We ended up at the bar around the corner from our humble abode, Top Shelf. Tuning out all the Top 10 cheesy music, shot glasses hitting the bar, and sultry whispers from boy to girl, I sat back and gazed at the endless possibilities life now had to offer. As I watched a girl daintily feed bar nuts into a cute boy's mouth, I had to consider that Mom could be right—the way to a man's heart might be through his stomach. Perhaps it was time to be proactive. I had lost too many possible boyfriends in college by not calling them back. My mother had never allowed me to make a call if the intended recipient was of the male species, but now that I was out on my own and an adult, I was going to be a hunter. So I began to assess the prospects at Top Shelf and immediately felt glum . . . How was I ever to find a desirable boyfriend/husband? I had grown up on Disney movies. I was waiting for my Prince Charming. Dark hair or blond . . . made no difference to me. But I was too cognizant of those random flaws that shouldn't matter. That one over there had a mole beneath his ear, the one by the stairs was biting his nails, the one talking to Tara had a bit of a mullet. (Hockey hair is so undesirable.) I knew that Prince Charming only existed in the movies, but what did I give up on? Where did I compromise?

As the night wore on, I thought about the road that lay

ahead. Robert Frost said, "Two roads diverged in a wood, and I—I took the one less traveled by . . ." Okay, so moving to NYC had not been so original, but I was determined to make my own path in this world from here on out. Although, as I felt myself getting sleepy, my current concern became finding my way back to my new apartment. What was my address again? Two roads diverged . . . and I was lost. The bar door opened to the sticky August night and I stepped out onto the sidewalk. But then the girls beckoned me back to do another shot at the end of the bar. Tara had her arm around Syd's neck—was it a friendly buddy gesture or a you-will-drink wrestling hold? There was a change in the air, like the wind shift in *Mary Poppins*. I looked at the dark sky and hoped for sunshine the next day. For the moment though, I was content to step back inside and bask in the amber glow (kind of like sunshine) of the numerous Amstel Light bottles lined up before us as we bonded.

September

Ever So Creamy Cheesecake

Easy Crust
>   Buy a ready-made graham cracker pie crust at grocery store

Filling
>   1 pound cream cheese (two 8-ounce packages)
>   1 cup sugar
>   3 teaspoons vanilla
>   2 large egg yolks, beaten
>   ½ pint sour cream

Preheat the oven to 350° F. Mix the cream cheese, ¾ cup of the sugar, 2 teaspoons of the vanilla, and the egg yolks together. Pour the filling into the crust and bake for 17 minutes.

Take the cake out of the oven and let it stand for 10 minutes to cool. Raise oven temperature to 450° F.

Mix together the sour cream, and the remaining ¼ cup of sugar and 1 teaspoon of vanilla. Spread this mixture on top of the cheesecake. Return to the oven and bake for 5 minutes. Be sure not to let the top brown.

Cool thoroughly, then refrigerate for a few hours and serve to your best friends with a smile.

"Hey!" I whispered. Okay, need to raise it up a notch. "Hey!!" I whispered/screamed. "I'm being robbed . . .

raped . . . pillaged and plundered! *Psst!*" Not one bruncher sitting outside at the restaurant in front of our building raised their hollandaise-sauce stuffed faces. I, in my pajamas and Earl Jean jacket (last-minute save), was leaning precariously over the rusty fire escape railing. I knew he, my assailant-rapist-murderer-arsonist-robber, would be throwing himself through my front door any minute. One more try, "Hey, help me!"

Where was the whistle, or at least a can of mace to throw on one of the daft brunchers' heads when you needed one? I grabbed my cell phone. 9-1-1-CALL . . .

"Nine-one-one, what is your emergency?" She had such a calm voice in my moment of despair.

"There is this man, a man trying to get into my apartment. He has a scratchy voice and is dressed in blue." I am such a detail-oriented person. As I proceeded to describe my would-be assailant, I pointed my left foot, reached down to the third rung, and grabbed the side rail with my right hand, while still holding my cell phone. (Note to self: Must get out of bed more often in time for those Lean and Lengthen classes.) I was ready to glide down the fire escape ladder, a modern-day, urban Grace Kelly. But as I lunged downward, my Chinatown tiger slipper dropped onto the plate of one of the brunchers. He looked up as if expecting rain, but then jumped up to catch me as I dangled from the bottom rung. Did anyone realize that fire escape ladders do not reach anywhere near the safe ground? As I finished up with the very nice emergency woman, I spun around, safe on the ground, only to find my assailant standing in front of me.

"Ahhhhh!" I screamed as only a woman can. Out from the front door popped the superintendent of my building.

"Charlotte!" my super interrupted. "This is Eduardo."

Great, now I had a name to put with his mug shot. "Eduardo is your utilities man."

"My what man?"

"The Consolidated Edison worker. He came to read your meter!" See how sick that sounds? "Your electric meter."

Two squad cars pulled up with the lights and sirens blaring. New York cop cars have two types of sirens. They have one annoying siren when they are "in pursuit" and another when they are "merely responding" to a call. Two cops got out, one of whom had his hand on his holster.

"Con Ed man? You?" I shouted as I spun around. My assailant nodded demurely. "Well, what was up with the scary-as-hell voice?"

"What scary voice?" he asked sounding as smooth as Barry White. The cops were looking rather confused.

"That one . . . I mean, well, what the hell is up with the jean jacket? What Con Ed man wears a jean jacket? Don't you have a name label? It's eighty degrees out, for God's sake! Who wears a stonewashed jean jacket?" I demanded. I turned to the cop, "What Con Ed man services without an official uniform? They should all wear an official uniform you know." I wrapped my Earl jacket tighter. The second cop had realized that he did not need to pull his gun and shifted his attention to the restaurant's brunch menu. By now all of the brunchers were paying attention. Funny how whispered screams of help did no good, but if you pointed out a fashion faux pas all New Yorkers snapped to attention.

⁂

My morning antics were the topic of conversation at our own late afternoon Sunday brunch. Some call Sunday the

Sabbath, while others call it a day of rest. It's considered by Christians to be the holiest day of the week. Whatever your religion tells you to observe on Sunday, we here in New York celebrate it a little differently. We gather and congregate at various outdoor cafes and eateries and celebrate the almighty brunch. The service typically begins around noon and can go on for hours, especially if Bloody Marys or Mimosas are involved. While many repent their sins through prayer, we here in the city eat and drink them away.

Growing up, the biggest day of the week for my family had been Sunday. Sunday was the day the entire family went to church, and better yet, went out to brunch afterward. And for somebody who preached the godliness of refined culinary skills, my mother really lived for Sundays. If this was a day of rest for the one up above, by golly, this was a day of rest for her too. She'd be damned if she would cook, clean, or do anything else on this day. I learned at an early age that Sunday was the day to repent and to stuff our faces, which I guess meant that I was destined to be a New Yorker.

After what seemed like one hundred Hail Marys and a million amens in church, we would cram into our beat-up, moss green Volvo station wagon and head to our favorite brunch spot. Now while most families go to civilized diner-bistro type deals that serve runny scrambled eggs, greasy bacon, and pulped-out OJ, my family strayed from the norm. We went to an all-you-can-eat, stuff-yourself-till-you-feel-like-you're-gonna-vomit type joint. Our slice of heaven was called Don Juan's El Paso Cantina. Yep, we had rice and beans, cheese enchiladas, and beef tacos all before 10:30 A.M. As kids we thought we'd died and gone to pork-out heaven. In that hour and a half, my brother, sister, and I would hit the buffet about fifty times and work our little bodies into food comas. You can imagine the fart contests in the car on the way home. My dad would coax the mariachi band over with dollar bills and make countless Julio Iglesias requests. Meanwhile, my mother would sit back in the cozy booth, sip her frozen fruity drink, and smile the entire time. This was her idea of heaven and we loved it too.

Now, as a certified adult, I didn't just go to brunch, I *did* brunch. Let's hear it for all the brunchers of the world! Could I get an "amen" from the audience? And now after a few weeks, I'd finally mastered the inner workings of the brunch system. Not only did you have to find the ultimate noshing spot, the even trickier part was fitting your entire congregation around one measly little table. But it gets worse. Everyone in your group had to be present, I repeat, *present* in order to get seated. All the New York hostesses just shake their haughty noses at the standard lies:

"My friend just ran to the ATM."

"The one who's not here isn't really going to eat anyway."

"She just called from the taxi, and she's stuck due to a huge accident in the park on Seventy-ninth Street!"

"She ran across the street for cigarettes . . . oh, I know she can't smoke inside anymore . . ."

Let's just say that my posse was "brunch challenged." To get six females out of bed, dressed, and out the door by noon is a tough feat to accomplish, especially when your group is usually hung over and lying in the fetal position in the living room watching reruns of 90210 on the FX channel. If you are just one minute late to an egg white omelet and turkey bacon sermon, your entire service could be delayed by as much as two hours.

But brunching goes beyond just eating; brunchers chat and chew at the same time, and some actually soak in the atmosphere around them (especially by watching young girls hang from fire escapes overhead); and thank God, because if my fellow eaters did not "love thy neighbor as thyself," well, then I could have been in a sticky situation today. I could have died before I had the opportunity to indulge myself in my last double half-decaf nonfat latte.

∽

*S*o naturally, my morning death-defying act was the hot topic at brunch. Tara actually rebuffed a smooth approach by a hot wanna-be-actor busboy to get a dose of daily drama that was not centered around her.

"Now you have an angry Con Ed man who knows where you live," she threatened. "He's probably pissed that you thought that he was a scary rapist trying to break in, and he might have gotten some vengeful ideas. You shouldn't put such ideas into people's heads."

"Stop! Stop, right now." As if I hadn't already had enough emotional damage for one day.

"She's got a point," Wade chimed in. "Y'all, I had this psycho rug-cleaning man who got mad when I questioned how professional his work was. I mean, there were gray edges on my supposedly 'clean' white rug, and I swear, I thought he was going to hunt me and my idealist rug cleaning beliefs down! I can still see him shaking his finger at me as I shook *my* finger at the still dirty rug. He was mumbling about his evil plans the whole way down my stairs."

"But you are alive today," I said, gulping down three swigs of my mimosa.

"Alive, yet fearful of rug-cleaning men. A scarring experience overall. Y'all, we really should be making this brunch at home," she suggested.

"What?" Tara asked through a mouthful of molasses-laced dark bread. I swear, I saw her use sleight of hand as if she was ready to abscond with a few rolls. "Wade, we just started our Cooking Club! And all we made was of liquid substance!" she groaned.

"Plus, that omelet that you ordered?" I pointed out. "Think of all the ingredients you'd have to buy." I knew that would get Wade as she was saving her pretty pennies for a cute top she was eyeing at Scoop. "Broccoli, onions, tomatoes, portobello mushrooms, shitake mushrooms, green peppers, red peppers . . . should I continue?" Wade shook her head as she sipped her fresh-squeezed orange juice.

"Don't forget the feta and goat cheeses," Syd read from the menu. I could see Sage's skinny stomach convulsing at the list of food.

"Fine, but y'all, we have to step it up next meeting. Make your mother proud, Charlie."

"We are not doing this for my mother," I reminded her. "We are doing this for ourselves."

"You mean you've actually embraced this concept?" Wade raised an eyebrow.

"Well, maybe. Come on, ladies. We are talented individuals! Plus, we have to have some skill in the kitchen so that we have something to register for at Williams-Sonoma when we get married." The other five nodded as we moved on to other topics.

&

Somehow, Sunday brunch turned into Sunday happy hour, which led right into Sunday cocktail hour at Top Shelf that night. Not a problem since the following day, Monday, was Labor Day—ironically named since we were celebrating a lack of labor. I was especially labor-free as I was still unemployed. We were stashing our coats in the corner when "he" walked in. By "he" I mean Mr. J. P. Morgan, who strolled through the door with his band of boys.

Mr. J. P. Morgan was someone I'd met during happy hour a couple of weeks ago. I had actually noticed his smile from the doorway of the bar. Really! It wasn't like he was in a spotlight or anything; rather, I just happened to find a clear shot of him from about twenty feet away, through a crowded bar, and with my nearsighted eyes. Fate! And his smile—well, did I mention that I noticed his smile first? Most girls say they notice a guy's eyes in those *Cosmo* surveys, followed closely by butts, with a few voting for hands. But smiles did it for me every time. I wanted a man who would smile at me and I would automatically grin back. You need that spontaneous happiness in life during traumatic moments, tumultuous fights, or just a gray winter morning. Mr. J. P. Morgan had an adorably crooked smile that reached his eyes. Ahh!

Tara had told us all the very first night we were in New York that the only way we were going to meet "Mr. Right" was if we attended gallery openings, society parties, and went to the grocery store on Sunday around 6 P.M., or happy hour after work. I quickly discovered that the grocery store concept was a farce. Forget what the glamour magazines tell you. They're all lying. You tell me, how are you supposed to make small talk in the vegetable aisle? I did happen to see one hot guy in the fresh produce aisle my first week here. With Tara's mantra in my head, I sprung into "available single girl" mode. Should I look sexy while perusing the cucumber selections? No that was too slutty. He would probably think I used them for God knows what in my spare time. Why not act coy while pinching the cantaloupe? I glanced down to my barely there A-cups and figured that the cantaloupe move was false advertising. In the end, all I accomplished was following him around with a bag of bagels and cream cheese in my hands. If he headed for the frozen pizza aisle, I suddenly garnered an interest in frozen tater-tots. As he headed for the healthy granola, I feigned fascination over the array of marshmallow cereals. When he headed for the shaving cream (no, don't touch that Clooney-esque five o'clock shadow!), I came dangerously close to picking up a can of shaving cream and asking him which would be the gentlest on my legs.

"Excuse me, do you recommend foaming gel or traditional shaving cream?" I'd imagine myself asking as I extended my barely clad leg in his direction. This fantasy ended quickly when I'd absently pointed my toe only to notice my unshaven ankle peeking out of my now bleach-stained sweatpants that sported my high school mascot, a donkey, on the ass. Attractive, right?

So after scrapping the grocery route, I decided that the easiest course of action for someone in my position would be happy hour. It was a no-brainer: alcohol and boys. This was going to be a walk in the park. First of all, Top Shelf was close to home: easy access from our front door to theirs. Second, the drinks were cheap as hell: two-dollar draft beers and mixed drinks for four hours. And on top of all that, we got dinner too! Happy hour was also girls' hour which meant we could eat all the chicken wings and blue cheese dip our hearts desired. Okay, so the place was a dive and it probably should have been called Bottom Shelf, but it didn't seem to matter.

But back to Mr. J. P. Morgan. There he was, and tonight I knew that I wanted to be with him and him only. He was perched on a stool sipping bourbon on the rocks and chatting with some work buddies. His tie was slightly loose around his neck, and his jet-black hair was tousled forward, falling just above his gorgeous blue eyes. Goddamn it, he really was a bona fide hottie. He's what the girls called "a true suit." Over the past couple of weeks, we'd danced—okay, it was a group circle kind of dance, but our hips bumped and he stepped on my toes at least twice. Could the toe stepping have been intentional? Must check with Tara . . . But to date, nothing truly significant had happened. He was a familiar face at what now was a familiar joint.

I surveyed his outfit: a striking navy blue Brooks Brothers suit, a button-down, hot pink, checked (extra starch) shirt, accented with a pair of shiny monogrammed cufflinks. Anyone could tell that he was a man who made deals over lunch. But the best part was that he was only twenty-four years old. That first night, Tara had done some dignified snooping. You gotta love older men! He looked like the type who would pay for the taxi, open the door, and buy you drinks. What a dream! Mom would love him and make blueberry pancakes and fresh-squeezed orange juice for breakfast when we visited on weekends. Dad would take him to the club for a quick round and an in-depth discussion about life goals over a glass of Scotch. Oh, I can just see the wedding now. Vera Wang, peonies and hydrangeas, pink striped tent, Nantucket. Now don't get me wrong, I'm not someone who plans this all out, like Wade—I just daydream really, really big.

As Mr. J. P. Morgan high-fived his friend at the bar, my bitch radar immediately clicked on. With my extra set of eyes,

I noticed several obstacles: a peppy-looking brunette smiling at him; a tall, curvy, dark-haired lady ("lady" due to the extra years on her which, in turn, made her not allowed in Top Shelf) who crinkled her eyes toward him in a flirty glance over her glass; and a bed-headed blonde who was exuding sex his way from another corner. If I just knew, had a sign from above, that he was destined to be mine, then I wouldn't have to sweat these competitors while I waited, hoping that he would see me and make his way over to join our group in the back.

Syd had ordered a Citron and soda and was gleefully telling us about her new job. Besides Macie and Wade having jobs (which didn't really count since they had lined them up before graduation), Syd was the first to get a job in NYC. As psyched as we were for her, it made the gut-wrenching, tummy-thumping feeling of employment anxiety pound a little harder.

Syd was the newest fake hair distributor on the block; selling wigs, falls, and extensions all out of a fancy looking toolbox like an Avon lady. "So I just go from salon to salon," she explained. "Indian hair is the ultimate in quality." Tara began to choke on her rum and Coke. "No, really. Jessica Simpson uses our products."

"Hairball," Tara quipped pointing to her throat, prompting herself to gag harder. Meanwhile, I was distracted following Mr. J. P. Morgan oh-so-subtly with my alcohol-glazed eyes. Suddenly my heart stopped. He'd turned and was making his way back toward us.

Typically, he and his rowdy Brooks Brothers buddies traveled in a pack, congregating around the pool table in the corner. But this time it was different. I held my breath as he made his way south to my end of the bar. Then I understood: he was trying to garner the attention of the bartender for a refresher.

He had been heading my way because there was an open stool, not because the open stool was next to me. He let out a dramatic frustrated sigh.

"Ha!" I laughed, not realizing it had been out loud. He swung his baby blues on me.

"Oh, sorry." I stammered. "Not laughing at you. It's just your sigh sounded like my dog, well, my parents' dog, well, not that you remind me of a dog . . ." my loquacious conversation petered out.

"Ha!" Now it was his turn. I was sure that my cheeks matched my Cosmopolitan. "I just can't get the bartender's attention," he grumbled, waving his hands like a high school cheerleader as the bartender breezed by.

"Hey, Tommy!" I called. The bartender spun around like a gold medal ice skater.

"Charlie, what can I get you?" I looked at my almost-full drink. Taking a huge swig, I said, "I'll take another of these and whatever he needs." Mr. J. P. Morgan gave me an appreciative glance, in which I basked, before he rattled off a list of drinks.

"Thanks," he said as he balanced the glasses and bottles as made his way back toward his group by the pool tables. I watched as he deposited the drinks—and then turned and headed back my way.

"So smile for me," he commanded.

"What?"

"Just smile." I faltered and then gave him my best Farrah Fawcett beam.

"Yep. That's what does it, Charlie." He remembered my name! Smartie!

"Does what?"

"Makes men fall to their knees in servitude." Oh, I liked

the sound of that. Suddenly, it was just him and me, talking and laughing. Our hands were on each other's hips and drinks were definitely gracing our lips. For tonight, I was J. P. Morgan's target and he was a heat-seeking missile ready to explode upon impact.

༄

*N*ow it's hard to tell if the deal closer was my sexy, albeit modest, rendition of Britney Spears's "Hit Me Baby (One More Time)" minus the school girl outfit, or if it was the five Dewar's on the rocks he'd sucked back within a two-hour span. In my grown-up, college-educated opinion, I always say screw the minor details and go with your gut. And my gut was telling me that the planets were aligned and the signals for me and J. P. were flashing go.

Well, as luck would have it, somewhere between Amstel Light sips and a lipstick check, Mr. J. P. Morgan whispered ever so sweetly into my ear, "Wanna go home, Charlie?" Did I wanna go home? Are you kidding me? I was home in bed with you about four hours ago in my innocent little mind. What took you so long? Home, sweet home!

"You read my mind," I casually tossed out. "Are you thinking my place?" I could hear it now, the girls screaming at me for throwing out a cheesy line, but there really was a method to my madness. The only reason I'd offered up my apartment was because I had my toothbrush, my sensitive-skin face wash, my clean April-fresh sheets, my Vicky's sassy lingerie, my matching mugs for that "morning after coffee for two," and my two-ply, ultra-padded toilet paper. I could look my best and be my best before, during, and after our glorious hook-up. Plus, there was no way I was going to be the one doing the walk of shame to the subway tomorrow morning. Snap! This was going to be the best night of my life. And with that, I felt his hand grab mine and we were off and walking down the street to my abode. My heart was four beats away from cardiac arrest. The kissing, the cuddling, the endless talking to the wee hours of the morning. This was it. I was gonna close the deal with this sexy older man, even if it killed me.

∽

*F*ast forward to J. P. and me, side by side, together at last, all warm and snuggly underneath my fluffy down comforter. Thank God I was wearing my lacy black g's with the hot pink flowers stitched on front. I could feel the glow just growing inside me. I have finally found Mr. Right, I thought. Mr. All-American. And all it took was one measly little month. This finding Mr. Right had been a walk in Central Park for *moi*.

Now all I had to remember was what Tara had taught me the other night. Shit, was it the right or the left side? I think she said, "Charlie, you are always in the right when you are on the right." So if I lie on the right side, I will elongate my torso, making myself look skinnier! Pretty simple rule. So with that I rolled over and assumed the right position. Poof! Fat be gone. And by golly, Tara was right. Within a few seconds, Mr. J. P. Morgan busted out with, "You are so tiny, Charlie!"

Okay, the lights were out, so maybe he couldn't really see, but he could feel and at that moment he felt a tiny me. And I felt, as he pressed his body closer to mine, that he was actually *not* so tiny. Holy cow! I'd hit the jackpot. Wait till the girls hear about this one tomorrow. I had a thing about no sex on the first night, but that didn't mean I was inhibited. If you find a talented man you should never deny him the opportunity to fully express himself. Somehow I ended up with my head down at the foot of my bed, hanging over the edge. I stared at our clothes scattered on the floor, which now seemed like the ceiling, and felt myself getting a head rush of a different sort! I was ready to squeal but felt like I didn't quite know him well enough to perform my high school cheerleader routine. So I flipped a leg over his head, sat up, and straddled him. He nuzzled my neck.

"You feel so good," he mumbled.

"Look into my eyes," I wanted to command. I was feeling romantic along with everything else. But, after ten minutes of panting and pawing like a college grad with honors, Mr. J. P. Morgan managed to come, basically by himself, despite the ounces of hard alcohol he had consumed. With no effort on my behalf, I mean not even a wiggle of my wrist, he convulsed, swore (oh-so-elegantly), and moaned my name one last time. I know that the male physiology is quite different than the female's, but I did give myself kudos in that he had to be sooo excited by my mere presence that he couldn't contain himself!

But back to the bigger headline of the night: J. P. had called me "tiny." I, Charlotte Brown had never been labeled "tiny." Nor have I ever been considered small boned. I was always the big boned, with a tiny waist and thicker thighs kinda gal. I was small on top, tiny in the middle, and I sported those athletic/soccer legs. So to hear this come out of a guy's mouth, especially from Mr. J. P. in the sack, felt pretty incredible.

"Um, you think so?" I asked.

"What?" he replied rolling back to face me.

"Uh, you were saying I felt good?" That was what he said, right? Was I talking too much? I guess these types of situations don't call for too much small talk. Who was I to think that I could get sexual accolades and a body compliment in one night? But I hadn't quite blown it because in between one of my over-analytical, self-deprecating moments, he chimed in and saved my embarrassed soul.

"Oh, yeah, Charlie. You felt really good tooonnniiig . . ." And then he was out. Fast asleep. That was it. Kaput. Finished.

He had wrapped up the evening without crossing the Ts. Shouldn't he have made sure that I too was fully satisfied before he passed out? Was I being hypersensitive? Maybe he had been hurt badly before, and therefore put himself as numero uno every time. Were his preppy good looks just the mask on a hardened interior? Could I ever be his top priority? Or would I wind up as one of those bitter Park Avenue wives in a fur coat and slippers taking the dog for a walk at 2:30 A.M., alone? Regardless, he still had me on the dotted line. Screw it. I had plenty of time to find out what made this Ken doll tick. I made an executive decision to stop psychoanalyzing the minor details of our first encounter.

Nevertheless, I was up all night staring at his every inch. You can learn the darnedest things about someone while they are sleeping. He tended to jump while dreaming, not unlike a dog, but when I'd lay my hand on his arm, he'd sigh and fall back into a deep sleep. He also talked in his sleep—kind of a singsong mumbling. I wondered what he sounded like singing in the shower. He had a little tattoo of a Tweety Bird on his ankle. Trust me that was a tough spot to inspect, but it's there. Little yellow wings. Teeny orange beak. So darn cute!

So here we were: 7:00 A.M. and Mr. Morgan and I were lying arm in arm, smooth leg with hairy leg, bedhead to bed-head. Ahhhhh! It was official. We had made it through the night. Not once did he say, "Oh Charlie, I'm sorry, I gotta go. Early meeting." Or "Hey Charlie, I have an appointment to get my hair cut." Oh, no. I could tell that this baby was all mine—it was written all over his face. I just was hoping that we'd continue the night before, move from the preview to the feature presentation. Then afterward, we could do breakfast. That would totally close the deal for us. A "couple breakfast" would make it officially official. Who cares about morning breath when you can share waffles and whipped cream together?

With his hair sticking straight up, he rolled over and handed me my one pillow, which he had snatched during the night.

"Sorry," he mumbled. Was he really talking about the pillow or our incomplete sex romp from the night before? (Note to self: Buy another pillow ASAP.)

"No problem. I can sleep on a floor, so I didn't even miss it," I soothed. I prayed that my mascara wasn't smeared all over my face as I resisted the temptation to rub my sore neck and wipe the sleep out of his left eye. God, his eyes were a great shade of blue. Not dismal gray but that steel color that someone like James Bond would have. I could imagine how deep in color they'd be when he looked into my own dull brown eyes and said "I do" someday.

"I think I have to go into the office today," he sighed.

"On Labor Day?" You could hear the disappointment in my voice.

"I have to log the hours now, show the big guys that I am eager, and I am," he added, "so that I can retire by thirty-five. I want to be able to go to my kids' Little League games." Oh, he has dreams! Oh, he wants kids (I forced myself not to ask how many). I was slowly learning about him, making my way to his heart. I ran my hand over his chest.

"Too bad I can't sneak you in my bag to work," he smiled lazily. Those half grins were so addictive. He swung his legs out of bed and paused. I reached under the sheets and tossed him his boxers.

"You know me so well," he joked. But I did! Immediately I could tell he didn't like walking around in the buff—so sad, but modesty is commendable. He walked toward the door and tossed me my undies (a true gentleman). We were in sync. I rolled over and onto the television remote. MTV's *Real World* switched on and the dysfunctional roomies' arguing blared through the room.

"Love this show!" J. P. declared when he returned. He leaned back against my teddy bear. Score! He was not moving for another, check the watch, eight minutes. I snuggled closer as he and I began to dissect each of the wayward roomies on the show. I was so getting beneath that hardened NYC male exterior! When the episode ended, I heard an imaginary bell toll, and this Cinderella gave Mr. J. P. Morgan her best Carrie Bradshaw wink as he headed out the front door.

❧

Forget the morning after. I always lament the whole day after. I mean, how do you follow up a night of good (sorta) lovin'? You don't want to stay in bed—too many memories. You don't want to go for any sort of celebratory lunch—you are now strictly watching your newly scrutinized waistline. You don't want to sit around watching TV—too much time to think. What to do? It was official, after such a night of highs, I was having a day of the autumn blues. Dr. Phil should do some advising on alcohol depression. Oh, the lows a little imbibing will bring one to!

So what to do? Why, clean! My mother would be so proud. I am actually a very thorough cleaner when the mood hits me. French maids had it right with the outfits. Talk about looking good and putting on airs while attending to daily duties. After dropping a tablet in the toilet (so laborious), I squirted some Fantastic on the counters. Fantastic, by God, is fantastic on those nasty red wine rings. Its label should proclaim such powers. But forget vacuuming—vacuums are so invariably expensive and therefore—not part of a New York budget, mind you.

And what is the pièce de résistance in apartment cleaning? Drumroll please for the Swiffer Sweeper, the new millennium's greatest invention! Only New Yorkers can truly value the sheer genius behind the Swiffer. New York apartments seem to be covered with dust bunnies and a thin layer of soot no matter how near the heavens one may live. How the soot gets in the tightly enclosed, air-conditioned apartments is one mystery. How dust bunnies the size of city rats accumulate in 400-square-foot apartments is the other mystery. No amount of sweeping or mopping will grab those bunnies or shine that soot. This is where the Swiffer saves the day. J. Lo must totally Swiffer (or have someone do it for her). With its highly technologically enhanced, lemon-scented, static cling–dryer sheet contraption, it snags the dust devils and licks the soot clean.

Deep in the doldrums with rubber gloves and scummy buckets, I had lit upon a wonderful idea—a two-step system to clean effectively. Step one: Dry Swiffer the designated area. Step two: Swiffer Wet Jet said area. But who knew the Swiffer Wet Jet that Macie had bought would be so complicated to assemble? I was determined, though, since I wanted my floors to shine. Mr. J. P. Morgan would want shiny floors to reflect his shiny polished loafers (could parquet floors shine?). I knew which parts of the wet Swiffer were the top, middle, and bottom (yeah, college grad!). However, the container that held the magic elixir was confusing. Did one attach it first? Did the narrow part attach to the top or bottom? How was it supposed to attach? Screw? Stick? And these damn blue dishwashing gloves protecting my manicured nails were not helping. I ended up just pouring some of the cleaning solution onto the floor and mopping it up by hand with the absorbing pads. The girls found me on the floor, staring up at the ceiling, waiting for divine intervention . . . my cleaning mood was finished.

"Incense? I hate incense!" Tara rolled her eyes as she walked into the apartment. Macie plopped down on the couch.

"Tara, sweetheart, that is the enticing scent of cleaning supplies. Smell the subtle tanginess of bleach? Can't you almost taste the oranges in the citrus window spray? And breathe in that mountain fresh air found in the bottle of mopping solution! We are in a plethora of clean smells, something we need to grow accustomed to."

"Ooh, I know a cleaning lady for seventy-five dollars an hour!" Tara volunteered missing the thrust of Macie's speech.

"I think the apartment smells like the Strawberry Shortcake dolls I used to eat," Syd tossed out.

"Eat?" we all questioned simultaneously.

"Um-hum," confirmed Syd absentmindedly. "I just loved their scent and would suck on the hair." I had a sudden image of Syd at two feet tall, sucking on one of those miniature doll's pink hair like a baby with a bottle.

"You were the type that probably ate glue too, huh?" theorized Macie.

"No, I am all about the smell, and glue smells like melted horses." We let that one go for another time. "But the Strawberry Shortcake dolls smelled delish. Lemon Meringue was my fav-or-ite," she declared licking her lips.

"Do you think she scoffed down some My Pretty Ponies too?" whispered Tara.

"Back to the cleaning issue," interrupted Macie. "There are four of us here! It wouldn't kill any of us to pick up a toilet brush once in a while—"

"I hate those phallic things. Maybe if the toilet brush was cleaned in between uses—" Tara interrupted back.

"Clean the cleaning supplies? That's funny coming from you! Just thank Charlie for doing all of this work."

"So, you didn't get laid, huh?" Tara asked me. She had this annoyingly uncanny sense. "Just kidding," she grinned. "Thanks, chickie!"

❧

After tidying our apartment, I decided to take a walk through the park in search of an answer about my professional life—or lack thereof. Midway across the Great Lawn, I had it (basically due to the fact that I was hungry). I had figured out my million dollar idea and I was a mere twenty-two! I, Charlotte Brown, would be the CFO of an up-and-coming company in charge of putting pizza stands in Central Park. Think about it. Everyone already flocked to the Popsicle stands in the summertime. They walked through the winding paths with blue and red stained lips. Weight-obsessed runners did the six-mile loop around a plethora of profitable hot dog stands. And the two-dollar pretzels were the favorite food of the plump park pigeons. So why were there no pizza stands? It was only logical.

New York City is known for its flat, greasy pizza. Marketing and presentation would be key. The stands would have yellow and orange stripped awnings, and we would use matching plastic plates. Chic, yet practical was my motto. Pizza Perfection . . . Slice of Delight . . . Metropolitan Munchies . . . Thanks to me, you'd be able to throw a little Frisbee, blade a few hills, and then grab a hot slice!

Buoyed by my own optimism that my ever-blossoming creativity would one day make me a self-made millionaire, I decided to walk into the Orange Bank near our apartment to open a basic, no-fee checking account. Time to establish myself as an official resident and bona fide adult. I had a whopping fifty dollars left in my wallet and figured it was enough to start an account. After all, you gotta start somewhere.

"So your present employer is?" asked the sweet balding banking man behind the customer service desk.

"None," I said.

"None? N-O-N-E?"

"Yes, none," I repeated definitively.

"What kind of company is this?" he asked as I saw him neatly printing "None" under "Employer" as if it were a Fortune 500 company.

"No, I mean I'm not working. Not working yet," I added.

"Oh, well, that is a problem. You have to wait until you have a financial backer for your business account." I wanted to ask him if a mom and a dad counted as references but decided otherwise. Still, I was not to be discouraged; I gave him an understanding smile and waltzed out with the dignity of a major CFO. I still had my brilliant idea to start my own business, thereby someday having the financial backing to open the said basic checking account. Duh, it was a no brainer!

$\mathcal{A}$ week later, I had yet to cash in on my multimillion dollar idea, but the mere lightning bolt of inspiration put me in the mood to rewrite my résumé a few days later. New York City rent would not allow for slacking off on the job hunt. Truth be told, I wasn't actually rewriting my résumé, but rather playing around with the format. Center the name? Ten point or twelve point font? To bullet or not to bullet? Bold the job title? Yes, "Camp Counselor" looked much better in bold print. How many tenths could I add to my grade point average without inflating it to a questionable level? After the six weeks of unemployment, I decided I would take any job thrown my way.

It wasn't that I hadn't been actively searching for a job. In fact, I'd been working every angle. First, I went the college alumni route, but that didn't really pan out. One thirty-something alum had informed me that she received an average of thirty phone calls a month from desperate recent grads. She estimated that I was lucky caller number one thousand in the current calendar year. In any event, she sounded hassled. (I could guess that her next "to-do" in her Palm Pilot would be to call the university and tell them to take her off the alumni phone distribution list.) She seemed to be taking her exasperation out on me because first she said that I had a "lack of work experience," and then she informed me that I didn't come off as "professional enough" on the phone! Rewind. First of all, don't give me shit about the work experience, lady—I just graduated. And second, I might not be CEO material, but I was sure as hell fit to be an "executive assistant." Obviously, she wasn't down with collegiate nepotism and therefore didn't help me. It was clear that I needed a totally different approach to the rat race.

My next tactic was much more successful and ultimately helped me land my first real interview at a television show called *Sunshine & Sensibility*. *Sunshine & Sensibility* was a daily nationally syndicated show seen by millions upon millions of viewers who consisted mostly of stay-at-home moms. It was a cross between a *Romper Room* episode and an Emma Thompson movie. A style show for the home entertainers. I was learning that friends of family can be great job connections, and that friends of family friends can be helpful too! Thank you Macie's dad, and thank you Macie's next-door neighbor's dad's coworker's sister.

"The neighbors on the right," emphasized Macie. "Not the ones on the left—they let their dog do his business all over our lawn, which drives my father crazy. But the MacCombers are wonderful. We share a volleyball net with them in the summer, and Mrs. MacComber lets my mother cut her gorgeous flowers anytime she wants." Point being that the MacCombers were generous people. I realized just how generous when Mr. MacComber called on his coworker's sister who worked at *Sunshine & Sensibility*. Mr. MacComber, without meeting me, went out on a limb and asked this kind woman to arrange an interview with human resources for me. Ta da! I had an interview at *Sunshine & Sensibility* with the head of HR at the network the very next day.

❦

"*C*harlotte Brown, nice to meet you," gushed the HR woman. "You come so highly recommended from Ms. Jones" (aka, Macie's next-door neighbor's dad's coworker's sister). "You also have a well-rounded academic background. But tell me about your work experience."

Gulp. Obviously my inflated grade point average hadn't overwhelmed her enough to skip the rest of my résumé. Which illustrious work experience should I attempt to elaborate on? Sailing instructor, babysitter supreme, or house cleaner ("Good money under the table," my mother had rationalized). Think positively! Think positively! I glanced around at all the useless certificates, not diplomas, on the walls documenting the special HR conferences that she had participated in, hoping to find some inspiration.

"Now Jane—Jane Dough that is," she paused to make sure I knew who Jane was. Jane deserved a single name like Cher. Jane Dough was the quintessential homemaker-homemaker turned gazillionaire. She had taken the stay-at-home woman's endless house chores and had turned them into "domestic arts." The rubber gloves with the diamond band . . . think Jane.

"Jane needs a new production assistant. Now, the person who takes on this role of production assistant will have many complex duties. She will have to organize the extensive tape library." I nodded. Little did they know that I could recite the alphabet forward and backward.

"She will need to make packets each day for the powers that be containing articles relating to our show and the network. Jane likes to read the latest about the industry *first* thing in the morning. The production assistant will also transcribe and log tapes from the shoots, file scripts and any contact information pertaining to guests on the show, and go on runs for any materials that we might need." Bonus! Time out of the office.

"She will aid the senior producers and the director for each and every shoot, especially when it comes to scheduling—arranging everything from arrival times to the lunch breaks for the crew, hair and makeup for Jane, the minutes allotted for equipment setup and breakdown, and such. And Jane likes it all printed on a Word document using Helvetica font."

"She will have to digitize the tapes for editing too," she continued. Digitize, what?

"Charlotte," she paused. "I'm just not sure you are tough enough. You seem like such a sweet and genuine person, but Jane can be, well she's demanding. She has the highest standards. She won't take no for an answer. I'm just not sure you can get the answers she wants and she expects. . . ." her voice dwindled as she looked down at my Payless loafers. What the hell did my choice in shoes have to do with getting this job? I crossed my legs and tucked my sturdily clad feet under the chair.

"617-555-1630," I said.

"Excuse me?" She replied with a confused look on her face.

"617-555-1630," I rattled off the number with the perfection of a well-trained kindergartener. "My parents' home phone number. Call them and ask them if I am tough and if I can argue to get my way. My mother always said that I would be a worthy opponent if God ever came out of the sky and told me no." And suddenly, the HR woman smiled.

I got the PA position. "PA" sounds so official, just as "administrative assistant" is now chic-ed down to "admin" (note the lowercase *a*). Why can't people just call it like it is? An admin is a secretary; yes, a secretary. Anybody who does not recognize this fact is fooling his or herself. Now a "PA" (note the capital letters!) is a production assistant, but in New

York reality PA stands for "PissAnt." At least secretaries have their own official day, Secretary Appreciation Day. Not so with PAs. I would soon find that my hell was called logging. Basically, I would spend my days grabbing videotapes from the library, cueing them up to particular random snippets, then rewinding, and then finally returning them to the library. Log, baby, log! But my name would be in the credits and that was all I needed to prove my worth to my grandparents.

Sunshine & Sensibility had a devoted following like few other shows. The host, Jane Dough, was not only the personality, she was also the creator and the CEO. As a true entertainer, she was also a moody diva—hence her nickname, "the Diva." Let's just say that "sunshine" did not radiate from her cheerful ass. Yet, she was sensible. How else would she become the poster woman for housewives around the world? She guided her cultlike audience through crafty yet chic household ideas with grace and ease. She tirelessly marketed herself in magazines, interviews, and board meetings with confidence and style, and to top it all off, she was as tough as a bull. Basically, the Diva was the perfect recipe for success.

Feeling as if I had been anointed by Jane Dough herself, I walked home that afternoon and into our second official Cooking Club meeting with my head held high. Five minutes later, in walked Wade (always early), and five minutes after that, Sage (always tardy).

"So . . . I got a job," I happened to mention. Immediately, the room went into an uproar.

"Congratulations, Charlie!"

"Here, here! Way to go." They hadn't even asked where.

"I'm going to be a PA at *Sunshine & Sensibility*." A hush enveloped the room.

"J. Lo religiously watches that show," Tara reminded everyone. I nodded.

"So, can you snag me some of that chic wrapping paper she always uses?" Syd asked. "Oh wait, the other day I saw her doing a segment on this fancy satin ribbon, could you get a couple yards of that?"

∞

The Cooking Club. God, it sounded so official. Well, so far it was proving to be anything but. You could call us the Bitch Buddies, the Whining Women, the Catty Cathys, the Chaotic Chefs. Those names seemed more fitting. Still, we had all tried to step up to the challenge. We all squealed as we revealed our dishes.

I had put a spin on my grilled cheeses by using garlic butter and roasting slices of tomatoes before placing them inside of the cheese envelope; Tara had made quesadillas; Syd had nuked some "baked" potatoes and diced some toppings (including a finger dish full of raisins); Sage had made banana bread out of her rotten bananas; and Wade had invented a nine-layer dip, an alternative to the popular seven-layer dip.

"Quesadillas?" Macie looked at Tara questioningly.

"You got some problem with my ethnic dish?" Tara challenged.

"No, but did you put anything inside besides cheese? And speaking of cheese, Charlie, I hope you wrote down every step of your complex recipe."

"Hey! I used cookie cutters to create these uniquely shaped finger foods! I call them Toasted Cheese Fingerettes." I had cut the toasted cheese sandwiches into the shapes of hearts and stars using the cutters I'd found at D'Agostino. I would forever stand by this signature dish. Watch out, Jane Dough!

"Sounds dirty. Yes, you brought the good ole Brown touch to this Cooking Club soirée," Tara joked. But we lost all spitefulness and began to ohh and ahh when Macie pulled out her delectable Ever So Creamy Cheesecake. To give her credit, she was the only one who had gone above and beyond, giving our Cooking Club an ounce (note the use of cooking terminology) of legitimacy.

"I've never seen so many forms of cheese in one room," moaned Skinny Sage. "Cheese for the cheese on our thighs," she muttered. But that notion was soon an afterthought as we all (at least five of us) dipped in eagerly. We hadn't taken to the cooking part enough yet, but we sure were good on the eating part.

"Hey, is cream cheese really a cheese?" asked Syd.

"Does it matter?" Tara responded with her mouth full.

"Just wondering," paused Syd. "I mean it is in the dairy aisle at the supermarket, but it doesn't go through the aging process that most cheeses do to get to moldy perfection."

"Syd, I truly appreciate your efforts to cultivate your culinary expertise!" applauded Wade. "We might actually get somewhere with this group." She beamed like a proud soccer mom.

After a quick toast, we all gathered around the coffee table munching away, and our conversation instantly went from sugar to spice. Yep, in less than ten minutes we managed to change the topic from food to men.

"So has he called?" baited Tara. She knew the answer but was playing pop psychologist. She knew it was better to get me talking versus stewing in my own boy wasteland.

"No. I did see him the other night though," I replied.

"Just see him?" Tara questioned.

"Well, I saw an awful lot of him," I smiled.

"So have you had a date yet?" Wade asked. "Or even a sober hookup?" Macie gasped at Wade's bluntness.

"Wade!"

"Sorry, I guess I just want to make sure Charlie isn't sugar-coating this," she mumbled as she took a spoonful of Macie's cheesecake.

"It's good. I mean we've hooked up twice now—"

"How romantic," gushed Sage.

"Phone calls?" Tara quizzed.

"No—at least not that I know of. Is my outgoing message friendly enough? Maybe my voice is too high and childlike." The girls nodded yes then shook their heads no in response. "He's sweet and cute, but just a tad, well, guarded I guess." I knew I was backtracking so I switched gears.

"Is there some sort of timeline or protocol here? I mean what should we as women be willing to accept? Or sacrifice?" Suddenly, we were in an episode of the Jenny Jones show. I was the host and the girls were my guests. It wasn't "Lesbians Turned Straight," or "My Momma Slept With Your Daddy." In keeping with our Cooking Club, tonight's topic was: *What Is the Recipe for the Perfect Guy?*

Did you go by the book?

Combine: looks, money, family, finance job, triathlete body

Add: a summerhouse and some country club manners

Blend in: a compatible religion and a dash of good ole Republican tendencies

Bake: until he is an ultimate golf player (ex-LAX player of course)

Or did you try to be creative and add some spice to the mix?

Combine: musical talent (at least the guitar), modern art appreciation, cooking skills

Mix in: political know-how (especially about those little war-scarred countries)

Add: a pinch of unemployment and starving artist

Cool: let sit until he looks good wearing a T-shirt over the long-sleeve T

Could you experiment? Could you mix the two? Who said the perfect chef followed each and every detail? My problem was that I seemed to burn every relationship somehow, somewhere along the way, every time: Brad—I was too overeager; Roger—I was too coy never returning his phone calls; Sam—I just couldn't get over his hairy lower back. Maybe I should play it safe and stick to the recipe. But whose recipe was I using?

As I brought the now-licked-clean dishes back into the kitchen, I willed my phone to ring. "Now! Okay, how about . . . *now!*" Those who talk to themselves supposedly have money in the bank, or are just plain crazy. I fell into a new category appropriate for the new millennium. Some of us talk to ourselves because a certain boy has pervaded all of our vital organs, multisponged cells, and viable neurons in the brain.

"Please let him be there. Please let him call. Call me, call me. One, two three . . . call!" Remember trying to turn the stoplight green with psychic magic? "One, two, three . . . ring!" I checked my cell phone. Was the ring working? Was the volume up? Modern technology actually works against the modern-day woman. We all now have cell phones, caller ID, answering machines, or voicemail. There is no way to not know if someone has called, if he indeed called. It is quite difficult to deny when someone hasn't called. That red light or little icon of an envelope can send your heart a pitter-patter like a love letter.

"What are you doing?" Macie said laughing. I stopped shaking my phone.

"Sometimes, well, I just think it can help grab a signal; a signal that may be lost in all those radio waves battling in the crowded NYC air." Sounded technical enough.

"Charlie, are you okay?" she asked, zooming in closer to me. I gave her my million-watt smile hoping that the glare would hide the dark under-eye circles I got when stressed.

"Sure!" I said as thoughts of Mr. J. P. Morgan's soft hands drifted through my mind. And was I whipped? Yep! Macie took a sip of her wine, and I gave the phone one last shake.

Maybe I gave him the wrong number, because it was a new number after all and didn't I used to be a little bit dyslexic when I was younger? I was never tested, but the words "being" and "doing" always threw me for a loop. The *b-d* thing. Or maybe he lost the piece of paper with my phone number on it on his way to work? He did tell me the last time that he's been putting together a big deal at work. Men can be scatterbrained. Maybe he doesn't have time to call me since he's a workaholic, in a good way? He does have to be professional . . . it's all cubicles nowadays, they can hear everything! Plus, cell phone reception can be sporadic in Manhattan. Sometimes Macie's messages are so garbled by the end of the night that you can't tell if she's calling from Mars or around the corner. And no, the shots we consume have nothing to do with that issue. Maybe the Sprint cellular tower was down in the area?

The single women of the world would be a lot saner if

someone would only take a retina scanner, a Breathalyzer, a disco ball, and enhanced ESP caller ID and morph them together with a cell phone. How great would that thingy be? To begin with, your cell phone would do all of the normal functions. It would allow one to make and receive calls (long distance included), call three-way (as if anyone ever does), and memorize and prioritize phone numbers. The ring tones would even help attract men at bars, as certain songs like ZZ Top's "She's Got Legs!" always do. At the bar, once the hottie had been attracted by your constantly ringing phone, you could wave the phone in front of him with a quick flick of the wrist and flip of the hair, and the retina scanner would download all of his pertinent information: age, dating status, job title, annual salary, penis length, apartment square footage. Once in the bathroom for a quick powder, you could flip out the tweezer arm of your cell phone to nip those errant brow hairs before exiting to make your final move on your selected hottie. You then have a night of extraordinary passion.

The next day, your phone would flash to alert you that said hottie is *thinking* of you, even if he hasn't called. All he has to do is get within twenty feet of his phone and think about you (good or bad) for your phone's ESP caller ID to alert you. That night, when you have not received the all-important call, you blow into the side of your phone and it registers your blood alcohol level. If your breath registers at anything above a giddy drunk, the phone will automatically shut down, preventing you from drunk dialing and making an ass out of yourself. Phew! Skip ahead to five long days later when he calls to toss out the ever-so-slight possibility of a drink sometime in the next year, and your phone lights the room with its disco ball mirrors. Like the fireworks in your head, your phone emits flashes of colored lights blinking and twinkling like stars in the sky. Make a wish! Your cell phone is your new best friend. Always by and on your side! All for $59.99 a month.

We all ended up buzzed and bouncing off the walls due to the cheesecake, and oh yeah, the wine, so we decided to hightail it to Top Shelf. Maybe Mr. J. P. Morgan would be there again, I thought, before doing my best to force him from my mind. We ordered apple martinis and somehow the clock over the bar changed from 11 P.M. to 3 A.M. in the span of "Waiting for Tonight," a goddamn J. Lo classic that always made me gyrate.

~

*L*ater that night, Sage and I stumbled back to 167 West Eighty-first . . . thank God we lived only two blocks and exactly fifty-five steps away from the bar. And good thing I was a champ at Frogger in my youth, since we had to artfully dodge oncoming taxis, limos, dry cleaning trucks, bread delivery trucks, high bike messengers, parked cars (yes, they are the nonmobile obstacles), and other nightly revelers to get across Broadway. We had left behind the dancing queens: Tara, Macie, Wade, and Syd . . . and damn, did we need some munchies.

We'd devoured the Cooking Club's creations before we had left, but thankfully, Syd's mother had bought about forty boxes of mac and cheese at Costco. And by the way, are the Kraft guys fucking kidding? That infamous blue box does not serve two to three people. That puppy yields one hefty helping for *one*, not two, not three, and sure as hell not one and an anorexic half. What's better than a bowl of mac and cheese and a good Lifetime Original Movie at three in the morning? Nothing.

"Bring out the milk and butter."

"Will skim milk work?" Sage asked. To give her skinny self credit, that was all that was in the fridge.

"Skim it is. I guess the butter can add the necessary creaminess."

"Butter, butter, butter," muttered Sage with her nonexistent ass sticking out of the refrigerator's shelves. "No butter!" she exclaimed, I swear with some glee.

"Ohh, you're kidding! The recipe is ruined and I haven't even turned on the stove!"

"No, wait! I got it!" In her drunken sense of reasoning, Sage pulled Macie's butter-flavored cooking spray from over the stove. Aha! One of her weight-loss secrets revealed!

"Eww, what are you thinking?" J. P. Morgan hadn't called, and now my mac and cheese was becoming a faint memory too. Sage's skinny ass was back in the refrigerator.

"Wait! Got it!" Her scream must have reverberated throughout the apartment building. She backed up and ceremoniously held up a jar of nacho cheese dip.

"We've got the cheese already," I protested.

"No, make the mac and cheese with the powder stuff, and then add the nacho cheese sauce for the creamy factor." I knew Sage had to be rocked to suggest such a fattening additive. Thus, we had our homestyle mac and cheese with a southwestern flair. Who said we couldn't cook! At least I had found one recipe that worked for me. Sage dumped the pot's contents into one large mixing bowl. We each grabbed a wooden spoon and settled on the living room floor with an episode of *Blind Date* in full swing. Legs spread, mouths moaning, warmness spreading throughout our bodies. What else do you need on a Saturday night? J. P. Morgan who?

October

Funeral Potatoes

12 large potatoes or one 32-ounce bag of frozen shredded
    hash browns
2 (10¾ ounce) cans condensed cream of chicken soup
2 cups sour cream
1¼ cups grated cheddar cheese
½ cup (8 tablespoons) plus 2 tablespoons butter, melted
⅓ cup chopped white onions
2 cups crushed corn flakes

Preheat the oven to 350° F. Peel potatoes and boil for 30 minutes
or just until tender. Cool and grate like hash browns into a greased
9 × 13-inch baking dish (or put hash browns into greased baking
dish). In a medium sized bowl, combine and gently mix soup, sour
cream, cheese, the ½ cup melted butter, and onions. Fold into
potatoes. In a small bowl, combine the crushed corn flakes and the
2 tablespoons of melted butter. Sprinkle on top of potato mixture.
Bake for 30 minutes.

    Serve up piping hot to all your ghosts and goblins. This sinful
treat is sure to spook up any dinner party.

"Lift, one-two, lift! Here we go, Bulldogs, here we go! 10,
9, 8 . . ."
"Syd!" I yelled before she got to the "off." "Focus. I don't

need a drill sergeant, a cheerleader, or an astronaut, I need muscles!"

"Hernia!" screamed Syd. "I have a hernia and I'm only in my twenties!"

"Drama queen," I mumbled under my breath as my mattress came crashing down on my left shoulder. "Please, Syd! Grab a handle!"

"You don't have any handles. How old is this mattress?"

"Brand new!"

"Brand new and no handles? I'd return it!"

"Focus, Syd, focus!" Syd had come home from work on her lunch break for a Fluffernutter sandwich, and I had snagged her to help me flip my mattress.

"Why are we doing this again?" she panted.

How to explain? How to explain that we were flipping a brand-new mattress due to the fact that the love of my life wouldn't spend the night anymore. A few nights ago the dilemma had begun:

"What are you going to be for Halloween?"

"What?" I had asked, a little hazy. I couldn't tell if my fogginess was the result of the two-hour kiss-a-thon with Mr. J. P. Morgan or due to the fact that he was pulling on his socks; pulling on his socks to leave; pulling on his socks to leave in the middle of the night.

"What are you going to be for Halloween? I'm thinking of the Hulk, although I don't think I own much green." As I struggled to pull on a shirt I thought of how the green paint would only complement and exaggerate his blue eyes.

"Are your toes getting cold?" I asked feigning innocence. "I'll pull out an extra blanket."

"What? No, don't worry. I have to go. I don't sleep well

here," he concluded waving his hands around as if to blame the sandman or someone. I couldn't help but think of last week when he'd stayed and snored himself into a deep slumber. I couldn't even wake him in the middle of the night for some dream-inducing nooky.

Now, from under my just-flipped mattress, I revisited the situation. He'd claimed that he couldn't sleep well through the night at my apartment, in my bed. At first, I wanted to blame the city noise. But he lived in midtown next to a hospital, so he was used to sirens and such. And we still hadn't had sex yet. I had tried to put out of my mind that men's sexual peak was in their early twenties, aka, now. Was it me? Did the abstinence speak to the depth or to the shallowness of our relationship? No, must be my mattress. I had always heard about flipping mattresses, but had never actually flipped one. So maybe mine was flawed and needed to be flipped—or something.

"Hernia!" Syd screamed again as the mattress fell on top of me. This time I was sandwiched between the box spring and mattress, so mission accomplished. Almost.

∽

*T*he first day of work at *Sunshine & Sensibility* dawned like the first day of school. I squeaked as I walked down the shiny hallway of the network's corporate high-rise in my new shoes.

"It will be a bit like high school," the HR woman had warned. "There's a lot of competition here. And sometimes that desire to succeed can translate into pettiness and yes, nastiness." High school? Nastiness? I pulled my skirt down a bit. I didn't need any stares about the "inappropriate length." How could I, I wondered, as a measly PA, be any sort of a threat to a high-ranking producer?

"And you are?" came a voice with a thick Boston accent from behind my cubicle wall. I stood up and peered over to see who was speaking to me. The "voice" did not glance up. She didn't even turn around. Staring at her hazy screen in her dimly lit office, she repeated, "And you are . . ." Like rhetorical questions, I hate lingering statements. I knew she wasn't asking me out of interest, but out of obligation.

"I'm Charlotte Brown," I said

"Charlotte. Family name?" she said.

"Umm no. Ahh, most people just call me Charlie," I said, figuring I might as well throw her some bone in the interest of female bonding.

"Charlotte, I don't like nicknames. I'm Margaret. Not Meg, nor Maggie, nor Marg, just Maaargaret. Oh, and don't bother me for things like paper clips. The supply office is just beyond the gym." That damn Boston long *a*. The Pilgrims left the fucking *Mayflower* four hundred years ago and some still wished they could kiss the weathered mast, or should I say, "Maaaast." I ducked back down after her whirlwind of crap.

Margaret seemed like she was in her early thirties (probably bitter about her single status—no shining diamond ring on her left hand) and somehow had reached producer status at an early age. She was therefore destined for greatness at *Sunshine & Sensibility*. I just hoped that she wasn't an example of the effects of a rapid rise to success. If so, I was screwed.

Besides hearing a couple of screaming matches between producers in the studio and the occasional, "What the hell were you thinking?" coming from Jane's office at the other end of the building, it seemed like a pretty normal morning. I sat in my cubicle and waited for someone—hopefully not Margaret—to give me some direction.

"*Psst,*" I heard. "*Psst!*" someone spit not too quietly. A head popped out of the cubicle on my right.

"Hey, new girl! Hi. Come here for a sec." I walked around the wall that encased our fifteen or so cubicles (and kept us peons separated from the bigwigs as effectively as the Great Wall of China). There, I met Julie.

"Charlie? Charlie Brown?" she asked, when I told her my name. I steeled myself for the obligatory laughter. I could mouth the next question: "Do you have a dog?" Julie even went so far as to waggle her hands at the sides of her head mimicking Snoopy's floppy ears.

"Nope, no dog, only the occasional best friend of dog sniffing around my bed if I'm lucky." Not particularly clever, but it tended to do the trick.

"So, not married either?" she asked. Okay, so TV people were nosey. I'd soon learn it was just part of the profession.

"Nope, uh, not yet," I repeated, as if marriage at an early age would be such a terrible crime in today's era. She, obviously single too, smiled.

I quickly realized that Julie was one of the good guys at work. She had lasted as an admin for five years at *S&S*, and I immediately knew I would need her help to survive my first day. She showed me around the studio, giving me the inside scoop on who was who and what was what. First, we went to what she dubbed the Craft Closet. This was the secret closet where the Diva kept everything from über-fancy ribbons and hot pink stationery to stacks upon stacks of chichi fabric and jars of knickknacks and buttons. You name it, it was in there. It was a craft-lovers' paradise. I drooled and I wasn't even crafty! Yet all I wanted to do was to start stuffing my pockets and run like hell. My mother would have peed her pants if she'd gotten a look at all the pretty goodies. No wonder she was a fan of the show. Deep down I felt like that evil little girl Veruca Salt from *Willy Wonka:* I wanted it and I wanted it now.

Julie didn't stop there. She showed me everything. Jane had a test kitchen where five chefs were constantly working around the clock to churn out fancy and delicious recipes for the Diva to use during one of her upcoming segments. She also had a handful of stylists who only worked on prepping and presenting the food, designing the invitations, and arranging the bouquets. It was absolutely insane. The place was a full-fledged sweatshop busting with extremely talented seamstresses, florists, carpenters, chefs, producers, directors, and PAs—all of whom wanted to please the Queen of Daytime Domesticity. The problem was that I had two left thumbs. I was doomed to be doomed on my first day!

"Hey, do you want to help me stuff the trick-or-treat bags?" Julie asked.

"The what?" I asked before realizing I was questioning my very first assignment. "I mean sure!" I corrected with the glee of a high-school cheerleader. "What do we need to do?"

"Well, Santo, our head stylist, came up with these cellophane bags for Jane's trick-or-treaters." After hearing the screaming from Jane's office, I couldn't help but wonder what evil creature she transformed into once the sun went down.

"We stuff her candy bags? You mean for the candy bowl at her house?"

"Oh, she doesn't use a bowl. She, I mean we, stack the bags in old-fashioned washtubs. It's quite effective." I couldn't wait to tell my mother that I, being one of the talented employees at *S&S*, could use my newfound skills to open bags of discount miniature candy bars. You know, just in case Jane couldn't handle the stress of it.

Having nothing else to do, I joined Julie at the craft table. We proceeded to mark up the cellophane bags with stamps (hand carved out of potatoes by the art department) and metallic orange ink. With a flick of the wrist, Julie dusted each wet imprint with silver glitter. We then filled the cellophane bags with classic types of candy. No slimy gummy snots in these bags! Only quality old-fashioned root beer barrels, Sweet Tarts, Mary Janes, and bull's-eye caramels filled these sweet sacks.

"Oh, that won't work," Julie informed me.

"What?"

"That bag of candy you just put down. Those rolls of Sweet Tarts need to be vertical."

"What?"

"Seriously." She giggled at my incredulous look. "Untie it and put the candy in a new bag because that one can't be reused. It will be too manhandled after you untie it and rearrange the candy." She spit out these rote instructions as if she was describing how to pour milk on breakfast cereal. After we stuffed the candies into their "proper" positions, we adorned each bag with a pumpkin cookie and a bit of raffia. For the last century, kids have been warned about eating homemade Halloween goods. However, mothers would be clamoring at the Diva's door in the New York suburbs, ready to shove these yummy handmade treats down their kids' throats.

Over our candy-stuffing bonding, Julie told me that I probably would never have a formal introduction to Jane. The rule of thumb around the cubicles was that she didn't like to be bothered by the lower staff. Speak when spoken to was the strict policy. Of course, this hadn't been included in my HR new-hire packet. Julie also quickly warned me about Jane's pet peeves:

No personal photos on desktop.

No colored push pins (only brushed silver).

No live plants.

No bananas anywhere in the office (it was known as "stupid fruit" to the Diva).

No wearing jeans.

No folders labeled by hand—only by a professional labeling machine.

No long stringy college hair (the Diva liked cropped, cultured dos).

I giggled nervously after her last point and played with my below shoulder-length locks. And God was I craving a banana (I was always the type to want what I couldn't have).

"What are you doing?" someone barked from behind me.

"Excuse me?" I answered with the utmost grace. It was Margaret.

"I think you can find something more productive to do with your time. If I were you, I'd make myself appear just a tad busier on my first day." Then she turned on her pointy shoes and went back to her cubicle.

"Sorry," I mumbled, "I thought I was helping." Shit, I *was* helping. Julie and I had stuffed at least seventy-five goddamn little trick-or-treat bags (all with vertically placed rolls of Sweet Tarts), and Maaargaret would rather see me inflating my newly donned corporate ass at my computer. I shuffled back to my cubicle in candy-stuffing shame.

I decided to keep low in my new little six-by-six space.

Back inside the compound, I dug through some of the more fun items on my desk. There was a fresh box of *S&S* stationery, a box of hot pink *S&S* pens, a name plate with my title strategically placed on the outside of my cubicle. I snuck a few pencils for Syd inside my bag. If my parents could see me now they'd be so proud. I was officially part of the workforce.

That night, so inspired, I brought home some of Jane's, or rather the head chef's, famous toffee. Tara snickered that I was already sucked into the Diva's universe as she popped one of the toffees I had left on the table by our front door into her mouth. I headed for my room and threw a mask on to detoxify after my stressful first day; I was exhausted. I warmed some milk like my mother had done when I had an upset tummy, and I lounged in my high school sweetheart's sweatshirt, ignoring the inappropriately placed worn spots. The girls had headed out, so I had the tiny apartment all to my bloated self. When someone knocked and let themselves in, I shouted "hi" from my fetal position.

"Hot. Very hot!" I leapt up at the sound of a male voice and looked around wildly for a blunt object. In my hasty search, I noticed a lopsided grin on my invader. He was standing in my living room. I didn't know whether to cover my holes, wipe off my mask, press stop on the Disney movie I was watching, or continue my search for the blunt object. Syd must have forgotten to lock the door again.

"I just wanted to come by and say congrats on your first day of work." Bells a'ringing! Were those angels singing? I still hadn't said a word. Mr. J. P. Morgan took about two steps with his well-formed lacrosse legs and, sweeping a hand under my sweatshirt, pulled me in for a long kiss. I pulled back first, I think, out of breath. On his nose was a smidge of green papaya mask. I wiped the smear away. He pulled off the sweatband holding my hair back off of my head.

"Rapunzel, Rapunzel. I like the curls," he mumbled running his fingers through my hair. "You look busy, so I'll head out. Just wanted to say hi and give you these," from behind his back he handed me three Gerber daisies. "Have a relaxing night." He kissed me once more, and then strode back toward the door as suddenly as he had come, leaving me off balance. On his way out, he grabbed some of the toffee before closing the door behind him. Standing there, still wondering whether or not I had said a single word, I heard a yell. Peering through the peephole, I could see Mr. J. P. Morgan, a distorted yet still cute version of him anyway, licking his fingers at the top of the stairs.

"Delicious!" he yelled. He liked the toffee. And he seemed to like me, green papaya mask and all! Things were looking up. I would nab this boy, and I would master that toffee recipe.

✍

"*F*or Pete's sake, who would ever buy this small plastic bottle of laundry detergent?" the Diva screamed from the studio. Day two had begun!

"Everyone knows that I would buy the economy size. You buy the large bottle and then dispense it into smaller, more discreet pour bottles. Who, I mean, *who* did this?" Who, I mean who, cares!? I wondered. Obviously millions of people cared because her show raked in gazillions of dollars. I sidestepped the tantrum and darted back to my cube, escaping back into logging hell.

By the end of the week, I was wondering if I had made a wise decision in taking the position at *S&S*. I thought that the new girl always got a break or two during her first week, right? Wrong. *S&S* was doing a segment on ice fishing. To begin with, I had a hard time envisioning Jane's padded derrière chilling on a frozen lake. Second, mean Margaret put me in charge of finding "fishing-related gear" for Jane (so much more important than candy stuffing). After about ten minutes of scrambling on the Internet and Googling the words "ice fishing" and "gear," I finally broke down and asked scary Margaret for some much-needed help.

"Umm, Margaret. Can I, I mean may I ask you a question?"

"What? I'm busy," she mumbled from her computer.

"Um, it will only take a sec."

"Fine, what?"

"Well, what exactly do you think I should be looking for?" I asked kindly.

"Are you kidding me?" she yelled. "Are you living in a cave? Do you not know what ice fishing is?" Oh dear Lord, big mistake to ask Margaret. Is ice fishing a recognized Olympic sport? Think, Charlie, think! She's making a scene. What to do? What to do?

"Oh, I just meant, what size clothing do I get for Jane?" I quickly rebounded.

"Do I look like her wardrobe assistant?" she barked.

"No!" I wanted to scream, "but Julie told me you started at *S&S* as Jane's wardrobe assistant five years ago!" I bit my tongue and actually think I tasted blood. I wondered if Margaret had been in this bad of a mood back then too. (Note to self: Don't know? Definitely don't ask!)

"Oh, and get those flowers off of your desk before Jane sees them," Margaret sneered. Was it another corporate bylaw or would Jane just take offense to my three wilting daisies from

J. P., which I had gently transported via the subway to my new job? As another few petals fell I whispered, "He loves me, he loves me not . . ."

⌁

J spent the remainder of the afternoon scouring the L.L. Bean and Eddie Bauer Web sites. I was looking for practical yet flattering styles of foul weather gear for incremental to severe cold. Why couldn't they make waders in a nice shade of blue (to match the Diva's eyes, of course). The beaten-down wardrobe assistant (about the twentieth since Margaret's humble days) had finally pointed me in the right direction and had warned me to get multiple sizes of each item.

"She'll flip if they are too small, implying that she has gained weight. Yet she'll flip if they are too big, implying that you couldn't predict the exact size of her ever-fluctuating waist. Just blame ill-fitting items on the cheap manufacturing found these days." He gave me a feeble smile of encouragement.

I found it strange that the retail companies claimed that they would "loan" the clothes to Jane, in return for proper accolades during the credits at the end of the show, but they still wanted them returned. Why? What were they going to do with them after she had worn them? Disgusting! I figured the heads of merchandising knew that they would make a killing by selling slightly worn fishing gear that had once graced the body of Ms. Jane Dough on eBay someday. I found the cutest knit hats on the *InStyle* Web site that were selling for $129.00 (yes, for a hat). I thought that the color would be perfect with Jane's meticulously highlighted hair (little did I know the wrath that would ensue about a month from now when I learned that Jane had a horrible allergy to wool, and therefore had to go hatless during the entire segment). I also called Skinny Sage in a panic when I realized how many colors long johns came in. Sage was a fashion guru who knew the latest trends yet somehow found those few precious items that would outlast one season. She was always trying to play up her skinny wrists and hide her emaciated rib cage with the hottest new things out there.

"Black. Black is such a safe bet especially since the tabloids have been covering Jane's weight gain." You could hear the scorn in Sage's voice. "And black hides a multitude of sins!"

"Black long johns? You're right, you're right." Black was New York City's official color! "And I guess nobody will really see them under all these other layers."

"But the key is that she'll know," Sage theorized. Just when I thought I was done, Margaret leaned over and dropped another bomb.

"Oh, and get gear for the cameraman, Jane's cousin who is also going on the shoot, and the two producers. But make sure to outfit them in colors different than Jane's. Remember that the colors should be complementary and not clash in case any of them end up in a shot. Oh, and make sure none of them will look cuter that Jane—maybe get some unflattering coat styles or something. Jane won't want to be outshone."

Outshone? On the friggin' ice? Didn't Margaret know that Jane would be worrying only about keeping her golden ass warm on the ice? I thought of ordering the Diva a bottle of whiskey to hide in one of her new vest's many pockets.

❧

*A*fter yet another particularly hellish day of *S&S*, Macie and I met for a few drinks. Taste, talk, sip, share, gulp, gossip, drain, drunk. Using each other as a crutch we stumbled back to our apartment. Juan was manning the door (well, the door next to our door). Juan was the most amicable of the doormen in the stately prewar high-rise next to our walk-up. He worked the oddest hours, had the brightest smile, listened to our endless babble and all the while minded his p's and q's better than the rest. He bowed as if we were about to enter the Plaza. We, of course, nodded to him grandly and waltzed (while hiccupping) into our building's stairwell. Up we went.

We entered our apartment to soothing darkness. The dim light inside the place was calming compared to the city's night glare. I guess one would say that our apartment had an urban quality to it. You know, a quality like the kind you find in seedy B-movies. Outside the living room (and consequently the dining room/my bedroom view too) was a pulsating red sign declaring "Manhattan Motel." The vertical sign was larger and higher than the five floors of the motel. But tonight, the red glare was sort of dim.

"Home at last," Macie collapsed on our too-short couch. "See, that Atkin's diet is working! I fit, I actually fit on our couch," she mumbled before turning over and curling up for the night. I grabbed a drink of water in some random J. P. Morgan mug (Note to self: What a coincidence!), kicked off my shoes (marring the walls in the process), and headed to the bathroom. I finally realized as I sat on the toilet mid-pee that there was something missing.

My soft butter yellow rug was missing from under my feet. It was probably my favorite item in our household. Lush, plush, and my favorite shade of yellow. Everyone knew not to dare wash the sacred bathroom rug. Did someone spill or drip? Maybe it was in one of the girls' hampers? Despite my dulled senses and rationalizations, I felt my annoyance start to stir. I finished my business and ran back out into the living room.

"Mace, Macie, the bathroom rug is gone!" I announced.

"What?" she moaned grabbing a shearling pillow. Suddenly she sat upright. Clutched in her hand was the exact ABC Carpet & Home shearling pillow that we had wanted to buy for our apartment but that had been way out of our price range. The shearling pillow that did not belong in our apartment. The shearling pillow that knocked some sense into us—and made us realize that we were *not* in our humble apartment after all! The dimmed red light was not our "Manhattan Motel" sign, but the softly blinking clock light on the VCR. Macie had not shrunken her thighs; the couch was simply wider than ours, which meant that my favorite butter yellow bathroom rug was safely ensconced in our apartment. Where we had come in ready to wake the dead, we now snuck out as silently as 007. The plaque 2C shone on the door; 5C was our apartment number. We were three floors off.

"Go!" We both sprinted up the stairs and collapsed into our apartment. I immediately ran to the bathroom and curled up on my snuggly rug. And it was there that I slept; slept spooning my snagged J. P. Morgan mug (not the man) the entire night.

⟡

*T*he next morning at *S&S*, hung over and during a brief reprieve from logging hell, I sat in front of my computer and tried to come up with some marvelous ideas for a Halloween costume. How is it that Halloween can stir such waves of excitement regardless of one's age? The discussions that surrounded what to dress up as carried the same weight as a discourse at an international summit. In New York, the whole month seemed to revolve around the childhood memories of autumnal Halloweens with wet leaves, chestnuts, mini candy bars, and winter jackets worn over costumes.

It was our first Halloween in the city, and we all wanted it to be memorable.

"We need to go above and beyond mere costumes," declared Tara.

"How are we going to do that?" I asked. "More memories at Top Shelf?"

"Charlie is right. Location is everything," Tara added. "I don't want my costume to be groped or spit upon in some packed bar setting. Maybe we should host a party," she suggested with a grin.

"You know we can't have parties. Not since those darn boys downstairs had the party where someone turned on the fire hose," Macie reminded us pointing to the water stain above our front door.

"We're not in college anymore," Tara said. "I'm talking about something different. How about a sophisticated party . . . a dinner party."

"And just who is going to cook this dinner?" I asked.

"Us!"

"Us?" I asked.

"We have a Cooking Club now. And Charlie, you can swipe some decorating ideas from S&S."

Suddenly, I liked the idea of being relied upon for styling suggestions. One week on the job, and my beautiful roommates already had confidence in me.

"We could . . . put candy corn in votives to hold tons of tea lights," I suggested. The three of them began nodding, so I continued spitting out ideas, "And we could carve those fake foam pumpkins, and serve ladyfinger munchies but make them look like chopped off digits . . ." My mind raced to recall each and every detail of the countless Halloween episodes from years past that I'd been forced to watch this past week at work. Macie began making a list of supplies, Tara began taking inventory of boys for invitees, and Syd began making ghost noises.

We ultimately decided on a dinner party of twenty-four, an intimate affair. We decided to send out an Evite that christened our dinner soirée the "Sinful Singles' Holy Halloween." Each of us six girls could invite four guests. I really only wanted Mr. J. P. Morgan; however, a part of me worried that he might be freaked out by such an intimate gathering. So I decided to alter the Evite a bit and added about fifty fake e-mail addresses such as manontop@aol.com, jockalot@yahoo.com, bigdog@ netzero.com. Then I thought that sounded like there'd be too many men, so I added a few hot-sounding female e-mail addresses: princess911@verizon.net, hottie1234@hotmail. com, sassygal@yahoo.com . . . Contrived? A tad. Scheming? Definitely. Desperate? Not yet! Though I did have a temporary moment of insanity when he replied as a maybe. Maybe? And, I noted ruefully, he was the only maybe. Even though we'd now met up at Top Shelf several times since that first fateful night, we had yet to have an official "dinner date." But that was fine, I reasoned, since I was trying to lose my freshman fifteen (yes, I tended to repeat the weight gain with each new phase of life).

A week before the party, the members of the Cooking Club met to revisit our assignments and take a few recipes for a test drive. Wade immediately jumped into teacher mode.

"Now, we all recognize that none of us is ready to tackle a

meat dish, aka, the main course, yet, right?" We all nodded, noting the gravity of our faults.

"It is only October though," Syd rationalized. "We've only had the Cooking Club since August."

"Syd." Wade had the patronizing tone down pat. "We are all on the same page here. We are Cooking Club virgins, and we shouldn't try to pretend we are experts at the various techniques—"

"Yeah, but speak for yourself!" Tara interjected. "I got pretty good at some other techniques when I was a virgin through practice, practice!"

"Cooking, Tara, we're talking about cooking," Wade admonished. "So, I will buy some stuffed chicken breasts at Zabar's. It's too early to subject our guests to one of our main course attempts." We all nodded again nonplussed.

"You know, chicken cutlets could make good fake boobs," pondered Tara. "Right size and consistency, you could mold them right under—"

"Macie, you're in charge of Funeral Potatoes, right?" interrupted Wade. She was bent on her dinner party mission and not going to be derailed by Tara's sexually errant brainstorms.

"They are divine and appropriately named," Macie replied. She was at the stove already, ready to whip up a sample of her dish. She had really risen to this challenge.

"Funeral?" Syd questioned.

"Think potatoes, dirt, corn flakes, grass . . . a sinful dish six-feet deep, or should I say under. At least six centimeters," she concluded holding up a brand-new Pyrex dish. "All of you, grab a peeler, a knife, or any sharp object you can find." We all hovered over the yellow Formica countertops wielding our instruments.

"A tad phallic," Tara observed. Syd was digging into the potatoes with swinging scoops of the peeler, each thrust sending a sliver of potato skin just inches from her face.

"I've been working on the railroad!" she sang. "All the live long day!"

"Syd, you peel *away* from you," I said giving her my best Jane Dough impression.

"These are tools of mass destruction you know," Sage sniffed, looking intently at the peeler. Anything to do with food was considered a tactical threat to her waist line.

"Blood! There is blood!" screamed Syd.

"That's it kids—abort mission!" Wade commanded. "Abort mission, I said."

"It's okay," Macie agreed as we put down our peelers. "You can use frozen hash browns in this recipe."

"Now you tell us!" Tara huffed, flexing her cramped fingers.

"Now for the rest of the dinner," Wade continued as we sat back down at the kitchen table. "Sage's making fat-free sorbet to cleanse the palate, Tara's making broccoli with some sort of sauce—"

"Mystery sauce," Tara winked, somehow making it sound sexy and mystifying.

"Syd—white bean salad."

"It might be white and brown beans. I'm not sure yet," corrected Syd.

"Okay, and I'm making the assortment of stuffed canapés . . . and Charlie?"

For the last week, I had been hiding out in the test kitchen at work hoping to perfect my ambitious contribution to our dinner party. After my very first day on the job, my mother had recommended that I find a cozy corner in the kitchen so that the good cooking vibes could "rub off on me as much as possible." I soon found that I was lured into the test kitchen not so much by the desire to hone my culinary skills but by the amazing smells that wafted through the sets. Who knew roasted cauliflower could smell so divine? The head chef was a great guy who let me drool (I mean observe) over his shoulder as much as possible. And he was my hero as he would often recommend shortcuts whenever he could. Case in point: my current task to perfect the Diva's famous toffee for our Halloween soirée.

"Charlie, you don't need a double boiler but if you use a regular pan, you have to watch the mixture every second and stir, stir, stir," the chef instructed. I just nodded along scribbling his instructions furiously. I didn't know if I had a double boiler. Nor did I know what I should be stirring the mixture with, a wooden spoon, a metal whisk, a plastic scraper, a spatula? Since working at *S&S*, I could now recognize the variety of utensils that could aid one in the kitchen—but I wasn't up on their exact uses. So I'd decided that I'd just use all four. I was determined to master Jane's toffee recipe for Mr. J. P. Morgan, or put on five pounds trying.

Now surrounded by my five best friends, I couldn't wait to reveal my plan.

"I'm making toffee!" I exclaimed a little too eagerly. "Mr. J. P. Morgan loves my toffee. It's his favorite sweet."

"You mean he loves Jane's toffee."

"Semantics," I conceded, handing out samples I'd snatched from work. Sage bowed out gracefully as always, but the rest were licking their fingers in delight.

"Way to step up, Charlie. You learned how to boil sugar?" Macie asked.

"Yep! Well, these are some of Jane's samples but I think I'm up to the task. Just, um, where do you get a candy thermometer?" All six of us dissolved into little girl giggles.

∞

"*T*o be or not to be? Or rather *what* to be?" An hour later, we were lounging in the living room, watching Macie mix her Funeral Potatoes while Syd mulled over a teen magazine, looking for costume ideas. Ever the eternal teenager, Syd figured that any magazine boasting glitter would have ingenious ideas when it came to fashion. She had nabbed the October issue by about September 10 and had been obsessing ever since.

"I still think we should do a group thing," suggested Tara, never one to shy away from group entertainment. "We could be a Brownie troop, Brownie troop 69."

"Cute idea, but I look pathetic in brown," negged Macie, sprinkling the corn flakes on her potatoes.

"I can't be a Brownie," threw out Syd with no explanation. After moments of silence, I asked the logical, "Why?"

"I had a bad Brownie experience."

"And?" all five of us asked.

"Well, I was working toward my Wilderness badge and, to make a long story short, my troop leader denied me the badge." Syd never had a short story; rarely did she have a logical one.

"Spill it, Syd-O," Macie said.

"Well, I like the outdoors. But nature and wilderness are not the same things," Syd shook her head. "Wilderness has the word 'wild' in it. Did any of you ever realize this?" Amid our shrugs, she continued, "Well, my troop went camping for forty-eight hours so that we could earn our Wilderness badges. To begin with, we didn't know I had an allergy to oak trees until I sneezed so hard and so loudly that the deer ran away before anyone got a picture for the troop scrapbook. Innocent mistake, right? Not my fault I have allergies," she sniffed. "And I didn't know what poison ivy looked like until every girl in the troop was wearing the leaf wreaths I had made in their hair. Itchy shit. And I took too long of a shower and flooded a red ant hill and all the little, tiny red ants floated into our cabin." I fought back a giggle.

"And since I wasn't a good swimmer, I had to wear my floaties on my arms in the canoe, which meant I really couldn't paddle, so Angelyn and I kept going in circles, so she threw up—which then made me jump up and we capsized. Angelyn swallowed too much lake water and threw up again, and became dehydrated so we had to go home after ten hours, not forty-eight. I didn't get the badge." Syd took a few deep breaths and managed not to let the tears in her eyes spill over at such miserable memories. Tara's eyes squinted as she bit her tongue to keep from laughing.

"I did earn the cookie badge. Surprise, surprise," she bemoaned patting her thighs. "I was my own best customer. It was the one measly badge I earned. And as if Brownie life wasn't trying enough, my mother just stapled my one badge to the sash. Everyone else's mothers sewed, but mine was sta-pled!" Macie tried in vain to cover up a snort.

"Stapled badges really don't stay on that well," Syd philoso-phized. "So no Brownies. I just want to be an angel. Is that so unoriginal?" she concluded.

"The white factor is questionable," muttered Tara, nibbling some of the corn flakes off of Macie's potatoes.

"But I could do the wings thing, and a halo, and lots of glit-ter," she mused, then switched to scouring the new dELiA*s catalogue for teenybopper ideas and trends.

"I was never allowed to buy a costume," Macie reminded us. "We had to make ours each year. Why spend money on those crappy plastic gowns?" Throughout college, she had usually slaved away on her Halloween costumes for weeks. Jane Dough would have been proud.

"Yeah, you only spend millions on the materials to make your costume," joked Tara.

"Well, you all will be amazed at my idea this year." Macie stuck her potatoes in the oven, then ran to her room and came back trailing a garbage bag. A few white feathers floated through the air.

"What the . . ." began Tara. Macie whipped open the bag. Inside was a pile of white feathers—a mound actually.

"Guess!" she cried with glee. "Guess what I am going to be!"

"Good God, a pillow? That's fitting with your buxom bust!" Tara laughed herself off of the couch.

"Shut up, Tara. No, I'm a chicken! See," she reached inside and pulled out a long strand of the feathers, "I saw this costume on a Web site for kids. You wrap the boas around your body, and this one is for the top of my head, and then I wear yellow tights and dish gloves on my feet. I even made a cardboard beak!"

"Where did you ever find yellow tights?" I asked.

"Aha!" she cried triumphantly. "I couldn't find them anywhere."

"Surprise, surprise," Sage chimed in.

"So I bought white ones and spray painted them yellow. Ta da!" Well that explained the mysterious yellow paint lines in the basement next to the washing machines. Sydney burst out in a fit of giggles. Macie's smile began to fall but then she thought better of it and began laughing too.

"Hmm, you'll be finger-lickin' good, I guess!" quipped Tara.

Syd turned to her. "So give, Tara. Who or what are you going to be? Let me guess—something French and something dirty?" We all just smiled. Tara had been a French maid (ruffles and all) umpteen times before. There should be a law against used and abused costumes.

"I just want to be recognized and remembered," Tara innocently claimed. Yeah, and if our party turned out as planned, there would be a list of men who would definitely remember her and not from her costume alone.

∽

*T*wo days before the big dinner, I decided to be Wonder Woman. I'd had a childhood love affair with Wonder Woman. I wore the Underoos with pride and I was forever sneaking out of the house in the starred panties and red and gold tank top. My mother had asked that, out of respect for the family, I wear either the tank top or the bottoms—the top with a pair of shorts or the bottoms with a T-shirt—but never sport both at the same time. Never one to listen to authority, I would cut out the cardboard crown, don the underwear (top and bottom), and sneak out through the garage. Who knew Wonder Woman lived on Mockingbird Lane? Needless to say, I had decided to revert to my childhood fantasy and don a cape. There were sure to be other superheroes out there tonight, but while Batman had his Batgirl, I would be secure with just my invisible jet.

My choice was also fueled by the fact that a few weeks earlier during our second rendezvous, Mr. J. P. Morgan had mentioned that he might be the Hulk.

"Hunk," I'd corrected him in my mind. I figured a green beast would be easy to spot at our party though even now his response annoyingly remained at "Maybe." When I'd bumped into him at Top Shelf a few nights earlier and ended up back at his apartment, I'd kept up the pretense of the Evite making it sound like it was a big old bash that we were having. Little did I know how foretelling my lie would be.

⁓

*F*inally, the big night arrived. We all stood by in the living room at 7:00 P.M.

"Where is everyone?" Tara asked for the umpteenth time. I looked around and realized that we were all standing in a line, facing the door. Macie was wringing her hands, and I was picking at my Wonder Woman wedgie.

"No one ever shows up to these things on time," I reminded them with the authority of an established New York socialite. "I mean, we're never on time to things."

"But we're girls."

"Are we hosting a 'Thing'?" Syd asked as she picked at the corn flakes topping Macie's Funeral Potatoes. Syd had initially had a mini conniption fit when Macie had taken the box of corn flakes from the cupboard and had begun to pulverize them. She was finally appeased when Macie bought her a box of Lucky Charms as a breakfast cereal replacement.

"Yes!" Wade shouted as if in mid-orgasm (out of character for her). "Girls, this is our first official Thing!"

"Another first. I don't know if I can contain myself. I haven't had so many firsts in a long time," pondered Tara.

Our Thing. Hmm. My first official Thing. I stood a little taller in my foil-covered boots just as the doorbell rang.

Somehow, our innocent invitees had taken it upon themselves to invite more friends—the whole word-of-mouth effect. No one likes to be alone in New York City, thus New Yorkers gravitate toward crowds. They surround themselves on all sides, buffering themselves from the taxi horns, police sirens, and other lonely people. And suddenly, our intimate Sinful Singles' Holy Halloween dinner party had turned into a Holy Shithouse Halloween. Within the first hour, the elegantly arranged dinner table and chairs, assembled from various rooms and a friendly neighbor's apartment, had been banished to the corners to make room for dancing. The delicately strung spiderwebs were torn and someone had eaten out the insides of Wade's canapés. Wade had doctored up some small menus announcing our festive feast:

Sinful Singles' Holy Halloween

October 31

We *dare* you to take a bite of our dinner . . .

Canapés

∾

White Bean Salad
Stuffed Chicken Breasts
Funeral Potatoes
Broccoli and Mystery Sauce

∾

Sorbet

∾

And hopefully, you will be alive to enjoy . . .
Tongue Tantalizing Toffee

They were now serving as coasters. Our first course had been stuffed into a plastic container (Note to self: Beans are not a group fave.), and the guys had dug into the Funeral Potatoes using coffee mugs instead of the etched glass dishes I had borrowed from work. But the Devil was cavorting with our resident Angel, and the male Tooth Fairy was dirty dancing with a Cinderella. Our first Thing was a success.

I barely heard the praise for my star-spangled butt as my attention was focused on finding my jolly green giant. Three hours in, as the clock ticked toward eleven, I finally saw a green entity. My Hunk had entered the building. I ran, lasso in hand, to the far side of the room, draped myself over his shoulders, grabbed his strong jawline and planted my most super-powered kiss on his gorgeous mouth. I was in a go-get-'em kind of mood. Forget the candy, I wanted the treats! He returned my kiss with a passion I could only equate to long-lost lovers on a deserted island. I swear it lasted so long I was breathing through my ears. He grabbed onto my golden-cinched waist and I simultaneously praised the weeklong water diet I had been on.

"Wonder Woman, wow!" I figured he was referring to my eagle-bearing cleavage. "You can take me down anytime."

Now! I was thinking, Now! I opened my eyes and . . . I wasn't sure what I was staring at.

"You're not the Hunk—I mean the Hulk."

"No, I'm the Boogeyman!" a green guy with a pimply-looking mask said with pride.

"Not the Hulk," I repeated, ready to cry.

"No, but I am in your dreams. And now you'll definitely be in mine!" Oh, the lines! He reached for me, but I wiped my hands on my fishnet tights (I'd modernized Wonder Woman a bit) and backed away. What the hell had happened to my Hulk? Figures I'd end up kissing a snot-covered slob. Feeling the need to redeem myself, and feeling slighted that Mr. J. P. Morgan had blown off my exclusive invite, I made my way through the throngs, seeking a cute boy to kiss. I knew Tara would be surrounded by such boys. True to form, she was backed, willingly, into a corner with five guys. I assessed the options and zeroed in on a Greek God.

$$\infty$$

"Who am I? Who am I really?" My train of thought during my sexual romps would be a psychologist's wet dream. For instance, now, with my wrists wrapped in Greek God's fake ivy, I was thinking about how far I had come in three months. True, I had not conquered the corporate world or received a marriage proposal, or wrangled any sort of commitment for that matter from Mr. J. P. Morgan, but I did have a little white square box of an apartment in one of the greatest cities in the world. The cutie on top of me, on the other hand, still hadn't moved out of his parents' house. He had explained to me that he just didn't feel the rush to join the corporate race, especially considering he had no idea what interested him. His major in Classics hadn't given him a clear direction. (Classics at my college had been the jocks' choice of study since they only had to read and write glorified stories about mythological gods—all of whom they desired to emulate.) Now he told me that he was seriously thinking about law school (an easy extra three years of prestigious noncommitment). But in part I envied his carefree spirit. I especially admired it when he'd captured my mouth in the middle of dancing to "Oh, What a Night!" We had snuck off to the bathroom and the *Grease 2* bowling song about "scoring" had blasted from my inner core. "We're gonna scorrre tonight, we're gonna scorrre tonight!"

Soon enough, the sink's ill-placed faucet brought me back from my drunken haze. That and Syd's voice shouting on the other side of the bathroom door.

"Charlieeeee!" she called, pounding on the door with her fists. "Phoneeeeee!"

I quickly held out my wrists to Greek God waiting for him to untangle the ivy, then plopped an apologetic kiss on his cheek. I stood, readjusted my crown, and gathered the other hastily strewn parts of my costume. I flung open the door and stepped out into the drunken masses. Syd handed me the phone and I pushed my way through the crowd to get to my bedroom.

"Hello," I answered.

"Hellloooo to you Miss Charlie-poo." It was J. P. Morgan. "Whatcha dooooing?" he asked, slurring his words. I looked down at my watch. It was midnight and he was definitely out partying. Wherever he was, he was completely piss drunk.

"Our party is still going on."

"Oh yeahhhhhh, the party." I wanted to scream. Had he not gotten the Evite reminder?

"Yep!"

"How's that *thiiinng gooooing?*"

"This *Thing*'s okay."

"Um, I just finished work." I could hear loud voices and clanking glasses in the background.

"Where are you now?"

"Whaattttt?"

"Where are you now?" Did I really need to yell? I was Wonder Woman. Wonder Woman didn't yell.

"Met some of the guys out, ew-up-rpp." What was that? Was it a burp? What, from too much Scotch?

"Are you going to swing by now?" Ever hopeful.

"Nah, don't have a costume. Sorry, babe."

"You don't need a . . ." and then I stopped. What was I doing trying to convince him? This was supposed to be our honeymoon-slash-wooing phase. He should have been running my way. Something rumbled in my stomach. Too many Funeral Potatoes, I thought.

"Gotta run! Someone is looking for me," I lied. I didn't tell him that I had been looking for him all night.

⌒

"*I* think I lost my costume," Syd mourned the next morning. We had found her passed out on the toilet at about 9:00 A.M. Her white gown had pooled around her ankles while glitter mingled with the drool escaping her mouth.

"Do you think it's drugs?" Macie had whispered. Just then Syd's head popped up.

"No, no drugs. Iss jusss bee'a—" She had slurred before falling off her heavenly throne.

Now Tara demanded, "What do you mean you 'lost it'? You were an angel, what could you lose?"

"Well, a pimp daddy walked off with my wings, and I think I gave Elvis my halo," she admitted before curling up on her bed in the fetal position.

"You are indeed a fallen angel!" Tara cheered. "Congratulations!" The comment actually mustered a blush from Sydney.

I was sitting on the couch twirling a hastily constructed ivy crown around my finger. God, a diamond ring would look so much better than this fake leafy thing. And I had thought it had looked so good the night before—must have been how those green eyes complemented the wreath. I tossed my hookup token on my bedroom door: the splendor and spoils of victory. It would hang there for about a month, until the dangling dust bunnies annoyed Macie to the point where she made some comment about resting on my laurels.

"What's up with you, Charlie?" Tara prodded as she shoved some cold leftover Funeral Potatoes into her mouth. "You look like someone died."

"Well, J. P. was a no-show—"

"Surprise, surprise," muttered Tara.

"And then I hooked up with some random Adonis." I continued. "Should I feel guilty?"

"Guilty? Nah," Macie dismissed. Macie was in a lotus yoga pose, sporting quite an afterglow from her own holiday escapades.

"You were spontaneous," Tara threw in.

"Would J. P. feel guilty?" I wondered aloud. Wait. Had he been hooking up? My heart hiccupped.

"Did he call yet?" asked Tara.

"Nope." I paused. "So what about Greek God?"

"What about him?" Tara demanded. "Mr. J. P. Morgan didn't show up. Nor did he call until almost midnight. What were you supposed to do, wait?" Syd rolled over and gave me weak thumbs up in agreement. I sighed. The drama of it all. After my escapade with the Greek God, I'd realized that not much had changed in the past few months after all—and I'd decided that I was going to change the fact that not much had changed. I was sick of no strings, college-style hookups. I wanted exclusivity. I didn't even know how to spell the word, but I wanted it.

"You were Wonder Woman, for God's sake! Mighty, independent—"

"And flying solo," I finished.

"Mr. J. P. Morgan needs to be kicked off his mighty throne," murmured Syd from her bedroom.

"Or knocked off the toilet," laughed Macie.

"At least I'm not pregnant!" Syd added.

"You were expecting to be expecting?" Wade questioned. Tara, Mace, and I rolled our eyes. Syd had this intense fear of becoming with child. She had an economy-sized box of pregnancy test sticks in the bathroom. At least once a month she would tear out of our little bathroom singing the praises of her empty uterus. You'd think that anyone with such a fear would just abstain from sex, but not Syd. No, her reassurance rested in that narrow white plastic stick. And don't think that she was above bragging about her expertise at holding the stick steadily under her flowing stream of urine. (P.S. Pregnancy Test Makers: Talk about lack of dignity in a stressful time, please advise.)

"Well, he did call last night," I ventured.

"And that redeems him? Did he actually come over to see you and spend time with you?" Macie, ever the realist, asked. I shrugged.

"You should be in the Salad Stage," she continued.

"The what?"

"The Salad Stage. You know, that beginning stage—when you meet someone exciting and everything is light and refreshing. Nothing is complicated yet. You're still honeymooning over the idea of a budding relationship. It's the best phase, the Salad Stage. And relationships, with food or men, are not supposed to be that complicated. They should be easy."

"I don't like roughage anyway," I assured her. "Can we change the subject now?" Macie picked a feather from under her left thigh.

"Okay," she said grinning. "Did I mention that I was a spring chicken last night? And damn, was I plucked!" Way to sum it up, Mace!

November

Better Than Ben Affleck Dessert
Serves 6–8

Crust

> 1 cup finely chopped pecans
> 1 cup flour
> ½ cup margarine
> 3 tablespoons granulated sugar

Preheat oven to 350° F. Mix the crust ingredients together with spoon. Pat into greased 13 × 9-inch pan. Bake crust for 15 to 20 minutes till golden brown. Remove the crust from oven and let it cool.

First Layer

> 1 cup powdered sugar
> One 8-ounce package cream cheese
> One 12-ounce tub Cool Whip

Mix the powdered sugar, cream cheese, and Cool Whip with electric mixer and pour mixture on top of cooled crust.

Second Layer

> 1 box Jell-O Instant Pudding, chocolate or vanilla
> 2 cups cold milk

Mix the Jell-O and milk with electric mixer slowly until it thickens.
Spread on top of cream cheese mixture.

Third Layer
    One 12-ounce tub of Cool Whip

Spread Cool Whip on top of Jell-O layer

Fourth Layer
    ½ cup grated Hershey Chocolate Bars

Sprinkle chocolate shavings all over the top of the dessert. Refrigerate for 2 to 3 hours.

Serve to your sassiest single ladies. You'll have even the biggest skeptics asking, "Ben who?"

In New York City, the fall is one of the friendliest times of the year. The air is not too humid, it's crisp and refreshing. There are usually a few last days of Indian summer spattered here and there. You can still dine at one of the hundreds of outdoor cafes that line the various avenues and streets, or you can cozy up in one of those quaint back garden restaurants in Little Italy. You can thankfully dress to the nines and not have to worry about donning a bulky winter wrap . . . yet. You can drink to Columbus, Halloween, the New York City Marathon, or to the Veterans.

True to form, my first November in New York arrived with a lot of hype and expectation. Holiday sales began right after Halloween, so window shopping was the sport of choice. The pre-holiday season allowed for guiltless shopping—it's better to give than to receive—shop, shop! One can't help but be optimistic as Christmas carols are blared from street performers' trumpets and keyboards at every intersection. Even the ringing of the Salvation Army's bells seemed to harmonize with the taxis' horns. Second to the sport of credit card swiping, one of New York's premier athletic events, the New York Marathon, always held on the first weekend in November, was fast approaching.

The city was so eager to capitalize on the marathon that it was practically boiling huge pots of carbo-loaded pasta for the runners who were about to descend upon the city from around the world. None of us, meaning me and my girls, was running. After our collective Halloween dinner party debauchery, we had all theorized about running it one day—one day in the distant future. But on Marathon Sunday, we all decided to meet at mile 25, located on the east side of Central Park South, for inspiration. Syd showed up looking confused. The cops had reworked the traffic patterns. The roads that ran east now ran west and vice versa—and the transit restructuring had drastically affected the city and its inhabitants.

"Good God, there are cops everywhere!" she fumed. "One of 'em wouldn't even let me near Tavern on the Green! Totally annoying."

"Syd, that's because it's the finish line and you are not a runner," Macie explained.

"Yes, but I always use the bathroom there after I have my soda and pretzel from the guy on Seventy-ninth Street, and he wouldn't let me near it!"

Meanwhile, Tara was cheering on the marathon runners as they went by. Most of them wore their names scribbled onto their shirts, and Tara, always good at getting close to people, was making intimate athletic connections on the sidelines.

"You go, Gary!" she screamed. "Shake those arms out or you'll cramp up! Go, Suzy, go! Hon, you can see your butt crack, hike those shorts up!" You could tell that she was going to be one fanatical soccer mom someday. "Come on, get going, Tyrone!"

"Jesus, Tara, I would break my stride to run over and deck you if you told me to 'get going' at mile twenty-five," scolded Macie. Tara just shrugged and unzipped her Juicy sweatshirt a bit.

"And why are you wearing a jogging suit when you are clearly not running?" Sage asked her.

"Why to blend in, of course. But I want to blend in and look good . . . not be puking in the bushes with my knees knocking and my hair matted down with sweat." She gave another thumbs up to a nearby runner who was in just such a state.

"If you really want to blend in, you need your name on your sweatshirt," suggested Wade. "Maybe you should have that top monogrammed?"

"I'd rather get my phone number tattooed on the back," Tara laughed, "8-6-7-5-3-0-9!"

✍

About an hour later, post a finish line photo op to remember our classic New York moment, we arrived at Top Shelf, ready to celebrate the marathon that we had not taken part in. Each and every bar on Broadway was packed, with lines out the doors due to the proximity to the finish line. It occurred to me that my father would have a field day making a math problem out of the situation. I'd figured you could calculate how many New Yorkers were *not* running the marathon simply by watching the bar bathroom lines. Subtract that number from the total city population and you'd know just how many runners had to be from out of state or from the other side of the world.

"I'd be pretty pissed if I was running, and the rest of the city was boozing," Wade remarked. "If I ran next year, would y'all come cheer me on or would you be scoping out the best bar stools?"

"Honey, I'd be standing on my bar stool and toasting your mighty fine running posture as you breezed by!" answered Tara.

Speaking of the sheer numbers, the bathroom lines on this Sunday afternoon were approximately twenty-five to forty-five minutes long. The boys' line, of course, moved efficiently. The girls' line, however, was stagnant. A fellow GBL (girls' bathroom liner) and I decided that the bathroom process was a lot like running the marathon: You trained your muscles beforehand—kegel exercises allowed one to hold it for as long as possible; once in the middle of the throng, you bonded with other participants—over the course of twenty minutes, we decided that we were supposed to be best friends after this trying experience; you begin to cheer on everyone else:

"Come on, you can do it!"

"Pick up the pace, go, go, go!"

"You're almost there!"

"Way to go, you are a speedy one!"

Some other GBLs gave us dirty looks as they exited. Apparently they did not appreciate such encouragement. But as we neared the finish line, with those metal stall doors in sight, the mental game kicked in. Just like the runners must surely feel, all of a sudden I could not go on. I began to groan, not sure if I could make it. I had made it so far, and now with the end in reach, I was not sure I was going to be successful! The cramps, the tears. But to make a long story short, my new best friend and I both made it and high-fived each other (after washing our hands, of course). I was as high as a kite and had not felt this good in a long time (granted because the oppressive pressure on my bladder had ceased). By the end of Marathon Sunday, after all the excitement and a few too many beers and Bloody Marys, we were all camped out on our respective couches, exhausted, a bit wired, quite light-headed, and not sure we were going to make it to work the next day. Runners, we can definitely relate!

∽

In addition to my vicarious runner's high, I'd recently been on a Mr. J. P. Morgan high as well. After his no-show at our Halloween dinner party, I had been willing him not to call (okay, maybe not with much effort—it was a short-lived endeavor). Then, the day after the marathon, he called and asked me to help him shop for a new tie. Although I should have said no and played hard to get, he did sound pretty darn sweet on the phone. He even apologized for not making it to our holiday get-together. I could tell by his tone on the phone that he wanted to see me, and that had to mean something. So I decided to meet him on the East Side the next day after work for our shopping date.

We headed toward the new Thomas Pink store on Madison Avenue, where I deduced that he was destined to be successful since he was willing to throw away more than $100 on a tie for a Thanksgiving dinner with family friends he didn't really know. We picked out a bold green tie with flecks of blue (to match his eyes).

"What do you need, C?" he asked fingering the cashmere scarves. What? Was he going to buy me something? Or was he simply inquiring if I was going to shop too? I could feel my credit card twitching in my bag, reminding me of my swollen balance.

"Oh, I really don't need anything," I said. "I have everything I want." I grabbed his hand. Did he catch my subtle meaning? Ugh, was that too over the top? He rubbed his thumb over the back of my hand as we waited in line. But contact was lost when his cell phone rang.

"Hey!" he greeted someone in a warm voice. Friend, girlfriend, cheating soul? "Yep. Nope. Done already. Hey, I gotta go, Charlie is with me." I practically gave myself whiplash as I spun around at the mention of my name. Someone on the phone knew who I was!

"Sorry, my mom checking in," he explained. His mom? I was mentioned to his mom? His mom knew my name? Would I call her Mrs. Morgan or Madge? Was her first name Madge? Where had that come from? What did I care? I was in love!

∽

Even though the month had started out with a bang (although the Marathon marshals didn't use real guns anymore), November's damp fingers soon began to grip the city. Dawn broke on Thanksgiving Thursday and I knew immediately that it was not going to be a good New York day. I could typically judge a day as being either "a good New York day" or "not a good New York day" after being awake for only a few hours. My methods were not as complicated as true qualitative research, but they were pretty reliable nonetheless. And there were no in betweens.

I had my doubts on Thanksgiving morning as I passed through our building's double door. I was forever wishing that we had a revolving door at the entrance to our building. On a good NY day, I could have breezed through it like Marlo Thomas in *That Girl*. (Remember her, the modern girl, so entranced with the New York skyscrapers that she was looking up at them during the opening credits?) On a not good NY day, I could have taken out my bad mood by slamming against the doors and going round and round. Somehow I knew that this childish move would put a smile on my face; kind of like when you hear the theme to *Sesame Street*, and you can't help but grin and hum. Unfortunately, our building sported run of the mill double doors with rusty locks and chipped paint. Even my grandmother could break those puppies down. In my opinion, safety wasn't the issue; it was more of a psychological necessity to have a revolving door.

As I strolled up the block, my gut was telling me that my very first Thanksgiving in NYC was doomed. The sky was overcast, the gray clouds spitting gray raindrops onto the gray skyscrapers standing tall next to the gray bare trees shadowing the gray concrete sidewalks. So what do I do when I'm having a depressing day like this? I head straight for the nearest food vendor of course.

My "happy" place was Moe's Deli. The location? A mere two hundred paces from my decrepit double door. The food culprit? Double-Stuffed Oreos and a bag of Jet-Puffed Marshmallows. I know, it's an odd match, but oh what a perfect recipe to clear those gray skies. And as my mouth began to salivate thinking about the marshmallows, I bit the side of my mouth. Nards! The acidic taste of blood filled my mouth. And, as if things couldn't get any worse, down I went. Literally. My heel caught and I pitched forward, landing splayed out on the filthy sidewalk. I was practically making an upside-down angel with the concrete.

"Jesus Christ!" I shouted. First, my Stila shimmer eye shadow fell out of my purse and went straight for the dog pee south of my right foot. Next a couple of my super-plus-sized tampons rolled down the sidewalk and straight into the sewerage drain. Not good because A, it was that time of the month and B, those cotton puppies that cost probably a penny to make are so expensive in the city. A box of ten costs like fifteen bucks and God knows, we all need more than ten to get through the five-day cycle. And as if it couldn't get any worse, my absolutely favorite to-die-for, must-have, and don't-kiss-without-it twenty-five dollar, juicy peach lip gloss spun out of control right under the homeless man who happened to be taking a catnap next to me. Could I get a little help here folks? I began to giggle like a crazy person. So ladies and gentleman, there you have it. A classic example of a not good NY day.

I stood up and quickly brushed off my soiled and possibly ruined pair of black pants, hoping that my quick reflexes would help me regain some sort of dignity. As I ducked under the awning of the building next door, I even managed to miraculously swipe my juicy gloss from underneath the homeless man. Call it divine intervention, or the almighty gloss gods, but the dear man happened to shift his entire body to the left mid-snore. Once he was belly up, there was my lip gloss, exposed and ready for rescue. I took a deep breath and reached out, somehow managing to find the tube within two stabs. Okay, things were improving slightly. I plunked myself down on the building's stoop to try to pull myself together. Smoothing out my hair and applying a quick coat of peachy nectar on my lips, I noticed in my now-cracked compact mirror (Note to self: Don't believe the seven years of bad luck hype.) that I looked utterly horrible. Then, out of the corner of my eye, I happened to notice a pair of more than five hundred dollar fuck-me Jimmy Choo stiletto shoes tapping right underneath my nose. I glanced up cautiously.

"Honey, can you tell your boyfriend that I have a package coming this afternoon, and that it is very important for him to keep it upright?" she said.

"Who? What?" I noticed that I sounded very much like the ditsy teenager I never was. My cheek throbbed and I felt like I probably had blood dripping out of my mouth like Countess Drac-u-dork.

"Yes dear. Juan, your boyfriend? Will you give him my message, sweetness? I figure you'll see him when he gets in." She nodded as if that was going to convince me.

Juan? Juan who? No, she couldn't be talking about door-man next-door Juan? I quickly realized that this high-flouting, sexed-out and sassed-up woman thought that I was the girl-friend of the doorman in her building! We girls liked to refer to Doorman Juan as our free apartment therapist. He would listen and nod so sincerely when went on drunken tirades at 2:00 A.M. in front of his building. From sex to work to parents, Juan knew all our torrid tales. And who cared if he hardly spoke any English? We knew he could feel our pain.

"No!" I screamed. "My boyfriend's name is J. P. Morgan."

"Yes, well whatever you call him. This is America and we all can have lofty dreams, my dear. I bet he will get there some-day. Ciao daaarling!" And with that final condescending "I'm better than you are so piss off" good-bye, the fuck-me stilettos were off down the block. I bet she was having a marvelous god-damned good NY day.

"She doesn't know what the hell she's talking about," I grumbled. I had a fantastic boyfriend. I had a J. P. Morgan. Not a Juan Morgan. But wait! I'd finally uttered that sacred word "boyfriend"! I, Charlotte Brown, had a boyfriend. Or did I? My mind began spinning out of control. Was he or wasn't he? I mean, we had never actually defined what we were. It wasn't like at bars or at parties he introduced me by saying, "This is my girlfriend, Charlie." So far, when we hung out with his friends at Top Shelf, he had only managed to say, "This is Charlie." It was always short and simple, but nevertheless, an introduction. Not too many details and so much left hanging. To think of it, J. P. Morgan and I really hadn't ever had the whole "me like you, you like me, so let's be boyfriend and girl-friend" convo. But, on the other hand, if an outsider looked at our relationship they would definitely say that we were "hang-ing out" with each other. That was good, right? I mean, when he's not canceling on me, or passing out on me, he and I do have a pretty darn good time together. Heck, his mother even knew who I was. That had to count for something. And since our shopping excursion for a tie, he and I had hooked up a cou-ple of times here and there. But, come to think of it, the last time I actually saw J. P. was last weekend at my place and that didn't really go over too well. (I'll explain later!) So in reality, he and I haven't spoken in about four or five days. Heeelllloo Charlie, reality check! If J. P. were really my "boyfriend," then he would be calling me every day. Heck, he'd be calling me multiple times a day. (I have *Swingers* on DVD and therefore I know that a week is way too many days past the two-day phone call etiquette dictated by the rules of the dating game.) I sighed. Definitely not a good NY day. It wasn't even 10:00 A.M. and I was already banged, bruised, and tamponless. And to top it off, I was alone, bleeding, poor, dizzy, dating a doorman, and hadn't even had a single cup of coffee yet.

As I sat on the stoop licking my wounds, I could feel my heart getting heavier and heavier. I started to do some deeper analysis on my relationship with Mr. J. P. Morgan. To date, he and I have met up a bunch of times, hooked-up a bunch of different ways, and sort of come within millimeters of having sex, yet we still hadn't consummated nor defined our sort of relationship. Was it just physical or was there a commitment? Does one plus one equal one, or does one plus one equal two? My dad would have a field day with the math.

Why do females always have to overanalyze relationships? Why can't we just be like boys—sleep around and not give a damn? You know what it is? It is straight-up confidence. That's what it is. As I rounded the corner kiosk, the plethora of tabloids caught my eye. Smiling from beneath a headline of lies, J. Lo radiated. No matter what her straits, that girl exudes the confidence of a shark in a pool of guppies. She goes around and swings her thing and doesn't give a shit about what anyone thinks. She is always looking out for the numero-uno player, herself. Now, would she play the male game? I think not. And with each J. Lo thought I began to get a little bit stronger and a hell of a lot tougher. My walk down the block even got a little sassier. I began to sing "I'm just Jenny from the block. I used to have a little and now I've got a lot!" Damn, that Puerto Rican princess was a genius. "Jenny from the Block" puts on her short shorts, gets out on the field, and just swings away. J. Lo would definitely tell me to get in the game.

Humming J. Lo tunes, I decided that I'd have to play by the boys' rules from now on. But even if I played the "man game," in order to actually win I needed a new strategy. I decided that a new system of bases was in order. You know the base system—the one you first learned about at summer camp that rates how far you have gone sexually or presexually. First base: kissing (whether just the simple kiss or whether tongue is involved is always a topic of debate). Second base: steps it up a notch with up and under the shirt action (or, for the chaste, French kissing comes in here). Third base: going down; yes, as in oral sex. Home base: the end-all, or at least the end of all virginity. However, while that rating system worked in high school, it no longer reflected my playing field. In real life the stakes were higher and the countdown to old maid status more imminent. Therefore, and since most of us skip ahead to sex pretty quickly these days, the base system should reflect more accurate relationship milestones. First base: dating, casual, yet full good behavior—flowers and all that. Second base: girlfriend and boyfriend status; the label is adopted by mutual consensus at this point and readily volunteered to others. Third base: the honeymoon is over and the pressure is on. Wedding invites include you as "and guest" or by actual name. As one of my good guy friends had recently admitted, "A wedding date? It's as good as being engaged!" And home base: "Da-da-da-da" (think wedding theme—or in the males' harmonic version, "Dum-dum-dumb-*dumb!*").

With my new system in place (but no resolution to the boyfriend thing) I steeled my resolve and made my way to Moe's Deli. Once there, Moe, who always knew what I wanted, handed me my much-needed cup of vanilla nonfat café au lait (aka flavored Folgers with a splash of skim milk and a scoop of calorie-laden vanilla powder). Nodding and smiling with my best look of gratitude, I took a huge gulp, skipped the marshmallows and Oreos combo, and went out to try to seize the day once more. There's nothing like a stiff cup of coffee to get my head screwed on straight in horrible situations.

I was fully awake now, but still not at optimal cheer level. Needless to say, the whole "work" thing was throwing me for a loop this time of year—another reality check of real life. Unfortunately, since Syd, Macie, Wade, and I were at the absolute bottom of the pecking order at our jobs, we had to work a full day the Wednesday before Thanksgiving, and a full day the Friday after. We only got measly Thanksgiving Thursday off. How generous of our employers! Growing up, we had become accustomed to so many winter, summer, spring, religious, Independence, Memorial, and Labor days off, that working around holidays came as a shock to the system. You'd think that my boss, the Diva, would want her employees to embrace and celebrate this all-American holiday, but nope. Thanksgiving was one of the bread-and-butter money makers for *Sunshine & Sensibility* and we had to work round the clock to keep the juggernaut moving, though rumor had it that we would be treated to a spectacular lunch the day after good ole Turkey Day. Having said that, I'd also heard that the Diva served up a triple oyster stuffing in lieu of a Jell-O cranberry mold in order to make her female employees fat. Apparently, she didn't like pretty, slim women in her presence. First, she worked us like dogs, then she stuffed us like turkeys. So we became not only disgruntled employees, but employees who were depressed and obsessed over their waistlines. I knew that come Friday, while the Diva was relishing in her turkey-induced lethargy at her farm in Connecticut, I would be sitting in my cubicle waiting for the phone to ring while shoveling her famous blueberry cobbler pie in my mouth. I also knew that despite my vigilance, the phone wouldn't ring and I wouldn't stop at one scoop of cobbler.

Thanksgiving happened to be one of my favorite holidays,

which made me even more melancholy. I knew that my mom had been up since the crack of dawn, stuffing the turkey; the smell was probably wafting through the house right now. Growing up, we'd all come out in our pj's and would gather round the stove begging Mom for a little taste of her famous chestnut stuffing. Just thinking about it made my stomach rumble.

Not to be defeated, Syd, Macie, Wade, and I had decided that we would finally christen our oven and make a grand, albeit cheap, Thanksgiving dinner at the apartment. When Tara learned that we were staying in the city, she didn't want to miss out on the "party." So she called her always-pregnant sister, who was hosting their family dinner, and lied, saying that she had to work too. "You know how it is, sis. They just work us to the bones! I just have to put in the face time if I want to move up. My boss was saying that she wanted a meeting soon, so I have to make an extra big effort in the next week or so."

I arrived home clutching my vanilla café au lait and surveyed the scene. Even as the "uninvited" guest, Tara had taken complete control. It was clear that she had hip-checked Wade right out of the head position in the kitchen and was now standing over the sink, preparing the turkey.

"Finally, I'm getting some!" she gloated as she stuck her hands up the turkey's butt and into the gooey depths of the innards. At the kitchen table, Syd was concentrating on making beer bread. I already had been banned from the cooking festivities after I'd bought cranberry juice instead of cranberry sauce for Wade's grandmother's recipe, but I figured at least the juice would come in handy for those dreaded UTIs. I'd tried to make good by piping up about my mom's stuffing recipe, but I couldn't remember if the stuffing had apples or sliced water chestnuts or both. Macie had put on the Macy's Day Parade in the other room, and I wandered in there like a rejected dog. No wonder Macie and my mother got along so well—every year my mother made a big deal about the parade. Just what is so entrancing about overblown balloons of old cartoon characters (sorry, Woody Woodpecker) floating in the chilly November air accompanied by piss-poor commentary from high-ranked correspondents? Tara, the talented imitator, was doing her best sing-song remarks from the kitchen.

"Now look, Dick, here comes Woody! Oh, he looks even larger this year! See how he is pointed straight up? For an old man, he sure is flying high." Macie clicked her tongue in disapproval. "Oh no, the Pink Panther is looking a little limp this year. Gosh, all he needs is just a good blow. I'm sure we can find a volunteer to fill the job," Tara giggled with a huff and a puff. I sat on the living room floor sipping my coffee and went back to stewing over the whole boyfriend issue. Sooner or later, I figured that either the vanilla coffee or fumes from the beer bread would lift my spirits.

"What's that smell?" Macie whined. I stuck my nose in the air thinking that disaster was imminent. "No, it's not from the kitchen," Macie deduced. "God, Charlie, can you not bring that nasty coffee into the house?"

Within three months I had learned that the most fragile relationship anyone will ever be in is that of the female room-mate situation. Unlike when we were in college, we now had real-life stresses: credit card late charges, tub drain blockage, dead houseplants, bland Thai takeout, coworker gossip, and lousy kisses, all of which only added to the precarious, bitchy communication naturally found between girls. I tried to smile as Macie made retching noises. She hated the scent of vanilla coffee. She said that the scent reminded her of her unsupportive soccer coach in fourth grade. Apparently the woman would sip vanilla coffee as she told Macie to "work off some of that extra weight" with some extra laps. Being a conscientious roommate and not wanting to give Macie the shakes, I usually tried not to expose her to vanilla coffee. But today was not a good NY day and I needed it bad.

"So where is J. P.?" Macie asked looking up from the television set. Why she hadn't thought to go down to the corner and watch the real shebang on Central Park West was beyond me.

"At home in Connecticut."

"Oh. And what's the latest?" I hated how my romance, or lack thereof, was like the headlines of the nightly news. Everyone wanted updates every twenty minutes.

"Ugh. I don't know. Remember how we left Top Shelf together last weekend?" Macie nodded. "Well, we came back here and I innocently suggested that we go into my room, where, you know, there is no distracting television set and no ESPN . . ." I paused. Macie smiled as Tara walked into the room. She wanted to hear the story too.

"So, have any of you ever heard about Lova-Rubba-Cumma, that lubricating massage oil?" I asked.

"Hell yes! They advertise on late-night infomercials," Tara exclaimed. "Charlie, you have some?" she asked raising her hand to her mouth feigning shock.

"Yeah. I had a wild moment and actually bought some in one of those West Village sex shops."

"They're *erotica* shops," Tara corrected. "Can I borrow it sometime?" I winced at the idea of sharing a used bottle of love oil.

"Well, I strongly advise against using it," I told them. "This is my gift to you from my inner circle of knowledge. I can attest that it can cause an allergic reaction, especially in that nether region, if you know what I mean."

"Why, what happened?" asked Syd as she came into the room, licking the bread batter from her fingers.

I sighed. "So I decided to be bold and I slathered this love juice all over my hands. By the way, it doesn't smell pretty—kind of like car oil overlaid with vanilla; it reminds me of the minty cod liver oil my mom used to make me take. Anyway, I reached down and began to stroke."

"Details, Charlie, details! I mean good God, you're using lubricating oil. I want Danielle Steel details!" Tara reprimanded.

"Okay! First he began to smile, his eyes were half closed, and then he moaned like a cat in heat. Lova-Rubba-Cumma is supposed to 'heat up slightly with a light loving touch.' So, like any pleasing woman, I thought I was headed in the right direction. Well, he then drew in a sharp breath and then another, and he moaned again. But this time the moaning began to sound more ragged and he began to hyperventilate! Now, I can be a maven in the bedroom, but this was a new reaction even for me. His eyes flew open and then, he screamed. Not a wow scream but an owwww type of scream. He leapt up from the bed pointing frantically at his genital region!" Tara bit back a laugh.

"No really, I was scared!" I protested. "There he was leaping and spinning like the best of them at the New York City Ballet. So at this point, I didn't know whether to throw the cup of water from my bedside table on him or grab his penis and try to rub the oil off of it. I finally just directed him to the shower and after that I couldn't tell whether the next scream was from relief or from the shock of our often too-cold water."

"Thinking back on it, I heard that yell." Macie said. "I just chalked it up to your—what did you call them—maven ways." I glared at her before continuing.

"It was terrible! Within two seconds, he had leapt out of the shower, wrapped himself in my towel, and fled the apartment. Yes," I confirmed before Syd could interrupt, "towel-clad, down the stairs and out the front door. And I haven't heard from him since."

"Devastating," Macie deadpanned.

"Horrific," Tara shuddered.

"Wasn't he cold?" Syd asked. "You know, shrinkage?" We stared at her.

"No, well, okay . . . Mortifying," she concluded with sincerity. Atta girl, Syd!

⟡

"Y'all?" began Wade. "Even though we are missing Sage, not that she'd eat anyway, I say that this here dinner is our official November Cooking Club meeting. I mean when have we ever even come close to such a cooking feat?" We were huddled around our cafe table surveying the remnants of Tara's cranberry sauce, Syd's beer bread, and Macie's slightly pink turkey. It had been a simple meal, but the pilgrims had prided themselves on Yankee minimalism. And as if it couldn't get any better, Wade brought out her dessert with a whopping grin on her face. The "Better than Ben Affleck Dessert" as she called it. Now, mankind has exalted the wonders of chocolate for centuries. Chocolate was rumored to be an aphrodisiac but either way I found it mood-altering. It wasn't that I wanted sex, at least not any more than I did before the pie, but at the very sight of all those chocolate shavings I slowly began to have a good NY day!

We fought spoon to spoon to dig into this delight. Each layer proved to be more rich than the last. I savored each bite—from the chocolate, to the pudding, to the surprising creamy layer, to the nutty bottom. The whole dessert made my life flash before my eyes—from childhood, when I would sing along with Mr. Cosby as I ate Jell-O pudding; to college, when my dirty talking hook-up brought whipped cream to bed one night (only to get too high on whip-its to notice my nakedness); to my present-day nuttiness over Mr. J. P. Morgan (my Abnormal Psych professor in college used to claim that craziness is correlated to genius).

Tara, on the other hand, seemed to be shoveling rather than savoring, quickly making her way to the bottom of the dish. Maybe this was my problem. Maybe I was treading too lightly in my relationship with J. P. Maybe I needed to forgo the baby steps and the little nibbles of romance. Maybe I needed to dig in and dive deep.

"My mother used to call this recipe her 'Better than Tom Selleck Dessert,' Wade giggled with chocolate uncharacteristically adorning her nose.

"God," moaned Tara. "He is the only man on the planet who actually looks yummy with a mustache."

"She would whip this up for her lady friends and they'd all sit around and discuss their erotic memories of high school boyfriends long gone. It was a welcomed break from husbands and kids."

"A precursor to our Cooking Club in a way," theorized Macie.

"Yep! They even joked that this dish should be called the Better than Sex dessert—"

"Wild and crazy women," quipped Tara.

"I figured that we needed to update the recipe with the times—no more Tom Selleck. Tom Cruise is too eighties and Brad Pitt is too blond for this chocolate masterpiece, so I decided on Ben," Wade explained.

I'd just finished spooning the last of the pan's contents into my mouth when Macie sang, "Last bite is the Old Maid's!" I coughed on the spoonful. Not that I was superstitious, but did I really need any more obstacles in my quest for true love?

"Hey, let's all say something we're thankful for," suggested Syd.

"Besides this?" Tara mumbled, wiping chocolate from her mouth. "If J. Lo had tasted this, she would have gotten rid of Ben a lot sooner!" With a deft flick of her tongue she did not miss a drop. The things that girl can do with her tongue!

"Each person has to list at least ten things," commanded Syd.

"Ohh, goody! Let's write them down," offered the ever-so-practical Macie. Syd passed out the paper while I distributed the pens, and off we all went, listing our thankful things.

Charlie:
- Cheap mani-pedis
- Unused Metro cards
- Page Six
- Good friends (albeit fledgling cooks)
- Caller ID
- J. Lo
- Neurotic yet loving family
- My butter yellow rug
- Mac and cheese

- Mr. J. P. Morgan (we'll see how long he stays on the list)
- Vanilla coffee

Macie:
- Bloomingdale's
- Tennis whites
- Fast elevators
- Flowers reappearing on semi-dead plants
- Sample sales
- Any Chanel makeup
- My mother
- My roommates
- J. Lo
- Our humble apartment

Wade:
- Rhyming poems (or nursery rhymes)
- Smelly markers
- Pearls being still in fashion
- Sunday afternoons in Barnes & Noble
- Dear friends
- Scented soaps (esp. those from hotels)
- My cashmere sweaters
- My sister
- J. Lo
- Free movies in Bryant Park
- Popsicles

Sydney:
- Newfound cooking skills
- Wine of any flavor

- Spell check
- Double features (for the price of one)
- My friends in NYC
- Reruns
- Starbucks
- Hospital scrubs to sleep in
- J. Lo
- Central Park (my reprieve!)

Tara:
- Boys
- J. Lo
- Boys (yes, I can put it twice)
- The female orgasm
- Roses from the man on the street
- New *People* magazines
- My family
- My ability to remember any cute boy's number
- My cell phone
- Yoga (the really hot kind)
- Ladies' night discounts
- My birth!! (You should all add it to your lists!)

It was touching to see what my best friends had put down and some of the items were very telling. For instance, I knew that Tara loved yoga not for the inner peace aspect, but for the way it limbered her up for certain nocturnal activities. Sydney's hospital scrubs were remnants of her high-school boyfriend, her first real relationship. She still refuses to go into detail about "him" other than that he was older, and a med student, but she still wore those scrubs as pajamas and a reminder of happy times. As for Wade, we'd all long been convinced that her love of Popsicles was purely phallic. She always goes for the really big round ones in the park, the ones that require your mouth to form the perfect "O" shape. She has a knack for sucking without one dribble. Demure southern belle, my ass!

To critique myself, I'd used up one of my ten valued spots on Mr. J. P. Morgan. Part of me felt like it was too early to be putting his existence on paper. I didn't even know if I could qualify him as my boyfriend yet (see inner-struggle from this morning), but he'd added a new dimension to my life here in New York, for better or for worse. Being superstitious, I was probably jinxing myself. However, I felt I couldn't help but acknowledge that man who had brought Gerber daisies, bedtime romps, and drama into my life. Who wants a flatline existence? I crave those peaks and valleys. Bring on the drama, I say!

Upon later inspection and after five glasses of cheap merlot, we noticed that Tara had added to our lists:

Charlie:
- Cheap mani-pedis
- Unused Metro cards
- Page Six
- Good friends (albeit fledgling cooks)
- Caller ID
- J. Lo
- Neurotic yet loving family
- My butter yellow rug
- Mac and cheese
- Mr. J. P. Morgan (we'll see how long he stays on the list)
- Vanilla coffee
- **THE GODDESS TARA'S BIRTH!**

Macie:
- Bloomingdale's
- Tennis whites
- Fast elevators
- Flowers reappearing on semi-dead plants
- Sample sales
- Any Chanel makeup
- My mother
- My roommates
- J. Lo
- Our humble apartment
- **TARA'S PRESENCE IN THIS WORLD**

Wade:
- Rhyming poems (or nursery rhymes)
- Smelly markers
- Pearls being still in fashion
- Sunday afternoons in Barnes & Noble
- Dear friends
- Scented soaps (esp. those from hotels)
- My cashmere sweaters
- My sister
- J. Lo
- Free movies in Bryant Park
- Popsicles
- **TARA, TARA, TARA**

Sydney:
- Newfound cooking skills
- Wine of any flavor
- Spell check

- Double features (for the price of one)
- My friends in NYC
- Reruns
- Starbucks
- Hospital scrubs to sleep in
- J. Lo
- Central Park (my reprieve!)
- **TARA IN MY LIFE**

⁂

In truth, I was thankful for Tara in my life. I was thankful for her birth, and I'm sure she popped out like the friggin' finale at a Fourth of July fireworks display. Fittingly, her birthday was two days after Thanksgiving and we celebrated the following Thursday after Sage had returned from her homey Thanksgiving break. Ensconced at Top Shelf with a free birthday shot in her hand, Tara had conceded to the bar manager that the green felt pool table might indeed be marred by her savvy dance moves, and then had chosen the back bar top with its bottle rings and cigarette burns as an ideal dance platform instead. On top of the bar, wiggling her hips, she moved as if the beer were sloshing through all of her limbs at once.

It was no secret that Tara had moved to New York City knowing that her *Sex and the City* fantasies could be fulfilled without guilt. If Miranda could be a successful lawyer/mother with a terrific sex drive, then Tara could certainly be an unemployed coed/hottie with unquenchable sexual compulsions. Now, drunken eyes were ogling from across the room. She stared back—she had chosen her target. I followed her superhero-like gaze and saw none other than Mr. J. P. Morgan's best friend staring back at her, enraptured.

"Oh, shit! Tara is crossing the boundaries!" I moaned to Syd. In the girls' code of life, as close friends, you can be friends with but not hook-up with someone's ex-boyfriend; you can flirt with but not give a blow job to another's brother; you can like but not love one another's boyfriend's ex-girlfriend; and you can do shots with but not get too close to a current fling's best friend. Too soap opera-y. Think about it logically! If girlfriend A messes up with boyfriend's best friend B, you get a huge fucking mess on your hands; if A and B fall in love, they will cast a shadow on your own wavering relationship; or if B dicks over A, questions of female solidarity arise and A will not understand why you're still friends with B. Loyalties will stomp all over your relationship anyway you twist it! Tara could not finger (literally and/or figuratively) Mr. J. P. Morgan's best friend (aka Mr. Goldman Sachs). No way, no how.

At this point, Tara had turned and was gyrating solely in his direction. Like a snake charmer, she was bringing Mr. Goldman Sachs hither. He was attempting some pathetic dance moves in her direction, but looked more like a Disney character tiptoeing on steroids. Think of Beetlejuice doing his uncoordinated shuffle. When his face reached Tara's crotch, she swiftly bent down (thus revealing her cleavage) and wrapped her arms around his neck. God, was Mr. J. P. Morgan watching? He had to be here, they never did anything social alone. Was he mortified that he and I had looked just as pathetic at our first memorable Top Shelf encounter? My headed whipped from side to side in sheer panic. Where was he? Coat check, nope; bathroom door, nope; dance floor, nope; the Tiki Bar outside, yes. Phew. I could just get a glimpse of him in my peripheral vision. But my relief was quickly squelched as I noticed he was chatting with a nondescript blonde. You know the type. She was short and petite (but you knew the squat factor would be an issue in her forties); she had shoulder-length hair without layers (too risqué) and had obviously once been a towhead but hadn't yet discovered the wonders of highlights. Not really cute, but pleasant enough with a huge, bonded-tooth smile plastered on her face as he probably engaged her with the details of some finance deal he'd recently closed. Not that I'm the jealous type, but all of a sudden my mind was filled with images of he and she, the two of them with two kids—no scratch that, no kids (no time due to their all-consuming love)—kissing each other good-bye in the morning light, outside of their suburban Connecticut house before he climbed into his BMW and she into her Saab, leaving plenty early for their executive jobs. I was torn—should I thwart the happy hook-up of Tara and Mr. Goldman Sachs or wreck the happy home of Mr. J. P. Morgan and bland girl? I had to call in reinforcements. The closest help was Syd.

I decided to send her after Tara while I headed outside to Top Shelf's Tiki Bar. I do love Syd, but Ms. Space Cadet can get sidetracked even during an emotional crisis. Before I descended the stairs outside, I looked back to see my partner in crime dancing.

"J. Lo!" she mouthed apologetically throwing her hands into the air. At least J. Lo could relate to the situation:

This perfect romance that I've created in my mind
I'd live a thousand lives each one with you right by my side
But yet we find ourselves in a less than perfect circumstance
And so it seems like we'll never get the chance . . .

Macie grabbed my arm as I felt the first rum-enhanced breeze from the Tiki Bar hit my face.

"Where are you going?"

"Don't you see?" I said tilting my head in the direction of the too-smiley dirty blonde.

"Oh."

"Not that I care."

"No, of course not. But, Charlie, maybe you need to think about you and Mr. J. P. Morgan." Did I do much else in my downtime? She turned my face away from the two.

"He's a frog."

"What?"

"He's a frog. *Ribbit*." She could always coax a smile. "He's a frog and you need to let him go. Your prince is out there waiting for you. Really. And while your prince is waiting, he is passing the time by rescuing kittens, feeding the homeless, and spending time with the elderly. He is trimming your future rose bushes and touching up the trim on your five-bedroom house. He is buffing your Porsche with ab-enhancing deep knee bends. Your prince is waiting. He is not wasting time by looking at others in the meantime. No, he is fine with waiting by himself, alone, not with some plain-looking blonde. Charlie, trust me, your prince is out there."

"Can't Mr. J. P. Morgan be a filler though?" I asked pathetically.

"No! His nuts deserved to be crushed!"

"I'm on top of things, really," my tone sounded as convincing as my mother when she was extolling the benefits of liverwurst to me as a child.

"Plus, I think he has plenty of issues," she continued.

"Like what?" I begged for more moral support.

"I've always thought that he had gay tendencies," she said. "See the way he just flicked his wrist while talking! For

Christ's sake, that's just not natural for a straight guy. He's got pleats in his pants, so he's hiding something." That got another smile. "Sorry to tell you, but he may have some VDs. He's ears are a tad pink and I think that is a sign of something serious." Macie was trying hard to remain stonefaced. "His feet are too small. For God's sake, he is stepping out of his Gucci loafers. And lastly," she took a deep breath, "I heard from a reliable source that his mother's father was bald. You know what that means." Instantly I envisioned Mr. J. P. Morgan with a shiny noggin. Not so cute.

"Charlie, are you happy?" she asked. I paused.

"I think so," I muttered. "I mean yes," I stuttered as Mr. J. P. Morgan turned and grinned my way. Part the Red Sea!

"*Ribbit?*" I questioned one last time.

"*Ribbit,*" she confirmed. She grabbed my hand and swung me into a ballroom turn. Giggling, I turned and curtsied to her just as Mr. J. P. Morgan sauntered up. His ears really were kind of pink.

"Where have you been?" he asked with that coy smile of his.

"Here." Duh! "It's Tara's birthday," I explained.

"Yeah, I heard. Looks like she's the one giving out the presents though," he nodded toward Tara and Mr. Goldman Sachs canoodling in the corner. Clearly Syd had failed miserably.

"What's up?" I said. So much for relaxed and cool conversation. I'd lost all of my advanced vocabulary attained from years of Latin classes. Macie's croaking noises still echoed in my brain.

"Wanna go get something to eat?"

Ah, dilemmas! What to do? Finally, the boy had invited me to go get something to eat and I *was* kind of hungry. An angel and devil, the angel looking suspiciously like Macie, floated above my alcohol-clouded swollen head:

Question: Do I need to rescue Tara first?

Angel: *Sweetie, it's her birthday and you should stay and celebrate with her. She'd rather remember turning twenty-three with you than with sweaty Mr. Goldman Sachs.*

Devil: *Who are you kidding, rescuing? She is fine, she is always fine. She is queen of this domain.*

Question: Should I give Mr. J. P. Morgan the cold treatment and make him lust after me?

Angel: *Follow the Rules. He is not worth your time. Go have fun with the girls.*

Devil: *He just came to you! He's asking you, not the pasty-faced blonde, to leave with him.*

Question: Should I be listening to Macie?

Angel: *She was being honest and trying to keep you from getting hurt. The frog hasn't called for a week!*

Devil: *Frogs have amazingly talented tongues!*

Question: Do I fall willingly for this line about food?

Angel: *You already ate two pieces of birthday cake, you are not hungry.*

Devil: *He is offering another kind of substance that you can definitely devour!*

Angel: *Sperm is filled with calories.*

Devil: *Party on!*

✇

The next morning at work, the e-mails were flying fast and furious . . .

To: Snoopy

CC: Sydrama, Macie-O-Gray, Wade.Brady, Sage The Rage

From: T-Dog Tara

Subject: Did the Deed?

So did you have sex or not? It's a straight yes or no . . . don't beat around the fucking bush . . . TELL US . . . We are all dying for the juicy details! It's my birthday week, and my wish is for you to give us all the goods . . . ASAP. Large, small, crooked, tongue, hot . . . ugh, talk to us Charlie . . . or else we will start the rumors flying!

To: T-Dog Tara

CC: Sydrama, Macie-O-Gray, Wade.Brady, Snoopy

From: Sage The Rage

Subject: RE: Did the Deed?

Oh my God . . . You slept with Mr. J. P. Morgan? What the hell are you thinking . . . holy shit . . . I thought he hadn't called you in a while? Wow . . .

To: Sage The Rage

CC: Macie-O-Gray, Wade.Brady, Snoopy, T-Dog Tara

From: Sydrama

Subject: RE: RE: Did the Deed?

Yeah, she did it! You go girl. I hope you smoked a cigarette after and basked in all your glory, you non–dirty blonde bombshell. So does he have any available suits for the girls to look over? You know I have to ask. Can't wait for the scoop!

Love, Syd

To: Sydrama

CC: Wade.Brady, Snoopy, T-Dog Tara, Sage The Rage

From: Macie-O-Gray
Subject: RE: RE: RE: Did the Deed?

Did the frog croak out his approval? Did he turn into a prince yet? Okay, just give the slimy details (no pun intended!).

To: Macie-O-Gray
CC: Snoopy, T-Dog Tara, Sage The Rage, Sydrama
From: Wade.Brady
Subject: RE: RE: RE: RE: Did the Deed?

!!!!!!!!!!!

(Sorry, I have little eyes peering over my shoulder, and I'm not sure who can read yet!)

—WB

To: T-Dog Tara, Sage The Rage, Sydrama, Macie-O-Gray, Wade.Brady
From: Charlie Brown
Subject: RE: RE: RE: RE: RE: Did the Deed?

Are you kidding me? Jesus—calm your hormones ladies. But I do have something to get this party started right. One word: AHHHHHHHHHHHH . . .

As you all know, a lady never reveals the dirty details. But my groin muscles are sorer than after my high school soccer championship, and the pain in my hip flexors means that I am hobbling down the stairs like an old lady. I have on my Frye's so that people will think that my gait is just that of a chic urban cowgirl. Yes, love hurts. Thanks for being so proud, Syd. Haven't felt so accomplished since I won that Latin award in H.S. Men, beware!

Love, C

December

Sledge Cookies
Yields 60

1 ½ cups (3 sticks) of butter
1 ½ cups granulated sugar
¾ cup packed brown sugar
2 eggs
1 ½ teaspoon baking soda
2 tablespoons vanilla
1 tablespoon cinnamon
2 ½ cups flour
2 ½ cups oatmeal
One 12-ounce package semisweet chocolate chips
One 12-ounce package butterscotch bits
One 6-ounce package butter brickle bits

Preheat oven to 350° F. Cream the butter and sugars together. Add the eggs, baking soda, vanilla, and cinnamon. Mix well. Gradually add flour and oatmeal. Stir in chips and bits. Drop spoonfuls of dough onto an ungreased cookie sheet and bake for 8 to 10 minutes. Do not over bake. Cool for about 5 minutes and remove from cookie sheets. Cool on racks.

Be prepared . . . these are not your usual chocolate chip cookies!

ecember danced in like Bing Crosby in wingtipped tap shoes. The days were so cold, so crisp and clear that you could almost lick the breeze. Feeling festive, I had passed one of those random shops on Broadway and had grabbed a postcard from amid the odd ensemble of tourist T-shirts and memorabilia. The postcard depicted imposing skyscrapers against a picturesque blue backdrop mimicking my surroundings. I scrawled a note to my parents:

> *City life is good!*
> *And Mom, I haven't forgotten—safety in numbers.*
> > *Love,*
> > *Your Urban Princess*

This morning, despite the frigid temperatures, I had decided to forgo the bus and walk down Broadway to Columbus Circle to catch the train at Fifty-ninth Street to head downtown to work. Early on, I had learned that four long crosstown NY blocks is a mile, and twenty short up- or downtown NY blocks is a mile. Most New Yorkers knew those stats for running purposes. I knew them just so I could count my occasional walks as legitimate exercise.

Before descending into the subway, I indulged in a Starbucks latte—partly for the caffeine and partly for the warmth. As I took a precious sip of my expensive treat, I heard the cheerful whine of subway wheels roaring by underneath. I sped down the stairs, screaming, "Hold the train!" as if I was saving a baby from being crushed, and squeezed on with only about four "how dare you" looks from those I'd smooshed. The commuters, padded in their winter down, had morphed into one large swaying blob. I found a seat that actually had another half spot empty next to it (half, due to the spread-eagle position of the man the next seat over), and opened up the tabloid-sized *New York Post*. Despite several months in the city, I still hadn't attained the skills necessary to fold a full-sized newspaper in the lengthwise way that made it possible to read without hitting other passengers with the black-inked pages. Other commuters seemed so uptown with their chic fold-and-flip style of reading. Taking another sip of my latte, I skipped ahead to the gossip columns on Page Six.

Three stops down, the doors gaped open to let a woman on. With her faux Burberry coat and golden Clairol boxed job, she squeezed toward me bumping everyone in her path with her three Macy's shopping bags. She approached the half seat, and courteously asked us to make room. I shifted my thighs to the side, and spread-eagled man reeled his knees in about two inches. She plopped down and immediately began fidgeting. She adjusted the right corner hem of her coat about fifty times in three minutes.

"Sorry, I just want to make sure that your muddy shoe does not touch my coat," she explained. Now her explanation would have been sufficient except for the fact that my shoes weren't muddy. It was a cold day, a cold dry day. And my new Payless shoes (so like the Tod's driving loafers) had hardly a scuff on the sole. I just smiled slightly and went back to my inner contemplation. A minute later, she was still at it.

"Don't you kick me!"

"What?" What was this psycho talking about?

"I can tell what you are trying to do!"

Again, what?

"Don't you dare kick me! You are messing with the wrong woman!"

"Ma'am,"—courtesy helps, right?—"I'm just sitting here. I have not moved! I'm just sitting here minding my own business, I haven't touched you."

"I can see your foot getting closer, don't kick me!"

"Hey," throw in a little attitude, "I was here first, and you sat down!"

"You didn't pay for that goddamn seat! You paid for the ride. You're messing with the wrong person." Good God, didn't I know it. "Don't kick me! *This* is New York!"

I knew where I was. Hell, I was no longer a New York virgin. I had been here almost five months, and therefore I was almost a resident according to tax law. Yet here was this woman giving me a geography lesson peppered with threats at 9:11 A.M. As the train slowed at the next stop, she stood, swinging her three shopping bags, and threw a Kennebunkport Red fingernail in my face.

"You are the most inconsiderate person. You are in New York now. Someday you are going to mess with the wrong person, and probably get hurt, get hurt bad!" I tried to ignore all the people staring as she walked off, and then buried my nose back in Page Six, and tried to concentrate on some celebrity's public misery. I felt almost nauseous. Where had I gone wrong in that exchange? It was supposed to be the season of joy. Good cheer. And instead I'd been verbally assaulted and humiliated in front of dozens of steely-eyed morning commuters. I felt my holiday mood rapidly disappearing.

I arrived at work and as soon as I'd settled at my desk, my dear mother called to reminisce about bygone Christmases. She had my work number and extension taped to the kitchen wall at home. I'd tried to explain to her that I couldn't gossip at work and to save it for our mother-daughter convo's during the obligatory 9:00 P.M. phone call every night. Yes, every night! She always wanted to know that I was safe at home and not lying dead out on the street. She'd apparently missed the professionalism point in the memo I sent, and too often took my curtness while at work as a rebuff. So, never one to give up, she usually called once during the afternoon as well.

"Oh, hi Mo—"

"Hi dear, do you remember that footstool you made me in woodworking?"

"Yes, it was relegated to the summerhouse junkyard of unappreciated art projects," I said with a tinge of sarcasm.

Without missing a beat, she continued, "Remember that batik wrap you made me? It turned my shoulders blue!"

Ha-ha. It was actually turquoise, thank you very much. "Yes Mom, and your point—"

"And remember the embroidered brick cover you gave me?" Her voice had a tinge of annoyance.

"Mom, that was for a doorstopper. You always complained that the doorframe in the guest bedroom is off-kilter and that Dad did not have the wherewithal to fix it! That doorstopper was so the door would not bang in the middle of the night!" Point Charlie. This was like a goddamn phone tennis match. What was in her craw today?

"Oh, well," she said, "I never heard the door do that. It probably bothers you since your bedroom is right there. But then again, you're never really home." How my thoughtful third-grade gift had been turned into a dig about my continuous absences was beyond me. Clearly, she was still upset that I'd missed Thanksgiving.

"Anyways, yes, Mom?" I prodded.

"It's anyway, not anyways. Anyway, I am so glad those days are over! Now that you are a working girl, no more homemade gifts!"

Okay, there went my idea of homemade soap sachets. Levette Chosser, the gift guru, had been on *Sunshine & Sensibility* the other day and shared the easiest recipe for scented soap. I figured I would whip up a batch for the holidays and put a little C-spin on the bars and use old cookie cutters to make funky little guest soaps. Oh well, I sighed, at least my grandparents would appreciate them.

I knew I definitely was bah-humbugging it when everyone swapped gifts later that afternoon at the annual *Sunshine & Sensibility* secret Santa party. I was given a gaily wrapped box with the words "Corporate Chic" emblazoned on the side. I held my lips in a polite bow of a smile as I lifted the lid. Inside was a mini lint roller, an aluminum box of peculiarly strong breath mints, a mirror that magnified by two hundred times, a mini can of static cling protection, and a pad of oil-absorbing powder leaves. What was this gift supposed to mean? Was my morning breath lingering all day long? Did I have a dandruff problem that was ruining my slimming black outfits? Did my skirt ride up and hug my ass in inappropriate ways? Was the oil sheen on my face reflecting off of others' computers making it impossible for them to concentrate? Did they think I was blind to these appearance ills and needed to have them brought to my attention two-hundred-fold?

"How wonderful!" I exclaimed with fake glee. "I can stick this . . . this Corporate Chic box in my desk drawer for those infrequent indiscretions!" I wasn't sure whether the nods were in agreement with me or with the appropriateness of the gift.

$\mathscr{T}$hings began looking up later that day when I left the office and my cell phone began to vibrate in my bag. I reached for it and saw Mr. J. P. Morgan's number flashing across my screen. Deep breath, deep breath, "Hello?"

"Gorgeous!" Pitter-pat, pitter-pat. "Where are you?"

"Walking home from a long day at work." He'd called me gorgeous!

"Well run your cute ass over here. I'm waiting for you at Hampton's Heiress." I had known that he would be frenzied at work during the holiday season—the stock market peaked and valleyed on so little as the publication of the Toys "R" Us catalog. Yet even after all of today's humiliations, it truly was turning out to be the season of giving. Jolly ole Mr. J. P. Morgan was making time for me.

"Be there in about ten minutes," I said casually, then factored in the newly descending rain. "Make it twelve." That gave me three minutes to grab a taxi to get home, five minutes to change, two minutes to cab it back across town to Hampton's Heiress, and a two-minute cushion for weather delays. Plausible.

Home. Changed. Cabbing. I had managed to hail a cab within the eight-minute time frame despite the freezing rain, but then the cab got stuck toward the east side of Central Park behind a car and carriage accident (the horse was all right).

"Mum, we might be here for hours," the cabbie told me. I didn't have hours! "You might want to walk, love." Feeling his good intentions, I took his advice. For five extra bucks, he gave me his old umbrella.

It took me twenty-three minutes to walk from the edge of the park to Hampton's Heiress. My feet were numb and I'd ruined my knee-high boots, stepping through the week-old snow banks. The chocolate brown suede was stained with white salt remnants. My mother would have said I was inappropriately dressed, but who bothered with tights and a winter coat and such when you were supposed to be inside at a warm restaurant, looking cute no less? My knees had taken on a raw pallor, and as I stumbled across the threshold, I huffed into my frozen hands hoping to thaw my Santaesque nose. My internal homing device steered me toward the back of the restaurant where Mr. J. P. Morgan was chatting with a homely brunette.

"Hey!" I threw out teetering on my frost-bitten feet.

"Beautiful!" he exclaimed. Bye-bye, homely brunette! "I've been waiting for you." Oh, the love! Should I bother to explain my tardiness, ruddy nose, ruined boots? Nah. A group of his friends approached and prepared to encircle. Must not lose body contact. I didn't need to worry though, since he had moved behind me and draped his arms over my shoulders, nestling me into his chest cavity. Sheer bliss. This was an intimate move, right? He was demonstrating our closeness to others, showing his ownership, and I was just fine being placed up high on his trophy shelf. I reached both arms behind me, back around his waist, and ran my thumb along the inside of his jeans' waist. He had the softest lower back. There was that dimple right where we humans used to have tails. Why hadn't *Cosmo* expounded upon that region?

"Be back in a sec, Charlie. Gotta run to the bathroom."

"See ya!" I watched him make his way through the crowd. Cute butt! And when he came back, I would see that gorgeous crooked smile—a smile all for me.

At first I was impressed with myself. Despite frozen inner thighs, here I was holding court with Mr. J. P. Morgan's boys.

We were joking and laughing . . . getting on so well that I didn't notice Mr. J. P. Morgan's absence at first. About twenty minutes later, my phone vibrated. It was Mr. J. P. Morgan.

"We decided to leave and are cross town at Gladiators." Huh? Who was *we*? Why wasn't I part of *we*?

"Come meet me," he said. I thought I just had. "Or just go to my apartment and get the keys from Tony and I'll meet you back there." Oh, feeling better. A formal invite.

Still cold and with my ego slightly bruised, I decided to meet him in bed. When I got to his apartment building, Tony, the doorman, looked me over a few times. I smiled, figuring that he just didn't recognize me in my frozen state.

"It's me," I threw out casually. No glimmer of recognition. "Charlie. C-h-a-r ," I began.

"I know how to spell 'Charlie,'" he barked in a foreign accent.

"Oh." I paused to shove some of my well-deserved McDonald's French fries into my mouth. (I'd made a quick stop at the McDonald's on the corner before strolling into J. P.'s lobby— I'd missed dinner after all.)

"You're not on the envelope," he stated. To gain access to another's apartment, New York doormen tended to write frequent visitors' names on the envelope of extra keys.

"I'm not?" Hmm. Food for thought. I was preferring the French fries though.

"You just saw me the other night!" I exclaimed. "Look, he just called me." I struggled to pull out my frozen cell phone and scrolled through my list of calls received.

"Never mind. Here," he conceded, handing me the tiny packet of keys. After that inquisition, I figured I would just hold on to this extra set for future use.

I pushed open the apartment door into a still darkness. I fumbled to find a light switch, finally turning on the matching table lamps next to the couch. For a bachelor pad, the boys' living room was quite nice. Though there were a few errant pizza boxes, the pillows on the couch were plump, the paintings on the walls were framed, and the plants were all alive. I wandered down the hall and turned into the first bedroom. Immediately I zeroed in on no less than five framed pictures of a stunning brunette. As my right arm began to tingle signaling an impending heart attack, I realized that I was in a roommate's bedroom, not J. P.'s. I ran from the room and stepped into the one next door. No incriminating pictures—then again, none of me either . . . yet. Maybe I would have to send him a personalized Christmas card. Crawling into his barely made bed, I munched on the few remaining fries. I buried my cold toes under his down comforter and my numbness soon turned into a raw slumber.

The next morning I awoke to something brushing my nose. Ready to kiss Mr. J. P. Morgan's fingers, I realized that my lips were touching cardboard. I rolled over to find myself alone in bed, next to an empty French fry container. Mr. J. P. Morgan had never come home.

"It's a happy day. A happy day," I repeated as my nose began to leak. It was going to be a horrible, no good, very shitty Christmas.

❧

*B*y Thursday I was still struggling to put the incident out of my mind (Note to self: Have sworn off French fries *forever!*) and I braved the windy hollow of the city streets on my way to Wade's apartment for a night of reality TV viewing. By the time I arrived and took off my layers, Wade was beating out the reality shows for the group's attention.

"Cookie swap? What's that? Wade, what are you talking about?" asked Tara in her typical sneer. She was bending over backward to embrace her inner-city gal and had a very low tolerance for the domestic traditions of suburban moms. Truthfully, the fact that she had been participating in the Cooking Club at all was somewhat shocking.

"Each Cooking Club member chooses a cookie to bake for our December meeting," Wade explained.

"I call Toll House!" Syd shouted, interrupting.

"No, you have to go beyond the typical chocolate chip cookies."

"But I use applesauce instead of butter. Now *that* is creative!"

"No chocolate chip cookies!" Wade declared. "Each girl chooses a *unique* cookie and bakes a dozen for each of the other girls. And right before Christmas, we exchange our specialty cookies at the meeting. Hence, the name *Cookie Swap!*" It was so annoying that Wade was a kindergarten teacher. That didactic—and never mind slow—tone got on all of our nerves. It made me wonder if her five-year-olds winced during reading time.

"Look," I said. "There are six of us, that means we each would have to bake six dozen cookies—that's 432 cookies in all!" Where was my dad? He would be proud. "We can't bake that many cookies in the shitty little Barbie doll stove in our apartment. We'd be baking for weeks!"

"And what am I going to do with six dozen chocolate, peanut butter, sprinkle, whatever cookies from all of you guys?" asked Skinny Sage. For once Sage had a good food point. I could see even the nonanorexics beginning to quake over the sticks of butter to be used in thirty-six dozen cookies (approximately two sticks per recipe means twelve sticks of butter per six dozen cookies—equaling seventy-two sticks of butter in one room at the same time). That sure was a lot of fat!

"Girls, cookies freeze quite nicely. Throw them in a Ziploc and you can thaw them for guests over the holidays," Wade assured us.

"When am I ever going to have an army of cookie-eating fiends around?" Sage groaned. Again, she had a point, if not a waistline to watch.

After numerous figures and fat calculations, Macie finally made a sensible suggestion. She figured that we should each bake only *one* dozen of our chosen cookies so that we would each get two cookies from one another's batches. Now that was doable. I could rationalize an eating binge of twelve Christmas cookies—144 cookies was a whole other matter.

"And," I added, seeing Skinny Sage's still-doubtful look, "any extras can be donated to Wade's little terrors! They'll be gobbled up during snack break."

"They are children, not terrors," Wade replied. It was her meek attempt to humanize her job, but all was lost as we began to dream of sugarplum fairies enlightening us all to our fantabulous cookie-baking potential. I knew my heartbroken self would be all over any of those "extra" cookies at our next Cooking Club meeting.

∽

*B*y this point, I was starting to suspect that Mr. J. P. Morgan and I just might be over. It was a girl-gut thing. I had felt the blow-off coming with the blustery winter winds. But now that it was here, it had been gentle—more like a retreating tide that leaves behind those foul-smelling mudflats. Tara had recommended that I remain stalwart and try a new blow job technique; Syd suggested that I try to "talk about it," but the "it" was the vague part (Tara again seconded her take-action plan); Macie just gave me the sympathetic "it sucks" nod. She was always one to admit defeat and move on. I, on the other hand, found myself groveling in the same old rut.

Later that week when he still hadn't called, I recognized that I had to start facing reality. I quickly put the kibosh on any extraneous depression-fueled eating—tough to do when the Diva's test kitchens were producing delectable holiday treats around the clock. In an attempt to shelter my waistline from such an assault, I began to write a letter to Santa wishing him, willing him, more like threatening him, to bring Mr. J. P. Morgan back to me in a red velvet bag. I didn't care if Santa went ballistic and swept through J. P. Morgan's apartment door (no chimney there), knocked him cold, and dragged him to my apartment in his overloaded sleigh with all the gifts for the other good boys and girls. I just wanted him back and snug in my bed. I had begun describing to Santa what went wrong, but it got a tad X-rated. I couldn't disgrace myself in front of lovable ole Saint Nick by going porno on the old guy! I scrapped that note, and tried to think of who else might possibly understand my pain and grant me my one wish this holiday? Ann Landers? The president? And then it hit me. Why the goddess of love connections, breakups, and makeups herself: J. Lo, but of course. I found a fan club address on the Internet and wrote:

Dear Ms. Lopez (aka J. Lo),

Merry Christmas! Feliz Navidad! *Now I know you get letters like this all the time, but desperate times call for desperate* measures. You know how it is. I am hoping that you can help me. Here it goes. I want my boyfriend back. I don't care if you drug him with your lyrics, entice him with your perfumes, lure him with your provocative clothes, or hypnotize him with your acting abilities (you could pretend you're a hypnotist). With your wealth of resources and with you being a believer in dreams, I hope you will answer my prayers. I thought we, he and I, were bouncing along all right until now.

We finally slept together a few weeks ago. You might think I was holding out since we began seeing each other in September, but I'm really not hung up on the morals thing. He had a problem at first with premature ejaculation and we got over that together. Then finally we had a passionate night with no leakage, but I erroneously decided to experiment with some Lova-Rubba-Cumma. You know, the sensual heating oil? Well, it didn't go so well and let's just say I won't be using that product again.

We finally sealed the deal on a night when the stars aligned and the angels sang (go ahead and use that for a song if you want). Now I know that orgasms through sexual intercourse are rare for any woman. I don't believe, nor do I trust, those girls out there who say that they have an O every single time. They are totally lying. Sex is an all-hands-on-deck type of deal. My mind, my body (nonbloated days), my senses (alcohol always helps), and my mood all have to be on the right page or this ship doesn't sail. But he was a talented soul and, by God, I had my first, non-self-induced, New York City, bona fide sex-induced orgasm even though we were in the missionary position (I figured we'd get experimental the next time). My head spun, my mind fluttered, my body convulsed, and I squealed. I'll spare you the upside-down, head-rushing details, but it was a *crescendo like I had never had before. I heard my entire life score in under thirty seconds! I now truly understand what you mean by "sunlight at night." In my post-wow tizzy, I realized that he would make an amazing older man, one I would be proud to claim as my husband when we celebrated our golden anniversary.*

Sadly, we have not had a next time, and I am doubting whether we will even reach the paper anniversary. He ditched me after inviting me out to meet up with him at a bar the other night (could that have been an accident?) and since then no phone calls, no e-mails, nothing, nada. So what is the problem? I am truly stumped. I honestly cannot pinpoint the one mistake I made. And I must say he was totally into it. He licked my toes and proclaimed that they tasted like Creamsicles (I think it was the cheap nail polish). Unless he is taking an acting class at night and testing out his new "coldhearted I-hate-you ex-boyfriend" scene on our relationship, I don't know where I screwed up. You can probably hear my angst in this letter. Jennifer, can you, will you help me? Please, I need your advice and inspiration more than ever.

Sincerely,
Charlotte Brown

❧

That night, I found myself in our kitchen preparing to cook the hell out of my cookies for the f'ing Cookie Swap. It was the last thing I wanted to do, but it took my mind off of a certain someone. They say cooking can be great therapy. There's something about mashing, cracking, beating, and balling. It's choco-thera-chippy. But I had to release all my tension through the wrists because our kitchen posed a bit of a challenge. It was basically a five foot wall comprised of a sink, what we called the Barbie stove, and some cupboards. For years when I was a kid, I had begged my mother for one of those EASY-BAKE Oven things. I wanted to whip up mini chocolate cakes (even though they tasted like rubber most of the time) and frost it with the pouch of white sugar. I dreamt of mixing and baking, basting, and broiling . . . okay, so my eight-year-old aspirations were not that sophisticated, nor were they ever fulfilled. My mother would not acquiesce. She was adamant about the fact that a toy oven would attract bugs. So she stomped all over my youthful dreams of cooking, and I fully blame her for my lack of skill in the kitchen today. Heck, I could have been the host of *Sunshine & Sensibility*, not the Diva. (I decided I'd throw this little zinger out to Mom on the phone tonight—payback for her snide comments about my homemade Christmas gifts.) But now, I had the Cooking Club to give me that all-important second chance at developing skills in the domestic department. It's never too late!

I spun in a pathetic twirl as my new favorite song blared through the stereo for the umpteenth time:

Shot through the heart [fist pump, fist pump]
and you're to blame, baby,
you give love a bad name.

Crouching down, I faced our miniature Barbie stove head on; so like that EASY-BAKE Oven I'd once dreamt about. This cookie project was going to take me hours. I'd already had to run out once to Bed Bath & Beyond to buy new cookie sheets; the hand-me-downs from my babysitter were too wide for the Barbie oven. Plus, I could only bake one sheet at a time. With flour in the air and in my hair, I mixed the brown gooey batter and even managed to separate the yolk from the white goopy part of the egg. I've never really been a fan of eggs, yet they appear in every recipe known to man.

My egg thoughts sent a new jolt of sorrow to my heart. I had dreamt about Mr. J. P. Morgan making me eggs once. My daydream went something like this: we would wake up after a late night out, me groggy and barely human, and he sweet and sexy, whipping breakfast up in the kitchen. My mother used to warn me, "Don't sleep with anyone before you marry them!" since I was such a bear in the morning. But Mr. J. P. Morgan wouldn't mind. He would wake up really early and begin to cook. Then he'd appear with a tray of scrambled eggs that he had dutifully concocted with a fork and a smidge of milk and pepper. He'd sneak in a spoonful of butter, not worrying about my cuddly hips. I'd smile sweetly with my eyes half opened and the eggs would soon be forgotten in lieu of a helping of morning sex.

The reality, however, was nowhere close, despite my poetic and imaginative scene setting. One morning, I *had* awoken to the smell of eggs—a smell, I confess, that I didn't even really like. Truth be told, I don't even like the taste of eggs (I just thought they'd look so pretty and sunny on a breakfast tray). Mr. J. P. Morgan's nose had twitched in his sleep and two nanoseconds later, he had left our love nest, jumping out of bed and leaving the covers thrown back and my nakedness exposed to the apartment. He had returned about twelve minutes later (about the time it takes to get the sports scores off the news broadcast), shoveling his roommate's leftover runny eggs into his mouth. I'd tried to smile sweetly with my eyes half open when he offered me a bite, but due to my squinted eyes, my mouth half missed the fork, and runny eggs dripped onto my boob. Tantalizing, right? I tried not breathing through my nose. I'd learned early in life that if you cut off the olfactory glands, your taste buds go numb. When he'd gone into the bathroom to shower for work, I hurriedly spooned the rest of the eggs into the pot of ivy his mother had hung above one of his windows. Interestingly, that plant had begun to die just about the time our relationship peaked. Coincidence? I think not.

Now at last, my first cookie tray was in the oven. Since our stove did not have any modern gadgets such as a timer, I had to rely on my watch: nine to eleven minutes. I settled on ten minutes and vowed to check the cookies at 4:17 P.M. Just as I was sitting down at the table with an issue of *Us Weekly*, my door buzzer sounded. The pathetic whine meant that someone was a-visiting. Since NYC is not a drop-by kind of town, I figured it was Syd, she always forgot her keys. I buzzed her up, cracked the apartment door, and returned to the kitchen to stare at my cookies through the yellowed oven window.

"You never stared so intently at me," laughed a familiar voice.

Holy shit! Mr. J. P. Morgan. I quickly tried to brush the hair from my eyes and felt the cookie dough from my fingers sticking to the too-long roots of my blondish hair. My heart pounded.

"I'm cooking," I sputtered. Duh!

"So I see. Congrats. Is this a newfound skill?"

There was no need to defend my nonexistent cooking skills. And forget being impressive. Now, with flour on my face, dough in my hair, and stained (from God knows what) sweatpants on my holiday-enhanced thighs, I had no chance of making him pine. Instead, I had to become the cold bitch.

The non-codependent, confident, self-assured woman of the new millennium. She-man, activate! I thrust out my hip and struck my best cool bitch stare with the wooden spoon jutting out from my side.

With a cool tone, I again announced, "I'm cooking."

"You already said that," he laughed. Laughing is not the correct response to the cool bitch stance. Damn!

"I happen to be doing extremely important charity work on behalf of all the single girls in NYC." Always stress being single as a positive. "What do you want?"

"Besides your effervescent holiday cheer, I need my extra apartment keys back." What a mother-f'ing jackass! He had come by to pick up his spare keys. How pathetic. How un-holiday like, especially since I'd only come by the keys while I was waiting for him at his apartment that night he'd never showed. What kind of person had the gall to drop by unannounced after an incident like that? Had he no shame? Then again, could it just be a reason to see me? (Have to salvage a glimmer of hope.) Whatever his motivation, I wasn't going to let myself turn into pathetic, lonely ex-girlfriend. Be strong Charlie, be strong.

I stomped to my bedroom and fished the keys, which were lying next to my sexy panties, out of my top drawer. How fitting! Lucky for him, I wasn't fishing the keys out of the toilet, where they'd almost ended up a couple of nights ago after a night out with the ladies. I sashayed back to the kitchen to a view of Mr. J. P. Morgan's incredible ass. He was bent over staring at my tasty little morsels in progress.

"Here!" The whole thing suddenly felt so juvenile. I wasn't even sure why I cared. He had disappointed me countless times. Even now, when there were a hundred different ways for the scene playing out here in my kitchen to go, I knew he would behave in the most thoughtless way possible.

The night before, when I'd been drowning my sorrows over a cup of Swiss Miss, Tara had actually forced me to check The List. Over the past few months, we had come up with the "Top Ten Romantic Interludes in NYC" (aka, The List) that we all were determined to experience with a man and/or have a man do for us; it had been tacked up on our refrigerator next to the Chinese takeout menu:

10. Watch the Macy's Day Parade together from the street with a cup of hot cocoa.
9. Enjoy the symphony in the park with a picnic basket and wine.
8. Have a portrait painted by a street artist at our lover's request.
7. Give a blow job while on the subway.
6. Watch our man, dressed in a suit, walk through the park toward us.
5. Enjoy a pizza and beer picnic at a city playground.
4. Take a tram ride to Rosie Island (aka, Roosevelt Island).
3. Have sex on a city rooftop.
2. Be presented with flowers bought off a street corner.
1. Circle Central Park in the winter by way of a carriage ride.

Number 7 had of course been Tara's suggestion. The rest of us doubted that we'd get a chance to check that one off The List due to the crowded-at-all-hours subway trains, but Tara was determined. "It's 'risky business' all right," she'd quip. The race, or should I say the dare, was on.

So far, Mr. J. P. Morgan and I had hooked-up on the roof of my building, but hadn't had sex outside of that one night in bed, so I couldn't officially scratch off number 3. Basically, he was a failure on the romantic front. It was December for God's sake, and number 1 was so obvious!

"Thanks," he said as I handed him his keys. "My sister will need them when she comes to visit this week." He had a sister?

I remained hopeful as he stood in the door. But he made no attempt to toss me a cute, flirty remark, or to invite me to his company cocktail party, which I knew he was dreading, and which I also knew was coming up this Saturday. Nope, it was over. And I needed him out. I walked to the door, opened it, and pointed down the long hallway with my floury finger.

"Bye!" I said with authority. He gave me his cocky smile (God help me!), shrugged his shoulders (so helpless, hmmm), shuffled out (so sad, ohhh, don't go!), and then chuckled (so cocky, ahhh!). Good God, would I never learn? I slammed the door and breathed in deeply.

Smoke.

Shit, the cookies were burning! It was 4:27 P.M. Damn you, Mr. J. P. Morgan! It was going to be a horrible, no good, very shitty Christmas.

&

Since Mr. J. P. Morgan had sabotaged my first batch of cookies, I had to start over and take another stab at the great cookie bake-off. I would stay true to our Cooking Club rule of "never, ever buy, just try, try, try." My cookie choice, the Sledge Cookie, had been in honor of my sixth-grade teacher, who'd introduced me to the recipe. She had taught us her infamous cookie recipe in order to cement fraction skills. I had failed both the cookies and math in general. This time, however, I could and would make her proud.

In my haste to mix a new batch of dough I knocked over a bottle of red food coloring. Not that Sledge Cookies require coloring, but in my disorganized, post-ex-boyfriend encounter state, I had pulled each and every baking item out of our cabinets. I figured that I might be inspired to add a creative twist or two to the recipe. Cooking truly is an art. If you wanted to be a real powerhouse in the kitchen, you needed to utilize that right side of the brain that was responsible for artsy-crafty things. But due to time constraints, I ended up sticking with the recipe line by line. However, when reaching for the brown sugar, I had knocked over the tiny red bottle, spilling its contents all over the counter, cabinet doors, stovetop, and floor.

Who knew that food coloring could dye items in different shades? A small drop of red will cast a pinkish hue, like that preppy shade that goes so well with green (note the once-white kitchen counter). Add about three drops, and you attain that rainbow red we all colored in grade school (see streaked cabinet doors). Add about five drops and you create that deep maroon found in velvet drapes in an old Newport mansions (observe said stovetop). Add a whole bottle, and well . . . blood. Think murder, decapitation, stabbing . . . a whole bottle of food coloring makes for quite a dark, shall we say rich red-blackish color. Yep, and that was our floor. I grabbed a paper towel and started mopping at the red dye. Ten minutes later I had the situation under control—except that the red dye had wreaked havoc on my nails! Food coloring is water-based according to the box, but it does not come off of skin that easily, nor does it wipe clean from cuticles or come out of nail beds. It had spread like some infectious disease. No amount of rubbing made it disappear.

✍

I remeasured, restirred, reheaped, and rebaked. This time, the cookies came out perfectly. Take that *Sunshine & Sensibility*! I was almost ready for Wade's crazy cookie swap. But, needless to say, my nails needed work. So, off to the local mani-pedi salon!

Nail parlors are a way of life in New York. They inhabit every street corner and are the poor man's lap of luxury. Any fool can afford a $10 slice of manicure heaven. The hand massages alone are worth your laundry quarters. Given the fact that you have no idea what the usually Asian manicurists are saying about you, and you have about forty minutes of sheer nonconversational bliss (including drying time), it's the cheapest place for therapy in all five boroughs. You talk, they listen, they respond in Chinese or Korean or Vietnamese and always nod sympathetically. If you can fit it into your schedule to go in one of the first few days of the week, MTW, before say about five o'clock, then you can usually get at least $3.00 knocked off the price—perfect for an indulgent cup of coffee afterward. As with sex, you have to reward one act of indulgence with another, right?

I had exactly two hours before the Cooking Club meeting began and since I had to fit in the emergency manicure, I wouldn't be able to indulge my shower drinking habit. It's a little routine we started back in college to get ourselves psyched up for a night out (my college roommate was convinced that the heat and humidity added to one's buzz). So before a party, I'll usually enjoy a beer or two as I loofah and lather. The shelf to my right in the shower can hold one bottle of shampoo, two conditioners (choice depended on the urban hair conditions), about three random body washes, and a bottle of beer—16 ounces or less. I decided to jump in the shower before I hit the mani-pedi salon to avoid the post-smudging factor, but after the shower I grabbed a beer bottle and slipped it into my mitten as I sailed out the door. When I arrived at the nail salon, the woman minding the front desk glanced at me, then my bottle. I nodded as if to say, "Happy Holidays," then settled in for my pampering. If rich ladies can take a nip or two while having their faces lifted, why can't a hip chick take a swig or two while having her nails shaped into squovals?

I grabbed the nearest bottle of red and the new issue of *Cosmo* and waited for the woman to signal me to the open pedi-spa bowl. Why red, you ask? Why the food coloring situation, of course. The shade of red I chose was called The Morning After. Here's hoping I would have a morning after with someone much cuter and kinder than Mr. J. P. Morgan someday soon!

∽

"*W*ow!" Macie exclaimed as I put down my platter of treats. The Diva had taught us a valuable lesson in entertaining: half of the battle is presentation. I had put my dozen Sledge Cookies in a bread basket lined with that swirly cellophane. I had baked a total of 36 nonburned, post–Mr. J. P. Morgan cookies, and had chosen the choicest twelve out of the three batches. I had even added a manila tie-on tag:

> *To the Dirty Half Dozen:*
> *I apologize in advance for any flour chunks.*
> *Enjoy!*

"Flour chunks? I'm not eating them!" declared Sage. Macie's and my eyes met and we began to giggle. Any excuse to get out of eating sugar-coated desserts! Sage was on the ball.

"Yum!" Macie said, biting a cookie. "These are divine, Charlie. You may be worthy of the most-improved award!" I smiled realizing that it was my first smile of the day.

"They have lots of oatmeal in them, so they are on the healthier side," I added pointingly to Sage.

"Not what I expected from you," Tara said, taking a bite. She closed her eyes in sugared bliss. "I just love sweet surprises!"

"And they aren't too hard to make. You add the best parts, the butterscotch bits, chocolate morsels, and butter brickle, at the very end and just fold them in. And I think the key is the smidge of cinnamon." I sounded like a regular Betty Crocker as I tried to distract myself from letting tears fall. I slipped off my gloves to reveal the plastic baggies underneath that were protecting my newly painted nails. Plastic baggies on one's hands and feet were the weirdest sensation of them all. Flashback to my mom shoving my baggy-covered feet into red or yellow rubber boots on rainy days before school. All day long my feet would squish.

"Fuck-me red, huh?" said Tara pointing to my nails. "Ho-ho-ho! Mr. J. P. Morgan might be lured back with that Christmas surprise."

"No, not likely. I think we may be over." My voice caught in my throat.

"What? What do you mean? He still hasn't called?"

"No, he, um, came by . . ." I sniffed.

"Did you drop to your knees?" Tara smirked.

"God, Tara, even you know that he's never been worthy of the godlike status Charlie's bestowed on him," scorned Macie.

"Nooo." Tara rolled her eyes. "Not because he's a god. She needs to be eye-level with the goods to perform the fancy tongue lashing I described before." She got down on her knees in demonstration.

"*No!*" I shouted a little too loudly as a few tears fell. I stuffed a cookie into my mouth so that I wouldn't accidentally bite off my own tongue. "No, he took his apartment keys back," I mumbled, wiping my nose. All five mouths were open, for once not awaiting food.

"Oh," said Wade, giving the only appropriate response to for the situation.

"What did you do?" asked Syd. Her eyes were wide as if watching her favorite soap. Even I felt tired of all the drama.

"I burned the damn cookies. But then I decided that I just . . . needed . . . to . . . start . . . over . . ."

My eyes began to fill up with more post-dumping tears when Tara belted out, *"Shithead got run over by a reindeer, walking home, from taking back his keys!"*

"Here, Charlie." Macie held out her plateful of cookies.

"Hmm?" Then I took a closer look at the plate.

"Gingerbread men, snowmen, and the man of them all, Santa!" Macie listed. I began to laugh. "Take your pick!" I grinned and took a deep breath to still my hysterical hiccups.

"Why can't I find the perfect recipe for a man?" I bemoaned, my mouth full of delicious crumbs.

"So you were burned this time. But we're going to keep playing with the ingredients and perfecting the proportions," Macie reassured me as she bit off Santa's head with a loud chomp. "In a few days it's a new year."

"Aren't the holidays a popular time to move?" Syd asked.

"Huh?"

"My point being that it is time to move on—a new year means a new man." Pretty profound for our Syd.

Macie held up her cup in a girls' solidarity toast, and even Skinny Sage gulped back a mouthful of fattening eggnog. I looked around the kitchen. Wade was rearranging everyone's plates, Sage was licking the frosting off of a glazed cookie, and Syd was sitting on the counter debating J. Lo's post-breakup remedies with Tara. It was a New York moment.

God Bless Everyone!

January

Sage's Skinny Soup

Three 16-oz cans fat-free refried beans

Three to four 14½-oz cans (or 1 large can, 18 oz) fat-free
   chicken broth, depending on the consistency you
   desire — thick or thin

Two 12-oz cans white chicken chunks (drained), or 3 cups,
   cooked chicken breasts cut up in chunks

One 15-oz can fat-free black beans, drained

1 large jar (16 oz) salsa (hot, medium, or mild . . . it's all
   up to your taste buds)

Two 15¼-oz cans white corn, drained

1 red bell pepper, diced

1 yellow bell pepper, diced

½ red onion, finely chopped

½ cup fresh cilantro, chopped

1 zucchini, chopped

Salt and pepper to taste

Toppings

   Tortilla chips

   Grated cheese

Note: The additional toppings will make the soup not-so-skinny!

Combine all of the ingredients, except the toppings, in a large pot
and stir. Simmer on low heat, stirring occasionally. Serve hot. If
you are not counting calories or just don't care, top it off with a few

tortilla chips and a handful of grated cheese. This soup can be served either as an appetizer or a main course. Don't forget to serve with either some ice-cold beers or frozen fruity margaritas. Enjoy!

Alleluia, it's finally January! I never thought I'd be praising the Lord for winter, but if this month didn't get here any quicker, my legs would have turned into a pair of honey-baked hams. For over a month, the nightly news had been covering the curse of Christmas calories. Oprah had even mentioned cutting back the festive fat several times in the past few weeks. You'd think that after twenty-two years, I'd be up to speed on how to prepare my body for the holiday hog fest. The problem was that my "shove your face with cookies, candies, stuffing, alcohol, and gravy" didn't stop until January 2; exactly two days after I'd had all the champagne I could manage to pop and exactly one day after I had inhaled bowls of chips and dip at my family's next-door neighbor's College Bowl Football party.

So for the New Year, we girls decided to call a truce with all the buffets and all the bartenders in the greater New York City area. We had decided to put on our helmets and hunker down in order to strategically plan our attack to fight off the January Jiggling Blues (aka, your ten-pound winter coat that seems to be still on you even after you hang it up in the front entrance-way). Yes, we were fighting the fat head on.

In this type of situation there was only one person who could come to our aid. So which one of the girls could answer our pathetic prayers and help us get rid of our holiday poundage, quick? Well, it was the one who knew food like the back of her Lean Cuisine microwave meal: Sage. The roommates decided that Skinny Sage was the one who would plan and implement our attack—killing the dimpled elephant legs right in their tracks.

"Sage," I wailed. "If I drink another vodka tonic, if I eat another damn Swedish meatball . . . I'll actually have to get pregnant so I can blame it on baby weight!" My stomach began to convulse just talking about it.

"Be quiet, Charlie," commanded Sage. Oh, the bulimic bitch we all loved to hate was in effect! The five of us had all shown up at her apartment, armed and ready to go. Wade had even taken drastic measures and come over in her brand-new workout gear.

"I didn't have anything else appropriate for the severity of the situation," she noted.

"I warned you!" Sage shook her head at all of us. "I knew this Cooking Club was a bad idea."

"Jesus, Sage," I said. "We didn't come over to get lectured. I can go to my mom for that. I came here to get your advice on how to stop watching my ass expand in front of my eyes!"

"Well, as you can see, it's a little too late for preventive action. So, we now have to fight the fat in a more drastic and militant way." Sage was the Cooking Club's very own General Custard (minus the egg yolk, sugar, and cream). She turned away from us and frantically began to rummage through her fridge. She reached deep behind the Pellegrino water, the fat-free yogurt, granola, and spray butter to where most people hide the cookie dough.

"Ah, here it is!" she squealed. I was expecting some sort of fat-free, calorie-less dessert. You can just imagine the look on my face when she pulled out a Ziploc bag containing five pieces of paper.

"You want us to eat paper?" I asked. I wasn't trying to be funny. Knowing Sage, she had found some newfangled diet from the other side of the world based on the nutrients found in trees or something.

"No, Charlie, we are going to get our bulbous butts to the gym!" she announced, pulling five gym passes from the bag. She handed them out as if they were tickets to Hawaii. No, not Hawaii, I wanted to scream. We were on our way to hell. (Note to self: Remember to ask Sage why the hell she keeps her gym passes in the fridge.)

⁂

*E*xhausted and starving after a grueling kickboxing class, we all made our way back to Wade's apartment for our monthly Cooking Club dinner. I could've eaten a cow at this particular moment. But given the urban setting, a nice filet would've been just fine. I had made my mother's creamy mashed potatoes for this month's meeting but ingeniously had added a little twist inspired by the chefs at *Sunshine & Sensibility*: horseradish! However, I'd first had to conduct some in-depth research to make sure that horseradish had nothing to do with horses (thank God) or radishes (second amen). My recipe cards for horseradish mashed potatoes were safely stuffed into my back pocket. Somehow, I always seemed to pick those recipes with three to five ingredients.

Wade lived in a doorman building, subsidized by her parents since they knew she could never afford it on her teacher's salary and her mother couldn't stand the thought of her living on her own in the big city without a doorman to protect her. Exiting the elevator, I was overwhelmed by the scent of garlic. "Italian," I thought. Great—my body was already craving carbs.

After a quick trip to the bathroom—how could I still have any water in me after sweating the Dead Sea during my workout? Must be retaining—I found the girls huddled around Syd who was clearly in the middle of sharing something interesting.

"I am training to run the New York Marathon," she confided. "I want to be a Road Runner in the Dust Busters group next fall. That's the group that runs six- to eight-minute miles."

"Sydney, I didn't know you were a runner!" Sage exclaimed. "Good for you!" Sage applauded anything that burned calories. She and Tara had once had a heated argument over the calorie-burning potential of sex. Tara claimed she could burn off at least three brownies. Sage had argued against the mathematical feasibility of it, but we all knew Tara's unusual potential when it came to physical exertion in the bedroom.

"Well, I don't really run that far yet," Syd continued.

"But you think you can do six-minute miles?" Macie asked.

"Hopefully. I ran about a mile today."

"How long did it take you?" Wade asked.

"Oh, about eighteen minutes. But I stopped to look for a bathroom. You know, they need more bathrooms in the park. And I'm not talking about those Porta-Potty type deals. They should put in really nice ones with running water and flowers . . ."

"And two-ply toilet paper?" joked Macie.

"Well, I had to use leaves," Syd concluded.

"Why did you have to use leaves?"

"I couldn't find a bathroom, so I went in the woods."

"The woods?" shrieked Tara. "There are no *woods* in Central Park."

"I just got off the trail and went under a bush. I couldn't help it!"

"The trail? You mean the road that they close on the weekend, right? That's not really a trail. That's a street. Did you know that? People could probably see you, girl!"

"I don't think so. Anyway, it wouldn't have mattered. I couldn't help it." Sydney shrugged. What I couldn't help was notice that her "running" jacket was hung on the back of Sage's front door. It was bright neon orange. I'm sure the salesman convinced Syd to buy the brightest for safety reasons. She was a sucker for gear. I was also sure that Syd, in her bright neon jacket, had been like a deer in a clearing as she squatted to relieve herself. The city is full of interesting people.

"Y'all, can't we at least sit in the dining room and eat our meal like civilized people?" Wade bemoaned.

"Wade, you don't have a dining room," I reminded her. From Wade's intonation, you would have thought there was a grand room beyond the doorway dripping with crystal and enveloped in soft candlelight.

When I thought about it, Wade should have been the one who worked at *Sunshine & Sensibility*, not me. It was right up her alley. She was always e-mailing me about work and asking what crafty thing Jane was working on or what new recipes Jane was whipping up in the kitchen. Wade had this craving to know everything about arts, crafts, and cooking. We all knew that she wanted to be a stay-at-home mom who threw lavish dinner parties and fancy luncheons at her gorgeous ten-acre estate in the country. Just like Jane, she wanted two Labs running in her backyard, a garden that was right out of a Monet painting, an über-wealthy hottie for a husband, and identical twin boys who would gush over her like she was the Queen of England. I think deep down inside we all wanted what Wade wanted, but we knew that she would be the one to get it one day.

"I did set the table though." Wade had a little bistro table in the corner (aka, the dining nook) of her living room. Who knew Julia Child could prove her mastery in such a confining space? But she sure had tried! Pots were simmering and the oven was baking, making for a cozy warm space at least.

"We're fine right here," determined Tara who was perched upon the kitchen's Formica countertop in her spandex and sports bra. "Plus, Charlie has news. Spill it, C."

"What's in this?" interrupted Sage. She was standing over a dish that Syd had brought.

"It's a Vidalia onion pie," Syd replied.

"A what?"

"No really, it's divine. Basically, you make a crushed Ritz cracker crust with drizzled butter, and add a filling of chopped onions mixed with heavy cream—"

"Stop right there! Ugh, the lbs!" moaned Sage in utter agony. "I thought you all wanted to lose weight! Lucky for you I brought something that's actually edible." She put a pot on the table and lifted the lid. Scents galore wafted to the top of the nine-foot ceilings.

"Mmm, smells good, Sage. What is it?" Wade asked as we all sat up to peak into the hot pot.

"It's my special soup," she began. Ugh. I needed a Big Mac, not soup. "I added some extra pepper, cilantro, a whole lot of salsa, and some other secret spices that I'll tell you about later."

"Spices? Is there anything of real substance to your soup? Like some big hunks of beef?" Tara laughed.

"Spices are a dieter's delight!" Sage enthused. "But there *is* chicken. I call it Sage's Skinny Soup and girls, trust me, it's to die for if I do say so myself."

"I brought horseradish mashed potatoes," I volunteered,

holding out my covered plastic bowl. I was quite proud of the feat. Mashed potatoes required boiling, mashing, measuring, and whipping. Four steps. Oh, how I had grown since August! My cooking stock was rising.

"Thanks!" said Sage as she lifted from my hand the blue bowl that contained my glorious potatoes. She then promptly lifted the lid of the garbage can and threw it in with a *thunk*. She wiped her hands on her jeans, as if cleansing them from filth.

"What!" I screeched.

"Mashed potatoes are definitely out this month and beans are in. Trust me, girls."

"But that is my contribution!"

"Was. And I thank you, but your back fat doesn't," chastised Sage. "You can still pass out your recipe card though." I looked to the other girls for help, but they all shrugged, helpless in the face of Sage's dictatorship. We'd asked for her help, after all. Growing up, everyone had that one friend whose mother was not to be questioned and never to be doubted. Sage was going to be that kind of mother. I sipped my skinny soup in relative silence that night. I'd been on a diet for one day and I was already struggling. I hoped this New Year wouldn't be one of starvation. Couldn't I find a man to love my extra poundage as well as me?

"So, did I tell you all that I have now perfected the art of going into work and functioning for the first half hour despite being still drunk?" Tara volunteered with the utmost pride. "I figure that hour is a trade-off for the fact that I don't take umpteen smoking breaks a day, because I don't smoke, and I don't take countless coffee breaks, because I don't gossip!" Macie snickered. "Well, not office gossip," Tara countered to defend herself. "No one there has any gossip-worthy drama in their lives as far as I'm concerned." We, on the other hand, always seemed to have drama in spades.

"Can we bring on the meat?" Macie interrupted.

"You mean because there is barely any in our soup tonight?" I retorted.

"Hey, first of all," Sage cut in, "it can be made in under thirty minutes. That's key when you live in the city. And secondly, it is healthy, nutritious, and within your recommended dietary constraints! What more could you ask for?"

"'Constraints' is right!" I grumbled.

"I see at least two slices of pie on those hips, Miss Charlie!" I tried to hip check her in the booth, but when I felt my thigh flap, I shut up.

"So Charlie . . ." Tara prompted again.

"Yeah, how was the romantic dinner with Mr. You Know Who the other night?" Wade asked. "Did you make me proud?"

I hung my head. "That would be a no?" she prodded.

"A solid no."

"What happened? That recipe is foolproof!" My head snapped back up and I glared at her. Then I started to tell the story.

⁓

*T*o spice up the New Year, I had made a firm resolution to get back in the game and win Mr. J. P. Morgan's heart once and for all—or at least get him to my apartment on a regular basis that is. I wanted commitment, I wanted dates, I wanted love with a capital (and cursive) *L*. So far, he and I had only had one real date—and Macie had even called that one into question. I'd argued that it counted since food was involved. One morning after, we'd gone to the corner kiosk and grabbed some breakfast. He'd had a greasy egg sandwich and I'd ordered an egg-white omelet (which the counter man scorned). J. P. had paid (willingly, not because I couldn't find my wallet in my huge hobo bag) and we ate, sans plates, by the stacks of the *New York Times*. It was a date. He paid. We chatted. We ate. And, no alcohol was involved. (Note to self: Figure out when we should celebrate our first anniversary . . . which hook-up counts?)

True, he had taken his keys back in the weeks before Christmas. But he'd shown up the first week of the New Year bearing pears. Okay, so he brought them for all of "the girls," not just me, but I thought that was sensitive of him, not wanting to leave anyone out. Macie hinted that she thought they came from some office party fruit basket, but it is the thought that counts. Right? Plus they were nice pears; you know, the ones wrapped in gold foil with the box lined with that annoying green curly paper stuffing. And he did spend the night afterward, in my room, in my bed, and God help me if he didn't sleep like a baby.

So in order to acknowledge all of Mr. J. P. Morgan's subtle efforts, I had decided to cook him dinner. A real home-cooked meal. I knew that he basically survived on frozen Egg McMuffins; his freezer was stocked with them (delivered of course). He and his roommates would take them out for any one of their three meals per day, nuke them, and stuff them down their throats. Needless to say, he needed a hearty meal that consisted of the basic five (or was it now six?) food groups.

After a few months of the Cooking Club, I was confident that I could pull off some more sophisticated recipes, especially one of Wade's scrumptious yet simplistic casserole concoctions. Wade swore up and down that casseroles, those famous dishes from the seventies, were making a comeback. We all pretty much pooh-poohed the idea until she brought a casserole to dinner one night and changed our minds—delish! Now with Wade's recipe for her mother's famous artichoke casserole in my back pocket, my mom's dreams would be fulfilled. Mr. J. P. Morgan's hunger would be satisfied. Love would be in the air. Oh God, I hoped he liked casserole! I summoned up my courage and sent an e-mail.

> **To: J.P.morgan**
> **From: Snoopy**
> **Subject: an invitation you can't refuse**
>   You.
>   Me.
>   Dinner at my apartment.
>   Saran Wrap.
>   (Not necessarily in that order.)

> **To: Snoopy**
> **From: J.P.morgan**
> **Subject: Re: an invitation you can't refuse**
>   Yum (on all parts)! I'm in.

I'd started my lovemaking mission in the kitchen. I whipped out the recipe card and examined Wade's very detailed instructions. Step one: *Open cupboard and take out* clean *casserole dish (a white china one)*. Nuts, I was already off to a bad start. There was no casserole dish, or even a clean dish for that matter, in our cabinets. Strike one.

I grabbed my bag and headed straight to the supermarket. Unfortunately, the chaos of Fairway, the mecca of supermarkets, overwhelmed me within minutes of entering. My first mission was to find a casserole dish. The nice store clerk directed me to aisle four for that fine little item. So far, so good. I then went in search of my main ingredient: artichoke hearts. I decided not to ask the same guy for help because I didn't want to seem like I was totally helpless, so I started going up and down the different aisles fighting many annoyed and agitated grocery shoppers. After ten minutes of searching aimlessly, I still hadn't found them. At first, I'd figured an artichoke was a vegetable, so I went to the canned veggie aisle. But after going up and down the shelves, they were nowhere to be found. I then ventured into the gourmet section and scrounged around the vats of olives. Still no artichokes. Flustered, bruised, and completely annoyed at this point, I threw in the towel and went back to the canned veggie aisle. I grabbed a couple of cans of green beans as a substitute and headed out of the chaos.

On my way home, I stopped by the local wine store. During the late afternoon the wine stores in New York tended to have wine tastings and not being a wine connoisseur, I had decided to educate myself. Half an hour later, a tad tipsy, and with a box containing four wine bottles under my arm, I felt prepared. The wine store owner was a bit perplexed as to which wine was best served with a vegetable casserole, so I had bought two not-so-cheap bottles of white wine and two definitely-not-so-cheap bottles of red.

The actual cooking process was not as traumatic as I thought. I had even scattered pieces of the Diva's toffee throughout the apartment for dessert—a bread crumb trail of sorts to my bedroom. Syd briefly burst my bubble when she came into the kitchen and asked what the green sticks peeking out of the casserole crust were.

"Beans!" I shouted. "Didn't you ever have veggies as a child?"

"Yeah, but I don't remember beans in Wade's recipe," she said as she stuck her nose closer to the dish. Goddamn, kitchen police!

"I couldn't find the artichoke hearts, so I grabbed beans," I explained. When she gave me one of her glazed looks, I continued, "They're both green!"

"Oh, right," agreed Syd. But her obvious lack of faith gave me pause. Did I want to be in the same boat as Syd when a recipe began to sink?

⁂

*L*ater that night, Mr. J. P. Morgan had seemed amused as I fluttered about, apron over my plunging wrap top and new jeans. The mismatched wineglasses were a bit streaked, and the cloth napkins smelled of spray starch. But I plastered on a big grin as I brought out the bubbling casserole, teetering on my one pair of Manolo Blahniks.

"You know, we could have just gone out," he said. Well, of course we could have gone out to a restaurant, if he'd ever bothered to ask me. But he hadn't.

"Oh, don't be silly. I'm loving this cooking stuff. I swear, I might become a pro someday."

"Are you Italian?" Why did men think that only Italian women could cook?

"I think somewhere on my mom's side," I lied. "I'm pretty much a mutt." Then I winced. Way to go, Charlie. Equate yourself to a dog! I unfolded my napkin on my lap, unlike my dinner date, and watched him take a minuscule bite of the casserole. I waited . . .

I knew I would see his eyes light up, his crooked grin widen, as he savored the taste of my exquisite meal. Unfortunately, his eyes crossed a bit, and he choked back a laugh.

"C, what's in this?" he asked.

"It's a family secret," I began.

"Damn, girl, put it back in the vault!"

What? What had gone wrong? I took a bite and almost choked, choked on my tears. It tasted nothing like Wade's dish had. There was a sour taste in place of the tangy zip. What could I have possibly done wrong? I looked up just in time to see Mr. J. P. Morgan blowing out the candles.

"Come on, let's go out, my treat. Let's grab some burgers and catch the end of the game across the street," he suggested, twirling on his scarf as if he were Cary Grant.

"But this was supposed to be *my* treat!"

"You can treat me later in bed," he hinted with that impish grin of his. Under normal circumstances, I would have melted, but domestic ambition had gotten the better of me.

"No, wait. I wanted to treat you to dinner," I began.

"Fine. Then you can grab the bill. Let's go," he said as he held a coat out for me. Struggling to keep my feelings inside, and struggling to get my arms into Syd's too-small-for-me coat that he had erroneously grabbed from the hook, I excused myself to go to the bathroom. Once there, I burst into tears. Macie, who was ensconced in her bedroom with the flu, snuck in behind me.

"What happened?"

"I don't know," I cried, trying to retouch my now smeared mascara.

"Did you follow the recipe?"

"Yes! Well, almost."

"Oh, Charlie!"

"I used green beans instead of artichokes. But they're both green!"

"Yes, they are," she sympathized. "But they're still different foods and that could change the flavor of the recipe, you know. Oh, I'm so sorry, sweetie. You tried, and that's all that matters."

"I guess not because now he wants to go watch the game, and on top of it all, he somehow suggested that I pay for dinner!"

"Bastard."

⚬

*B*astard, bastard, bastard, is all I thought as he high-fived his three buddies at the bar where we were now dining. I squinted across the packed table that we were sharing with nine others. Was he cute? For the past four months I had thought so. I squinted harder. Maybe I did need glasses. No, he was cute. The three blondes by the bar staring at him confirmed it for me. So he didn't like my cooking. Was that such a big deal? I could hardly blame him, after all. I reflected again that I'd been a tad emotionally scarred by all those Prince Charmings in the Disney movies. They'd ruined generations of women by building up our expectations and selling us on something we could never have. Disney had franchised everything else; why couldn't they produce a line of Prince Charmings, $19.95 plus shipping. Could J. P. Morgan ever be my Prince Charming? One of the players scored and he turned and flashed me that oh-so-perfect smile. But as I watched him lean over and take a slobbering bite of his burger, I had to wonder . . .

"So the dinner was a disaster!" I concluded, conjuring up my best Susan Lucci dramatics.

"Did he at least come back for dessert?" Tara asked.

"Yep. And . . ." Here I smiled in spite of myself. "I think we are beyond *just* sex."

"No," sighed Sage.

"You didn't," moaned Wade.

"She spooned! You did! Just tell us!" Tara pleaded as she jumped off the counter.

Spooning. Such a simple concept, yet so hard to perfect. I swear that both parties not only have to be willing, they just have to be . . . a particular fit. The ability to spoon properly requires a little bit of fate mixed in with destiny. Kind of like cooking. Some things just blend together beautifully regardless of proportions. Chocolate and peanut butter, turkey and cranberry. But some combinations can't be forced.

When spooning is right, it doesn't matter how tall or short the participants are. It doesn't matter how fat or thin. No matter what your body types, you almost melt into each other. You are not hyperaware of each other, staying awake for hours locked in one position. No, it's like falling into a warm bath or nestling under a featherbed. You can't feel any unwanted body hair on either body. No body part goes numb or gets that tingling feeling from falling asleep. Rather, the warm breath on the back of your neck is like a baby's sigh or a puppy's snore. Contentness at its best.

"We spooned!" I shrieked.

"And . . ." Tara prodded.

"Well, it was the first night of *real* cuddling."

"And . . . did you sleep like a satisfied baby?"

"No . . ."

"You didn't sleep? Oh, is he a pillow stealer?"

"No, I mean I didn't sleep, but not in a bad way at all. I think I was just so excited that he had me in a bear hug and didn't let go or relax his grip once! The tension in his forearms was divine!"

"For how long?"

"What, you think I timed it?"

"For roughly how long, Charlie?" demanded Tara. I could hear my father now, "It always comes back to math." I could make him proud with this one.

"Fine. We started spooning around 10:37, after forty-nine minutes of nooky—"

"Does nooky include sex?" asked Syd.

"For God's sake!" Tara answered for me.

"And, I finally got up to go to the bathroom at 1:31." There was silence. "Two hours and fifty-six minutes." I looked around.

"You got up? Honey, what were you thinking?" asked Wade.

"I had to go," I reasoned.

"In the middle of your first spooning encounter? No, you hold it," scolded Sage.

"I had to go!" I wailed. "If I don't go to the bathroom after sex, I get UTIs!"

"Oh, so nooky does include sex," concluded Syd, nodding to herself.

"Good God, did you at least weasel your way back in?" asked Tara. I think my face must have fallen, because Macie put down her glass of water and threw an arm over my shoulders.

"No. He had flipped over and was hugging the pillow," I said. I didn't bother to add how I had pondered the situation from every single angle; had debated how to mattress dive my way back into the spooning position. Nor did I mention that he had stolen both pillows, yet again.

"He did flip a leg over mine mid early morning."

"Atta, girl!" shouted Tara.

"Did you get any sleep at all?" Macie asked.

"Nope!" I said raising my can of Red Bull. "But the spooning was worth it." The girls nodded. End of subject.

∽

*L*ife seemed to seep from the city in the last days of January and there was a lag time full of gray, cold days. The East Coast, where New York not-so-silently lies, began to be pounded by wet winter storms from the Atlantic.

Forget the fluffy white stuff you see in the movies. It might come down white, but in New York, within a matter of minutes, it is transformed into black, sticky slush. But it's not the snow, or lack thereof, that bothers most of us city folk. It's the frigid, nail-biting wind that gets your goat. Try coming around the corner of our street onto Broadway, only to be pummeled by winds so fierce and biting that you feel tears come to your eyes. Soon your mascara-streaked cheeks reflect the gray tones of the slush underfoot. And to add insult to the injurious bitter chill that constantly runs through your veins, think *Marshmallow Woman Takes New York!* And you thought *Ghostbusters* was an overexaggeration! Hell, fellow commuters on the subway literally bounce off your puffy (yet warm), not-so-stylish jacket. Desperate times call for desperate fashion measures. So if that means bulking up and looking ten pounds heavier topside, so be it. Survival of the fittest takes on new meaning in winter.

When the temperature dropped to Arctic levels in the city, I realized that the change of season was going to be a severe shock to my system, especially January mornings. They were the absolute worst.

But I was already about twenty-one days late. No, I was not late for the big *P* (aka period), but rather, for sending out my holiday thank-you cards. My mother had drilled it into my head, that if the gift giver is not present, a thank-you card must be sent. I had finally pumped out my last four cards when I realized I was out of stamps. Not wanting to lose momentum, I decided that I had to brave the bitter cold morning to go purchase some. As I left our building, our maintenance man was watering the sidewalks with a hose. I almost pointed out that he was creating a hazard as the wind chill was about fifteen below zero, but I was bolstered by his ambition, and just gave him a holiday smile.

A post office truck was parked a few blocks from our building seven days a week. So useful! It had a lifting side panel through which you could buy postal supplies. Today, a large postman was leaning out of the side, grinning into the January sun like he was basking in Aruba.

"Hi!"

"And what can I do for you?" he smiled. Maybe Santa spent the off months between Christmases in the postal system.

"I need four stamps, please."

"That's it?" he asked. "No envelopes today?" I grinned at the obligatory random question.

"Nope. Just four stamps." He handed me a small leaf of bright first-class stamps. As I handed him the money, I looked at them more closely. They were colorful. They were large. Colorful and large and sporting enormous Hanukah menorahs.

"Oh, excuse me?"

"See, you need those envelopes to go with those stamps, right?" he laughed, and I swear his stomach shook like a bowl-ful of . . .

"No," I stopped myself. "Um, I just, can I have some other picture?"

"Oh, you have a problem with the religion depicted on the stamps?"

"Oh, no." I didn't have a problem with the religion, just the picture. "I just, well . . ." I did appreciate the pink back-ground with purple flames blazing brightly above the sacred candles, but I was sending the four remaining thank-you cards to my severely Catholic grandmother, my former minister, and one each to my newly divorced yet equally small-minded aunt and uncle. With family, I always put the stamp upside down— the universal message of love being sent through the mail. I knew my granny looked for this love with each letter, and I knew she would completely notice the menorah. And since they would be on my Christmas thank-you cards, I wouldn't want my granny to think I was converting.

"Don't you have flags or something?" I almost saluted. The once-jolly postman looked ready to bite my head off. He snatched back the stamps and handed me four others.

"You'll probably have a problem with these too." I took the stamps and fled the postal truck, feeling sure that I was now off the "Good Boys and Girls" list at the North Pole for next year. Who knew Santa was Jewish to boot? As I rounded the corner, I glanced down at the stamps folded in my mitten. Thurgood Marshall stared me in the face. He had given me Black History Month stamps. Perfect! New York City was home to all types. This included a politically correct postman who was dispensing life lessons about open-mindedness through a small panel in a white truck on the corner of Amsterdam and Seventy-fifth Street.

With thank-you cards mailed, I decided to tackle the next item off of my to-do list—buy new underwear. Shoving my hands into my pockets, I trudged a block to the bus stop. I thought the New Year deserved new, cotton, no-panty-lines underwear. And I thought J. P. might appreciate the purchase as well (as would the operating attendant in the emergency room after I got hit by a bus while daydreaming).

I took a childish swipe at my running nose as I pushed through the bodies toward the back of the bus. As I looked up to scan for a vacant seat, I found myself staring right into the eyes of Tom Funger. Shit. Shit! Did I have a second to pinch color into my makeup-less cheeks? Tom Funger had been my two-week pre–Mr. J. P. Morgan fling when I'd first arrived in New York City. Back in those early virginal NY days, I'd found the whole social scene so overwhelming. I mean there were so many boys to look at, never mind meet. So one night, I happened to run into Tom, who'd gone to school with us. Tom was Tom. At school, he was an unassuming nice guy—one you'd never look twice at. But, oh how things had changed for good ole Tom. He had stepped up quite a bit since I had seen him last (when was that . . . sophomore year, at Bugger's Bar?). The day I ran into him, he was wearing a crisp, ultrastarched Thomas Pink button-down and brown suede Gucci loafers—what a fast learner! He looked good—good and familiar. And there was something reassuring about familiarity in such a huge, impersonal city.

We'd hooked up and gone on two dinner dates, but I'd soon decided after that despite his snappy new attire, Tom was still fairly uninspiring and therefore I shouldn't waste my time. Plus, he had small hands. Now I know what you are thinking, but it's so not true. I wasn't worried about the hands and penis size correlation—I'm not that shallow. The problem was that my manicured hands ensconced, no eclipsed, his! I felt like I was holding a little boy's hands, and the pedophile ramifications scared me. Plus, with a name like Funger . . . I just knew I couldn't be called Mrs. Fungus, I mean Funger, for the rest of my life. And being a traditional girl, I wouldn't *want* to have to choose to keep my maiden name. Charlie Brown-Funger. Mrs. Brown-Fungus. So I never called Tom back. No reason was given, no good-bye was said, no excuse, no nothing. And now here he was on the same bus. There was absolutely no escape. The bus was packed, and we were standing smack dab in the middle. With a quick lick of my chapped lips, I turned and gave him my cheeriest smile.

"Tom, hey, good to see you! How are you? What have you been up to? I've been super busy." Smile, smile. I think I gave too much information away in that first conversational strand. I took a big breath.

Shit. Shit. Shit. Watch him be happy and about to pop the question to some young New York socialite.

"Hey, Charlie." Was there any enthusiasm in his voice or did I just hear bitter contempt? Was his smile genuine or mocking?

"Long time no see!" I quipped. He just nodded. "So what's new with you?"

"Not much," he said. "I'm just on my way home. I brought breakfast to a sick friend." Oh, he was a humanitarian. Did I know this when I didn't call him back?

"I think you might know him," he went on. "J. P.?"

Did I know him? Of course! Wait. How did Tom know that I knew him? How did they know each other? Had J. P. mentioned me? And if he had, did he say that he just "knew" me or that he "*knew*" me in a deeper, more soulful sense?

"Sure I do," I said, trying to sound like he was a dear yet casual acquaintance. "So he's, um, sick? Like deathbed sick?" I swallowed a heaping sense of panic.

"Probably just a cold," he answered. "Good seeing you, Charlie." Tom waved as the doors opened and he pushed his way out through the crowd. I stared distractedly after him out of the bus window. I gave him a slight wave like the prom queen I never was. J. P. was sick! Not that I was excited over his pain, but maybe he was too weak to pick up the phone (he hadn't called since our dinner, despite the spooning). His was an older, heavier cell phone.

A new plan for the day was forming in my mind. As we approached the next stop, I scurried up the middle of the bus to the front and jumped off to run back uptown. Back in the apartment, I grabbed the leftover container of Sage's Skinny Soup. Nothing like soup for the ailing. Like a top spinning out of control, I was back out of the apartment and back on the bus downtown before you could spell "pathetic."

⌘

J. P. didn't answer the door right away. I began to think that his illness was probably just a bad hangover and that I was the fool in waiting, the fool with soup in her hand.

"Charlie!" he said as he opened the door. Did he sound surprised or startled?

"I heard through the grapevine that you were sick, and I thought that you could use some soup!" I responded cheerfully trying to mask the fact that my sudden appearance could be considered stalkerish. I smiled. How could a disheveled, bathrobe-wearing, two-day-beard-sporting patient look so cute? How?

"Thanks," he answered, still standing in the doorway. I waited for him to invite me inside.

"Let me heat some of this up for you," I suggested.

"Microwave's broken." Did he not want me to come in?

"Silly. I know how to use a stove," I laughed. Thank God I did! Thank you Cooking Club!

Ten minutes later, I had warmed up the soup.

"This is quite good, Charlie," he commented. I didn't tell him that Sage had made it because I also now had the recipe to go with my growing arsenal of cooking skills.

"Here," I said pressing a cold washcloth compress to his forehead. "You really are warm," I murmured. I disappeared back into the kitchen and opened a couple of cans of soda to leave on the counter.

"Let the fizz, the carbonation, leave the soda. Flat soda is good for your upset stomach," I advised as I walked back into his living room. I walked by his comatose body on the couch and turned on ESPN on the television. Figuring that his lack of conversation was due to exhaustion, I put my coat back on to go. Food, sports, and now for a little loving . . . I could be a true Renaissance woman. As I leaned in for a kiss good-bye, he shrank back into the pillow a bit.

"You shouldn't have come over," he said.

"No, no problem at all."

"I might be contagious, C."

"I'm not worried," I answered as I planted a well-placed kiss just below his ear.

As I walked back up Broadway, I began to wonder if I should be worried. He had said that I shouldn't have come over. Huh. I had just risked my health and I wasn't sure that J. P. had recognized or even cared about my sacrifice. Luckily, I didn't have a chance to wallow too much because a sale sign at the Gap reeled me in off of the cold sidewalk. I had hit upon the motherload of all post-holiday sales. (Note to self: Never again shop at full retail price.) Once inside, I dug through the bins and found about eighteen pairs of thong (not g-string) underwear, all for the mere price of about $23.50, not counting tax. What a relief, especially to my swollen credit card debt. Dumping the load on the counter, I gave the Gap woman a post-holiday smile. I had done some freelance retail work at the Gap during college vacations and knew the stress involved.

"Whew, it's cold," I said to no one in particular.

"It must be important for you to keep warm," the Gap woman remarked.

"Warm? What?" I inquired. Did she not notice that I was buying thong underwear and not wool sweaters?

"I mean, it must be important for you to keep warm with your bundle of joy," she said smiling. I looked down. The only bundles of joy were in my hands and they were in brown and white striped bags.

"My bundle of joy?" I asked, still confused. The woman behind me gasped audibly.

"You're not pregnant? Oh my gosh. I'm so sorry."

My cheeks flushed despite the January winds whisking through the ever-revolving Gap door. Didn't she see that I was buying medium-sized underwear and not XL? What could I say? For God's sake, my jacket was unzipped, so it was not my marshmallow frumpy down jacket either.

"Um, that will be $25.76." My friendly Gap woman went into serious retail mode. I stood there for a second. Should I demand an apology? Did I want her to acknowledge her error yet again? My post-holiday sale buzz deflated. I scowled as I signed the sales receipt. Who was I kidding anyway? Why would J. P. be excited about cotton underwear? I took out my cell phone. The screen stared back at me blankly—o missed calls. Couldn't he, shouldn't he call to say thank you? Didn't I deserve a simple phone call?

Experts say that the holiday season can cause severe depression. I left the Gap feeling low, and cold water seeped into my boot as I sank into a slushy gray snow bank at the corner. I looked up hoping to find some divine intervention as the snot running from my nose froze to my face. I felt like a used tissue—an apparently pregnant used tissue. As "Oh, Come All Ye Faithful" blared from the Hallmark store, I burst into tears.

I made a list of resolutions (yes, a tad late) right there on the corner of Broadway and Thirty-fourth:

Get over Mr. J. P. Morgan

Find *true* love

Lose twenty pounds (or at least seven)

Order soda not tonic in mixed drinks

Research a cheap yoga class

Cry only due to circumstances like those in *Terms of Endearment*

Ascend the corporate ladder at *Sunshine & Sensibility*

Take a pottery class (cheaper than psychotherapy)

Pay off credit cards

Forgo dry cleaning and take up ironing

Brew own morning coffee
Read a classic novel (perhaps *Moby-Dick*?)
Cook a scrumptious casserole
Get over Mr. J. P. Morgan
Rule the world

It was all plausible. I crossed Broadway feeling determined.
Optimistic.

The New Year had officially begun.

February

Sweet Cinnamon Buns with Tongue-Tickling Icing

Icing

> 12 ounces cream cheese, room temperature
>
> 6 tablespoons unsalted butter, room temperature
>
> 3 cups confectioner's sugar

Buns

> 2 cups sifted all-purpose flour
>
> 1 tablespoon baking powder
>
> 1 teaspoon salt
>
> ¼ teaspoon baking soda
>
> ¼ cup vegetable oil
>
> ¾ cup buttermilk
>
> 8 tablespoons (1 stick) butter, softened
>
> ¾ cup granulated sugar
>
> 1 teaspoon cinnamon

Prepare the icing in advance, as it has to chill for 3 to 4 hours.

To make the icing, beat the cream cheese on medium-low speed for about 1 minute with an electric beater with paddle attachment. Add the butter and beat for about 2 minutes, until smooth. Add the sugar, beating on low speed until combined. Mix on medium for about 1 minute until smooth and fluffy. Chill the icing in the fridge for about 3 to 4 hours until firm.

Combine flour, baking powder, salt, and baking soda in bowl. Stir in vegetable oil. Add buttermilk and mix.

Knead the dough on a floured surface until smooth. Roll dough out with a rolling pin into a 15 × 8-inch rectangle.

Preheat oven to 400°F. Lightly grease a 9-inch round baking pan.

Spread the butter over the dough. Combine the sugar and cinnamon, mixing well, and sprinkle over the buttered dough. In a jelly-roll fashion, roll up the rectangle starting from one long side. Pinch the seam to seal.

Cut the roll into 1½-inch-thick slices and arrange the slices, cut side up, in the baking pan. Bake for about 20 minutes until lightly browned.

Gently spread the chilled icing over the cinnamon buns while they are hot.

Serve these sweet cinnamon buns piping hot to your favorite loved one. Save any extra icing to frost your mate with this tongue-tickling delight (wink, wink)!

"I don't care!" She shrieked from inside her office. "This is absolutely atrocious and whoever picked out these hideous red roses does not, I repeat, does *not* belong on my staff. Do you hear me?"

"Yes, Jane. You are so right, Jane," Donna, *Sunshine & Sensibility's* neurotic executive producer, replied softly, attempting to quell Jane's tirade. Her head was nodding like one of those dashboard bobbles.

"Don't nod!" Jane snapped. "If you agree, then this should never have happened. Why do I always have to do things myself?!" She sighed with the dramatic flair of a community theater actress.

"This will never happen again, Jane. I promise," Donna swore.

Donna Murphy was in theory the most powerful person next to Jane. Yet time and time again, Jane made sure to emphasize Who (with a capital *w*) was truly and solely in charge. Case in point: Donna had just been reduced to the role of a six-year-old being scolded. The Diva was in full-on diva form and everyone in the office knew to either duck behind the partitions when she passed or stay hidden in the shadow of the now-damned roses.

"Roses are unoriginal, Donna!" She ranted on. "They are cliché. They are stale, boring, and insipid. So basic, so bland. Katie loves roses, Kelly loves roses; actually, no, Kelly probably loves daisies. For Christ's sake, you should have known this. Roses are trite. Red roses are thoroughly uninspiring. Most of all, they're pedestrian." Pedestrian? Who used the word "pedestrian" when referring to anything other than a person on foot?

"So, what are you doing right now?" Jane demanded.

"Um, I'm sorry," Donna stammered, looking confused. "What am I doing? Whatever it is, I can change it."

"Donna, what you are doing is wasting my time and you of all people know that I don't tolerate this type of behavior. So get out of my office and fix this. Do you hear me?" And with that, Jane slammed the door behind Donna's shaking behind.

The entire office had heard the big bitch fest go down and you could just feel the black cloud hovering over the rows of cubicles. I swore I'd heard a clap of thunder erupt and the Wicked Witch of the West laughing from inside her lair. As I peeked over the edge of my cubicle, not a soul was to be found. No one was hovering near the staff lunchroom searching for an errant triple caramel fudge brownie, no one was giggling over wedding Web sites, no one was rearranging the dishes in the studio on Set A. Everyone had assumed his/her high-alert status—hide and hide good.

Jane's tongue-lashings typically occurred once or twice a week. You would think one would feel sorry for Donna, but she had taken this abuse for three years, and we all figured she had enough zeroes in her salary to compensate for the verbal abuse. To make matters worse, Donna herself would morph from meek to maniacal about five minutes after the initial rant ended: Jane yells at Donna, Donna apologizes, Jane slams the door, Donna turns on someone else. It was pretty much status quo. Compared to the other girls and their jobs, my office dynamics were the most abnormal. Some would call them unbearable and downright cruel, but I kept reminding myself that this was a job hundreds of thousands of people my age would die for. The HR lady hadn't been kidding when she'd warned me it was going to be tough. And the unwritten understanding was that if you didn't like it, you could leave. However, there was a silver lining to Jane's sweatshop: Apparently, if you made it here, you could make it anywhere in the television biz. Rumor had it that Jane was notorious for molding the careers of some of the greatest television minds around. Oprah, Jay, Kelly, Dave, Katie, even Ellen's shows were filled with Jane survivors. And with the typical employee's tenure being about a year to a year and a half, I figured at the rate I was going, I'd be able to move up the ranks pretty quickly.

Things quieted down after the fight, but I could still hear feet scurrying around the office at a more frantic pace than usual. True, we were often in panic mode, but today it seemed a little different. I glanced at the "official" calendar that was given out at the beginning of each month that listed all the shoots and edits and the days they were scheduled. In bold letters under tomorrow's date it read "Red Says I Love You." It had been a last-minute change, but everything around here was last minute. It was television, after all. The viewer at home would never know the difference, but the programming board was always getting shuffled around like a deck of playing cards. I just kept thanking God I hadn't planned the segment Jane was bitching about.

"Did you hear that?" Julie said as she came out of her office.

"Who didn't?" I said. "God, I feel sorry for the person who's going to suffer the wrath of Donna over that one."

"Yeah, to be on Jane's or Donna's shit list is not good, especially the day before a taping day," she said.

"Totally. Even I know that Jane hates red and I haven't even been here that long. She made me return the red bathrobe I ordered for the bathroom remodel shoot. Now at least we all know that she hates roses too, because they are just so 'pedestrian.' Have you ever heard anyone use that word in that manner?"

"Nope. Just another diva-ism." Julie shrugged.

"Well, back to work on my expensive treehouses. Did you know that we're showcasing none other than singer extraordinaire Willie Nelson's two-story pine tree monstrosity?" I asked.

"And Jane is going to climb trees?"

"No, Jungle Jane has a fear of heights," I reassured her.

"You'd think she'd like to climb higher toward her divine throne."

"She never does heights. She won't even climb a stepladder to put plates in plate racks high on the set wall. So, we're going to replicate the treehouses on the ground."

"You're kidding!"

"Nope. The art department has drawn up blueprints, and

the wood experts have arranged for specially treated cedar to be flown in from India by next Friday. And Nancy in postproduction is creating some sort of digitally imaged film for the house's windows to replicate the trees we need to have simulated outside. I'm supposed to be researching the shape and shade of poplar leaves."

"Oh goodie!" Julie clapped.

⌇

*J*ane strove to be the first to show or do anything on *Sunshine & Sensibility*. Her motto was "Create and cultivate." We (the royal we) were supposed to come up with the "Wow items" that would pique her creative interest during our Wednesday brainstorming meetings. It was a pretty tough feat to accomplish, but if you were successful, there would be no stopping you. I knew that in the end my treehouse segment would not just showcase Willie Nelson's humble abode. No, Jane would find some way to improve upon it. So I'd gotten a jump start on her and come up with a list of "out of the box" ideas. So far I had:

Humble Projects
⌇ grow organic vegetables in the treehouse's window boxes
⌇ affix retractable eyelet curtains to skylights

Grand Projects
⌇ add a wraparound sun porch
⌇ install an elevator powered by solar energy

Mid-brainstorm, I was interrupted. "Charlotte!" Donna screamed as she ran past my cube.

Now what? It was the bolt of lightning I was dreading. But wait, why did it strike me?

"Um, what? Yes Donna. I'm right behind you." Run, Forrest, run! I grabbed pen and pad, my treehouse list, and scurried down the hall after her. I knew that this wasn't going to be good. Donna never wanted to speak to me, at least not directly. Come to think of it, I don't even think she'd ever spoken to me. Little beads of sweat began to collect on my forehead and my mouth suddenly became dry and pasty. What the hell did I do? Okay, just breathe Charlie, breathe.

As I walked down the corridor to her office, I could sense everyone staring at me. I tried to keep my head low and walk fast to save face, but the whispering soon followed. Was this a good sign? Was this bad? Did my ass have a blaring yellow sign saying, "Kick me and kick me hard?" Apparently so. As I rounded the corner into Donna's office, I could hear her still trying to appease Jane.

"I understand, Jane, I *fully* understand," she said as she hung up her phone. Then she turned to me. "Sit down, Charlotte." I sat up straight upon hearing her enunciate each syllable of my given name.

So far, so good. I planted myself in the steel chair (cold metal cleverly disguised with an oh-so-warm brushed silver look) over in the far corner of her office. Distance makes the heart grow fonder, right? I sat there silently while she took notes. After what seemed like five minutes of senseless writing (could her pen move any further down the page?) she looked up and smiled. The grin on her face resembled one of those evil Disney vultures coming in for the kill.

"Thanks for coming in so quickly, Charlotte," she said sweetly. "As you may have heard," her eyes rolled sarcastically, "Jane has a little problem with the flowers *you* picked for today's segment." Hold up! Rewind! The list of treehouse ideas wilted in my hand. I looked around the office—had someone else come through the door? I sure as hell hadn't had anything to do with the damned red roses. For God's sake, I wasn't even the flower arranger! Generosa was the one who went to the flower market, picked the stems, brought them back in her company-paid-for SUV, and arranged them for the set. And how exactly was I involved?

"Now you're new . . ." Correction. I had been at *S&S* for five months. A record in my early employment career path.

"But we can't have such, ah, devastating disasters like the one we had this morning. Jane is quite upset, and with good reason," she continued. Ah, yes. She's totally right because a hissy fit over red roses is entirely justifiable.

"So I need you to clean up the mess you made." This finger pointing was starting to jab me in the all the wrong places. I was seething but I held my tongue.

"Now Jennifer is arriving on set tomorrow for the Valentine's Day shoot at ten A.M. We obviously won't have time to really rehearse since your mistake has made the planned rehearsal today ineffective. Now Ms. Lopez will be expecting everything to be in place . . ." Wait a minute! My heart stopped in my chest. Jennifer. Ms. Lopez. Put them together and you've got Ms. Jennifer Lopez! And I didn't even do the *New York Times* crossword puzzle!

"Jennifer Lopez is coming here? Here to *S&S*?"

"Yes, Charlotte. Now I'd like you to refer to her as Ms. Lopez. You just reminded me, I need to send out an e-mail asking everyone not to say hello to her, not to ask her personal questions, and not to ask her for an autograph. Anyway, I need you to find flowers that will please her—flowers that will evoke Ms. Lopez's independent and fierce spirit."

Had she picked the right girl or what!? I knew the answer to every possible J. Lo question. Panic evaporated into excitement. This was going to be my "Wow item," my tour de force, my magical moment to shine. You could bet that I was going to milk this assignment and come out on top.

"I'll get on this task right away, Donna. You can count on me." Why did I have to revert to such cheesy and subservient catch phrases? "But what about Willie Nelson's treehouse shoot?"

"Treehouses are nothing new. We'll be scrapping that piece," she scoffed as if we'd been working on that concept for minutes instead of months.

"But what about the wood from India?" I asked.

"Cancel it." Little did she know it was en route on some enormous tanker in the middle of the Atlantic Ocean. She looked up at me and held my gaze. "The flowers, Charlotte? Please?" It wasn't a polite please, it was more like a get your ass moving please.

"No pedestrian flowers for Ms. Lopez," I recited and caught myself before I actually saluted.

◆

That night I rallied the troops at the apartment for an emergency meeting of the minds.

"My job is on the line at *S&S*," I explained. "But I think I may also have a chance to become the next shining star. Can you guys take the day off work tomorrow?"

"I don't even have a vacation day yet, Charlie," sighed Macie. "Not until the end of year one."

I'd known it would be a lot to ask Macie considering that she'd never missed a day of class in college. Come sleet, snow,

105-degree temperature, or hangover, reliable Macie was never absent. She saw "sickness" as a sign of weakness and weak was something she was not. She would have been perfect for the armed forces—she was so disciplined and dependable. That's probably why my mom loved her so much. But right now, she needed to Save Private Charlie.

"My kids go crazy when I'm not around," rationalized Wade.

"I have an important appointment at Brown Sugar about our new Beyoncé Bootylicious Extensions," whined Syd.

"I have a Pilates training class every Tuesday morning," chimed in Sage.

"Family emergency? I'm in," cheered Tara.

I held my hands, Wade-teacher-style, to silence the group, which had now evolved into a chattering mass of explanations and excuses. "Girls, who do we aspire to be? Who do we pray to each night? Who is our coach, our mentor, our idol?"

"J. Lo!" They exclaimed in perfect sync.

"And who is going to be on *Sunshine & Sensibility* tomorrow?" I called in full cheerleader mode. All their mouths dropped open.

"J. Lo," whispered Syd in pure disbelief. They all started talking at once, rehashing their Tuesday agendas. There was no way they were going to miss an opportunity to meet Jenny from the Block herself.

"Wait. It gets better. To make the visit a success, I've been put in charge of coming up with the perfect flower to decorate the set. They'll be a decorative backdrop for when J. Lo concocts her mother's favorite recipe—some cinnamon bun thingy."

"You're in charge of flowers? That's all you have to do to

score points at work is decorate the set with the right flower?" asked Macie.

"You have no idea how essential the flower selection is."

"Okay, J. Lo loves two flowers," recited Tara. "She had gardenias at her first wedding and peonies at her second. Who knows what she wanted for the Ben nuptials, but I think she might have had both at her private ceremony with Marc Anthony."

"Now would we be bringing up bad memories with those selections?" I asked.

"That girl changes men like the weatherman changes his mind."

"She can be fickle about men, but I bet our lady sticks by her flowers. Can you have both on the set?" Macie theorized.

"Well, Jane likes simplicity. But I can have both ready to go," I reasoned. We made plans for the girls to arrive at the office at 7:30 A.M. I planned to stash them in my cubicle and then let them watch the taping from the sidelines. With so many charity auction tours coming in and out of the office, I figured no one would think twice about a small gaggle of girls coming through.

⁓

$\mathcal{T}$uesday morning was chaotic. Ms. Lopez's limo was late, so the buzz around the studio was that she had hopped into a taxi hoping that the New York cabbie could make up the time. Oh, the lengths our lady would go to—riding in a germ-ridden cab like a commoner! But more important, J. Lo probably knew (or sensed) that Jane despised tardiness. Luckily, the extra minutes bought us some much-needed time, leaving us girls a few seconds to primp. The six of us were hanging out in the receptionist's office when J. Lo arrived, waltzing through with a single bodyguard but sans entourage (they were probably still delayed in the limo). Like monkeys in a tree, our heads turned and watched her saunter down the hallway with every assistant in the building at her heels.

As she shed her coat, I noticed she was wearing all white. From her head to her toe, she was a winter wonderland. Gone were the days of short shorts and gaudy headbands from her P. Diddy days. The two-piece, perfectly tailored suit must have been couture; it was stylish, sleek, and fit her body like a glove. It wasn't too tight, but was tight enough to flaunt that fabulous female figure. There was no loud jewelry (although I bet she missed that million-dollar pink diamond) and no low, plunging necklines. Yep, J. Lo, Ms. Jennifer Lopez, was a vision of taste and style when she stepped into the S&S offices.

"The gardenias are out!" I whispered to the troops. "They won't show up well on camera against her outfit."

"Bring on the peonies," Macie whispered. I left the girls with Julie and ran off to Set A to fluff the peonies. Two minutes later J. Lo walked in arm in arm with Jane, while the makeup artists waved brushes over their faces with last-minute strokes.

"Oh my God, Jane!" J. Lo gushed. "These peonies are just absolutely extraordinary!" Little did she know what a pretty penny those peonies had cost the company. "How did you know that they are my absolute favorite?" she asked. Of course Jane just smiled and nodded. "Not many people understand the virtues of peonies," J. Lo went on. "They appear delicate but they're actually quite hearty. Their simplicity is so beguiling. They have so much more to offer than the common rose."

"Did anyone get that? I mean did anyone get that!" Jane screeched in true diva fashion. To give her credit, she didn't put on that much of a façade. She glared toward the back of the set, toward the cameramen shielded in dark anonymity.

"We may have to have you say that again when we're rolling," Jane explained to J. Lo. Little did Jennifer know that Jane expected her to recite it word for word.

"Got it!" called a lone cameraman. "I was getting some B-shots of the flower vases and picked it up then Jane. No problem."

"Wonderful," sighed Jane (along with the rest of the crew). "You must know that Queen Elizabeth the First suffered from anthophobia."

"Oh? What's anthophobia?" J. Lo looked genuinely concerned about this long-lost member of the royal family.

"It is an unusual psychological disorder—a fear of roses."

"Ahh. I also adore gardenias. They are my second favorite flower. I often have them put in my trailer when I'm filming. The scent is heavenly." When I heard that comment, I was off like Flash Gordon. I ran to the potting shed and grabbed the extra gardenias we had on hand. Back in the craft room, I put Suzi to work creating a display that would bring tears to a socialite bride's eyes.

❧

J. Lo's segment with Jane was taped flawlessly. She admitted to not being the most divine cook (like she had time, I wanted to shout), but explained that over the years she had perfected her mother's cinnamon bun recipe. As she and Jane stirred, mixed, and whipped them up, they extolled the virtues of being a domestic goddess.

"A wonderful person is a true hostess—always taking others' comfort into consideration before their own. My mother would have these buns piping hot at least once a week before we headed off to school, before she even had a chance to stir a spoonful of coffee crystals into a cup. Now that I'm a tad older—"

"Wiser, Jennifer, not older," corrected Jane.

"So true," she laughed. "I find that my houseguests enjoy waking up to the warm scent of cinnamon! They're licking their lips before they can rub the sleep out of their eyes! Now on Valentine's Day," she smiled, "I plan to serve these to a loved one in bed. These are no ordinary cinnamon buns, Jane—wait till you taste my tongue-tickling icing. I'm sure your viewers, being crafty, can come up with a use for the extra icing. If you know what I mean, Jane?" She suggestively licked a dollop of icing off one of her fingers. Jane gave a slightly nasal laugh and switched the focus to the nonstick baking sheets available on her Web site. Gotta love network TV!

"Now, Jennifer, would you ever buy that prepackaged cinnamon bun dough?" Jane prompted.

"Jane, you could buy store bought—it's easy and predictable. But I think going that route is way too cookie-cutter. And who wants the basic standard in life? Life's too short for store shelf goods and I think there really is a difference. I encourage everyone to roll up their sleeves from time to time and bake from scratch. It's such a treat for the people you care about. Cooking is like love: don't go for what's easiest or expected if you want to end up with something genuine, flavorful, and unique." My mouth dropped open in awe. She was speaking my lingo. She was speaking to me.

"I'm very impressed," Jane beamed in response. "You hear that ladies at home? Even Jennifer Lopez is a traditional woman at heart. She toils in the kitchen to keep her loved ones happy."

J. Lo's eyes lit up and she shook her head. "Oh no, Jane. You got me all wrong, girl. I've rewritten my own traditions. And while it's true that I do enjoy whipping up culinary treats for my man, in our household it's a two-way street. We have two cooks in the kitchen—my honey makes the best arroz con pollo, you know, and he gives the best foot massages. I've been burned before, and not just in the kitchen. I've finally realized that the best relationships are between equals—and it's not just about sharing domestic tasks like cooking. It's about equal emotion and devotion on both parts. That's the way it should be, Jane." J. Lo turned directly into the camera and gave a sassy wink into the camera and turned back to her cinnamon buns. We all stared, love-struck—she was amazing.

As I watched the two of them cook and chitchat on the monitors, it finally hit me. It hit me like a two-ton truck. J. Lo was absolutely right. What she had just said to Jane snapped me out of my romantic bubble and right back into reality. Here I was, chasing and pursuing Mr. J. P. Morgan like a lovesick puppy. I was the one initiating the calling, the cooking, the spooning, the private one-on-one time. I had bent over backward to win this man's heart, and what had I gotten in return? Sure the sex was good (okay, great even), but at the end of the day I'd wound up with an overdone burger and soggy fries in a dive bar in front of some basketball game. That and utter ingratitude for my nursing efforts. Good God, Charlie! It dawned on me right there, on the ice-cold set of S&S, just days before the most overrated, yet romantic, day of the year, that I was the one who needed to be pursued, wined, dined, loved, canoodled, romanced, snuggled, kissed. I deserved all the things I wasn't getting from him. I wanted individualized love, just like an à la carte dish. Time to put Mr. J. P. Morgan's prepackaged self back on the shelf! How could I have let my inner diva die like that? Bravo, J. Lo! Thank you, J. Lo! The master had awakened her eager apprentice, me, to her wise ways. And it was time for a change.

∾

*A*fter two hours, Jane announced that shooting was finished (as usual, she did so before the director had come to the same conclusion) and after a few photo shots of the two of them holding up the sticky buns for publicity, Jane and J. Lo walked off the set. I timed it perfectly to round the corner from the hallway at the same moment. My arms were filled with the art-fully wrapped gardenia blossoms. I held my breath so as not to sneeze all over the bouquet.

"Um, excuse me, Ms. Lopez, we thought you would enjoy these gardenias we had in the back," I whispered. Who was I? Can you say, a three-year-old meeting Santa for the first time?

"Um, I know that you really like gardenias . . ." my voice petered out as J. Lo focused her attention on me. At the same time, Jane was looking me up and down, up and down. She probably had no clue who I was. I had purposely tucked an *S&S* pencil behind my ear in case she should wonder if I was a studio intruder about to attack her prized guest.

"Thank you!" J. Lo gushed. "What thoughtfulness. Jane, you have the most wonderful staff. What is your name?" she asked me.

"Charlotte, Charlotte Brown. But most people call me Charlie."

"Well, Charlie, I'm Jennifer, and thank you for my first Valentine's gift of the year." I swooned. I was officially on a first-name basis!

"Yes, thank you, Charlotte," smiled Jane. She actually smiled, and not her fierce, fake, gummy version. She looked genuinely pleased, and pleased was what got one far here at *Sunshine & Sensibility*.

"Very thoughtful," she winked. A conversation with J. Lo, a wink from Jane; I flew like an angel on Ecstasy back to the girls. They were hidden away in an editing booth with Julie watching reruns of the taping. They squealed with delight when I shared my successful encounter. They squealed even more loudly when I pulled out a plate of J. Lo's handmade cinnamon buns from behind my back.

"Should we really eat these?" asked Syd.

"They're full of fat, I'm sure," muttered Sage.

"That's not what I meant," replied Syd.

"What do you mean?" asked Wade.

"Well, we could auction them," she suggested.

"What?" we all asked in sync.

"No, seriously. Some radio station here in NYC auctioned off Justin Timberlake's half-eaten waffles after he joined them for breakfast. They sold on eBay for oodles of money!"

"Maybe we should just bronze them," deadpanned Tara.

"Can they do that with food?" inquired Syd. Macie just rolled her eyes, as she and Wade grabbed a gooey pile from the plate. Good thing no one from sound was around to record our moans and groans as we ate the glorified goodies; our sound clip would have been mistaken for a track from the late-night porno channel. We decided then and there to make J. Lo an honorary member of the Cooking Club and declared our clandestine snack our first ever Cooking Club meeting on the go. We girls do know how to get around.

❧

*A*fter an exhausting Tuesday, the following day—aka, Valentine's Day—was standard. I got off early and wandered home with my eyes watching the subway grates (there are actually true stories about women falling through, never mind ruining a pair of heels) in order to avoided glancing into the dimly lit windows of the restaurants along the way. Too depressing. Each window was a showcase for lovers galore. I mean, Bloomingdale's should try to make their windows so appealing. Okay, so I took one peek. Under a sconced light, two lovebirds sat gazing at each other, feeding each other, holding each other's hands, whispering sweet nothings . . . it was like *Lady and the Tramp*. I couldn't bear the agony. I deserved to be front and center in one of those cafe windows twirling chicken alfredo as my man twirled my long locks (minus the horrible black roots I was sporting). But no. Mr. J. P. Morgan had conveniently disappeared this month even after I'd brought him soup. No phone calls, no lovin', no spooning. I wondered if men actually put a note on their calendars to remind them to cool things off before high-pressure holidays: "December 15: Must dump girlfriend *now* in order to avoid holiday gifts and Valentine's hoopla!"

I'd known so many girls who were in a "loving" relationship, yet when the first of the year rolled around, they were suddenly single! And not because their respective boyfriends had found a new catch with the New Year. No, these boys romped around loving the single life until after February 14th, when they suddenly managed to find love once again. My problem was that with no boyfriend to keep me busy around Valentine's Day, I sat around eating the chocolates my parents had sent to me (by myself) and gorging on the half-price chocolates at CVS (by myself). I felt sure that when the dogs did come around sniffing, my butt would be too big for them to envision it in a bikini during a romantic mid-winter getaway.

It was hard to keep up my new J. Lo–inspired burst of empowerment in the face of all this romantic bliss. Inevitably my thoughts wandered to Mr. J. P. Morgan, even though I knew the writing was on the wall. I hadn't "officially" been dumped. But then again, if I was honest, we hadn't ever been "officially" dating. He *might* have called me his girlfriend when I wasn't around, but I knew better. I had a sneaking suspicion that my attempts at cooking for him last month—the dinner, the soup—might have been the final straw. He probably saw how inadequate I was in the domestic department and realized that I wasn't relationship material.

At least Doorman Juan blew me a kiss as I passed his building. I smiled but was too exhausted to return the love. I trudged up the flights of stairs bemoaning my fate with each step: not one loving card, not one loving phone call, no flowers, no spooning . . . ugh! I resolved to concentrate on the benefits of being single. No one to steal the pillows in the middle of the night! No one to commandeer the remote control! Best of all, my legs could go unshaven for weeks! This wooly mammoth pulled herself into the apartment and flopped on the couch.

"Too trampy?" Tara flounced out of the bathroom. She had on a tube dress that looked as though it was supposed to be a top only.

"What's that made out of?" I asked.

"Lycra!" The top did look a bit shiny, like a scuba suit.

"Oh, nice I guess."

"Not too much back fat showing?"

"Go without underwear, then there won't be any lines, just curves."

"So true! Pure genius!" She ran back into the bathroom singing "I'm going to get some, I'm going to get some . . ." Great. I was a genius. I was going to be alone forever with my calculating brainy self. I kicked off my knee-high suede boots. No self-respecting brainiac wore such trendy footwear.

"Want some ice cream?" Macie asked, poking her head out from behind the kitchen wall.

"What kind?"

"Beggars can't be choosers!"

"Hey, if I can't pick a decent boyfriend, I can sure as hell be picky about my ice cream!" I snapped. I was about ready to burst into tears. Macie, God bless her, brought out a tray. She swooped down with the elegance of June Cleaver, and to my surprise put a smorgasbord of flavor options in front of me.

"Vanilla if you are feeling bland, M&M if you want some diverse flava, Oreo if you need to be sweetened up, pecan praline if you need some sticky-finger licking, and rainbow sherbet should you need some childhood innocence." She grinned at me. J. Lo's sticky buns may be the perfect way to tempt a man, but ice cream is the single girl's best friend.

Just as we'd settled in with a clinking of our spoons, the door buzzer rang. I still hadn't gotten used to that harsh-sounding foghorn; I jumped every single time. Macie leapt up and buzzed them in.

"You don't even ask who it is?" I asked.

"You can't hear anybody on that thing. Everyone sounds like they have some foreign accent."

"Most people do in New York."

"True!" she agreed.

"But I still always ask who it is."

"What, you figure potential bad guys will be warded off by your ferocious voice?" she laughed.

"Yes. Well, no."

"Ha, but—" The bell rang. Whoever it was had actually climbed the stairs.

"I got it," I scoffed. "You know, since I have the vicious voice." I made a pathetic attempt at a Zorro-type sword move as I removed the chain and flung open the door. In a full lunge with my arm poised in a defensive move, I came face to face with Mr. J. P. Morgan. In his hand was a bunch of red roses.

"Whoa, hey," he said taking two steps back and holding his hands up in a surrender stance. He gave me that adorable lopsided grin, "Don't kung fu me!" he laughed. My stomach dropped. I stood back up. I suddenly felt lightheaded. Bright spots appeared in front of my eyes like fireflies or paparazzi flashbulbs. But I wasn't in a fairy-filled forest nor was I posing on a red carpet. I was staring at my sort-of boyfriend. Who was standing smack dab in front of me with roses in his hand on Valentine's Day.

"Hey," I mumbled running my hand through my messy hair. I hadn't looked in a mirror since lunch and I was sure it must be a disaster.

"Here," he said thrusting the roses my way. All the tingling in my fingers stopped. Here? That was all he had to say after almost three weeks of nothing? Here? My eyes left his face and wandered down to his extended arm. In his left hand were the said red roses. They were a dull red and were even wilted around the edges. Obviously the man at the bodega on the corner had not done a good enough job pulling the rotting petals from the stem. He must have been really busy to sell this sorry looking bunch to J. P., or J. P. had simply not cared enough to pay attention to what he was buying. The buds were barely open on their short stems. Besides, every girl knows that true Valentine's Day roses are always *long* stemmed. Not only are they long stemmed, they are in full bloom. Not only are they long stemmed and fully bloomed, but their fragrance envelopes all those lucky enough to be standing near them. I took a deep breath. All I smelled was Ms. Fignucio's cooking from down the hall. I took another deep breath—this one to steady my nerves.

"Huh," I sighed. I could hear J. Lo in my head whispering, "Who wants the basic standard in life . . . the cookie cutter . . . life's too short for store shelf goods . . ."

"Can I come in?" he asked.

"Actually, we're in the middle of something."

"We?" he asked, looking over my shoulder. I closed the door partway behind me.

"Um, what do you want?"

"These are for you!" he said with the eagerness of a schoolboy.

"Thanks. But actually, no thanks."

"No what?"

"No thanks."

"Oh, just take them, Charlie. Don't be this way."

"Are they a peace offering?"

"A piece . . . no, I want more than just a piece," he chuckled, giving me that flirtatious grin again. I took the roses and leaned forward for a sniff. Nope, no scent at all.

"You know," I began, looking toward the ceiling for divine

inspiration and to keep from crying, "Roses are so, so unoriginal. They're cliché, trite, uninspiring. And even worse, they're pedestrian."

"Pedestrian . . . ?" he questioned.

"Pedestrian," I stated emphatically. With a final flourish, I dropped the sad bundle on the floor and daintily stepped on them with my tiger slipper. As I felt the blooms smoosh and the stems snap, I stomped with greater force and a bigger smile. Thank you J. Lo! My inner diva had finally arrived.

"Oh, okay," he paused. "I guess I should go?"

"Yes, please." My mother would have been so proud of my graciousness and tact. One nonverbal blow-off deserved another. I tried to close the door in his surprised and confused face, but unlike in the movies, the door bounced back open and hit my elbow. The crushed roses were in the way of a dramatic finale. I kicked the mashed mess out of the way, slammed the door, and stalked back over to the couch where I flopped down on the cushions. As I reached for my ice cream, Macie began to clap. She leapt to her feet, whooping and hollering.

"Spoken like a true diva! Good for you! I am sooo proud."

"Yep," I sighed.

"Don't you feel good?"

"Nope."

"Don't you feel vindicated?"

"Not at all."

"Why not?"

"How does one crushed bunch of flowers make up for three weeks of mental anguish, days of staring at my cell phone, and hours of fingernail biting?"

"Not to mention a million minutes of roommate therapy," she added.

"Are you trying to make me feel better?" I asked as tears began to flow down my face. Great, at least I was getting a cheap facial.

"Sorry." Macie ate another spoonful of rainbow sherbet, broke open a pint of chocolate marshmallow swirl, and handed it to me. Just what the breakup doctor ordered.

I couldn't believe he would just show up. Why now? As I headed into a deep pit of wallowing, Macie got up from the couch, scooped up the petal mess on the floor, and disappeared. I slowly sucked on a spoonful of ice cream. Did he find himself alone on V-Day and start reminiscing? Did he remember that morning we'd woken up and couldn't even leave the bed? And when we did, we ended up on the floor and then on the kitchen counter? I couldn't make a peanut butter and Fluff sandwich for months without thinking about him. Why couldn't he have just called me once over the past few weeks? If he had only picked up the phone once I might have given in to his pedestrian red roses. Ugh!

"Macie! I don't think I'm ever going to get married. He doesn't want me, nobody will want me," I sniffed. My nose began running at this point. "I'm going to be an old spinster with eight cats who will only feign love for me because I feed them canned food, and speaking of canned food, I am doomed to eat canned SpaghettiOs for the rest of my life since I can't even make a simple casserole!"

"Okay, it's all ready!" Macie's calm voice interrupted my panicked tirade.

"What's all ready? A life of eternal loneliness?"

"Come on. Come see." She emerged from the bathroom and held her hand out like the mother hen that she was. Feeling about two years old, never mind two inches tall, I stood up, grabbed her hand and followed. She gave my hand a squeeze before opening the bathroom door. We were met by a cloud of fragrant steam and Macie had written *"I am a princess!"* across the foggy bathroom mirror. I smiled and then saw that the bathtub was filled with voluptuous suds. Floating on the bubbles was a smattering of red rose petals.

"A bath of rose petals, exotic rose petals, to smooth the skin and the ruffled feathers of my fair princess," she grinned. Leave it to Macie to find a better use for cheap roses. I sat down on the toilet.

"Thanks," I said. She bent down and removed my tiger slippers as if they were made of glass.

"And to make the picture complete . . ." she hit play on the old boom box we kept on the toilet tank. Suddenly Steve Perry's voice filled the air:

"Don't stop believing, hold on to the feeling . . . yeaahhhhh . . ."

I stopped for a moment to reflect on what a good friend she was. I had met Macie the first day of our freshman year. During orientation, we had been assigned to certain themed dinners depending on our schools. I had applied to the School of Medicine with grand aspirations of being a doctor like my grandfather. I had aced frog dissection in high school and was positive that I could handle any gory pre-med courses thrown my way. However, no one had warned me about organic chemistry. That night though, I made my way to the freshman orientation organ-themed dinner, Organ-tuous Organza, wondering what would be served as the main course. Everyone else on my hall was in the College of Arts and Sciences and was being treated to a buffet, fitting since they were the undecided majors. I ended up in line behind this short, stunning girl. As we wound our way toward the blood-red soup she suddenly turned to me, "I'm Macie. Wanna go grab some pizza?" That's all it took—Macie's spontaneity coupled with my dislike of red soup.

From that moment on Macie and I were best friends. She was my practical friend, but practical with a wild side. She could party with the best of them while getting top grades at school. She was never one to disgrace herself with silly late-night antics. She never blacked out. She never regretted anything, sexual or otherwise. She was my heroine! Especially now.

"Remember that breakup mix you made the second week of school?" she asked.

"The one I made after I was dumped by Billy the Toga King?" I asked.

"Remember, we warned you that he didn't look so gallant without his polka-dotted sheet."

"So true, so true. But regardless of the fact that I didn't have your support, I did manage to survive the demise of my three-day romance with the help of ABBA."

"Well I'm glad you said that because I've resurrected that mix for the occasion."

With that perfect timing of hers, Macie turned up the radio and those sweet words that eased my pain so many times came blaring through the speakers.

You can change your mind, I'll be first in line.
Honey, I'm still free, take a chance on me . . .

You gotta love friends. Change is good and I decided to implement a whole slew of changes, especially when it came to you-know-who. Thank you, J. Lo and thank you, God, for friends.

Lying back against the tub pillow that Macie had somehow produced out of thin air, I felt my taut ligaments loosen. If Macie could rearrange a pathetic bunch of flowers into a bubble bath, I could rearrange my love life—I could! I drifted in and out of consciousness in between ABBA choruses. After about an hour, I wrestled the bathtub plug loose with my shriveled-up fingers. I sat naked and cross-legged in the tub and watched with the utmost satisfaction as the petals swirled down the drain. The drain made a satisfying sucking noise as it swallowed each petal with hungry vigor. I loved the idea of Mr. J. P. Morgan's roses wallowing in the New York City sewer system far away from my soon to be freer, happier self.

March

Give It to Me Guacamole

5 ripe (soft to the touch, but not too soft) avocados, peeled
    and pitted
½ cup hot salsa
¼ cup finely chopped red onion
¼ teaspoon chili powder
Finely chopped cilantro to taste
Dash of hot sauce
Garlic powder, to taste
Lemon juice, to taste

Mash up the avocados. Add the rest of the ingredients and mix.
Serve immediately with tortilla chips and some ice-cold beers on a
beautiful early spring day!

"God, I am so frickin' pale!" I happened to catch a glimpse of my pasty-white stomach in the bathroom mirror as I got out of the shower. At least I was manless at the moment. I wiped the steam off the mirror in order to get a better look at myself. But as the remainder of the condensation evaporated from the edges, it revealed something that was so ghastly, so horrible, that I couldn't even keep looking.

It had been four months—okay, maybe more like five months—since my body had seen the light of day. Ever since the leaves changed and the winds shifted in October, neither my thighs nor biceps, nor breasts nor butt had been exposed to direct sunlight. While long strolls along the snow-covered paths of Central Park and ice skating on the rink at Rockefeller Center are fun, they don't melt away those extra pounds acquired from holiday Krispy Kremes. The transition between two seasons can be startling and downright unkind to your body image.

So here we were. It was March and my skin had hidden behind bulky sweaters and oversized coats for way too long. Overall, I would say that on a scale of one to ten, I was an eight—at least on the inside. Mentally, I was faring much better since the horrible V-Day incident. I was no longer crying randomly at those diamond engagement ring commercials set in Italy. Nope, I was much better. However, my outside self had taken a severe beating. On a scale of one to ten, I would have to be a two right now. Snow White may have been revered for her fairness, but what I was dealing with was not pretty.

As I continued to inspect my fair flesh, I happened to notice the light dappling my right thigh. Like sunlight on the water, a trail of dimples was forming interesting patterns on the back of my leg. I whirled my body around so that my backside was facing the mirror and shifted my head to get a better look. Up until this moment, I don't think I'd ever really, and I mean really, looked at the back of my thighs or butt in a mirror. Sure, I'd caught a glimpse or two in the Bloomie's mirrors from time to time, but everyone knows to dismiss those images since the mirrors are distorted and the fluorescent lights are misguiding. But today I saw them, and it wasn't pretty. Gone were the smooth buns and the ripped soccer legs from my teen years.

Hello baby cellulite! So depressing. Sweet Jesus, was this what J. P. Morgan had been staring at during our sexual escapades? Those vile little puppies were not there a few mere months ago. At least, I don't think they were. Wouldn't I have noticed such a drastic change in my body's topography? I felt my neck for evidence of a chin wattle. As I got ready for work, I begrudgingly accepted my newfound friends, but also recognized that something needed to be done and it had to be done quickly.

Maybe it was due to the crisis in my bathroom or maybe because the train operators were in a good mood, but the subway gods were in my favor and I got to work early enough to do a little private research on my "dimple debacle." First thing I decided to do was to Google the word "cellulite." Ah Google, the search engine for all your needs. It is the most fantastic tool on earth. I felt an itch to Google Mr. J. P. Morgan but I suppressed it. Naturally, I had already Googled him months ago and found two sites extolling him: one about his high school soccer prowess and another with a small pic from his company Web site. I still had to fight the urge to check out the merchandise even though I wasn't really in the market anymore.

Instead, I was instantly inundated with links to everything from wacky creams to strap-on gadgets that promised to help the cellulite-crazed woman rid herself of those nasty little suckers. At first, it was overwhelming. Not only did every site claim to have the ultimate cure, but most of them also had a money-back guarantee. Thank goodness! It would be horrible to be dimpled and poor! Okay, so which one was it going to be? The cream claimed to sting a little after the initial application. I wouldn't mind a little burn for the cause. The strap-on thingy said it had to be worn for a minimum of two hours every day for a week in order to see the best results. Who the hells wants her

ass jiggling for one hundred and twenty minutes a day? I definitely didn't. After fifteen minutes of searching, my head began
to ache. There were just too many things out there and I had
absolutely no idea which one would provide the best solution.

Just as I was about to throw in the towel, the answer to my
prayers appeared. It came in the form of one of those annoying
little pop-up advertisements. There it was in all its glory,
smack dab in the middle of my screen. Typically, these things
annoyed the crap out of me, but this one was intriguing.

☺☺☺☺☺
BODY WOES GOT YOU DOWN?
NEED A LITTLE GETAWAY TO MAKE YOU FEEL BETTER?
FOR JUST $299, WE'VE GOT THE PERFECT CURE FOR YOU.
INTERESTED? CLICK HERE FOR MORE DETAILS!
☺☺☺☺☺

The happy faces were a little cheesy but I was curious, so I
proceeded to click for more details. What appeared on my
screen was the saving light at the end of dimple tunnel.

**To: T-Dog Tara, Sydrama, Macie-O-Gray, Wade.Brady, Sage The
   Rage**
From: Snoopy
Subject: Die Dimples!!!
Get your bags packed hot mommas . . . we're going on a jour-
ney. I found this fantastic travel deal. For just $299, we get air
travel, 3 nights hotel, meals & DRINKS at one of three possible
destinations.

Oh, and by the way, today I noticed some cheese on my thighs and this is my version of a cure. What better way to get rid of those fat pockets than a little tanage? So no excuses . . . you gotta help me rid myself of my ailment. Are you all in? This is our first grown-up girls' getaway! How could any of you resist such a weekend?

Love The Dimple Killer,

CB

To: Snoopy, Sydrama, Macie-O-Gray, Wade.Brady, Sage The Rage
From: T-Dog Tara
Subject: Re: Die Dimples!!!

Holy shit! Count me in! This is just what I need. I am so over NYC right now. I could use a little sun tan and a big piña colada! I'm totally bringing my big straw hat and my Jackie-O glasses. Get that puppy booked, Charlie!

Love the Dimple Killer Accomplice,

T

To: Snoopy, T-Dog Tara, Sydrama, Macie-O-Gray, Wade.Brady
From: Sage The Rage
Subject: Re: Re: Die Dimples!!!

Me too! I'm in. But I'm bringing the sun block—30+ for everyone! Perfect timing. But girls, think ahead. Lay off the diet soda starting now—it will bloat you for weeks!

XOXO,

Sage

To: Snoopy, T-Dog Tara, Sage The Rage, Macie-O-Gray, Wade.Brady
From: Sydrama
Subject: Re: Re: Re: Die Dimples!!!

Me too! Me too! I'm in! Where do I send the check?

∾

$\mathcal{T}$he Cooking Club convened later that night. Sage had whipped up some sinful guacamole to get us in the mood for our tropical getaway. Consistent with the theme, Macie had concocted some of her equally sinful chili-nacho dip.

"This is my mother's good ole stand-by when she has guests coming over last minute," she told us while mixing the bubbly concoction on the stove. "All it takes is a can of chili, with or without meat depending on what you like, and a jar of that queso dip you find in the chip section at the store."

Now we could have been tough on Macie about the simplicity of her recipe, but all I'd managed to contribute was two six-packs of Coronas and two limes. Who was I to throw stones at glass houses? So March was officially the "Mexican Fiesta" month for our Cooking Club.

"Guacamole has the good fat, not the trans fat," Sage lectured as she shoved a carrot-full into her mouth (no chips for her). We gathered around the kitchen table and began inhaling by the pound.

"God Sage, this guac is heavenly," Syd chimed in with her

mouth full. "Mmmmm, it must be the lemons. Oh yeah, gotta be the lemons. It's just so zesty. Fantastic!"

"What about the zesty nacho dip, girls?" Macie asked, sort of offended that no one was raving about her contribution.

"Um, it's tasty. A tad too spicy maybe?" suggested Tara. Macie glared, then smiled as she realized that Tara was actually conversing about seasonings—a big step for her.

"Okay, so let's talk trip. What about Miami?" suggested Macie.

"I want to go on a trip afar," Sage whispered like a movie star.

"Miami is at least three hours away, but okay, what about Jamaica?" Wade asked.

"Been there, done that," Macie said.

"Ditto," Sage agreed. "Done that twice, although I only remember one trip." Sage's skinny little body could only handle so much alcohol. However, each and every blackout seemed to erase that fact from her long-term memory.

"Hold on for a second, girls," I interrupted. "Before you get too excited about your destination, there's a catch with the package I found. We've got three lovely destinations to choose from and only three." I could see their minds begin to wander. "You ready to hear your choices?" They all nodded their heads in unison.

"Okay, first up, there's the sunny island of Puerto Rico. It's close, warm, and clean. Or we can sunbathe on the exotic spring-break beaches of Cancun. But wait, there's more. How about what's behind door number three? We've got the gorgeous Florida panhandle destination of Destin." There was dead silence in the room for a good ten seconds and then the girls begin to chime in one after another.

"Cancun?" I called out.

"Too college," Macie sighed.

"You need a passport to go there, don't you?" Syd asked.

"Destin?"

"Too dirty."

"Too old ladyish," Tara whined.

"I think the Rico would be great!" Syd blurted out while double dipping in the guac for the tenth time.

"What?" we all asked in sync again.

"The Rico, you know, Puerto Rico," she said mid-bite. "Choice numero uno. Plus, it could be a sign that we are eating Spanish/Mexican type food. Don't you think?" At that moment, we all knew. The Rico it was to be.

❧

*T*he next day at work, I booked everyone's travel on my credit card and coordinated the trip. So, it was official. Two weeks from today we would be sunning our bodies in the Rico. Watch out PR! Here come the Six Sinners to Be . . .

As I sent out the grand announcement, an IM popped up on my screen. They needed to make those thingees less obvious to nosey cubicle neighbors. I already had the audio turned down, but I swear those flashing boxes look like a nuclear alert from the Pentagon.

J.P.M: What up?

Holy shit! Where had he come from? And more important, what kind of question was that? Text messaging could make an Ivy Leaguer sound like a dunce. What kind of update did he really want? Was he asking about my well-being or my dating status? Did a mere two words warrant a real juicy answer or a curt, clever reply? Was he looking for a loophole to worm his way back in or was he trying to be the "nice" ex by keeping sporadic communication going?

I sat for a moment pondering how to respond—*if* I responded, that is. I chewed my lip. Maybe I'd better just ignore him. After all, he'd barely mustered a hello. But what if he had something important to say—an apology perhaps? I thought hard, and then it clicked! The perfect reply.

Snoopy: Going to Puerto Rico with the girls.

Ha! Let's see what he says to that! I was moving on. I was a jet-setter leaving his rose-strewn ass in the dust.

J.P.M: Don't you burn easily?

What the hell? He hadn't even known me last summer during tanning season! Did he just assume since he had seen my Irish self in all its buff glory that he knew my melatonin level? How could he so easily have twisted my fun news into something that grated against the very fibers of my being? Good God, wait until he saw my tan! (Note to self: Determine at later date if he deserves to see my tan.) Or, was he simply being concerned about me?

Snoopy: No worries. CVS has aloe on sale in economy size. Will be fine.

Would I be fine? I jotted down a note to myself to visit the drugstore and a psychiatrist. Somehow, after only six words,

Mr. J. P. Morgan had me obsessing again. Was I really taking this trip because I deserved it, because New York winters suck, because my body needed pampering, and because I wanted time with the girls? Or had it been fueled all along by a sense that I wasn't good enough, that I needed to be hotter, thinner, tanner, for the next time I bumped into my now ex at Top Shelf?

"No!" I told myself firmly. "I am broadening my horizons. I am a woman of the world! Tanned, toned thighs are something I want for me, not for Mr. J. P. Morgan."

❧

*H*e had, however, gotten me thinking about my lack of a base tan. Everyone knows that it's important to acquire a base tan before you head out into the sun. Besides lathering yourself with SPF 15 sunblock, you should always prep your skin with slow exposure to Mr. UV Ray. He is relentless when it comes to the burning department and it is important to take preventative measures. So the night before we left on our big spring-break adventure, I decided to get a jump on the tanning process. I couldn't go the fake-and-bake route because the lights in the tanning bed irritate my skin (I'd had a totally bad prom experience after a visit to the sun-bulb gods). So I decided to give the whole spray tan thing a whirl. Although it's always a dead giveaway during the winter months, I figured that I had the perfect excuse to try it since I was going to Puerto Rico in the morning.

Luckily, I got the last appointment at Sun Sensation, a place down the street from our apartment that had five new spray machines. It was pretty reasonable too, only twenty bucks for each of your first three visits. Cheap and chic! I got there about five minutes early and when I arrived the place was packed. Twenty dollars per visitor times fifteen waiting white bodies plus the five already spraying equals a multimillion dollar idea. I needed one of these franchises! (Note to self: Am getting suspiciously math-minded like dear old dad.) I checked in and the young girl at the front desk handed me a surgical-type mesh cloth cap and a pair of matching booties.

"Um, what are these for?" I asked her.

"Oh, you've never spray tanned?" She responded snidely and quite loudly. What? Had everyone in NYC spray tanned? Yes, judging by the crowd I'd say so.

"Um, yes, totally. I mean I've done it before. I've, um, just never done it here," I replied. Shit. I'd just lied to this girl about spray tanning. What was I thinking? Who the hell lies about spray tanning? But, whatever, how hard could it be? Undress, walk in, press button and spray. Voilà! You're in, you're out. No big whoop.

After signing the release form, I turned around and noticed a dozen sets of curious eyes staring at me. Totally self-conscious, I grabbed my spray tan gear and took a seat on the couch. As I was waiting for my big moment, I took the time to inspect the different types of tans that were in the room. What kind of tan was I looking for? Dark, medium, light? Rumor on the street was that these machines have a setting button or something that lets you pick the type of tan you want. Well, the first thing I noticed was that there were a couple of veteran "sprayers" in the house. The guy and girl next to the door were sporting really good even glows. Both their faces and legs were nicely bronzed with a real-looking tan! Not bad, I thought. That would be a nice color to kick things off in the Rico. Moving across the room, I then spotted a few others who looked like they had just a hint of color. They obviously took the less-is-best approach. They were sporting more of a faint cocoa-brown kind of color and it looked pretty good.

I took on my Nancy Drew persona and bent to tie my sneaker. Once at a lower level, I inspected all the exposed knees—one of the spots that will give away fake tans at a quick glance. None of their knees were too dark. Good. I roved over behind the bench. What about inner arms? One girl stretched and I saw she was a tad bit paler on the inside than on the outside of her arms. Don't like that look at all . . .

"Charlotte Brown?" The young girl snapped from behind the counter.

"Yep, that's me!"

"Room six. Down the hall and it's the last door on your right."

As I got up and gathered my tactical spray gear, I happened to catch a quick glimpse of two women who were chatting it up over in the corner by the television. These women were straight out of the "spray tanning gone wrong" pamphlet. Now that's what I did not want. They were flat-out, no-joke Oompah Loompah orange. Did they think they looked good? I wondered. Clearly they must if they were here getting sprayed again. As I walked down the corridor to my room, I was beginning to have doubts about my little endeavor. Was it worth it? What if I turned out like an Oompah Loompah? Was it light, medium, or dark that I wanted? Should I bag it and just take it slow in the sun once I got to PR? No, there was no turning back now.

Once inside the room, I figured I had nothing to lose. Worse-case scenario, if I didn't like how it looked, I could go home and scrub the stuff off. Right? I proceeded to take off all of my clothes and meticulously put on my booties and cap. After a once-over in the mirror to make sure my hair was securely inside the mesh casing and my toes were properly covered, I decided it was go time. Damn dimples! I opened the door and stepped inside the tiny two-by-four contraption. On the outside, it sort of looked like a phone booth. Pretty unalarming. But once I got inside, it was a completely different story. It felt like I was in one of my high school gym showers. The floor was a wet and it smelled like raw bacon. I couldn't see out, but I felt like someone could see in. Needless to say, it was sort of creepy, but I figured it was worth it for the cause.

I closed and secured the door and proceeded to look for the on button. I searched all over, but there was only a little green light thingy to the left of the door. Should I push that? Or did it go on automatically like those toilets that flushed when your butt moved? There I was: alone, naked, cold, and confused. After five minutes, I accepted the fact that I was an idiot for not asking for explicit instructions and decided to just push the green light. That had to be the right button. Right? And before I could say "right," the machine started to rumble and shake. All of a sudden, a giant burst of air followed by a wet concoction began to stream out from all over the place. This warm, wet bacon-smelling shit was hitting my butt, my face, and it was even invading my crotch. Nothing was off limits. I tried to protect my face from the direct line of fire and in the process my mesh cap flew off.

"*Heeeellpppp!*" I screamed. "Somebody, turn this machine off! It's attacking me," I pleaded from inside the spray monster's lair. Every time I tried to open my eyes to find the door handle, a gust of spray would attack. This thing was on the offensive and there was no end in sight.

"For Christ's sake, could someone please turn this thing off? I beg of you!" It was apparent that no one could hear me down the hall. Maybe they were all outside the door laughing at me. I assumed the "duck and cover" position and helplessly waited like a wet rat trembling in the subway corner waiting for the enemy to retreat. This thing had me by my cap and booties. And then finally, it just stopped. There was no more rattling, no more spray, no more nothing. It was absolutely dead silent.

I opened my eyes and couldn't see a thing. It was like the bomb had dropped and dusted everything in its path. I crawled around on my hands and knees in search of the door. I was hacking like a cat with a fur ball lodged in its mouth. Determined to find the door handle, I frantically skimmed the walls and stumbled across the latch on my last attempt. Once the door was open, a giant cloud of brown smoke billowed out and into the changing room. The dust quickly disappeared and it was time to assess the damage. I walked over to the mirror as the remaining spray tanning remnants settled onto the carpet.

Once again, Mr. Mirror revealed something that was so horrible, so ghastly, that I burst into tears. Holy shit, I was a f'ing Oompah-Loompah! *Noooooo!* I instantly reached for the stack of towels on the counter and frantically began to rub the stuff off.

"Is everything okay in there?" the young girl called from the other side of the door.

Oh, shit. Think, Charlie, think. "Yes everything's fine. Sorry, minor confusion. Um, the door got stuck. Out now! No problem. Thanks though."

After six towels and a couple gallons of spit (Note to self: Never be the mom who uses her own spit on her kids.), my fake tan slowly seemed to be coming off. The towels were saturated with the brown substance and my body appeared to be regaining its normal creamy color (yes, my opinion had changed—I was creamy, not pasty). Later on, I would find out that what I'd just done with the towels was what spray tanners called the blotting phase. If I had only asked for instructions at the beginning, I would have known to wipe my body with the towels in a circular motion in order make sure the product was blended evenly. Mortified about the entire experience, I quickly threw on my clothes and ran out of the place.

When I got back to the apartment, I went straight to the shower in order to wash any other spots that I might have missed. After scrubbing myself raw with a loofah and some apricot scrub, I slipped on my robe and went straight to bed. Thank God it had only cost me twenty bucks. So I'd have four fewer beers or one less buffet brunch in PR. No big whoop. But what was that yeasty bacony smell? The stench was sure to be a male repellant in Puerto Rico. Good going, Charlie! As I fell asleep, I rationalized that the worst was behind me and that in less than eight hours I would be on a plane headed to paradise. Rico here I come!

❦

"*L*adies and gentlemen, please prepare for landing. Make sure your seat belts are securely fastened and that your seat is in the upright position. We'll be landing in approximately twenty minutes at San Juan International Airport. Welcome to Puerto Rico." The divas were in flight!

"I am so excited," Macie yelped from behind her work portfolio.

"Can ya put that work away now? Our destination is in sight!" Tara scolded from behind her issue of *Cosmo*.

Wade gushed from the window seat behind me, "It's soooo beautiful. Palm trees swaying in the breeze, waves lapping at the shore—"

"Those waves are sucking that sand like I am going to be sucking some gorgeous Rican's toes!" Tara laughed.

"Those piña coladas are gonna go down nice and smooth," Sydney chimed in while putting on a fresh coat of lip gloss. "My goal is to see how many of those cute little umbrella drink thingamajiggies I can collect this weekend."

"Ah, such lofty goals," sighed Tara. "Girls, we've got some heavy-duty dancing to do. And I'm all about finding a forbidden lover."

"What about you, Charlie?" Macie asked.

"Um, you know, I just want to relax and read and stuff," I said.

"Hey, you've been awfully quiet the entire plane ride. Is everything okay?" Macie asked.

"Oh, yeah, sorry. I'm just really into my book," I said with my best poker face. "It's a how-to book on planting the perfect summer garden. The Diva wants us up to speed on the newest garden designs from Paris and London, so she bought the entire staff this must-read. Fun, Fun . . ." I cracked a smile and burrowed my head deeper into the pages.

"Aren't you going to be hot in that bulky sweatshirt and wool pants?" Wade asked as she reached in between the seats to inspect my one hundred percent wool wide-leg black pants. They were the bottom half of the DKNY pants suit my mom had given me for Christmas, not typical resort wear for a tropical destination. However, it had been cold in the city when we left.

"Sweetie, you're totally going to sweat your ass off when we get there. You'll be dripping the minute you step off the plane,"

Macie confirmed from across the aisle. She began to rummage through her duffel bag and pulled out a tank top.

"Here you go!" she said. "I always carry the essentials in my duffel just in case they lose my bags." That was Macie for you—always prepared. Whatever you needed, she most likely had it in that bag of hers. Water? Check! Tweezers? Check! Tampons? Check! Luna Bar for nutrition? Check! Adorable hot pink tank top? Check!

"Thanks, I'll put it on once we land," I said. That should hold them off for a little bit. Once they found out what was lurking underneath my sweatshirt and wool pants they were going to die. Ugh!

The brochure had said that the El Juan Hotel was only about a ten-minute cab ride from the airport and that upon arrival you'd be greeted with a tropical beverage. There had been three crucial requirements when we planned the trip: First, it had to be cheap. Second, it had to be easy to get to. And finally, it had to offer a plethora of free fruity drinks. Having so far met all of our criteria, we were six happy babes en route to a fabulous adventure.

Wade assumed the shotgun position in the front of the cab so that she could work on her Spanish with the driver, while the rest of us sat in back and soaked up the scenery outside the windows. The sun was shining and the windows were open, allowing the warm air to blow against our smiling faces. Syd was hanging out the window like a dog in heat, Puerto Rican heat that is. As we sped along the busy highway, I closed my eyes and took a deep breath. I could feel the tension in my body begin to melt—along with my now-soaked shoulders inside my sweatshirt.

"*Buenos dias. Me llamo Wade.*" Good God, Wade had

assumed the persona of a tour guide. She held the PA microphone in the front of the cab like a pro.

"You know, the one and only J. Lo's family is from the Rico," Sydney called out as she reached up and grabbed the mike from Wade.

"It's fate. We can all forget our dimpled asses and flaunt our delicious booties at the pool."

"My looovveee don't cost aaaa thinggg . . ." we all sang in perfect unison as the cab sped down the highway.

About fifteen minutes later, as we drove up the windy entrance to our hotel, we all decided that our first order of business was to get our bathing suits on and hit the beach immediately. An adorable bellhop first escorted us to our junior suite, then gave us a tour of the compound. As we passed by two big funeral parlor–type wooden doors, he told us that the nightclub that lurked behind them was one of the best in the San Juan. Then he led us outside along the seashell-strewn path and pointed to towers of beach chairs. As we stood gaping at the ocean-filled horizon, still clad in our NYC apparel, he demonstrated the genius of the beach chairs' design. Each was rigged with a little white flag on the back of the headrest.

"All you have to do is raise this flag," he began, flicking up the flag with one finger to show us how, "and a waitress, they're the ones you see in the blue and yellow shirts, will come to take your order." We all glanced at one another, at the ocean, at the beach chairs, and at our hands. Apparently we all had the same vision—a Venuslike waitress emerging from the sea to bring us endless rounds of drinks, all because she had been signaled by this white flag. I surrender, I surrender! Sheer brilliance! This hotel deserved another star just for this flag contraption thing. So far, so good.

Some of the girls immediately pranced off to soak their toes in the water while Macie, Sage, and I plopped down on our beach chairs to soak up the first of many rays.

"Charlie what a fantastic idea," Sage said. "I can't believe we're here. This is unreal."

"I know. This is exactly what the doctor ordered," I sighed.

"Hey, get those pants off. Here, I brought SPF 30 sunscreen if you need any," Sage said.

"Oh, no thanks," I replied hugging my still wool-clad legs. Sage began to strip and lather her skinny little body. She then plugged in her iPod and lay back with her eyes closed.

"What's the matter with you, C?" Macie asked as soon as Sage couldn't hear. "You've been acting strange ever since we left JFK this morning."

"You really, and I mean really, want to know, Mace?" I asked seriously.

"Totally! I mean, of course," she said in a more somber tone. Her expression went from eager-beaver expecting some illicit sex tale, to concerned mother anticipating a heart-wrenching phone call.

"And you promise not to say anything to the rest of the girls?" I asked even more seriously.

"Promise," she said with her right hand in the air.

"Okay, here you have it. I went spray tanning last night to get a jump start, and well, it didn't turn out quite like I thought it would." And before she could reply, I rolled up my pant legs to reveal the disgusting evidence. My body was infested with tons of uneven orange blotches. They were all over my legs, my arms, and my stomach. And the area that had been hit the hardest was my crotch. Of all the places on my body, it had received an unusual cluster of dark splotches. No joke, I looked like a leopard with an STD. As if I needed to give prospective guys any more ammo not to go down there. One look at my spotted crotch and they'd run for cover from this beast.

"Jesus, Charlie, that's nasty," she said.

"Thanks. I know it's a disaster. I've tried everything to get it off."

"Sorry. Hmm. Oh, I know! Did you try lemon juice? Or how about nail polish remover? I've heard that works."

"Really? I'm desperate. I'll try anything."

"I think we have lemons up in the room," Macie said.

"Why would we have lemons in the room? I know they have complimentary ice, but lemons?"

"No, Syd got them."

"Didn't she think they could make the lemonade at the pool bar?"

"She was convinced that she needed to bring a little of the Cooking Club on-the-go to Puerto Rico, and actually smuggled the ingredients for Sage's guacamole on the plane."

"But you can't bring fresh produce between countries!"

"Tell that to Syd. She's probably infected the Rico with some random lemon bug disease."

"And isn't guacamole usually associated with Mexico?"

"Syd's not too up on her geography, I don't think. Earlier on the plane, when the pilot said to look out north to see some godforsaken river, she looked up at the plane's ceiling. Come on, let's go upstairs."

We ran up to the room and began to prep for our emergency spray tan removal campaign. I cut the lemons while Macie squeezed the juice into one of the hotel glasses. After the last lemon was polished off, we began the delicate process. First we started off with a tiny test patch around my ankle. At first I didn't notice any difference, but Macie persisted and then all of a sudden the spot began to disappear.

"It's working!" I screamed with relief.

"See, I told you it would work," she said. We both grabbed washcloths and got down to business.

"I can't seem to get these crotch spots to disappear," I moaned after a half hour had passed. "If I keep scrubbing my inner thighs are going to be raw and it will look like I had a bad waxing job."

"Forget your crotch. Maybe some real sun will cover those last spots. We'll hit that hotel gift shop and snag a new sarong. Problem solved!"

I finally smiled. I loved this girl! No spots, a bit of shopping, and tons of sun. My vacation had begun!

∞

"*R*emember, ladies, we shouldn't gorge on this poolside food. We're in swimsuits!" directed Sage. I put down the menu and raised my flag.

"Sorry, Sage," I said. "I have to eat in this sun. I am sweating off the pounds as it is. You know, it's important to stay hydrated and keep your blood sugar up in this heat." Syd nodded in agreement as she reached for my oil-slicked menu.

"Well, since we're in the tropics, I'd recommend that we take advantage of all the exotic fruits they have to offer," Sage suggested as she slid off her chair and headed over to the pool to join in the morning aerobics class already in progress.

"Do you think we gross her out?" wondered Macie.

"Nope, we just speak to her inner devil," Tara responded. As if she had heard us, we heard Sage give a few retaliatory "whoops" and "yeehaws" in chorus with the aerobics instructor. The water in the pool churned like the ocean during a hurricane.

"Fruit, huh? Do banana daiquiris count?" Macie asked without batting an eye.

"What about apple martinis?" suggested Syd.

"I'll stick with rum punch. It's full of tropical fruit!" I offered.

"Their strawberry freeze has real strawberry seeds in it. They were stuck in my teeth earlier," volunteered Tara. "Good thing I have a tricky tongue!"

"Do Cosmos have any fruit in them?" asked Wade, ever the true New Yorker. We all laughed as a blue-and-yellow clad waitress approached.

"I'll take a fruit plate and some French fries please," I told her. I figured the good and the bad would cancel each other out. I scanned the pool looking for hot natives. To our right was an older couple. She was knitting while he did the *New York Times* crossword puzzle. Every once in a while, she'd stop, reapply some of that blue zinc oxide that we all had to wear as kids to her nose, then pick up her knitting again. Knit-purl, knit-purl. Across the pool, however, was a group of boys descending from the restaurant steps. Excitedly, I poked Tara and she immediately went a-wandering.

She came back scowling. "A) I think they are about sixteen. B) They are way too giddy about a pool volleyball game. C) Two of them are wearing cut-off jean shorts. We have got to get you some glasses, Charlie."

"This tropical sun must have blinded me," I shrugged. "Just wait until we hit that nightclub."

That night, after we had changed rooms twice (first room change due to an errant, incriminating-looking, small, black hair found beneath the sheets of the bed; second room change due to the "luxury view" of another hotel's back wall out of our windows), we headed down to Caliente, the nightclub. As we walked up, the club's wooden doors were almost bouncing off their hinges. I swear, they still looked like the entrance to a funeral parlor but now the frosted window panels on the sides were pulsating bright neon colors. Now I was thinking Disney. The bellhop was right about its popularity though. The line to get in wound itself all the way back to the slot machines in the casino.

"Not waiting!" announced Macie.

"Come on, Mace! I curled my hair!" protested Syd. She had tried to use some of her company's hair extensions. Tried. Enough said. We were squabbling in front of the doors of Caliente when our bellhop from the morning approached us.

"*Buenos noches.* I told you, yes?" He gestured at the club.

"Yeah, but who wants to stand in this line? The party's in there," Tara said, pointing toward the doors, as if he didn't know.

"Oh, for hotel guests, you no wait! Come. You have *la llave,* your key." It was as if we were true American princesses. The hulky bouncers smiled, stamped our hands, and opened the doors. We were almost blown away by the bass from the music that boomed out the inside.

"*Gracias!*" Wade tried to shout above the music. Inside, the lights swirled, the music pumped, and people danced. Everyone was moving some part of their bodies. A man in the hall was nodding his head, two girls by the edge of the dance floor were swiveling their hips, the boys behind them were cranking their necks back and forth following the girls' rhythm, and the people on the dance floor were letting it all loose—their whole bodies convulsing in time with the music.

"I love this Latin flavor! So sexy . . . *Viva Caliente!*" screamed Tara.

"You love any ethnicity as long as it's of the male species!" Macie shouted back. Tara began to move. It started with her head tilting, then her shoulders began to sway, then her hips stirred. She grabbed Sage's hand and headed toward the dance floor. Macie, Wade, Sydney, and I grabbed a drink and took our positions at the crowded bar.

"It reminds me of a really loud ice-skating rink!" screamed Macie.

"Yeah, and we're the shy girls on the side of the rink who will only watch everyone else skate!" I shouted back.

"They never did *that* at my rink!" shouted Wade pointing to a woman stripping on the stage. "It's like Cancun on steroids!"

"Ouch!" Syd moaned as a couple making out stumbled into her. "That's it. It's too crazy here. I'm going!"

"No, wait . . ." I began, but stopped when I realized that Syd wasn't talking about going back to the room. Rather she was joining the other hedonistic dancers.

Syd considered herself a self-trained dancer. Last year, she had bought a tape off the television. For two easy installments of $12.95, she had purchased Britney Spears' choreographer's latest dance moves: a step-by-step instructional video to make one move like the pros. The girl was a bonafide "As Seen On TV" junkie. In the months we'd been living with her, she had also bought the following:

hand sewer (for her multiple Girl Scout projects)

food dehydrator (for those city camping trips)

micro shaver (just the image of nose hair falling on the commercial . . . 'nuf said)

spray hair in a can (not sure who that was for)

edible hair wax (hmmm)

laser pointer light (for all of her important hair sales meetings)

shrinkwrappers for food and clothes (never seen a cucumber wrapped so tightly)

rotisserie oven (chicken was Syd's dish for our next Cooking Club meeting)

jar opener (not a bad purchase)

Twisty Turner for creative ponytails (Syd rivaled sixteen-year-olds)

Bedazzler to rhinestone her wardrobe (*Flashdance* anyone?)

meatball maker for perfect two-inch meatballs (We had forty-two such meatballs crowding our freezer)

To give her credit, she had mastered one of the more difficult routines on the dance video. Feeling more and more confident, she had started to add her own creative dance steps as well. The end result looked something like John Travolta dancing to an Eminem song. Fingers in the air, toes pointed to the side.

Tara and Sage were now up on a little stage dancing with each other and garnering quite a bit of attention. Both had a rhythm unknown to most white girls. They were indulging every man's fantasy and giving a little girl-on-girl action. Trying to be sly, two guys had grooved their way toward them and, using the old sandwich move, were gyrating behind Sage and Tara's backs. Tara, with her male radar, shimmied her butt back a bit and reached behind her, drawing her new partner closer. He was tall and dark and carried an air of mystery given the fact that he wore black sunglasses in this dimly lit cavern.

After a couple hours of Nelly, 50 Cent, and Usher, we gathered the troops, along with their various dance partners. It took us about fifteen minutes alone to find Syd. Somehow we had overlooked her on the stage. She was off to the side by herself humping a skinny pole with her gyrating hips as if it were Elvis's leg. Tara's original dance partner with the sunglasses had somehow been ditched (surprise, surprise) for a hunkier version. But Mr. Shades had now decided that I was second best.

"You no dance?" he asked me. "*Como se llama?* What's your name?"

"Oh, I'm Roxi," I said. "With an *i*." Gotta maintain some anonymity. I figured that I could have an alter ego here in the Rico. "I dance. But I need a little Britney or J. Lo," I feebly explained.

"Rrroxi," he purred. Oh that Spanish rolling *r*! "I love J. Lo!" he enthused. Hmm, on second thought . . .

In the casino, the two of us somehow lost the rest of the gang as we discussed how J. Lo had built a formidable empire in such a short time and at such a young age.

"Come. Let's go to the pool," he said grabbing my hand.

"Oh, no. I don't want to swim," I began to protest.

"No swim," he continued, obviously unwilling to take no as an answer. "I get us some food." This man knew magic words.

Outside was pure perfection. Talk about a tropical paradise. Here I was, a slightly sunburned Charlie Brown, cuddling on a lounge chair with a lusty Latino, with the moon out, shooting stars falling above our heads, palm fronds whispering, and waves crashing in tandem on the beach. To complete the picture, we had a bowl of plantain chips and guacamole between our legs. My mystery man informed me in broken English that he had some connections at the hotel. He was feeding me a chip when a bit of guacamole tumbled off onto my shoulder.

"Oh, how elegant," I mumbled, smiling, with food in my mouth. He didn't seem to mind though. He dipped his head and with his tongue, licked the morsel off my shoulder. And he didn't stop there. He wound his tongue up the side of my neck causing me to giggle. (Note to self: Gotta control the ticklish-ness.) I held my breath as he found his way to my mouth and captured it with authority. I began a mental list in order to rationalize what I knew was about to happen:

1. I'm on an island.
2. It's all part of the vacation package.
3. He's cute . . . I think.
4. He cares about me—he fed me!
5. I've never had sand in my pants.
6. What happens in the Rico, stays in the Rico.
7. I'm sure he has more than just dance moves.
8. He can croon sweet Spanish nothings in my ear.
9. Tara would do it!
10. Rrroxi with an *i* would do it!

My mental check list quickly ended at number ten due to the fact that I couldn't concentrate any longer. Sunglass-clad Don Juan's tongue had gone from nibbling on my ear down to my navel. Good-bye chips and guacamole. Hello Latin lover. At that moment, I decided to let myself go and settled on rationalization 6: What happens in the Rico, stays in the Rico. Enough said!

The next morning by the pool, I kept squirming in my bikini bottoms.

"Nice sunglasses," Macie remarked about my newly acquired shades.

"You've learned the truth about sand, huh?" laughed Tara.

Following our great romp on the lounge chair (great cushions), my new friend and I had ended up on the sand the night before. It was like *From Here to Eternity*, or a poorer version of it. The tide had made its way in and I had lost one of Syd's sandals. She hadn't thought to ask for them back yet, and I was still basking in my post–hook-up glow, so I wasn't going to tell her. But Tara was right. I had ended up with sand in crevices where sand should never go. Even after a shower this morning, I was still digging sand out of my ears. Plus, as if I hadn't had enough skin irritation already, the sand had rubbed my butt raw! Like an old-fashioned diaper rash, my bottom was pink and not too happy in my wet bikini bottom.

"This . . . is . . . going . . . to . . . drive . . . me . . . crazy!" I forced between my gritting teeth.

"We need to get you a drink," suggested Sage, raising her white flag.

"Help me, daiquiri gods!" I shouted. "Do we think a daiquiri will freeze my itching ass?"

"Might as well try," suggested Macie, always rational and positive. She was going to be a great mom.

"Charlie, what do you want?" Sage asked as the waiter approached.

"I need your coldest, largest strawberry daiquiri with an extra shot or two . . ." I began.

"Rrroxi, how are you this morning?" I lifted the sunglasses off of my eyes.

"Wha . . . ?" I squinted up at the man in the blue and yellow shirt.

"Did you sleep okay?" At this point, the other five girls flipped over onto their backs simultaneously, suddenly wide awake.

"Did I . . . ?" I started.

"It's Hector," he began to explain, sounding a bit dejected, "from last night."

"Oh, Hector. Didn't recognize you without your sunglasses," I said pointing to my eyes as if he didn't understand.

"Those are for night," he said as if it were obvious.

"Yeah, um, I'm fine, thanks," I stumbled.

"So R-r-roxi wants a daiquiri, yes?" Now that rolling *r* sounded like a stutter.

"Yes. Yes, uhm, *por favor*."

"Be right back," he said way too cheerfully.

"That is the man of mystery?" laughed Sage.

"They shouldn't be allowed out during the day," I bemoaned, ready to cry. Really! I thought I'd had a man of mystery, sunglasses and all, and that we'd had a passionate night on the beach, but now some island god thought it was funny to send him back to me in the broad daylight to highlight his pox-marked skin and gel-laden hair, and to show me that he is a waiter—not some son of a rich Puerto Rican mogul like I had envisioned. "And of course he is not wearing sunglasses when he is supposed to wear sunglasses!"

"You said he was attentive, though. And here he is bringing you a drink right now!" Wade said, nodding toward Hector, who was headed back our way.

"But now I feel like a dirty old man on the Hollywood streets too late at night," I wailed, "because I have to pay for this service. And I have to leave a goddamn fifteen percent hotel-mandated tip!"

⁓

*T*he next afternoon, the stewardess closed the plane door and proceeded to give the obligatory safety instructions over the PA system. Sad but relieved to go home after a weekend of debauchery, I nestled back into my spacious first-class seat and took a giant sip of my free glass of champagne. What a way to end a sensational trip! Although the rest of the divas were back in coach, Macie and I were in the front of the plane enjoying the good life. We did feel a tad bit guilty for taking the upgrade, but my parents had given me some of those frequent flier upgrade coupons before the trip. And as all young New Yorkers know, one has to take advantage of coupons! To be fair, we'd drawn straws to see who would join me upfront and Macie was the lucky winner. But I promised the other girls that we would bring them each a glass of yummy champagne during the flight. We all know how good it is to have friends in high places, especially if the friend is named Dom Perignon at 35,000 feet.

Somewhere in between devouring the fresh corn-crusted salmon and licking the hot fudge brownie plate, I decided to visit the girls. Macie was raving about the thought put into the overall presentation of the brownies, so I had to go show them. On top of the five or so glasses of bubbly I had managed to suck back, I somehow convinced the flight crew to give me four extra desserts as well. And after hearing where the goodies were going, they even gave me a fancy platter to deliver them with.

Way in the back of the plane I could barely see the girls' heads. They were all clustered together right next to the bathrooms. Poor things! Fortunately, I had something that would cheer them up. Two steps away from presenting them with their first-class treats, I glanced down to find every single one of them sound asleep. Syd's head was planted face down on her pull-out tray. Tara was snoring, her hands tightly clutching her *InStyle* to her chest, her sunglasses perched on her nose blocking out the cabin lights. Sage, who had an entire row to her tiny self, was sprawled out. But her foot was doing that twitching thing that dogs do when they are dreaming deeply. And although Wade was off in dreamland too, she appeared wide awake. Her eyes were half-open and her body was perched perfectly erect in her chair, poised as always. They didn't look too comfortable, but their poor bodies deserved the rest. Over the course of seventy-two hours, all of us had put ourselves through some serious mental and physical tests. After a weekend of crazy dancing, endless drinking, swimming, laughing, and chitchat we were all exhausted. And we had some good stories to boot. I left the desserts on an empty seat next to Syd and headed back to first class.

❧

*A*s the plane made its initial descent into the New York area, I could barely make out the city skyline from my window. I realized that I was actually looking forward to getting back to the city. What's more, I realized that I hadn't thought of Mr. J. P. Morgan once in more than seventy-two hours. I felt that deserved a toast. I motioned to the stewardess.

"Were you beckoning me?" She spit with the *b* in "beckon."

"I didn't want to wake the others, you know with that pinging sound," I apologized, pointing to the call button. "Could I have another glass of champagne please?" She looked at me from underneath her fake lashes. Was she thinking to herself that I didn't look like I belonged in this double-wide, leather-backed seat? Was there a limit on alcohol consumption in first class? As she sauntered back to the kitchen area I quickly skimmed the in-flight magazine to make sure there wasn't an imbibing maximum.

"Miss?" The flight attendant was back holding up two bottles. "We don't have anymore champagne, but we do have white or red wine."

"Perfect! I'll take . . . white, please." Note the dramatic pause as I tried to feign interest in the bottles' labels. Then the seatbelt sign rang. Nuts. It was official. My first-class status was coming to an abrupt end. Good-bye, warm cloth napkins. Good-bye, freshly baked foccacia bread. Good-bye, free bubbly. I closed my eyes in dismay.

When I opened them, I was given the final ultimate treat. It was a stunning vision. Right smack dab in front of me was the Statue of Liberty. I pressed my forehead against the plane window to get a better look. It was a magnificent sight to see. There she was in all her feminine glory. With my glass in hand, I turned to face the window in order to make a toast. This one's for you, Ms. Statue of Liberty. Her gown was a bit ragged, streaked with the city's finest grime, but her face was regal, complete with an aristocratic nose. Her smile was tired (New Yorkers tended to stay up way too late working and playing) but suggestive, like she had been up to something while everyone wasn't looking. I winked at her. Here's to many new adventures, to never giving up, and to finding true happiness. I closed my eyes and proceeded to drink the entire glass of wine in one sip. It was a sign. Charlie, I thought, you can be anything you want to be and do anything you want to do.

As I tightened my seatbelt and made sure my seat was in the upright position, I felt an odd rumbling in my throat. That last glass of wine wasn't sitting so well with the glasses of champagne that had come before it. My stomach lurched. Oh, God. Don't tell me this was going to happen. I flew out of my seat and ran toward the bathroom.

"Excuse me, miss," the flight attendant spit the *m*, if that was possible, "You're going to have to take your seat. We are just about to land and the captain has turned on the fasten seat-belt sign."

It was as if she was reading a manual to me. Did she not see my face? If she just looked at me she'd notice that this wasn't your ordinary bathroom visit. I didn't have to do number one or number two. No lady, this was number three. Back off or I was going to pull the trigger.

"Yes. You're right. But I promise, this will only take a minute," I urged her with one hand over my mouth and the other on the bathroom door. But before she could respond, it was too late. Up came the wine and the champagne, all over the cabin floor. Okay, in hindsight, maybe I shouldn't have had eleven glasses of alcohol thirty-something thousand feet in the air. But up until this point, I had felt fine. And as the last drop of the bubbly backed out of my mouth, I looked up to find every single first-class passenger staring furiously at me. By now, they'd probably figured out that I wasn't your typical first-class passenger. This wasn't the mile-high club I wanted to join. The flight attendants looked mortified. Oh well, what are you going to do? It was fun while it lasted.

April

Glorious Greasy Pizza

Go ahead and treat yourself this month:
  Call Domino's for delivery!!!
  Order a large pie and have it delivered right to your front door.
  Quick and easy!

It was April and thus far, I had avoided all of the city's subtle dangers: broken heels, pigeon dung, construction-site catcalls. I had even avoided the more infamous city dangers: muggings, rapes, accidentally falling onto the subway's third rail. My mother's philosophy of "safety in numbers!" always resounded in my head whenever I took the subway late at night or walked home in a drunken haze by myself from a bar (usually from the one just across the street mind you). But in New York City, it's easy to develop a false sense of security. I mean at 4:30 in the morning, the city is still wide awake and doing its daily jumping jacks. And not just in Times Square, which is constantly aglow—even down in the city's respectable "villages," people are out and about chatting, strolling, smoking, fighting, drinking, puking, laughing, and loving even at the wee hours. Still, I always made sure to walk in well-lit areas, letting the fake yellow light wrap its arms around me. If I ever got a tad spooked, I'd just pull out my powerless cell phone and talk as if I was in the midst of the most animated conversation, a conversation with my big buff boyfriend (a boyfriend is always much more intimidating than a husband— he just is!). And for most of the year, I never had to look over my shoulder, never heard eerie footsteps echoing my own, and never had to blow the safety whistle tucked deep into my purse courtesy of dear old dad.

So when I was first confronted with a potentially dangerous situation, you can imagine how my mind went spinning out of control. Just like a Lifetime movie, the epilogue was already scrolling across my mind:

> Charlotte Brown never reached her full potential as a production assistant at *Sunshine & Sensibility*. Sadly, she was cut down in the prime of her life. Her still devoted ex-boyfriend, Mr. J. P. Morgan, never fully recovered from the shock. After her death, he spiraled out of control, never married (or procreated), and has spent the last fifteen years wallowing in New York's Psychiatric Hospital. Her friends left New York City, unable to bear the thought of toasting without her during their nightly revelry. Her charming apartment is now a museum one can visit Mondays through Wednesdays; her favorite socks still lie on the floor. If you or someone you love has experienced such harassment as Charlie, don't hesitate to contact Mail Protect before it is too late.

Yes, Mail Protect. "Mail," not "male." I had taken it upon myself to collect our mail daily. No one else ever seemed to bother, so inevitably when one would finally open the little brushed silver door in our lobby, magazines and bills would avalanche onto the floor. A tad embarrassing. There was one old biddy from our building who was always in the mailroom and always scowled in my direction when our box spilled overdue notices on my shoes. One day she actually said, "I don't think it's fair to make our postal person cram letters into our boxes like a complicated jigsaw puzzle."

What?

"I was in the Congo for the past month doing medical research," I explained. Was that a real place? I stuck my tongue out of the corner of my mouth and tried to look at the ceiling in a contemplative way as I bent down to scoop up our mail, hoping to look like I was debating the molecular structure of DNA. In reality, I was biting on my tongue so that I wouldn't stick it all the way out at her.

So I had taken it upon myself to try—stress *try*—to go to the mailbox each day when I got home from work. It wasn't easy though since I never got fun letters; instead we received utility bills (aka, arguments over who'd watched a Pay-Per-View movie that month), credit card notices (want even more debt), credit card checks (who thought of that wonderful idea?), the occasional notice of a new Barney's promotion (like I could afford to shop there), and endless magazines (full of more desirable can't haves). We often got a pack of local businesses' coupons too. I tried to be efficient and clip or keep the coupons on hand should I ever need two carpeted rooms cleaned for $19.95, or a car service to any of the city's three major airports, but the only result was a drawer full of these handy irrelevant discounts. (Note to self: Must start using coupons to lower credit card debt.)

So it took me by surprise on a random Thursday when I received a letter. Actually it was a postcard. The generic type. White with no picture or address lines.

"Yes!" I initially thought. Some fun mail! However the message scribbled on it seemed a tad cryptic:

Have a great week!
L_ _ _ _ _

_ _

The two-word name underneath was illegible. It began with an *L* so immediately I thought it said, "Love, So-and-so." Love? Could it be? Would I even let myself daydream that Mr. J. P. Morgan had sent me an anonymous love note to try to mend things? Did he even know my street address? All he probably knew was that he could get some on the Upper West Side! No, I stomped on that thought more quickly than I usually stomped on the cockroaches crawling across our floor. Then who could it be from?

"Hey, Tara!" I shouted as I entered the apartment and dumped the other mail in the overflowing basket on the floor. "Take a look at this, would ya?"

Tara emerged from her bathroom wrapped in a towel, with a mask on her face, shaving cream on her legs, razor in hand, and curlers in her hair. She looked like Mrs. Robinson getting ready for a big day out, but it was 9:34 P.M.

"You going somewhere?" I asked.

"Nope, just felt like this tired hag needed some sprucing up."

"Hmm, the sandman is going to have some fun with you tonight, gorgeous! But here. Take a look at this and tell me what you think." I tried to act nonchalant and headed toward the kitchen to get a Devil Dog (the perfect soul-soothing food).

"Who's this from?" Tara asked as she turned the card over in her hands.

"Um, I don't know."

"Freaky!" Tara exclaimed stopping me in my tracks. "I mean, your name and address is written in one handwriting and the message on the back is in another. Whoever wrote your name and address has handwriting like my grandfather's chicken scratch." Immediately, Mr. J. P. Morgan turned into a big burly seventy-year-old stalker. A sleazy dirty old man (but still not lacking in strength or sexual desire). I spun around and grabbed the card back from Tara.

"Where's the postmark from?" she asked. Good thinking. Then I could obsess over all the predators I knew in all fifty states.

"Let's see . . . New York, New York. And it was sent yesterday in the P.M."

"Not much help then." My mother would agree since she claimed this city had more than its share of psychos. Once again, it looked like Mom was right. Damn!

"What could this name be?" Tara mused. "L . . . Lenny, Larry, Lionel, Len . . . Ludacris."

"Yes, the rapper Ludacris knows who I am and where I live."

"No, not the rapper, just a guy who's renamed himself to fit his personality."

"Tara! Stop! I'm a little freaked out here."

"Could it be a woman? Lenore, Linda, or Lynda with a y, Lydia, Lindsey, Leslie. Gee there are a lot of L girl names."

"Tara, focus. We are not naming a baby. We are naming my stalker. Do you think it could be a woman?" My seventy-year-old man had just gained birthing hips and a pouty mouth. And trust me, she did not have eyebrows like Charlize Theron in Monster.

"Now wait, who else in New York would send you a post-card?"

"That's the problem. Who would?"

"Have you had an appointment recently? A facial or something where the technician is following up with a kiss-ass note versus a phone call? My mother always says a note is more personal than a simple call." I nodded, absently thinking that my mother would agree.

"No, I've been so dirt poor I haven't been able to afford a mani-pedi even on the cheap package days," I responded as I bit down hard on one of my polishless nails.

"Hmm, well I'm sure it's nothing—"

"You think? I don't know!" I said doubtfully.

"We'll figure it out. But my mask is beginning to hurt because it's been on my face seven minutes too long. Huh, freaky," she called as she sailed back into her bathroom beauty parlor. I flipped the card over and over before realizing that I was contaminating it with my fingerprints, and then threw it back into our pile of mail. At least Tara knew about it, should I be found dead on the sidewalk tomorrow with a Starbucks Grande nonfat cafe latte in hand.

I figured that I had a right to be suspicious and a tad neurotic. After all, Jane had received a dangerous liaison-type of letter too just last week. It was as if the mail gods were throwing lightning bolts. The positive side? I just knew she and I were destined to connect in some way. Maybe we would bond as we took our seats by the witness stands during our stalker trials. Yes, we would be fearful for our lives, but would testify to rid the world of two treacherous predators.

A new and oh-so-demanding responsibility of mine at work was to sort through the entries we'd received in response to a recent contest on water feature décor. It was amazing what people could do with a little H_2O, colored lights, and plastic tubing. Sadly, Polaroids just don't do fountains and birdbaths justice. Amid the envelopes, most of which were vellum or Crane's twenty-pound weight, was a cheap, see-through, business-sized envelope. But in place of Jane's followers' usual hand calligraphy or embossed labels was a chicken-scratch version of our studio's address. I was surprised that the post office could read the scribblings. And where the return address should have been, there was only a seven-digit number. A phone number? As I ripped open the envelope, I realized that I had torn into a personal note to Jane. My first panicked thought was that she would see I had not used a letter opener. My second was that this was no ordinary pen pal note. Within reading the first couple of lines, my face flushed with embarrassment. I made myself do some yoga breathing (thank you, Buddha) as I scanned the rest of the letter to see if I had inadvertently opened a letter from Jane's long-lost jungle lover. No, the seven digit number on the outside of the envelope was more than just a phone number . . . it was a convict's calling card. Jane had gotten a love letter, or lust letter, from an inmate. And was this incarcerated boy imaginative!

Somehow, he was referencing Jane's body parts, which she hid well beneath baggy tops and conservative skirts, with the familiarity of an ob-gyn. He was quite a prolific writer, creating picturesque similes comparing her cannolis to the male anatomy. In his letter, he had her tossed on her kitchen counter, noting how the green Corian would highlight her eyes. And the things this man wanted to do to her knees! *Cosmo*, listen up! His step-by-step sexual instructions were just as detailed as Jane's step-by-step cooking directions, though his suggested finale would set off more than smoke alarms. To top it off, at the end of his letter, he suggested that she use unsalted butter in her recipes as he thought the unnecessary salt might cause his blood pressure to soar, leading to a lesser performance in the kitchen. His idea of cooking was rated by X's versus stars.

"Honey?" I had asked. That truly was Jane's assistant's name. And, Jane's assistant was male. "Um, I think I may be in trouble here."

"What's up," he had murmured, not looking up from the careful eraser marks he was making in the Diva's daily agenda. He brushed away the eraser's pink dust with his one painted fingernail.

"I, um, opened a personal letter that was meant for Jane," I squeaked.

"What! Who was it from? The Donald? She'll flip if you tore into his one-of-a-kind envelope." I held out the shredded paper-thin one.

"No, this isn't from Donald. It's from inmate 457–9989."

"Ugh," Honey sighed, finally looking up. "Not another."

"What? She gets these often? Shouldn't we notify the police?"

"Number 457–9989 is at Rikers Island. He's there for life and then some for a string of rash serial killings. Actually, he spends part of his time at Bellevue too since apparently the murders made him go mad." Honey spun his finger near his temple for the full effect should I not understand the idea of a crazy man. My mouth dropped open. The Diva was in danger.

"There's no way he's eligible for parole," he assured me.

"How do you know?"

"I've worked for Jane for eight years, and I have connections," he said with the conviction of a CSI officer. Yeah right, I thought, eight years with connections and still a servant to the Diva's every mood.

"Plus, all of his victims had blond hair."

"But so does Jane," I reminded him, picturing her perfect coif.

"No," Honey said lowering his voice to a whisper. "She's really a red head. But she thought the hair would objectify her too much as a sexpot."

"Sexpot? Jane?"

"She really does have good legs you know. Better than mine," he continued, stretching out his waxed legs from under his capri pants. "Have you seen any of her early pictures? She could have modeled. But she wanted to be taken seriously as a television personality and bona fide cook. So she went the Betty Crocker route, hence the blond locks." Honey waved his hand dismissively as if let down by yet another blond wannabe. Honey had given up his golden-tinted locks in exchange for the new "in" color—copper. I nodded, my head busily trying to absorb all of this personal information. Jane was becoming more human to me. Honey took the letter, opened a low desk drawer, and threw it on top of a mounting pile of similar chicken-scrawled envelopes.

"Are those all from him?" I asked.

"Yep." Honey slammed the drawer shut as Jane came whisking around the corner.

"Honey! Now!" the Diva had bellowed. My two-second humanized vision of Jane was replaced by that of a cartoon giant whose head spun around in time with her pansy-smooshing sneakers.

What blew about getting the note on Thursday was that Friday was a workday, meaning that I had to leave my building. Had it been Saturday or Sunday, I could have curled up in the safety of my couch and lost myself in a Lifetime made-for-TV movie. I might have been able to get a few clues about how to protect myself, how to put my soon-to-be-attacker away for life, how to argue against his/her parole, and how to get on with my now scarred existence.

Instead, I donned my faux Burberry hat and pulled it low as I exited the apartment the next morning. I made sure to wave to Doorman Juan on my way out so that he could be a witness for the prosecution at my murderer's trial. I walked with my head down (nothing new as a New Yorker) and felt paranoia swirling all around me. It snuck through the protective barrier in the cab, and it squeezed through the closing elevator doors at work. Smiles became sneers. I had never noticed how the magazine guy in the lobby smiled with only one side of his mouth, how the security guard's whole face squinched up when he said hello (suspiciously happy), and how the Diva's total lack of smile could be construed as criminal.

"You look horrible," Julie commented as I walked in, my head whipping left and right in true surveillance form.

"Not feeling so hot," I responded. No need to connect her in any way to my impending murder.

"You!" Jane hollered at me in the hallway. "Let's gooooo!" Julie rolled her eyes. The Diva was pissed.

"Wooden bowl!" she bellowed. "Is it so hard to find me a wooden bowl?" I had been tagged to put the apples in a wooden bowl—repeat, wooden bowl—on the set's kitchen counter.

"Why would anyone put them in a crystal bowl?" she snapped. "Just what I need—the set lights reflecting off the bowl and blinding my viewers! Plus, think of the image of my hips as I pass behind this bowl. Let's make Jane's hips appear even wider! Do I have to think of everything?" Wow. I rushed forward with the wooden bowl, reminding myself that one didn't get to this level of success without being detail oriented.

"And you," she continued as the finger swung toward me, "Never use yellow apples again. Actually, go to the test kitchen and get some Granny Smith green apples. Yellow doesn't look good near my skin." I nodded and ran off. It wasn't that Jane was simply shallow; she just knew that a bad image would turn people away from buying into her cult. And we wouldn't want that! Shit, now I couldn't remember what type of green apples she wanted. Were there many types of green apples? Thankfully the kitchen chef knew what I meant when I smiled and asked for the "green apples."

I finally lost it before lunch and burst into hysterical hiccups when Margaret tapped me from behind, causing me to jump a mile high and slam my big toe into the copying machine while doing my rendition of a karate kick.

"Gosh, aren't we jumpy today," she snickered. I tasted blood from my tongue, which I had just bitten. "You should know better, you know." No, I didn't know.

"What's that, Margaret?"

"No copying between 10:45 and 12:30," she informed me. "Everyone knows not to use the copier then."

"Why would that be?" I asked.

"Jane doesn't like to be bothered with the noise during her lunch break," she spat as if I were some first grader. Luckily, Margaret began to back away as my hiccupping grew worse. I gathered my stack of papers and ran to the HR woman's office. Feigning food poisoning (an absolute sin to the staff at S&S), I took the rest of the day off. Hat lowered to my chin, I hobbled home as quickly as possible.

✑

*A*s I entered my apartment building around noon, I began to assess my neighbors. One never feels alone in New York, but on the flip side, you rarely ever feel part of a close-knit community. I knew some other young girls lived in our building because they had winked at Macie one night while she was making out in the lobby area.

"Great, now I'll be seen as the slut of the apartment building," she moaned.

"Don't worry, darling. I will do my best to dethrone you. I've been thinking that the couch in the lobby looks comfy, but the plastic would probably stick to my ass," Tara grinned. Macie didn't seem amused.

We also had a couple who lived next door to us. We weren't sure of their ages since Manhattan practically had Botox in the air. We did know that they didn't approve of our late-night antics. We'd received a note under our door back in November that read:

> *Please be more respectful of your neighbors. With shared walls, we cannot only hear but feel the vibrations of your headboards banging incessantly against the wall late at night. We*

would appreciate it if you could curtail your activities or move your bed.

Thank you, the McManns, apt. 5D

"I can't put my bed anywhere else in my room—there's no space!" Tara, the guilty party, had objected. Syd was doubled over in a fit of giggles.

"Maybe we should pad your headboard like on *Trading Spaces!*" she had suggested.

"Whatever. I've heard her high-pitched groaning before! They're just morning people," observed Tara. "It's a nice way to start the day, but in my experience the guy usually already has his mind on impending work issues, preventing him from focusing completely on me." The problem however was soon forgotten after Tara ditched her flavor of the month later that week.

We did have one spooky guy in our building and I still hadn't figured out if he was always drunk or just slow. He also lived on our floor. One afternoon, he had passed by me and I'd given him the obligatory, neighborly "How are you?"

Rather than playing the polite game, he'd turned around and said, "Not so good. I was beaten up last night." His face was indeed bruised and banged up. I had tried not to wince. He didn't elaborate as to whether he'd been beaten up in a bar brawl, beaten up because he'd fallen down some stairs, or beaten up by some crazed girlfriend.

"I'm so sorry!" I squeaked. What else do you say? He stood there staring at me with his two enormous dogs who could have easily eaten me. Did management really allow such dangerous-looking pets in the building?

"Feel better!" I'd exclaimed as if he had a runny nose and hurried on my way. Thinking back, this encounter had taken place outside of our apartment door and he knew where I lived. Maybe my sympathy hadn't been enough, or maybe he was now in love with my kind ways and wanted more!

⁓

This, I reflected as I lay huddled on the couch, was the longest Friday of my life. I couldn't risk going out tonight; my assailant might be hiding among the throngs in a stale beer shroud. I couldn't even think about all the days that lay ahead. What to do?

Suddenly it hit me. Why, redecorate! Our apartment deserved a snappy spring makeover, just like a Cinderella in waiting. Jane had been espousing the wonders of spring cleaning and reorganization all week. I turned to the piles of catalogs in our basket for inspiration. (I wasn't about to touch today's mail!) Sadly, the Pottery Barn catalog was usually too steep in price and lacking in originality, so I set it aside. I wavered over the dream catalogs: Neiman's, Saks, and Hammacher Schlemmer. Who wouldn't want an electric hot air balloon to get to work? Putting down the catalogs, I took a deep breath and dug down deep into my inner core of creativity. I stood back and assessed the layout of our humble abode. It was a square, no actually, more rectangular space. One wall was unusable because our front door was smack dab in the middle, another wall contained the one outlet into which the TV was plugged. Well, I could use an extension cord and wind the cord along the baseboards and put the TV in the corner. Much better!

"Noooo!" a scream came flying through the front door. "What do you think you are doing?" Sydney was standing in the doorway with a panicked look on her face, as if she had walked in on the worst scenario imaginable. Her wide eyes mimicked my sixth-grade teacher's when she'd discovered me reading test answers off of my elbow. Did you know that it is physically impossible to kiss your elbow? Well, it is just as difficult to read notes from your elbow—hence my thwarted efforts.

"What?!" I screamed back. Hysteria has a way of spreading. "What the hell is the matter, Syd?"

"You cannot, *cannot* use an extension cord in our apartment!"

"Why the hell not?" I demanded. Why was I still screeching?

"Because they cause so many fires!"

"Stop yelling! They're perfectly safe—you just can't plug like eighteen million cords into one!"

"No!!"

Okay. Roommate lesson number one: know when to just back down. Some months later, I would realize how serious she was when she whispered, "Cords! Check the extension cords!" to Kurt Russell as he was searching a burnt-out shell of a house in *Backdraft*.

I hadn't shared with Syd that Mr. or Mrs. Death was waiting for me somewhere outside of our apartment, so she couldn't be blamed for making me age another few years. And what did it matter anyway, since it didn't look like I would reach the age of twenty-three? Our TV was destined to remain in its one and only spot. I was fine with that, really. When faced with one's mortality, the little things didn't matter so much. Someday though, should I live, I planned to invent a TV with an extra-long retractable cord already attached. Kind of like a vacuum, just for neurotic nitwits like Sydney.

Back on the redecorating front, I was now limited to the last two walls in the apartment. Currently the couch resided along the wall that faced the windows. So I changed the couch to the wall that had the windows. True, we wouldn't have the cityscape of the blinking hotel sign in front of us, and I couldn't watch the naked singing woman across the way who had an interesting way of ironing in the morning, but already the room looked completely different!

When we'd moved in back in August, the four of us had made some simple decorating concessions. Since we were out of college and entrenched in real life, gone were the framed Monet prints that we'd bought at the co-op for fifteen dollars each. Gone was the initial futon inherited from Macie's older brother. We had splurged over the winter for a Jennifer Convertible sofa. I owned one-fourth of a plush couch! Well, actually it was a loveseat. Which, at this point, I must take issue with. Actually, Tara had been the first one to raise the point about a week after the new couch's arrival.

"Loveseat, my ass! Okay, so I hooked up with Ben on the loveseat," she'd informed us. Syd, Macie, and I had turned and looked at the new sofa with a bit of repulsion. No stains were visible to the naked eye, but each of us probably had the same vision of naked butts rubbed along the brushed cotton finish. "You can't properly kiss, never mind make love, on that thing," she continued. "Ben's legs hung over the arm at his knees, my elbow kept hitting the back cushion, which does not come unattached—did we know that when we bought it? But the bottom cushions do slide off and flip off, as Ben and I found out as we groped toward the unattainable." So much for my thoughts of simply flipping the cushions.

"Do not blame the couch for your lack of orgasms," reprimanded Macie, still eyeing the couch with hesitation.

"Only 64 percent of women ever reach an orgasmic state and most do so by their own hand," quoted Tara.

"Sweetie, you just keep trying. This Ben guy, maybe he can break the curse!"

Tara believed she had been cursed from ever experiencing orgasms during sex by an ex-boyfriend who turned out to be gay. His being gay was not an issue for Tara—it was that he had proclaimed himself a follower of witchcraft. Meaning, he had the power to cast spells and, after they broke up, Tara believed that she was doomed. Though she hadn't given up on trying!

Unfortunately, Tara had been cursed before. During college at Georgetown, she had lived in a row house in Washington, DC. Her castle was little more than a ragged, party-torn townhouse whose scaffolding was barely tied together in order to extract rent from eager coeds (whose parents were footing the bill). In order to make the worn-down house a little more presentable, she and her roommates had adorned the windows with plastic window boxes filled with flowers: bright pink geraniums at $1.99 a piece planted every six inches. However, Tara and her beautiful geraniums had an enemy. Two houses down lived Helena Humperstein, aptly named, who was at least eighty years old and she had lived in her red row house at least that long. Needless to say, she did not appreciate the college spirit at her age. Nor did she appreciate Tara's torrid fight with her umpteenth boyfriend that first September.

Tara was "not allowed" to brawl in the house (House Rule 6, right after House Rule 5: No piggies are allowed to eat leftovers not belonging to said little piggy!), so she'd taken her issues outside, right in front of Helena's house. Tara's dramatic fury was soon upstaged by Helena leaning out of her window muttering under her breath (this was after she went after the male coed neighbors with a Wiffle ball bat—their bat, mind you). The syllables were indistinguishable (even to Tara, the linguistics major), but the guttural noises couldn't be denied. Tara ended her riot act, grabbed the boyfriend, and dragged him back to her place. And the next morning, the geraniums were dead. One day alive, next day gone. Life, so short. Helena, so freaky. Tara, so cursed.

I put all thoughts of Tara's, Ben's, and whoever else's bodily fluids from my mind as I finished centering the couch against its new wall. I stood back and suddenly, in my mind, rich silken drapes appeared above the windows. The Diva had hung similar drapes on the set last Tuesday. I envisioned ours falling in soft billows and puddling on the floor like the trail of a luxurious ball gown. I then began to ponder the color. A sky blue—no, a deep wine red! Why does everything tie back to drinking? How amazing they would look. However, reality quickly set in. Unlike the Diva, TV hostess extraordinaire with millions of advertising dollars on her side, with a budget like ours, we would be lucky to be able to afford her cheap signature line of sheets. Maybe Mom could sew us some balloon curtains from those puppies. (Note to self: Call Mom to see if she knows what balloon curtains are.)

Next up, the white walls. Until I marry, I have come to terms with the fact that I will be surrounded by white walls. Harmonious and serene. And boring! Most apartment buildings in the city will not let you paint the walls even if you promise to paint them back to their boring old selves. And our lovely little multiethnic walk-up was no different. Our super was the building's sniffer. He'd roam the halls investigating and sniffing for any foreign scent. Whether it be pot, burning cookies, kitty litter, wet dogs, or paint fumes, he knew it all. So white walls it was.

I surveyed the rest of the space and reflected that in years gone by, the ritual of getting married was designed to outfit you for grown-up life. Hence, bridal showers, which in theory gave you the goods you'd need to set up your first apartment or house. But these days, with women getting married later in life, bridal showers had become redundant. What we needed instead were Real-Life Showers, which could be thrown for girls when they first moved out on their own. Who wouldn't benefit from registering for home goods upon entering the real world? After all, that's when you really need them. Think about it. When you move into your first apartment, you rack up a tremendous amount of credit card debt within the first couple of weeks buying just the bare essentials. From knives and plates, to toilet brush cleaner and bath towels, there is so much stuff you need at the beginning. My own wish list would have included:

Flatware (fancy word for kitchen utensils)
Sheets (at least 300 thread count)
Towels (who knew the bath size cost so much?)
Silk flowers (that is, if no one signs you up for one of those amazing month-by-month fresh flower delivery services)
A compact microwave (versus the vintage, big-ass one you inherited from the 'rents)
Cappuccino maker (frothy milk and all)
Pant hangers (yes, they add up)
A vacuum (no reason for the insane cost)
Stainless steel step-open wastepaper basket (instant kitchen chic)

Cloth shower curtain (mildew problems be damned)

Throw pillows (just a few with tassels to dress up that college futon)

Wine rack (for the necessary collection)

(Note to self: Be sure to bring up Real-Life Shower idea at work. Could totally be a Wow segment for the Diva.)

As I settled back down on the couch, my domestic inspiration drained, I found myself wondering who would protect me in the event that my stalker came calling. My father was miles away, 289 miles to be mathematically precise, and our super would only rise from the subbasement depths to defend me if my attacker stood in the way of Krispy Kreme's doorway around the corner. A boyfriend would have been the obvious choice, but I was all alone in that regard. Mr. J. P. Morgan had worked out religiously and had a body to do the bragging for him, but would he be willing to defend me if he saw me on the street in need of help?

Maybe this stalker episode would bring us together again. He'd be so concerned that he'd rush over to guard my humble door. Very movie-esque. I'd boil him coffee (Note to self: Does coffee really boil?) and serve him some of my newly learned Cooking Club delights like the cinnamon buns. I'd brush his bangs out of his sleep-deprived eyes and his lips would catch the ends of my fingers. With that innocent finger kiss, we'd get it on right there in the hallway. The McManns from 5D would ignore the sensuous noises in the name of love, and the old man in 5B was a recluse anyway—no problem there. The romance would ignite again. Every cloud has a silver lining, right?

Exhausted from the drama of the detailed fantasies in my mind, I headed for the kitchen. I needed one of the cool-down pints of ice cream in the freezer. Yet when I opened the door, all that was left was one tiny cup of Tasty Treats. Apparently Sage had come over and spring cleaned our fridge. Ugh! Tasty Treats was definitely not ice cream; it was a newfangled trend of dieters. Someone, somewhere, had "invented" (because it's obviously not a natural process) ice cream that had no calories, no fat, and get this, no carbs. The name itself leaves something to be desired because all I could think of was dog snacks every time I heard it. But the line of salivating girls outside any one of the Tasty Treats kiosks in the city often resembled a pack of eager puppies. Famished, I snatched the cup and scoffed down the appetizing air in about eight seconds flat. In the midst of licking the last dribbles off my spoon, my cell phone rang.

"Charlie, how many points have you eaten today?" Sage asked.

"What?" I answered licking my guilty lips.

"How many points? You couldn't have given up already!"

That's right. The points. Sage had coerced us all into joining Weight Watchers a few weeks ago after our bathing suit experience in Puerto Rico, and she was determined to get us all following the point system. She'd found that Weight Watchers could be a tad discriminating however. After we'd all sent in the paperwork at her insistence, Sage had gone to a meeting to survey the scene and reported that the looks she got from the other women in the class could have burned off her saddlebags right then and there. Now I could see why these overweight women might have a problem with a tiny little thing like Sage. She was most likely sitting at attention in the front row, taking notes mind you, asking all sorts of annoying calorie-laced questions. Skinny bitch, is what they were probably thinking. And apparently, the Weight Watchers leader had taken Sage aside afterward and said that she couldn't in good faith put Sage into the program. Sage had been crestfallen but somehow she had still been able to get her hands on the literature and was now reveling in her newfound glory as the points drill sergeant.

The other night when we'd been watching TV, she'd reprimanded Wade. "Five points!"

"What?" asked Wade.

"Five points."

"What is?"

"That cracker that you're munching. Did you even *know* you were eating a cracker?" Watch out Dr. Phil.

"Yes, Sage. I know I am eating a cracker," Wade said using her slow kindergarten voice. "I'm frickin' hungry!"

"Five points hungry? You might try to satisfy your hunger with a handful of butter-free popcorn instead," suggested Sage.

"Sage, A) these girls do not have a microwave, B) I like butter on my popcorn, and C) I want my cracker!" Wade was screeching at this point. I have a theory about teachers. They hold all their anger inside during the day, their patience being tried minute-by-minute. But let them out of school, and they are ready to yell at the littlest infraction. Wade behind the wheel of a car was scary. That sweet southerner could curse like a truck driver. Yet when around kids, she was a sappy version of Peter Pan combined with a smidge of the *Romper Room* lady. So Wade had continued to stuff her face full of crackers while Sage gritted her teeth and tapped her fingers on the table. I'd been convinced that Sage's taps were counting out 1, 2, 3, 4, 5 over and over again to make her five points point very clear.

"Yep, Sage, I've been counting," I said now, calmly, into the phone. "I've had about seventeen out of my twenty-five points today and I think I'm going to bank the other eight points."

"What do you mean 'bank'?"

"Well, if I don't use up those eight today, I can drink an extra beer or two this weekend!" Check out that math prowess, Dad! Too bad this newfound mathematical ability hadn't spilled over into my lack of financial common sense.

"You can't bank them!" Sage sounded disgusted. I could feel the spit coming through the phone. "You have to moderate your solid and liquid intake across the board. By not using up your points, you will begin to see those dimpled thighs disappear!" I knew Sage should never have come to the Rico with us. Those discerning eyes missed nothing!

"Fine, fine," I mumbled as I opened the cabinet to search for eight points worth of something. "I'll talk to you later. I've got to find some more points to shove down my throat."

"Trust me, C. I'm only doing this to help you."

∾

$\mathscr{S}$till in the kitchen, I was alone, tired, apparently being stalked and yet, I was still hungry. Points, schmoints. Sage was turning into a real pain in the you know what over the whole Weight Watchers situation. What began as personal goodwill gesture toward our bodies had now turned into a one woman war against our physical well-being. Something needed to be done about Ms. Sage, aka Sage the Starver. She had turned into a nasty food dictator, and it was time for us to rise up and revolt against her suppressive eating regime. As my annoyance meter began to rise, my stomach began to cramp from being empty (or maybe from having ingested a chemical substitute for ice cream). How had it come to this? I felt sure that J. Lo wasn't somewhere counting points. Nor did she allow her friends to critique the size of her signature hips. The food madness had to stop. It was time for an emergency Cooking Club meeting and I needed to gather the troops, stat!

It didn't take much to convince the rest of the girls to join me over the weekend in my anti-point campaign. They were all pretty much starving as well and had wanted to throw in the towel a long time ago. But none of us had had the courage to take on you know who. So we joined forces, and without Sage's knowledge, agreed to make whatever the hell we wanted for tomorrow night's April meeting. No limits, no restrictions. We could even order in! Screw the points. Sage could try and curb our diets, but she couldn't curb our ferocious appetites.

~

The following night, Lieutenant Sergeant Sydney started things off with a formidable ground attack. She decided to use the "shock and awe" approach and her initial assault consisted of a one-two punch. First she cooked up some tater tots (the shock part of the operation). Then she boiled a double, not single, packet of Top Ramen (the awe). Some might say that hers wasn't a strong first strike, but those carbo-laced noodles coupled with a few fried tater tots added up to some serious saturated fat. Syd—mission accomplished.

It was now General Wade's turn to lead her troops into battle. As a teacher, Wade had nerves of steel; she understood that keeping a firm resolve was half the battle. So after a few quick deep breaths on the couch, Wade got up and reached for the cordless phone on the wall. In the matter of ten seconds, she had locked, loaded, and fired on China Palace. There was absolutely no way that the point system would survive a large order of extra fried General Tso's Chicken. Oh yeah, extra fried. Kaboom! Mission accomplished.

As for Major Macie, she decided to go all-American on our asses. Oh yeah, red, white, and blue, baby! Her attack was clean and quick, just like Macie herself. Her method: the triple threat. A McDonald's Big Mac Value Meal: Coke, fries, and burger. Oh, and she super-sized the whole damn thing. Atta girl! Her order was guaranteed to contain over a million devastating points. The special sauce, two beef patties, and three buns alone had the potential to wipe out an entire block of point followers. Mission accomplished.

Next up, it was Lance Corporal Tara's turn to take on the axis of evil. She didn't waste any time pulling out her secret weapon. It was nothing new, but it was oh-so-vicious. She implemented her infamous hangover signature move. While sitting on the counter in front of us, looking innocent and sweet, she whipped out her cell and dialed her food accomplice: Taco Mamma. It was a risky move on her part, but pretty darn brilliant. This mom and pop joint not only had the potential to ensure devastating blows to the conscious calorie counter, but it could also really do a number on your arteries. Now Tara could have compromised the entire mission by going the grilled chicken and dry corn tortillas route, but we were confident that our girl would not sell us down the healthy river. As the words came out of her mouth, we all threw out the V sign with our fingers, signaling victory. She ordered the mind-blowing, bomb-dropping More Cheese Please Enchilada Platter. It contained five gooey cheeses, fried tortillas, and a pint of double refried beans topped with sour cream. Mission accomplished.

Thirty minutes later, all our food had safely been delivered to our front door. Seated in a tight circle on the living room floor, it took us no time to fill our plates and begin devouring our sinful, fat-infested meals. Not one of us was remorseful about what we had done. We were just happy to have some real food in our systems. Plus, up until now we'd done our best with the Cooking Club rules, but sometimes rules need to be broken. Just as we were licking our fingers and finishing up our greasy grub, the buzzer for the front door went off.

"I'll get it," Macie jumped up to buzz in whoever it was.

"Who is it?" I asked.

"Oops. I didn't ask. It's probably Sage. My bad." She plopped back down onto the floor.

"Whaaaaaatttt? Are you crazy? It could be L!" I jumped up off the floor and began to panic.

"Who the hell is L?" she asked with a perplexed look on her face.

That's when I remembered that I hadn't given the rest of the girls the full scoop on my stalker situation. We'd been so wrapped up in our food crusade for the past twenty-four hours that I'd completely forgotten to tell them about my would-be assailant.

"What the hell are you talking about, Charlie?" Syd asked.

"Ladies, I have a stalker! That's what I'm talking about," I announced, springing to my feet and frantically looking around for possible escape routes. I pointed Macie toward the pile of mail on the counter. She reached over to pluck out the threatening hate mail.

"Is this it?" Macie asked holding a brightly colored postcard in the air.

"No," I said. "Wait. What is that one?"

"It's for you," she continued. "Oh, 'Wish You Were Here,'" she read from the front. The script letters ran atop a picture of a large sailboat passing some white sand shores.

"For me? Who's it from? Read it," I commanded, momentarily distracted from the intruder coming up the stairs.

"C. In Club Med soaking up the sun. Gotta get a tan to rival yours. You should see these sunsets. Cheers, J. P." Macie raised her eyebrows.

"He sent me a postcard?" I cried, grabbing the card from her hand. He sent me a postcard? A) That meant that he had planned ahead and taken my address with him on vacation. B) That meant that he was thinking of me. Was he missing me? Did he really wish I was there, or was the postcard just the first one he grabbed? Maybe Club Med only had "Wish You Were Here" postcards as a sort of advertising. He had signed off "Cheers." Was he wishing me well or was he toasting that Club Med was all-inclusive? Did the all-inclusivity include hot vacationing girls to hook up with?

"Huh," Macie concluded, still digging through the mail.

"Yeah," I said in shallow breaths. "Huh."

"Oh, you mean this one," Macie exclaimed as she pulled out the plain yet threatening postcard from beneath a Kmart flier. Terror immediately wiped a tanned J. P. from my mind. If I were dead, I couldn't daydream and contemplate his future intentions.

"Okay Charlie, is this like the burglar slash Con Ed man incident?" Syd questioned from the living room.

Bam. I pointed to the door like a little kid. *Bam, Bam.* The knock was much louder this time. Hopefully, the tyrannical knocking would convince them of the severity of the situation.

"Shit!" I started to panic. "Call 911. Hurry up, let's hide in my room." We were stuck. There was no place to go. The killer was going to get five for the price of one. I could just see the front page of the *New York Post:*

Five Found Dead in 5th Floor Walk-up
The L Killer Strikes Again!

"Everybody remain calm. I'll go assess the situation." Tara got up, fixed her hair in the mirror, and headed straight for the door. She didn't appear nervous as she headed down the hallway. I had no idea what she was going to do. She didn't take a weapon with her.

"Whooooo isssss itttttt?" She asked in a very peculiar English accent as she peered through the peephole.

And without missing a beat, the nameless, faceless person responded in a matching fake English accent: "Ittt'ssssssss mmeeeee." Our attacker obviously had a sense of humor, but this was not a joking matter. If I was going to die, it was going to be on my terms.

"Okay, stop fucking around you asshole!" I screamed from my room. I was totally freaked out at this point. Who did this person think he/she was? "We've got some pretty big ass men in here who are ready to kick your butt!" Enough was enough. I sprang from my room and as I ran down the corridor I grabbed an umbrella for a weapon. But before I was all the way there, Tara decided to open the door. What the hell was she thinking? I hadn't even had a chance to get into my attack position. Shit! And just as I was about to swing away and beat the you-know-what out of this dirtbag, a very familiar voice yelped from behind the pizza box she was holding.

"It's me! It's me, Sage. Don't hit me!" Sage slowly poked her head out to the side. She was visibly shaken by what had just gone down.

"Jesus Christ!" I heaved. "I almost took your head off with the Gust Buster. You scared the crap out of us!"

"I'm sorry. I just wanted to surprise you guys. I came bearing pizza as a points' peace offering. See? I even made this darling white flag out of a paper napkin. Cute, huh?" she said waving it back and forth in the air.

"Why? Are you actually giving up the points fight?" I asked as we walked back to the living room.

"Well, I'm not giving them up totally. I just wanted to put them on the back burner for a couple of days."

"Um, as you can see, we put them off too!" I gestured to the floor, and she gasped at the empty plates and boxes full of delivery.

"Yeah, I can see you guys were hungry. I guess that means more pizza for me." She took a seat on the floor, flipped open the box and immediately delved into a slice of pie.

"Good God," she mumbled, her mouth full of sauce and cheese. "New York has the best pies. This is delicious!" Sage could actually make pizza comparisons? I didn't think she had ever tried the deep-dish delight in her life.

"So fill me in," she continued. "What was with all the dramatics at the door?"

"Hey guys, stop it," I cried as Tara and Syd giggled. "This is serious." I went back to the coffee table to get the incriminating evidence. As I spun around, Sage was talking to Macie through a mouthful of pizza.

"Yeah, she's so sweet. So that's the real reason why I decided the heck with the points," she said.

"Who's sweet?" I asked.

"Oh, Laurie sent me a nice apology note," Sage continued. "She wrote that she was proud of my health consciousness . . ." Great. All Sage needed was someone encouraging and applauding her weight obsession.

"Who's Laurie?"

"You know, Laurie. She's the girl who led the Weight Watchers meeting I went to. You know, the one who basically kicked me out. It was nice of her to slip me the book though." Sage spoke of the points book as if it were the Bible.

"Laurie, her name is Laurie?"

"Yep, not sure of her last name. She was nice though. A bit thick around the upper arms however."

"Laurie is the Weight Watcher's chick?" I asked again.

Good God! It couldn't be? Could it? I grabbed the death note and carefully reread the loopy writing for the thousandth time:

Have a great week!

L - - - - -

- -

It was. L-a-u-r-i-e was the first word and the second word was "W-W." It was a postcard from Laurie at Weight Watchers. The girls broke out in laughter. I, on the other hand, collapsed on the floor in a points-heavy pile. The postcard was an automatic mailing in response to my paperwork from the Weight Watchers center down the street. Relieved, but severely embarrassed, I crawled back to my room, still clutching the card, and slipped into bed. Lying there in a self-induced Cooking Club food delivery coma, I passed out due to all the excitement and too much General Tso's. As I drifted in and out of consciousness, I realized that although I might not be super-skinny, I sure as hell was going live a little bit longer! Point well taken.

May

Hey Blondie!

16 servings

¼ cup (4 tablespoons) of butter

1 cup brown sugar

1 egg

1 cup flour, sifted

¼ teaspoon salt

1 teaspoon baking powder

1 teaspoon vanilla

½ cup walnuts

Preheat the oven to 350° F. Grease and flour one 8 × 8-inch pan.

Melt the butter in a saucepan. Add the sugar and stir until sugar melts. Remove the pan from stove and let cool. Add the egg and blend well.

Mix the flour, salt, and baking powder in a separate bowl. Slowly add the sugar mixture and the vanilla and nuts. Mix until well blended and spread in prepared pan.

Bake for 25 minutes or until a toothpick inserted in the middle comes out clean. Cool and cut into 2 × 2-inch squares. Serve warm or cold to your hungry little sweet-toothed friends.

Saturday. 9:30 A.M. Hungover and in search of the perfect cup of coffee. Syd was in bed grousing about her head. I had volunteered to get the victim some morning nourishment to quiet her moans. I was standing on the corner of West Eighty-second and Columbus contemplating where to get bagels and coffee when I happened to notice an attractive couple canoodling in front of me. They looked as if they were plucked right out of a fashion magazine. Poised and beautiful. They were both wearing matching bright pink Polo shirts with the collars turned up just right. Their jeans were ripped in all the right spots making sure to show the right amount of skin. And their hair was just the perfect shade of light brown with subtle natural-looking highlights. I couldn't see their eyes because they both happened to be wearing the exact same fashionable metal Ray Ban sunglasses. They were so disgustingly hip and chic. I then glanced left and saw an adorable family sitting on a park bench eating ice cream. The mom was wearing a stunning, chocolate, buttery leather jacket that hugged her just right in the waist and just so happened to match her buttery chocolate brown Bugaboo stroller that likely carried the cutest baby on the Upper West Side. I was surrounded by fashion greatness. Were all these people tourists? Is that why they were so perfect, so neat, and so pressed? It wasn't Sunday, and therefore church protocol hadn't been involved in their outerwear decisions. I sighed. I didn't know if I was truly cut out to be a New Yorker; I just didn't have the panache. I stood and stared at a billboard promoting Spring Fashion Week—now come and gone. Had I learned nothing from the nightly news reports from those glamorized runway shows? I glanced around. It would be just my luck to have one of those do's and don'ts *Glamour* photographers snap my picture at this very moment.

As I continued my quest for coffee and food, I shoved my

hands deep into my sweatshirt pockets and decided that I really had to do something about my fashion efforts. As big as Manhattan seems, it is actually only four miles wide and sixteen miles long. And despite the numerous residents and thousands of commuters who invade the sidewalks each day, you inevitably run into someone you know. My second week in the city I had run into Pookie Saltmarsh (yes, her real name) with whom I'd gone to nursery school. She shrieked, I smiled. We traded numbers and hugged. Luckily, I'd felt inspired to motivate and take a shower and put on something halfway decent that day. Otherwise I knew I would have heard from my mother that afternoon. I could just imagine the phone call:

"Tootsie Saltmarsh said that you saw Pookie. Charlie, why did you have on those ratty corduroys with the hole in the knee? If you need new pants, I can go look at Marshall's here at home. I can see if there's a sale on bras too." My mother was always on the hunt for the perfect panty sale.

"Mom, how did Tootsie just happen to bring up my pants?" She of course would miss the sarcasm.

If I was ever going to be a true New Yorker, I really needed to make a bona fide effort in the fashion department each and every time I left the apartment. But that certainly wasn't the case right now. With every step I took I would notice another hip, trendy person walk by. A "hobo-esque" stunningly beautiful model-type woman donning the most gorgeous leather Balenciaga bag on her shoulder was doing the catwalk into a restaurant on the corner. The bag was the exact same one that Jessica Simpson and the Olsen twins owned. I knew this because I had seen pictures of them each carrying one in *US Weekly* last week. And just as she escaped my view, a hot guy with one of the best vintage army jackets I had ever seen darted right past me. God, why was everyone so fashionably perfect here? I definitely stuck out like a sore thumb. I still had pasta sauce remnants from last night's dinner on my wife beater. My boobs were bouncing because I wasn't wearing a bra. I had black mascara circles around my eyes because using just soap doesn't get it all off. On top of all that, I could have sworn there was a hole in my underpants. I was a train wreck. I could have possibly pulled this look off in the East Village, but here on the Upper West Side I felt totally inadequate.

Looking around, I realized that my situation was even worse than my freshman year at college. Worse than Ashley Hancock, who would get all dressed up for English Lit at 9:35 A.M. The rest of us would stumble in with last night's hook-up's lacrosse cap on our heads (not for show, of course), ripped high school sweatpants, and the required blue and white flip-flops. And then Ashley would arrive. Her hair always had the proper amount of under-curl. Her pleated pants had the perfect dry-cleaned crease down the middle. She had every pastel cashmere cardigan sweater there was and they were always placed evenly over her shoulders tied in a perfect square knot. And the patent leather loafers she wore were never scuffed and were never, I repeat never, without two shiny perfect pennies in the tongue. God knows she was ready for the corporate world at age ten. We would all raise our eyebrows when she donned the pearls, obviously it was a wacky Wednesday or something. I didn't think much of her look, but she always did look put together.

Now here I was four years later, in a baseball cap (remnant of a college hook-up long gone) and flip-flops in one of the most stylish cities in the world. Ashley would have survived in this city without a hint of static cling. I, on the other hand, was not so sure if I could be so Holly Golightly. I was not city chic. And how could I ever expect to find my prince looking like a slob? What should I do? Why, hit the sample sales of course!

"Macie, what are the newest sales coming up?" I called as I charged back into the apartment. I handed Syd the coffee and patted her on the head. As she winced, I went into Macie's room and plopped on her bed. From under the covers Macie recited, "Bonbons, Monday through Thursday, promises sweet deals on intimate wear; a spot on Thirty-fourth Street boasts about its D&G and Gucci deals starting Tuesday through Sunday; and Diane von Furstenberg is having her once-a-year deal Monday and Tuesday only."

DVF! The Diane von Furstenberg wrap dress is timeless. It has survived the fashion cycle throughout the decades and while its price has amply increased with soaring inflation, any female New Yorker will tell you what an investment the wrap dress is. You can throw it on with sensible shoes and look corporate chic, and then deepen the V at your neck when happy hour kicks off. And boys love it not only for the flattering tie at the waist but for the easy access.

"Diane von Furstenberg is a genius and a goddess!"

"Yes, Charlie, I agree. But please, don't bounce. We'll go Monday before work." Like a good little girl who had been promised new shoes, I stopped bouncing on the bed and high-fived Macie (whose head was still under her pillow). I immediately dialed my bank account to assess just how much damage I could do.

∽

On Monday morning, Macie and I both feigned doctor's appointments and high-tailed it to midtown. At 8 A.M., there was already a line outside. My blood began to pump a little faster. Macie smiled at me. God bless her. She always knew what I was thinking. We were delving into the inner sanctum of New York life. As we stood close to each other, not really having a choice since the line seemed to be constricting, whispers floated above our ears.

"This line is nothing like the one at Burberry."

"The boots had been marked down from $1,473 to $975, how could I pass that up?"

"What are these women waiting for, a casting call?"

"Whose sale is this one . . . ohhh!"

"Head right for the size 6 rack, it is always the most picked over."

Macie and I nodded to each other. Point noted.

"Violet is in this spring," Macie reminded.

"And you know I love anything navy," I responded.

"I think if we are investing in DVF, we have to take a chance and grab some of her wilder prints," she suggested.

"You grab anything that will work for either of us and I'll do the same." Before we could strategize anymore, the door opened from inside. A hush fell over the entire line. I craned my neck but couldn't see anyone. It was a climatic moment, and we were the chosen few. They let the first twenty of us inside. We tramped up three flights.

"How am I going to look good with this sweat pouring off of me?" I asked.

"Sweetie, once wrapped in a discounted wrap dress, that sweat will look like a glowing sheen!"

We both hushed as we walked into a cavernous room with large windows filled with racks of brightly colored clothing. I could hear a little kid in my head shout, "Ready, set, go!" With a nod to Macie, I set off. Should I go to the cheap racks or the pricier ones first? I followed Macie's lead and we hit the expensive items. Under her breath, Macie explained, "The more expensive items tend to have the greatest markdown. Therefore, they're ultimately feasible. And they will be the first to go."

We ravished the left quadrant and then headed toward the right. My left arm was aching under the weight of the polyester frocks. Meanwhile my right arm was robotic as it slid hangers along the racks quickly and grabbed discerningly. Slide, grab, slide, slide, slide, grab.

"Come on, let's try these," Macie commanded. We twirled around looking for the curtained trying-on area. There was none.

"So where do we . . ." I began and then stopped. A woman in front of us had dumped her items on the floor and was struggling to get her shirt off. I gave an "okay let's join them" shrug to Macie, and we weaseled our way toward one of the few mirrors. We had both planned ahead of time and worn easy access pants, loafers, and button-down shirts. The pants meant that we could slide them up and down with ease while kicking off our shoes (no shoelaces permitted!). The shirt meant that we wouldn't have that frumpled, bed head look after having pulled our shirt on and off countless times before we showed up to work. No smeared makeup on these faces! Time was of the essence as Macie and I threw on dress after dress.

"Nope!"

"Hugs your hips."

"Not your color."

"Don't even consider it!"

"Ripped armpit."

"Panty lines."

It is wonderful to have a truthful friend, one who would never intentionally cut you down. Macie's brutal honesty was her way of saving me pain and suffering later; in this case, fashion pain. We both tried on about eight or nine items of clothing in a mere five minutes and on the last try I hit gold. I found a hot little black and white leopard print number that fit me like a glove. It hugged me in all the right spots. I mean, the dress was magic. Diane was a fashion genius. For the first time my legs looked like they came up to my waist. I felt absolutely beautiful. Excited about my find, I put my pants back on, slipped my shoes back on, buttoned my shirt halfway up, and grabbed Macie to head back to the racks for a final round.

"Ahhhh!" I grabbed Macie's arm as a blood-curdling screamed echoed in the high-ceilinged room. Had someone just stolen a DVF dress out of someone else's arms, like a baby stolen from its mother? Suddenly the gaggle of half-dressed women by the large loft windows screamed collectively and rushed to throw some article of clothing over their fronts. Macie and I hedged our way over to look. Above, on some scaffolding on the building next door, about fifteen men were looking down at us. They were all sipping coffee and looking in the windows as if they were enjoying the most recent Maxim flick on an Imax screen. One actually waved to us.

"Hope they enjoyed the show," Macie muttered. "Come on, we don't have time to waste."

About thirty minutes later, we stood in the cash-only line with four dresses each. The total was about half of my rent money, but the savings were something to be proud of. I suspected my math happy Dad wouldn't quite see it my way, though.

I ran to work and crept through the back hallway to get to my cubicle. It was the secret route for all late arrivers. Julie had tipped me off on it a few months back. I was only about an hour and a half late, but I don't think anyone noticed. Plus, I'd brushed my teeth with some of Syd's Brite Smile this morning to make it look like they'd been freshly cleaned by the dentist. I did tell them it was a dentist appointment, right? Whatever. Out of breath, I slumped into my chair and noticed that there was no flashing red light on my phone indicating the usual slew of messages from perturbed coworkers. Luckily, I'd also happened to leave my computer on last Friday so it sort of looked like I'd been there all along. Flying toasters flittered across my screen. Breathless, I shoved my DVF bag underneath my desk in order to hide the evidence and went straight to work. Or so I thought.

Bling! (My IM went off.) It was Tara.

> **T-Doggie: you are going to die**
> **Snoopy: why???**
> **T-Doggie: i got O'Divine-d.**
> **Snoopy: you got what? what's that?**
> **T-Doggie: you'll see tonight at Cooking Club . . . trust me . . .**
> **it's fantastic!**
> **Snoopy: OK. see ya tonight.**
> **T-Doggie: oh hey, I'm bringing the dessert . . . it is a coordinat-**
> **ing dessert btw. ciao baby.**

Tara could be so elusive. I figured that's what made her alluring to the male species (that and her talents in various other areas). Even our Cooking Club, a domestic venture, could not remain demure in her presence. Tara could never be part of something without adding her own thumbprint, her own signature, her own spice.

⁕

"So I just had the most orgasmic time at O'Divine!" Tara shrieked with joy as she unveiled her new platinum blond hair as well as a plateful of matching blond brownies. The recipe was appropriately called, Hey Blondie!

"Y'all, what's O'Divine?" Wade asked the question on all our minds. Considering that Tara was involved, I imagined some gentleman's club or Chinese rub and tug.

"My new beauty salon! Oh and girls, these divine treats are not store-bought like my hair," she laughed. "I made these from one of my dear old great-grandnanna's secret recipes. They are absolutely sinful, but so worth it. Trust me." She passed out the blondies, all the while tossing her hair back and forth in an odd, deliberate way to make sure we really noticed the lack of underlying roots.

"Hey, girls, I also brought something sweet for tonight's Cooking Club meeting," Wade chimed as she walked back into the living room. "I thought it would be cute to make homemade dark chocolate brownies. What complimentary desserts—the blonds and the brunettes." She walked around handing one to each of us. Tara eyed her as she went around. You could sense a little cooking competition in the air.

"Now, my chocolate brownies are really rich because I used *real* cocoa beans. Did you use margarine or butter in your recipe, Tara?" Wade quizzed as she handed her a brownie.

"Butter!" Tara cheered. "Nothing but the best ingredients in my recipes, Wade."

"Good girl. You've been taking notes at our meetings."

Wade sat down to enjoy her own sweet treat. "Mmmm. So good. If you can tell, I mixed in some finely, and I mean finely, chopped walnuts too. I didn't want the walnuts to dominate the chocolate in the brownie, so there's just a hint. Oh, but if anyone is allergic to nuts, don't eat one." She just couldn't get out of teacher mode. "Okay, so what did I miss?"

"So what's so great about O'Divine?" Macie got us back on track. O'Divine. What a weird name for a hair salon. Where do they get those names anyway? And why do most stylists have horrible hair? Not just bad styles mind you, but frizzed, burnt, discolored hair! Tara had been verklempt recently after a botched meeting with a home-coloring kit. It said auburn on the box, but it was more like a burnt pumpkin with yellow splotches. Yet now, after O'Divine, she was glowing, literally and folically. Her hair was back to the brilliant blond she loved, and boy was she beaming. I usually saw this type of enhanced state only after a late Friday night date or an energetic ride on the cardio bike.

"Oscar is, ohmigod, o'divine, o'orgasmic!"

"What are you talking about? An orgasmic Oscar? Because of that?" Wade said pointing to Tara's do.

"You have to go! Just go. Oscar is the owner of the salon. He gives you highlights for under one hundred dollars and he gives the most amazing head massages. He can actually cradle your head in one hand, and then rub his thumb gently over your throat as he rubs and tugs your hair with the other!"

"Totally suspect, Tara. You're saying that this man, Oscar, basically has you in an exposed position, ready to thrust his thumb into your windpipe and snap your neck in the wash basin while you're mid-orgasm? He sounds more like a serial killer stylist to me," Sage scoffed.

"Come on, girls, it would take *Matrix* Keanu mixed with a little Hannibal Lecter to pull that off," Tara joked. "Seriously, O is amazing. He gives your shoulders a full rubdown, pressing on those spots that hold all of your tension. Then he goes for the armpits—"

"Stop! Who goes for the armpits?" Macie asked. "A boyfriend never goes near the armpits! A husband of forty years never goes for the armpits."

"Yes, shave before you go. It's totally relaxing, the armpit massage. Trust me. Then he goes back for the head and rubs your ears. Now I have had my ears sucked and kissed before, but he sticks his fingers inside your ears, and rubs gently behind your lobes and—"

"This is turning into a Harlequin romance novel!" I squealed. "Who is this hair man?"

Okay, I admit it, I was entranced. Entranced and extremely interested. Hell, who wouldn't be interested in highlights, a blowout, and a full rubdown for under a hundred dollars? The girls and I had been facing the harsh reality of the astronomical cost of foils in the city. It was pretty outrageous what they charged especially since at the end of the day the hair folks were basically using bleach from a bottle and wrapping our hair in the cheap foil from Food Emporium. A process that probably cost them a couple of bucks could cost us upward of three hundred.

For the past few months, we'd all had hair anxiety. Personally, my roots were kicking. I even heard one of the girls at work whisper "nice roots" to a coworker as I walked by them in the bathroom. It was getting pretty noticeable, but it wasn't due to lack of effort. We'd all been hard at work trying to find someone who was good and cheap. They didn't have to be great, just good and cheap, dirt cheap. I was really strapped in the cash flow department especially after this morning's DVF purchase. But it looked as if our hair prayers had been answered. Tara had done the dirty work for us and found us our ideal hair man.

"So he's cradling my head and rubbing, and his wet thumb slides gently over my lips. I'm totally ready to suck the thing for Christ's sake! Then water dribbles down my chin and I swear it is the juice of life. The whole experience was just so fucking unbelievable. Doesn't it look fabu? Oh God, he's great. Don't know if he's straight, and I don't care!" Tara threw her hands into the air. We were all salivating for more at this point as well as salivating for more of her grandnanna's delicious blond brownies. I had a weakness for nuts in desserts.

"Oh, but wait. There's more!" she went on. "It's the best part, the drying. You toss your head upside down between your legs, and he brings the hot dryer toward you. He tousels and shakes your head and you just have to let go. He then pulls your head toward his crotch—"

"What!" I yelled. "His crotch?" I bit into another nut.

"Yes, girl, and there's a nut on your lip," she responded. "Now here's how it goes. O is standing, and you're sitting with your head upside down, your head is just about crotch level. Personally, I think he does it for leverage, so that he can give your hair ultimate volume. How else can he tousle effectively?" Tara paused in deep contemplation.

"Now I don't know if he had a hard-on, but I think he did. It was hard to tell because he wears those damn tight Euro pants, so he might just have had a big package." She nodded at Sydney's and Sage's agape mouths.

"Yeah, those Euro pants," she went on. "Actually, come to

think of it, I don't even know O's ethnicity. He sort of looks Latino, but has a slight French accent. Oh yeah, and those striking dark Italian eyes. On top of that, I can't figure out his age either. He's way too wise to be our age."

"Stop, right there," I interrupted. "The hairdresser is too wise for us? This man who is violating you with his fingers and his crotch is wise?"

"Yep. And he wasn't violating me. I was letting him!" You can rationalize anything when conscious choice is involved I guess. Tara handed out O's business card as if it were the password to some illicit, underground after-hours club.

"Oh, for God's sake," Macie mumbled as she grabbed the mauve-colored card. But I noticed she quickly flipped open her cell and entered O's digits. A man like that did not have a number, he had digits. So figuring I had nothing to lose, coupled with the fact that Tara walked by me humming, "I see your true colors shining through . . ." I made an appointment with O for the following Saturday. Who couldn't use a little cheap hair amusement? (Note to self: Avoid the inexperienced mistake of using the word "cheap" in a sentence with the word "hair.") Plus, maybe some alluring highlights would be just what I needed to complement the fashion makeover I'd started at the sample sale and help me find a spring romance. As luck would have it, Mr. J. P. Morgan had left me a message just the other day:

"Hey Charlie, it's me. Just checking in. Haven't talked to ya in awhile. Are you avoiding me? Yeah right! You wouldn't do that. Okay, give me a shout when you get off the couch. Ahhh, just kidding. Call me."

It wasn't the most inviting message, hence I hadn't returned it. So far I'd done a good job of ignoring him. But goodness knows my hair had to be ready for whatever was thrown my way, especially if it was him.

◦◦

*T*ara was right. O was o-mazing. He took well over five hours, but I didn't mind. I spent three hundred glorious minutes the next Saturday afternoon at O'Divine and I relished every second of it. I must admit that the night before, I'd had some serious issues over what to wear to my big meeting with O. Most hairdressers make you take off your shirt and don a lovely black polyester cape-smock, as they call it in the business. Normally, I would have worn just a plain old T-shirt and left it on underneath, but not today. Today was special. I decided to wear one of my new tank tops sans bra. It screamed sexy yet chic. Well, the top went right out the window once I set eyes on my new hunky hairdresser. O was tall, dark, and handsome—either Italian or Spanish, I couldn't quite tell. He had dark brown eyes, dark brown hair, and dark olive skin. He was built long and lean with that typical European male body—you know, the type of body that can wear a Speedo and actually look hot in it. I quickly stripped down to nothing except my jeans and put on the silky smock. The thoughts racing in my mind were straight out of a Danielle Steel novel. I wrapped the ties tight around my waist in order to flaunt my tiny midsection and even went so far as to make sure that the V-neck was plunging to give my boobs a boost. (Note to self: That smidge of bronzer to the breast line worked!)

I sat in the chair and O did his thing. First, he fluffed and examined my hair. Now he didn't need to do that much with it. In my opinion, it was actually pretty plain: straight (no random kinks) and mousy brown (dishwasher blond in the summer). Somehow it worked for me. But just five minutes into my hair consultation with O, I suddenly envisioned him as an artist and I as his naked muse. He was clearly a Monet in the making, going on and on about faint hues, lowlights, highlights, and all. And during the hours of foiling, O went one step further and even tried to engage me in salon small talk. Unfortunately, I did not have much to contribute. I didn't really mingle with celebrities much at *Sunshine & Sensibility* (except for the brief J. Lo encounter) and besides, talking about work put me in a bad mood. As for NYC chitchat, I still didn't really know the city well enough to trade banter about restaurants or clubs. More importantly, I did not have a boyfriend to dish about with my hair stylist. But here I was at O'Divine with an exotic-looking man running his fingers through my luscious locks, so I figured I might as well indulge him and embellish my boring life. Who the hell cares, right? I have an active imagination. And with that, my mouth began to sputter nonsense. After the first couple of fictitious sentences, I even began to get hot and bothered about my imaginary life.

"He works in finance and loves it!" I gushed. "The firm is so lucky to have someone like him considering what hours they put these poor young guys through. But he really enjoys staying late and seeing a project through." I knew I had O's undivided attention just by the look in his dreamy Italian eyes. He was even nodding with a genuinely interested look on his face.

"We've been dating just over a year . . . What? Marriage? Oh, no [insert laughter], we're not to that point yet. I mean, um, I want to be established in my career before I have to spend hours pouring over bridal magazines. Right? Don't you agree?" Okay, was he buying it? I wasn't sure, but in the mirror's reflection I envisioned my hair in an elegant up-do perfect for a tiara, a subtle one, and topped off with a simple ivory veil. And, even though O's newest follicle masterpiece wasn't anywhere near completion, I knew my radiant highlights would shimmer underneath the twinkling Christmas lights hanging from the ceiling of the tent at my December wedding. I slipped into a deep wedding haze and, for lack of anyone else to think about, began to envision Mr. J. P. Morgan standing at the end of the aisle waiting for me. As I walked toward him holding my father's arm, guests would ring little bells that hung on robin's-egg-blue taffeta ribbon. I'd happened to catch an article in last months *S&S* magazine that highlighted unique wedding favors and bells were one of them.

"You know, he's thinking about moving into his own place," I went on. "He's sooooo tired of roommates and is looking to buy . . . Oh, you own too! Yeah, he's thinking loft space." Think fourteen-foot ceilings, hardwood floors . . . Good God, can you imagine? I could.

"You're done!" O's husky voice proclaimed. "Give me fifteen minutes and I'll wash it out." Exactly fifteen minutes later, he led me to a plastic-covered chair in the back of the salon. Was this the finger-in-the-ear scenario I'd been promised or the finger-on-the-neck rub down action? Sweet Jesus, I wanted it now! My domestic dreams vanished in favor of graphic images of raw, rough caveman sex complete with beauty parlor bubbles and spray hoses. Seconds later, the moment I had waited for arrived. O leaned me back and cradled my head in his mammoth hand. He then placed a towel lovingly under the nape of my neck. Oh God, I was already quivering.

He was so gentle with me. I could have sworn his hands were shaking—or was that the rattle of the subway underneath? I didn't care. What I did know was that my innocent loins were trembling from the sheer excitement of what was about to happen. Warm water streamed through my junked-up hair. And then came his fingers. All ten of O's digits proceeded to massage my head with an exotic banana-scented shampoo. I closed my eyes and was instantly transported to a rainforest in a third world country. I could feel the air. It was like a warm blanket, thick and soothing, while our naked bodies were moist and sticky. I envisioned his luscious tongue twirling and licking his way like a curious serpent around my body exploring every crevasse and every hole. O and I continued our mating ritual while make-believe monkeys howled their approval from the trees. Jane Goodall, that *Gorillas in the Mist* chick—I think she was a blonde, so she knows what I'm talking about. Uh huh. It was very jungle lovin' at O'Divine and I was into it.

O's thumb roved and ravaged for what seemed like eternity. In the ears, over the lips, down the neck, into the armpits (yes, the erogenous zone of the new millennium). Tara was oh-so-fucking right. I was again relieved that I hadn't worn that ratty old T-shirt. Wait, were his fingertips rubbing my ribs or were they seriously reaching for my breasts? At that moment, O's thumb slid over the outside of my left breast. He was careful not to go too far over toward the nipple region—now that would have been too much for me to handle. But good God, he knew the female body so well. And suddenly . . . oh man, there it was! I'd just had my very first O'Divine orgasm. No joke! It started down there and went all the way to the top of my head. And all it had taken was a couple of fingers, some shampoo, and a strapping hairdresser.

But wait, it didn't stop there. After the rinse, he glided me to his love lair (aka his chair) and sealed the deal with the blow-dry. I sat down and bent over placing my head in between his legs. Okay, it was sexual. My head was firmly entrenched in his crotch. After the ten-minute head massage I felt I owed him at least this subtle gesture of gratitude. Up, down, right, left, went my lifeless head. It was thrashing around like a ragdoll's. I could sense his penis about two inches away from my mouth. I know, totally gross, but I was so relaxed yet wound up that I couldn't have cared less. His hand tightly gripped my blond locks as he moved my head, and at this point I was ready to have him drag me across the tile floor to the waxing table and have his way with me. Finally he flipped my head back to its normal position—head rush—and smiled slyly. "Your man is a lucky guy."

"What? Huh?" I mumbled. "Oh, yeah. Um, we have fun."

Back into the chair, I looked into the mirror. My new blond hair was brilliant. I had gone from a mousy brown to a sun-kissed bona fide beauty. I felt like a supermodel.

I tipped O handsomely and promised repeatedly to return very soon. O had rocked my world and lord knows it had been awhile since anyone had done that! After what seemed to be a way too long hug and a kiss on the cheek, I was out the door.

I knew that this hair addiction was going to cost me. Most women get highlights every couple of months. Well, after this out-of-body experience, I was going to have to make hair trips every couple of weeks. As I was walking across the street to catch the crosstown bus, a construction worker whistled and shouted "Hey, Blondie! Looking good!" The fashion and makeover gods were smiling down on me now. Look out New York, Charlie is back and looking good. Money well spent. Snap! Double snap!

That night we all decided to go out for a big night on the town. I was gung ho to whoop it up mainly because I wanted to flaunt my new blond hair and my new hot DVF dress. By Sunday morning, I knew the makeover had worked because I woke up to find two phone numbers written on Top Shelf napkins inside my purse. Score!

Out in the living room, Tara was still passed out on the couch. She was face down next to a bowl of Ramen soup, obviously a late-night attempt at a snack. I was definitely beyond Ramen soup, but after last night I wasn't beyond finding a new boyfriend. Thanks to my new do and new chic clothing, I had gained some much-needed confidence in the dating and overall style department. No more daydreaming about walking down the aisle with J. P. Morgan for this girl. What I needed was a new fling.

Macie wandered into the kitchen and immediately sensed my good mood.

"Did you meet someone last night?"

"Perhaps," I said coyly. "I think I'm ready for a spring fling! Do you remember Natalie?"

"You mean the Natmare?" Macie asked.

"Yeah, she e-mailed me the other day," I said. "Apparently she wants to set me up." Macie just raised her eyebrows in that annoying motherish way, and walked out of the kitchen hugging her coffee mug to her chest.

There was no real rhyme or reason to the time-honored rituals of dating, but after being semi-single for nearly a year in New York, I figured that if opportunity knocked, I had better let it in. Natalie was a sometimes-friend from college who last week had e-mailed me out of the blue. I decided that it couldn't hurt if I called her.

"Charlie! Hey, how are you, Chuck?"

Her use of the nickname "Chuck" alone should tell you just what kind of "friend" she was. Natalie, aka the Natmare, and I had had Spanish together all four years in college. We had skipped the entry-level courses freshman year and instantly had been put on the intensive fast track. For four solid years, I rose before dawn to drag myself to the 8:15 A.M. classes. My *r*'s didn't quite roll that well early in the morning, but the Natmare and I worked on projects together (she had a better accent than I) and traded notes. Once in a while, she would hunt me down at one of the local bars with a, "Hey Chuck! What are you doing here?" A) I am not a Chuck—chuck is a smelly, faded, basketball sneaker—and B) What was I doing there? Had she drunk so much that she'd completely lost sight of where we were and what the purpose of a bar was?

Now once again, Natalie had tracked me down, this time in the city—with a blind-date proposal. I generally tried to be open-minded about all relationship prospects. I mean, in theory, you do get a free meal with every date. Plus, most males come with friends, and one of them is bound to be at least nice looking if not cute. Either way, I was feeling good these days and it was time to put myself out there.

"Do I have a *winna* for you!" She'd gushed at me a few days before. Ugh, that Long Island drawl. Who calls boys *winnas*?

"Really?" I'd asked.

"Yes!"

"Oh." It was an enthusiastic "oh," I swear.

"Okay, so here's the deal-io." What? "I don't know him all that well. Hottie works in a hedge fund on the floor above me.

I've gotten to be good friends with the admin on their floor and she raves about him. Ivy says—"

"Who?"

"Ivy," my ears perked up, "the amazing admin!" That quote should go on Ivy's résumé, I thought wryly. "She says that he's down to earth, smart, well-liked, and he went to Columbia too." Hello! Now my ears were open. An Ivy League degree was the cherry on top of the white icing on top of the chocolate cake. Score!

"So, Nat, why did you think of me?" I'd asked. This was the true mystery. I'd bumped into her once last fall and given her the brush off in a way that I hoped made it seem like I was merely drunk and clueless.

"Why you're great, Chuck! I love doing favors for good college friends." Was she being taped or something for one of those blind dating shows? *Take a Chance on a Loser!*

"And I know you like the cute, rich, brainy types." How did Nat know my type? Had I mentioned Mr. J. P. Morgan back in November? All she knew about me was my meager Spanish proficiency!

"Well, that's nice." What else could I say?

"So, do you want me to set it up?" Big, deep breath.

"Sure, why not? I'm adventurous." I had reached a new low (but also a possible high) as of four minutes and thirty-two seconds ago, when I had decided to converse with Nat.

"Now that's the old college spirit!" She cheered. What were we, fifty or something?

I sighed. Tara was going to have a field day with this one. She could not stand the Natmare. Macie had always tried to be politically correct about Nat until Nat spilled a full glass of cabernet on her at a career center function during our senior spring. Then Nat landed on Macie's black list—not a place anyone wants to be. We ended the phone call with Nat promising me, promise-promising me, to call back as soon as she had any sort of details.

About five minutes later the phone rang. Promise fulfilled.

"Chuckie!" Ugh! Could the nickname get any worse? Now I was that psycho-killing redheaded doll with the awful bowl cut.

"Okay," she began. "So first I need you to e-mail me a picture."

"What?" What!

"Well, Ivy said that Hottie's friend, Joe, wants to see a picture of you before we give Hottie your number."

"Ivy, the admin, Joe, the Hottie's friend," I recited. Too confusing. "By the way, what is um, Hottie's name?"

"Brad. Think Brad Pitt!" Oh, genius. "So send me your pic and I will pass it along." I felt like I could hear her taking shorthand notes about this whole process. Yes, it was beginning to be a process.

"Do I get his picture?" I said with a sneer.

"Actually, you can see his pic in the advertisements for his firm. They're on buses all around the city. Can you believe that hedge funds advertise? Gives you an idea of how bad the economy is." Nice political slide-in. So his picture was on a bus. Classic. Was that cheesy or not? I needed an outside opinion.

"Here's my e-mail address . . ." Nat began to prattle on as I immediately IM'ed Sydney.

Snoopy: Hey . . . pronto need a reply fast . . . Being set up on a date, and potential date's image is on the side of NYC transit buses. Cheesy?

SydSister: [mind you, in under 3 seconds] You've got to be kidding! Okay, could be considered cheesy. Is he posing? Did he have to put on makeup? Or was his picture pulled from the annual Christmas party? That would be considered outside admiration, not self-promotion. Need more details.

Snoopy: [reply in under 1 second] You are the maven on Fifth Ave with all the major bus lines. Be the best roommate ever and check out some of the passing M1s and M5s, will ya? Ugh!

SydSister: No prob, due for a latte. Going out to check out the goods.

Your Loyal Bus Hunter, S

Thank goodness for Syd. I knew I would get candid feedback soon. In the meantime, I had some time to reflect on the whole situation. Here I was, being set up by my former college Spanish partner, with a guy recommended by some sort-of friend-secretary in her building, and now I had to send my picture. I was being screened! God, what had my dating life come to? It was not supposed to be this complicated. It used to be much simpler. Boy meets girl, boy calls girl, boy marries girl. Done.

Still, I realized that it was time for new beginnings in my personal life and there was no time like the present to start. So I had Syd take a picture of me that night with her digital camera. Of course, I'd had to put on one of my new DVFs for the "candid" shot. I wanted to look hot for Hottie's friend. As soon as I got into work the next morning, I e-mailed the pic to the Natmare.

⁓

The following weekend I went out on my blind date with Brad, and from the moment I met him, I knew I was in trouble.

Not that he wasn't cute, he was. He had sandy brown hair and ice-blue eyes. He was of medium height and had good-sized hands. But, and there's always a but, he gave me an odd smile when I opened the door to our apartment.

"You don't look like your picture," he began. Was that a good thing? And I thought the picture had been for his friend's eyes only!

"You know how fierce that New York sun is," I joked referring to my new blond streaks.

"Yeah. I don't really go for artificial things," he said looking behind me. Was he calling me artificial or a thing? Did it matter? Not wanting to give him any more ammunition, I suggested that we go.

"I looked at this neighborhood when I changed apartments," he began.

"Oh? I love this area, very neighborhoody—"

"I didn't like it. Too cliché," he interrupted. I decided to just stop talking. Plus, I had to concentrate on keeping up. He was walking about two steps ahead of me.

"So where are we going?" I asked.

"I thought we'd walk to that bar, Un Sacco di Baci, for drinks." Walk? Who walked in NYC, especially on a first, never mind blind, date? We did. We walked about fifteen blocks in relative silence. We were definitely off to a bad start.

When we got to Un Sacco di Baci, it was actually quite charming. At first glance, I could tell that it wasn't your typical meat market–type dating spot. There were darling little rustic mosaic-tiled tables for two lined up along the outer walls with tiny candles flickering in the middle of each one. It seemed like the ideal place to sit down, have a real conversation, and really get to know someone. I was also completely won over by the name, which Brad had translated for me. It meant "a bag of kisses" in Italian. My first impression of him began to waver as I sensed a more romantic side of him. But that quickly changed once again when he did a quick lap and declared that we would be leaving because "no one was there." I apparently wasn't enough of "a someone" for him to stay. We then walked back from where we had just come, and ended up at a trendy new hotel with a restaurant in the basement. It was dimly lit, which was all right considering that I had decided on the walk back that his ice-blue eyes were actually quite freaky—too light and too intense.

"So, tell me about your family," I began, attempting to initiate a sane conversation.

"I have one sister, but I don't really like her."

"Why?"

"She's fat," he answered.

"You don't like her because she is fat?"

"Yeah, she eats a lot. I can't hang out with her. And she drinks a ton too." I reflected that she sounded much more like my type of person than this tool. I could feel the blisters forming on my toes from all the walking. I took a long sip of my wine.

"So do you go on blind dates much?" I asked.

"Never."

"Oh."

"I dated my ex-girlfriend for a long time."

"How long was that?"

"Ten and a half months," Brad nodded gravely.

"That is long." I tried to look serious, serious and interested. "What happened?"

"Well, I have a medical condition," he began. "I'm a

nymphomaniac and she couldn't handle it." His eye color was getting more intense by the minute.

"Would you like another round of drinks?" asked the waiter.

"No," Brad answered, "we've had enough. We've each already had one." Was he joking? That was it? I certainly could have used another drink, but I'd definitely had enough of this boob.

"I actually have to get going," I said, excusing myself and standing up.

"You don't want dinner?" he asked. That stumped me. I had no idea where the sudden interest on his part was coming from. Then his left eye began to twitch. I took it as a sign that his serious medical condition was beginning to flare up.

"No, I don't want to get too *fat*," I emphasized. I ducked outside and promptly hailed a cab for the ten blocks back to my apartment. I felt I'd earned it after such an excruciating encounter. If this was what men and the dating world was going to be like post–Mr. J. P. Morgan, I think I'd rather become a lesbian.

⌇

*T*he date had lasted a total of an hour and fifteen minutes and as soon as I got home and the girls took one look at my face, they all rallied to go out. They didn't even pause to ask for a recap. They just instinctively knew what to do. We jumped in a cab and headed down to Alphabet City to find a place to eat and imbibe.

"We're splurging on the cab tonight because you deserve it! Don't forget, we're all fucking princesses!" shrieked Tara.

"Cinderella dressed in yella went upstairs to kiss a fella,

how many kisses did she get?" sang Syd mimicking the old kids' jumping rhyme while making kissy faces on the cab's window as we idled in downtown traffic on Broadway. Suddenly she stopped and waved.

"Who are you waving at?" asked Macie.

"Cutie over there," she answered pointing to a convertible BMW.

"Hmm," Tara said from the front seat. Being stuck in traffic allowed her to lean out the window and get a better glance.

"Yale license plate holder!" she reported.

"Who *really* puts a custom license plate holder on his car?" Macie asked.

"Cutie with the hat, that's who," answered Syd. "Or maybe it's his dad's car and his dad's alma mater."

"Oh, he is cute," Macie commented. "Your type, Charlie."

"Exactly!" Tara exclaimed. All of a sudden, her door opened and she shot out of the cab. The cabbie's mouth dropped open.

"Tara, what are you doing?" I shouted out the window. But she had already glided up to the convertible and had engaged the cutie in deep conversation, walking slowly alongside the car as it inched forward. Our cabbie spluttered and motioned at her to get back in the car, and as I watched her work her charms, the cutie laughed, throwing his head back. Syd gave me a wink. "Tara's working for you, Charlie." My face was glued to the window next to Syd's. From what I could make out, he was really good-looking. I could see that he had a little dimple on his left cheek and his smile was slightly crooked but that his teeth were perfectly straight (totally had braces). He also had brown hair and was clean-shaven. Got to love a clean-cut boy! But the best part was the adorable pair of round metal glasses he wore. He must be an intellectual. Yale plus glasses plus dimple equals cute in my book.

"She wouldn't dare," I theorized. But then Tara whipped out her cell phone. "Oh, yes she would!" I moaned as I realized she was giving him my number. Cutie grinned and went along. Tara skipped back to the cab between moving vehicles.

"All set!"

"What? What is all set?" I demanded.

"He's going to —" my cell phone began to ring.

"You have to answer it!" Tara screamed. Even Macie nodded in agreement. Syd accosted my bag and fished out my blinking phone. She flipped it open and shoved it against my face.

"Hello?" I said as she banged the phone against my head.

"Hey. So this is supposed to be the beautiful one in the cab near me. Do I have the right number?"

"Yep. I guess so." I grinned. He had a good phone voice. Tara was motioning to me to talk more. What else was I supposed to say?

"So I've never had anyone come up to me in traffic before and give me a number," he continued. "But I'm going to take it as a New York moment and go with it."

"Uh-huh. . . . It's a first for me too."

"So, would you like to go for drinks one night soon?"

"Okay."

"Great!" he gave a little laugh which made me smile even more. "I'll talk to you soon, Charlotte." Bonus! He'd called me by my real full name. So far he was polite and funny. Not a bad combo.

"Wait!" I cried.

"Yeah?"

"Sorry. I just thought that I should know your name? It's only fair. Right?"

"You're right! Dan. It's Dan."

"Okay, thanks, Dan. Bye!" I said as I closed my phone. I tried to glare at Tara but Syd and Macie were whooping it up too loudly for me not to crack a smile.

"That should make up for earlier tonight and restore your faith in finding love in New York!" Tara exclaimed. Of course traffic had begun to move just as I'd hung up the phone. I watched Dan's taillights get lost behind the multiple cars heading downtown. I was already envisioning myself in the copilot seat of that BMW. Down, dreams, down!

"Dan and Charlie . . . sounds good!" murmured Syd. Obviously I wasn't the only one who dreamed.

"Dan the Man!" dubbed Tara.

I sat back in the cab with a smile on my face. Who says blondes didn't have more fun? This fake one sure did.

June

Thai Chicken Salad

5–6 cups cooked and diced chicken breasts

One 20-ounce can pineapple chunks, drained

2 cups green seedless grapes, sliced

One 8-ounce can water chestnuts, drained and sliced

1 cup sliced celery

1 cup diced unsalted cashew nuts

2–3 tablespoons curry powder, to taste

1 cup light mayonnaise (You want to coat the salad, not
   drench it.)

salt and pepper, to taste

Mix all the salad ingredients in a large bowl, using 1 cup of mayo and adding more as necessary. Refrigerate for 2 to 3 hours until salad is chilled and serve. The salad will serve 4 or 5, depending on how hungry they are.

If you want to step up your salad a notch: Cut 2 cantaloupes or 2 papayas in half. Scoop out all the seeds and wash the fruit. Pile the salad in the fruit. Serve immediately.

"Shopping time!" called Tara from the living room.

"I cannot move. Just can't," I moaned from my bed. My inner thighs ached and my butt felt bruised. God, even my toes throbbed.

"My toes even hurt!" I whined.

"Probably from your dance marathon last night with Buddy, the bar back," she teased.

"Who?" I asked.

"Buddy, the bar back! Your enticing moves drew him out from behind the bar, but his international dance steps left your shoes a tad scuffed," she explained pulling one shoe out from under my bed.

"Not my new Stuarts!" I groaned. "God, I paid full price for those."

"Never pay full price," Tara quipped. "Speaking of which, this morning is perfect for a trip to the flea market and Canal Street." She drew back my curtain to reveal a shocking glare of early morning sunlight. Cheap shopping was one way to try to cure a post–dance-a-thon hangover.

"Come on!" She pulled back my duvet cover as if she were a mother on a mission. I reached over to hide under a pillow when I noticed the blinking light on my cell phone signaling a new voicemail. Could it be my rotten blind date from the week before? Natmare calling for the post-date recap? I'd been dodging her calls at work for over a week. Could it be Mr. J. P. Morgan? Sadly, my alcohol-laden mind was slow to block such detrimental thoughts.

I reached for my cell and pushed the envelope button to retrieve my messages.

"Message one received Friday at 11:30 P.M. from an unknown number . . ." Unknown number at 11:30 at night? Suspect. Okay, it was definitely not Mr. J. P. Morgan unless . . . unless he was calling from a different desk at work, which was totally possible because he did most of his work in random conference rooms late at night . . . Oh, the inner workings of the deranged female love-punked mind. Ugh, the suspense was killing me! Really, it was probably just another annoying telemarketer.

"Uh, hey Charlotte, this is Dan . . . you know the guy from the car in traffic." Oh my God, it was Dan! Dan the Man from the BMW was calling me and leaving me a voicemail.

"So I was just calling to say hi and see what you were up to." He was calling to see what I was up to! He was interested in me. Points for Dan.

"And I was thinking that we could maybe, um, get together if you have time in that busy social calendar of yours." Listening to his message, my heart started to flutter. First of all, his voice was just as sexy as I'd remembered—a tad throaty, but very strong and convincing.

"In case you lost my number, I'll give it to you again, but I don't expect you to call because the ball is in my court. Right? Well, here you go . . . I hope you had enough time to get a pen and a piece of paper: 646-555-5555. Okay, well in case you missed that, it was 646-555-5555." I grabbed the only thing I could find, a lip liner pencil on my nightstand, and scribbled down his digits on my hand.

"So Charlie, hope all is well and I look forward to hearing, I mean talking to you soon." I flopped down on my bed and began to squeal like a schoolgirl.

"Dan-Dan-Dan!" I repeated over in a cheerleader type of mantra. "He called! The guy from the BMW called!" I screamed to the roomies. Funny how a phone call from a cute boy could banish post-drinking blues in a snap. Syd came running in holding two rather large cantaloupes.

"Who called?"

"Dan, the enigma. You know, the guy from the car. He just left me a message."

"That's fantastic, Charlie. I love it. So what did he say?"

"You know the usual, but he was so cute about everything. He was like, 'I don't expect you to call because the ball is in my court,' and stuff like that."

"Oooh, I like him. A man who puts the woman first. He could be the perfect guy, Charlie. The first couple of spoonfuls are looking good." She tried to balance the big balls of fruit in each hand.

"Why are you holding cantaloupes, Syd?" I asked.

"Oh, it's my turn to make the main dish for our Cooking Club meeting tonight. So I'm trying something fresh and healthy: Thai Chicken Salad. It's my mom's recipe and she's all about presentation so she told me to serve the salad inside a half of a cantaloupe. I know, it sounds all frou-frou, but at least it looks legit. And really, it's actually quite tasty. It's got pineapple, grapes, curry, mayo, and water chestnuts. Sounds good, right?"

"Sounds great," I said. "I'm starving. I could use a little chicken salad to pick me up. Well, maybe later that is," I concluded as my stomach lurched in tandem with the pounding in my head.

"Did you say Thai chicken salad?" Tara poked her head back in to my room. "It's a perfect day for it because Charlie and I are going shooooppppinnggg on Canal Street. God, I love themes! You ready to go, girl?"

"Sure thing!" I sprang off my bed and no longer felt the aches and pains. "I'll pick up some chopsticks for tonight's meeting . . . It's all about presentation, right Syd?"

"Our mothers would be so proud!" she yelled from the kitchen.

"Do you need anything else while we are down on Canal Street?" I asked Syd. "Bok choy, peanut sauce, how about some green tea?" I was on a roll for the Cooking Club rendezvous. Dan's phone call had transformed me into a giddy and excited schoolgirl in a matter of seconds. You gotta love the energy of possibility. Bring it on, Dan!

"No, I'm all set in the kitchen," she said wiping her hands on her apron. "But you should totally pick yourself up a cute cheap bag or something for your big date with Danny boy. Oh, but you can do one thing for me."

"What's that?" I said.

"Don't be late for dinner," she said in her best mother voice while waving a finger at us. "Okay, off to cut more cantaloupes. Ta-ta."

❧

*O*ur favorite Saturday ritual was to wander around the neighborhood flea market. It was window shopping at its best. You could search for that perfect three-way lamp (which you didn't need) for your couch table (which you didn't have) that would rest on your antique Persian rug (which you couldn't afford, even at a flea market). From one-of-a-kind crystal broaches and vintage Chanel bags circa 1950 to perfectly handcrafted mahogany dressers and antique tiled mirrors, the flea market was a shabby chic paradise where you could strike gold. And when you found it, you could haggle the price down, and then walk away needing "more time to think about it." Our standard big splurge was on a cup of steaming cider made from pressed apples trucked in from the country. The flea market was one of the rare places in NYC where you could show up in dirty sweats, with a baseball hat thrown over gnarly hair, and scuffle around in last year's boyfriend's flip-flops without shame.

Having temporarily lost Tara somewhere between the faux Tiffany jewelry and the discounted makeup, I wandered up and down the aisles by myself. Just when I was admiring a pair of chandelier earrings made from broken mirrors (Note to self: Street trash transformed by pure genius), I caught a familiar whiff of exotic perfume. Now, I'm not one to notice other women's scents, except for one. Back in February, I had accosted the makeup artists at *S&S* after J. Lo's appearance. Not only did I aspire to dress like J. Lo, cook like J. Lo, and love like J. Lo, but I wanted to smell like her too. Alas, Monique the makeup artist said that Jennifer had arrived at the studio smelling oh-so-sweetly, and that Monique's own collection of powders and sprays didn't contain anything close.

I spun around, nearly sloshing myself with cider, and there hidden behind tinted Fendi glasses, checking out the vintage New York photographs, was her highness, J. Lo herself. I blinked and looked again. It was like looking at one of those snapshots you see in tabloid magazines where someone famous is doing something so normal. She was accompanied by her sister, Linda Lopez, an entertainment reporter for one of the local New York television stations. I bit my lip to keep from squealing. Where was Tara? She would die right now! Unable to control myself, I inched closer to them to try to listen to what they were talking about.

"Scarves, pashminas, wraps, but where's the caffeine? I need a caffeine fix. What about you?" Linda asked her big sis.

"Sounds good. But I hear the apple cider they sell here is supposed to be amazing," J. Lo responded.

How about that? J. Lo liked the same flea market pressed cider as I did. This was getting better by the minute. I followed closely behind them as they snaked in and out of the different vendor setups. As they made their way toward the cider stand, they slowed down to check out the offerings of different dealers, which gave me the perfect opportunity to continue my eavesdropping. The girls were going to have a conniption fit when they heard about this tonight at the Cooking Club meeting!

"God, I love flea markets. No one's even noticed me yet," J. Lo commented as she slid her arms into a vintage, faux fur-trimmed jacket. She gave a sigh of pleasure as she spun a 360 in front of a small mirror. I quickly crouched down in the stall next to them to pretend to admire some worn-looking purple cowboy boots. I didn't want to be the first gawker of the morning.

"Remember how Mom and me used to comb these markets on weekends?" J. Lo said as the sisters headed my way. "Hey, look at this antique crescent end table. Can you see it inside the front door in Miami?"

"This one? With all those dings? Honey, it's so scarred! Take off those sunglasses before you pull out your wallet," Linda laughed. J. Lo slid her oversized rims up on her head while scowling in a playful manner.

"No, but imagine it refinished. Sometimes scars . . . they just take some extra care, you know?"

"You and Mom. Helpless romantics!" Linda chided.

"God, Mom and I used to walk these markets from one end to the other," J. Lo grabbed her sister's hand and they continued to walk. "She'd look at each and every piece. There was this one time, when it was probably ten degrees below zero, and I had tears frozen to my face because I had just broken up with Ty—remember him?" Linda nodded. "Mom knew better than to indulge me about that breakup, but she did pass on some valuable advice. While eyeing a three-legged chair, she managed to tie her whole philosophy of bargain hunting to love." J. Lo peeked inside a Victorian armoire before continuing.

"I can still hear her: 'Jenny, there is a distinct difference between vintage and junk. Vintage has been gently worn but it's classic, timeless. It's solid, with a good structure and a beauty that defies the glitz of trends,'" J. Lo twirled some sequined purses by their straps.

"Ah, Mom and her flea market wisdom," her sister joked.

J. Lo pinched Linda's cheek and said in a mock-parental tone, "'Jenny, you don't want to grab something or someone just because they are shiny and new. Just because something looks pretty on the surface doesn't mean it's well-made, you know? You need to do your homework, honey, and figure out if it's a solid investment for your future. Most importantly, does it make you smile?'" Linda began to smile. Still in character, J. Lo continued.

"'There's that sunshine we can't be without, *mi hija*. Smile! It makes people wonder what you've been up to!'" Both sisters began to giggle like teenagers.

"All of that over a three-legged chair?"

"I don't know if it was the chair or Ty that set her off. But she didn't stop there—"

"Oh, no!"

"Oh, yeah!" J. Lo began waving her finger in the air. "She was like, 'Now, beware of plain old junk—junk that has been damaged beyond repair. Even though it may have some redeeming qualities, it will never be what *you* want it to be. Don't waste your money . . . don't waste your time.'"

"God. Some of us are just drawn to those shiny or damaged goods, aren't we, sis?" Linda said with a knowing smile. J. Lo glanced down at a set of cracked Limoges teacups and gave a sad smile. I practically tripped over a barrel full of old flower-pots and gardening tools. Had that been a poke at J. Lo's past dating scandals? Oh, this was getting good.

"Yep, a discerning eye is crucial in *all* areas of life," J. Lo said. "Two ciders please." The apple man ladled out the cider into two paper cups. He barely looked up—obviously not recognizing the singer's true identity.

"Now, about that table back there. What do you think, seriously?"

"Jenny, if it will make you smile, grab it. Otherwise, never settle for anything less."

"Right," J. Lo said. She walked back and took a second look, running her hand around the edge. As the table wobbled like a drunken sailor, she wrinkled her nose.

"Nah, I think I'll pass. No buyer's remorse here, you know?" And with that final thought, the two sisters turned and walked away.

I was stunned. I couldn't move. One, because I had just seen Jennifer Lopez in the flesh at my flea market. What were the odds? And two, what J. Lo had just said to her sister had somehow resonated with every aspect of my life. She'd hit the nail dead on. I was having another J. Lo epiphany. Yes, I'd had one a few months back, but sometimes we do need to be hit over the head twice. Was I really willing to settle for anything that didn't make me smile? I stood there in silence soaking in the true diva's words of wisdom, when suddenly someone grabbed me from behind.

"Where the heck have you been?" shrieked Tara, her hands filled with plastic bags. "I have been trying to find you. You're *never* going to believe who's supposedly here."

"J. Lo," I muttered still in a daze.

"You saw her? Oh my God. So she really *is* here. I totally didn't believe it when I heard these two girls gabbing about her. Where'd she go?" She spun around widely, straining to look.

"Over there," I said, pointing toward the entrance to the flea market. Tara grabbed my hand and we raced to the front. We got there just as J. Lo and her sister were getting into a black sedan.

"Nuts! We missed her," Tara said disappointed.

Tara might have missed her, but I sure hadn't. I was lucky. J. Lo had given me the secrets of her ineffable spirit and success not once, but twice. But this time around it was different. This time around I was going to take action.

For the past eight months, I had been so caught up with Mr. J. P. Morgan's pretty package that I had lost sight of all the wonderful things *I* had to offer. I'd been so caught up with the idea of him, that I'd overlooked a million glaring flaws. I'd even let that asshole Brad make me feel small even though he was clearly a fool. I was finally ready for someone of true value— mostly because I was ready to value myself. I had to stop trying to close the deal on worthless items. I had to take charge. With each empowering thought, I could feel myself grow stronger and stronger inside. Good-bye shiny objects, good-bye junk. Hello vintage, hello timeless! Thank you, Jennifer.

*I*nvigorated and renewed, Tara and I decided to head downtown to scour the knockoffs on Canal Street. At least on Chinatown's Canal Street I knew exactly what I was getting. And so did most city tourists. Busloads of women from the Midwest roamed the streets with their big bouffant hairdos and high heels carrying huge garbage bags full of knockoff handbags and accessories. You could buy everything from faux Louis Vuitton and Prada, to faux Gucci and Versace. The reason these hot items were in such demand was that no one, especially in small-town USA, could tell the difference between a real and a fake bag. That's how good the knockoffs were on Canal.

As Tara and I pushed our way through the swarms of people, we could hear the potential buyers negotiating deals bigger than those in the corporate boardrooms of the financial district. They carried wallets stuffed with twenties and singles ready for business. They were the masters. They would grab six bags for under one hundred dollars! Then, with the aura of success wrapped around them like a fake pashmina, they would heft the bags through the crowded street. And crowded it was. Even the tourists learned quickly how to walk and push like a New Yorker down here. Elbows out, head down. I was being jostled back and forth as I blindly followed Tara's jacket.

"Ouch!" I cried as I was struck by the rubber wheel of a baby carriage.

In New York people with babies think they rule the city streets. I had seen more than one mother/nanny shove a baby carriage, complete with baby, off a street corner into traffic as if they assumed the cars would stop and the streetlight would change. The babies would squeal in glee at the colors flying by—yellow taxis, green delivery vans, red sports cars, and blue bike messengers.

"God, who would bring a baby to Canal Street?" I asked Tara as I narrowly avoided being sideswiped by a cart loaded with knockoff T-shirts. Unfortunately, the woman with the baby carriage overheard me.

"A woman who has a baby, that's who!" she spat as she maneuvered her carriage, its wheels obviously designed for the high trails in Lake Tahoe rather than the New York streets.

We stumbled into the first few makeshift shops and found that most of the walls were covered in sheets—a sign that undercover cops were attempting to crack down on the hot merchandise. In order to avoid any confrontations, the sales-people usually just covered up the goods until they knew the coast was clear. It is illegal to sell knockoffs, but that doesn't scare them straight; money is what talks down here. Tara tried to peek under one sheet and immediately had her hand slapped by a five-foot-tall Chinese woman.

"No look! No, no!" she chastised. Tara shrugged.

"Do you have any white Louis's?" she asked casually.

"No, no have."

"Come on," she said sweetly giving the irritated woman a wink. "I know you have them," she pressed, then turned to me. "My friend Sara got one down here last week." The woman's expression didn't change. Tara spun in a two-foot radius lit-tered with about a hundred bags. She picked up a blue tote with tan plastic straps.

"Can you put a Kate Spade label on this?" she asked.

"No, no do labels."

"Yes, you do!" argued Tara.

"No, never."

"No, never," mimicked Tara. She let out a dramatic sigh, annoyed at the stalemate. We walked out and headed to the next shop. Again, all the "expensive" bags were covered with sheets. There must have been a big raid down here recently. With every step we took, my J. Lo high was being squashed by a lack of Canal Street success. One woman stood by the door of her store rattling away on a walkie-talkie. Her eyes were darting back and forth faster than the city traffic. All of a sudden a loud command barked through the walkie-talkie. The undercover cops must have been prowling nearby. The woman leapt into the air like a professional ballerina and grabbed the metal gate that covered the storefront at night. As it came rumbling downward, we bent over and ducked into the store. The door crashed to the ground.

"Oh no you don't!" screamed a bleached blonde with a southern accent who was already inside. "You are not locking me in here!" She ran full tilt toward the descending gate. "You are not trapping me in here!"

"Quick! Over to the back wall!" Tara commanded. We both knew that this dark den could be a blessing. With the gate down and the cops at bay, the shopkeepers would likely be more willing to show us the really hot items. As the southern blonde fumed, Tara sidled up to the leaping saleswoman and casually asked, "So, do you have any white Louis's?" Not that she really wanted a white Louis Vuitton handbag, but Tara knew those were the magic words these days on Canal Street. That one phrase meant that you, the consumer, knew your fake bags. You were asking for the newest item on the line. However, given the mysterious inner workings of Canal Street, white Louis's were probably already passé. The woman paused, looked us up and down, then motioned for us to follow her.

She pushed against the back wall and a door popped open as if it were a magic passageway. We ducked down and passed into the inner sanctum. Around us were bags piled high, made of see-through plastic, clothlike plastic, and faux leather (aka plastic). Like bunches of brightly colored balloons, they even hung from the ceiling above. Party time! But the woman didn't stop there. She wiggled her finger again, and pushed against another wall. This time we passed through a door about three-feet high and beyond was the room of all rooms. Everywhere we looked we saw bags made of faux skins, with real brass buckles and flexible straps (not hard ones). Paradise found! Yet with a foray into Utopia came complications—decision-making time; something I had to become better at.

"Got one!" called Tara shouting across the closet sized space. In her hand she held an odd shaped bag—part hobo, part clutch, with a twist of a tote. It was classic beige—good for spring or fall.

"Can you put a label on this?" she asked the saleswoman as she pealed out a couple of tens.

"You want Gucci?"

"No, I want Kate Spade," Tara answered.

"You give me bag." Tara turned over her new possession. Then she said, "You meet me outside."

"What?"

"Outside now." We scuttled back through the shop and out the door like mice from a city sewer. We stood being jostled on the corner as the woman reappeared, walked outside, and motioned for us to follow. Halfway down the block she handed the bag off to her cohort and ducked into a side alley. About ten more steps down the street, the mystery man stopped and handed us the purse in a brown paper bag.

"It's like an illicit drug deal," I whispered to Tara. She shushed me immediately, I guess fearing that I would jinx the transaction. Seconds later, the guy was gone and we were left standing with our prized possession.

"Ah, I feel so complete," Tara sighed.

"And it only cost you twenty bucks," I replied as we walked back to the main strip.

Happy that we had made at least one deal, Tara and I continued our bag quest or so we thought.

"You want? You want pet?" A man shouted at us.

"Oh look! Turtles!" I squealed with glee. We crouched over a bucket with about an inch of water in it, full of inch-long turtles. Bright green little suckers. They were clambering over each other in an attempt to escape. They knew that if they didn't make it to some rich kid's Upper East Side apartment for a life of luxury, they'd be dumped into a park puddle or into a pot of boiling water at some sketchy restaurant. Bags weren't the only things you could buy on Canal Street; alongside the fake stuff, you could get the real stuff too. Between live clucking chickens and smoked whole ducks, and a sea of assorted fresh fish and itty-bitty turtles, Canal Street went from one extreme to another in a matter of blocks.

Now a pet was a luxury in this city. I couldn't have a cat—it was against single girl protocol. And New York dogs were pampered more than the socialites on Madison Avenue, which led to expenses that city newcomers like myself could not afford. During the winter, their precious paws were covered in cloth (probably mink lined) to protect their pads from the salt-covered, icy sidewalks. And during the summer, the dogs congregated on the street corners waiting for Doggie Day Camp to begin. Vans would arrive to take them for a ten-hour romp in the countryside.

Then, after their fun-filled day, they would be returned to their owners—the ultimate door-to-door service. Not to mention organic dog food, real leather collars, and vet bills. So what did that leave for the young girl starting out in the city?

A man was waving a green net in my face. I followed the fluttering mesh and must have made a nodding motion because next thing I knew, I was holding a water-filled baggie with a turtle in it.

"I'll love him, and hug him, and call him George!" I whispered.

"Now what the hell is that? I was saying that you should get a green bag, not a turtle," Tara pointed out.

"Meet George," I announced and held the bag up proudly.

"No way in hell. Do you know what kind of diseases those things carry?"

"What do you mean?"

"Like hot tubs, turtles are silent carriers of deadly bacterial . . . bacterial stuff," Tara cried.

"Oh," I said. George pushed himself against the bag. He must have seen the bling-bling on the table next to us. "Oh."

✑

About an hour later, none the handbag richer, I decided that I had to head back uptown, "Or else George will roast," I rationalized. The water in the bag was quite tepid. And George was no longer pushing against the bag so ferociously. His lack of luster mirrored my own lethargic state. One had to be in top form for Canal Street, and I was fading fast when my cell phone rang. I didn't recognize the number.

"God, could you not have 'We Wish You a Merry Christmas' playing as your ring in June?" Tara groaned.

"Hello?" I couldn't hear anything above the local din. "Hello?"

"Hey."

My stomach dropped. It was Mr. J. P. Morgan. I almost stumbled into the pretzel cart.

"What's wrong? Your face is ghost white. Are you going to be sick?" Tara asked. I covered my right ear and attempted to shove the phone into my brain. I waved her away.

"Hey," I repeated.

"How have you been?" It was incredible how such a simple phrase could make my stomach do a complete nose dive. For God's sake, I'd almost dropped George. I tried to think of all that had happened since February.

"Good. I've been good. I bought a turtle!" I said in a sickly cheerleader voice. A turtle?

"A turtle?" Tara mouthed.

Pause pause pause. I panicked, wondering what to do. J. Lo's words of wisdom echoed through my mind: "Just because something looks pretty on the surface doesn't mean it is a solid investment for your future. A discerning eye is important in all areas of life." I should let him make the effort, right? I stared at Tara, trying to send her mental SOSs but she backed away, obviously still thinking I was going to be sick. And she was nearly right.

"U-ahh-hack," I cleared my throat, a compromise of sorts.

"Have you been sick?" he asked. Sick? It was June! Anger crept up inside me. He should have been wondering about my physical well-being during the flu season. And here he was, suddenly concerned in June? *Pause pause pause.*

"You don't sound good," he reiterated. He might as well have said that I didn't look good. I turned to face a dim sum window. My hair was a bit frazzled from the heat, I glowed a bit from our shopping efforts, and the circles under my eyes were a tad dark but I might have simply smudged my mascara. All in all, not too bad, really. And this time, I wasn't going to let him rattle me.

"No, I'm fine—fabulous in fact!" Why settle for mediocrity?

"You seeing anyone?" And with a thud, there it was. Why are guys so direct? We girls would have chatted about the weather, the upcoming sale at Barneys, and the newest reality star or celebrity scandal before asking the loaded question. *Pause pause pause.* Shit! Now I'd paused too long for credibility on the boyfriend story.

"No, um, no. Been dating, but no dance stars yet." He laughed. Ohh, I was being witty.

"So Charlie, wanna grab some dinner? I miss seeing you." Wait. I grabbed Tara's hand. She promptly pulled loose to look at a tray of watches. He missed seeing me—in terms of how I looked? I'd been told I was cute before. Or did he miss *me,* meaning my intellect and conversational skills, my overall depth of character? We never did talk much though. Did he miss the whole package? Was I a package deal? I thought frantically about what to do. I knew I should keep him guessing, make him beg—

"Okay!" Partly out of curiosity and partly on account of that undeniable tug he always seemed to have on me, I gave in. Screw it. So much for my game plan.

We decided to meet later on at a new spot in the Meat Packing District. Sitting quietly next to Tara on the subway home, my mind whirled. I was still in shock. It had been months since I'd seen J. P. Why had he called? Could it be that finally, after all those months of hoping and strategizing and trying to make it work, he had finally realized that I was the best thing that had ever happened to him? My heart convulsed, my stomach tightened, and my fingers twirled the top of George's bag in an old nervous habit. Sensing that I was in no state to deal with the future of a turtle, I handed him off to some cute kid on the train. He grinned like I was Mrs. Claus and despite my toe-tapping jitters, I couldn't help but smile. I felt a surge of hopeful empowerment. This time I was in control. I was the one with the discerning eye. My fairy godmother had come a-visiting this morning, and I was Cinderella on her way to the ball. Yes, I was a fucking princess and I was going to get my prince!

❧

That night I stressed over what to wear. According to the Zagat's guide, our restaurant had "sublime ambiance" that was "ready for romance." Perfect! I finally settled on my darkest and tightest jeans, which the flamboyant salesman at Saks had claimed would lift and tuck, all for a mere $186 plus tax. I topped them off with a flouncy, feminine, top.

"You going to go park yourself on top of a wedding cake?" Macie asked raising an eyebrow. Okay, so my top was a tad bit frilly, but it was adorable nonetheless.

"He's too thick to go Freud on me. He was only an American studies major," I scoffed.

"That's my girl!" Tara called from the kitchen.

"Well *this* girl wants you to remember one thing," Macie said with that motherly tone. "Remember this, Charlie. You are smart, witty, kind, and might I add pretty damn hot in those jeans," she said slapping my butt. "You know that, right? You have come a long way since February. Be strong tonight, you hear me? You call the shots." She gave me a big hug. "Now knock him dead! Oh, and it better be worth it because you're missing Syd's mother's Thai chicken salad tonight and, more importantly, our Cooking Club meeting, missy."

"Oh, she got a hall pass from me!" Tara yelled from the kitchen.

"Save some for me," I said walking to the door. "I might be back sooner than you think."

∽

I arrived at the restaurant, which had a smoky lounge atmosphere lit by old gas lanterns. I squinted through the dim light to scan the human shapes draped on the banquettes. I was early. He was late. Sigh. Strike one, or should I say strike one hundred and one. To calm my nerves I sat right at the bar and ordered a beer. The bartender watched me guzzle the thing. She laughed and said, "Do you want another?"

"Thanks, but I don't think I have time." It must have been comical, the way I kept glancing at the door.

"First date?"

"No, old one. I mean, ex-boyfriend who's been sniffing around. It shouldn't be so traumatic, but he called me . . . and I don't know what he's thinking . . ." I petered out.

"Been there, done that," she said. "Just relax. You've already been through the hellish part, right?"

"True." Maybe this bartender was Oprah in disguise.

"That him?" she asked, nodding toward the door. I turned around and there he was! Cute as ever. Slightly tousled hair, lopsided grin, pink tie nestled perfectly against his starched collar.

"Hey."

"Hi."

"Hey." Yikes! It was like a scene out of an awkward preteen movie.

"I need a drink!" he exclaimed, sliding onto the stool beside me. Was his sudden thirst due to my scorching beauty? Was he nervous? "Hellish day." Oh. "Did you just get here?"

"Just," I nodded sliding my right hand under my leg. No need for him to see the damage I'd done to my manicured nails while waiting these last twenty minutes.

"You want a drink?"

"I'd love one." The bartender came over and asked me what I'd like. She must have been one of those actresses-in-waiting because her facial expression was perfectly nonchalant, as if I was just another barfly on the wall.

"Amstel, please. Thanks," I added and she gave me that extra little grin. Such support! She could start a new group: BAAD—Bartenders who Aid Anxious Drinkers.

"And I'll have an Amstel and two shots of Goldschlager," he added with his usual charming smirk. Ugh. He knew I hated that particular shot. I'm all for fantasy but how the idea of swallowing flakes of gold is supposed to be magical beats me. I swear the gold flakes make me constipated (never mind how they feel going down).

The shot arrived and I swallowed with a grimace. He laughed. Strike two. Any decent guy would have A) offered to order me a different kind of shot, and B) empathized with my pain, not encouraged it.

"Let's bring these beers to the table," he said, then turned to the bartender. "I'll settle up please. I owe ya for two Amstels and two shots." Shit! What to do? The total was really for three Amstels. My forehead felt tight. But the bartender didn't even miss a beat.

"No problem!" she said. And as J. P. headed over to the hostess, she gave me a wink. Who said New Yorkers weren't friendly or sympathetic?

"Ahhh, thank you," J. P. said as the hostess seated us at a quiet table in the back. "Please. Sit here, Charlotte." J. P. stepped to the side as he pulled out my chair for me. "Comfortable?"

"Um, yes," I replied. "Thank you."

"Don't you think this is a great place for a date?" he asked, gesturing to the room at large.

"Um, yes," I answered. He smiled at me and winked. Was I supposed to wink back? Okay, what the hell was going on? First of all, he was pulling out my chair for me. Secondly, he'd called me by my full name for the first time since I'd known him. Where was all this chivalry coming from? Lastly, he had referred to the restaurant as a great "date" place. I didn't even think he knew the meaning of "date." Were we even on a date? One thing was sure, this date, or meeting, or gathering was getting stranger by the second.

Maybe in the past few months, J. P. had realized the errors of his ways. Could he be new and improved? Maybe he had come to admit to himself just how much I meant to him . . . just how much he missed me. Lost in my soap opera daydream, I nibbled on a few nuts, eagerly anticipating the next scene.

"Excuse me," he said suddenly, standing up. "I have to use the restroom. Do you mind?"

"Um, no. Go ahead." When he got up to hit the bathroom, I frantically searched for my cell phone in my purse. I had to call the girls.

"Pass me the chicken salad, pleassseee . . . Um, hello?" Macie answered, her mouth obviously filled with food.

"Hey, it's me," I whispered.

"Charrrlieee?" she mumbled, still eating. "Is that you? Shh-hhh . . . girls, girls be quiet, it's Charlie. She's out with Ass-hole. What's up, girl? You are missing out on some good food tonight!"

"I know, I'm sorry. I wish I was there." I pictured the Cooking Club scene that I was missing. "Okay, so J. P.'s acting weird. I mean he's being all nice and stuff. What should I do?"

"Nice? Are you sure you're out with the right guy?" Macie laughed. "Just kidding. Okay, well, um, just see how it goes. But you know what they say, old habits die hard. He could be putting on a show just to win you back and—"

"Shit, he's coming back from the bathroom."

"We've saved you some of the chicken salad—"

"And it's legit, grown-up chicken salad, Charlie," called Syd from somewhere in phoneland. "Like an adult version of tunafish!" I smiled.

"We're even using cloth napkins," Macie said. At that moment I knew that we really had grown up quite a bit in the last year, especially if we were willing to spend our sacred laundry quarters on washing cloth napkins.

"Gotta go," I told Macie as I quickly hung up the phone and threw it back into my purse.

"Sorry I took so long. There was a line in the men's bathroom. So who were you on the phone with?" he asked.

"Oh, um it was work. Nothing major. You know, they wanted my opinion on a shoot that's happening next week," I said trying to sound convincing.

"Work? That's a first for you, C," he said with a laugh. "They want *your* opinion? Little do they know, or should I say, little do *you* know." He flagged down our waiter. "Could I get a

Johnnie Walker Blue on the rocks? Hey, you want anything?" he asked, sounding more like his old self again.

"No, no thank you," I replied, a little perplexed. Had he just said what I thought he said? Had he just flat-out insulted me? Maybe the little boy's room had let Superman change back into his plain old Clark Kent self. It was one thing to pass out on me mid-hook-up, not return my phone calls, bring me wilted red roses on Valentine's Day, and never take me out on an actual date when we were supposed to be dating. It was a whole other thing to insult my intelligence. Macie was right, old habits do die hard especially for jerk-offs like him. I realized then and there that it was over, and I meant *over* over. This was my moment to make a decision and luckily he had made the decision much easier. I didn't want him to want me back.

"You know what, J. P.? You're a real jerk!" I said with some venom as I got up from the table.

"Excuse me?" he said.

"You heard me," I said as I turned to walk away. "You're a jerk. And I am such an idiot for meeting you tonight. I can't imagine why I ever thought that wasting another minute of my time on you would be a positive thing, or that you might actually have decided to turn into a decent person. You are the same person you've always been. A complete asshole."

"Charlie, for Christ's sake, come back here," he whispered following close behind me.

"No!" I snapped, walking faster.

"You are so sensitive sometimes. Jesus, I was friggin' joking."

I stopped dead in my tracks and began to lay into him right in the middle of the restaurant.

"Joking? God, J. P., if you're not smart enough to know the difference between a joke and an insult, you're going to have a pretty lonely time in this world." I could feel my face getting red and my voice getting stronger with every statement. "What's amazing is that I spent so much time and effort believing that you were a decent boyfriend, never mind a decent human person. Every time you didn't show up, every time you didn't call, every time you gave me a lame excuse as to why you had to be somewhere else rather than with me, I thought it was because I had done something wrong. But in fact, it wasn't me, it was you. This whole situation has been a colossal waste of my time, my energy, and my cooking skills. And you know what else? I'm done."

With every word that came out of my mouth, I felt a heavy weight being lifted from my heart. J. P. stood there stunned.

"Someday I hope you're lucky enough to meet another girl as great as me," I said. "But my guess is that most of the truly great and talented women in this world are discerning enough to see you for who you really are." I opened the door to the restaurant and stepped outside into the warm June air. I turned around and met his baby blue eyes one more time.

"This girl passes, thank you. Good luck, J. P., and good-bye."

As I headed to the subway, I felt amazing. With each step I took, an overwhelming wave of relief was washing over my entire body. For the first time in ages, I felt good. No, I felt great. I felt whole again. Relieved. Revived. This was what J. Lo had been talking about—being discerning and decisive about what you want and what you deserve. I had finally found my inner diva's voice and boy, was she loud.

As I reached for my cell phone to call the girls, it began to vibrate before I'd even flipped it open. Surely Mr. J. P. Morgan wouldn't be calling anytime soon. I glanced down. DAN THE

MAN flashed on the screen. I couldn't help smiling—Tara had been editing my address book again.

I answered. "Hello?"

"Hey there, taxi girl! What are you up to?"

"Nothing," I baited. "Just coming back from seeing an old friend for a drink."

"Well, I know I left you a message, but I thought I'd try again." Imagine that—an up-front, honest man who wasn't afraid to call twice. I loved it!

"So anyhow, would you like to grab dinner next Friday?" Dinner? Did he just ask me out to a formal dinner? This guy was too good to be true.

"Sure!" I smiled, loving the way his voice sounded—warm, with traces of happiness. I could even hear it through my crappy phone. Plus, he'd offered food, an actual meal! It was a real date. Finally! Life could be such a melted mess at times, but as long as there was a cherry on top, I was biting. And Dan was the cherry on top.

July

Fourth of July Flank Steak

Steak Marinade

    2 lemons

    1 cup soy sauce

    ½ cup red wine

    6 tablespoons Worchestershire sauce

    ½ teaspoon garlic powder

    4 scallions, chopped

    2 teaspoons black pepper

    Dash of salt

    3 pounds flank steak

Cut the lemons in half and squeeze their juice into large Ziploc bag. Add the rest of the marinade ingredients into the bag. Put the meat inside the bag, close, and refrigerate for up to 3 hours to allow sauce to penetrate the meat. Grill steak as desired. Serve with roasted potatoes, garden salad, and red wine. Simply delicious!

July 1

Ludlow Management Inc., NYC

Re: Lease Renewal Application

Dear Tenant(s):

    Greetings! It's that time of the year. We are pleased to

inform you that your lease is up for renewal. We would greatly appreciate it if you could inform our offices as to whether or not you intend to stay for another year. You have exactly 30 days from the date of this letter to give us your response. The current value of the rental will increase by $200 for the next year.

If you have any questions, please do not hesitate to call us. Thank you for being such wonderful tenants and we look forward to hearing from you.

Cheers,

Ludlow Management Inc.

Wonderful tenants? Cheers? Were they talking to us? When I first saw the certified letter taped to the front door of our apartment, I immediately thought that the rats were at it again. Think hairy, think twitchy eyes, think skinny legs, think bulging guts, think bulging *beer* guts. Our rats were not the vermin who controlled the inner workings of NYC apartment buildings. No, our rats were the sleazy old men who were firmly entrenched in the higher echelons of our management company. You've heard horror stories about landlords in the city and 99 percent of the time the stories are true no matter how ludicrous they sound. From no hot water to no heat, from broken windows to broken pipes, or any combination of the above, our humble city's apartment walls could whisper some pretty horrific tales through their cracks.

Rather than an invitation to renew the lease, I had assumed we were getting an eviction notice.

We were consistently a week or so late with the rent check each month (never could find that book of stamps when you needed them), so it wouldn't have been a shock if good ole Ludlow Management had finally decided to come after us. At the beginning of the month, one could typically find at least one apartment with an eviction letter taped to its door. The notices were the only clear form of communication we, the tenants, could ever expect from Ludlow.

✧

*B*attling the landlords was pretty much the only thing that tied the neighbors in our building together. I never saw many of the other tenants, but when I did it wasn't "Hi" or "Good day," it was, "No hot water? Me either." "Did your floor get fixed? Mine neither." "Did Ludlow call you back? Ditto." However, the rent angels had spread their wings over our particular apartment and had protected us from any sort of harm. Or rather, Tara had worked our Ludlow leasing agent, Stephen, back in August and let's just say she had a way of getting things done.

With the letter in hand, I plunked down on the couch. It was unbelievable that a year had come and gone so quickly. There were so many things that I still hadn't done. I hadn't even been up to the top of the Empire State Building yet. Who wanted to wait two hours or more to stare into pea soup? Plus, I was certain it was not just an urban legend that a penny dropped from the top of the Empire State Building could bore a hole six centimeters deep into the sidewalk. NYC was perilous enough without falling change!

Only a few nights earlier, I'd had a momentary lapse of sanity: I began to think about moving home. That's home, home: like with mom and pops. It was only a fleeting thought, which I'd attributed to all the emotional turmoil of late. True, I had Dan the Man to look forward to, but the encounter with J. P. had only served to highlight all the drama and mistakes of the past twelve months. At the very least, there was no chance J. P. would follow me to my hometown where there was not a stock market ticker within fifty miles. I would be safe in my childhood bedroom hiding behind my eyelet curtains, and my parents would welcome me back into the fold. After all, my mother did worry about who would push her wheelchair when the day came. She often threatened to haunt me from the grave if I ever put her in a nursing home. And she'd be only too happy to have us all together again, congregated in the kitchen while she served up delicious meals.

Actually, I had become quite fond of my own kitchen, or at least our feeble attempts to better ourselves in the homemaking department. We had all improved quite a bit. Sage could smell food without bitching about the sins of sampling, Tara had perfected sauces other than the ones she'd relied on for bedroom uses beforehand, Macie had become quite the baker as long as icing was involved, Wade had stepped up her already decent skills to using double boilers and basters, and even I had mastered about three basic recipes. Syd, well, she was a bit of a lost cause, but she still persevered in the salad department.

My thoughts were interrupted by the sound of keys opening the front door.

"Is anyone home?" Macie yelled.

"Yep, I'm in the living room."

She plopped down onto the couch next to me. She smelled like City Summer. City Summer—a cross between body odor and faint cheap perfume. They say the New York winters are tough, but I think the summers are far worse. The minute you walk outside, it's like you shouldn't have bothered to shower. Straight hair goes curly. Sweat beads appear on your skin. Your deodorant fails. Mascara melts. Face powder evaporates. And that's just what happens to women! The summers are even more torturous for men. You'd see throngs of guys, their suit jackets slung over their shoulders, a giant sweat stain in the middle of their backs. As for the cheap perfume smell, it was due to the amount of time people spent trying to escape the heat by flocking to the air-conditioned shopping meccas of the city. No matter how diligent one was, there was no avoiding the perfume sprayers canvassing the aisles of Saks, Bloomies, Bendels, and Barneys. Even the employees at the Gap got aggressive during the summer. So, if you took the heat-induced BO and covered it with a fine misting of perfume-of-the-moment—voilà —you had New York City's own eau de perfume, City Summer.

"Macie, you need a shower!" I said, pinching my nose.

"Is it that bad?" she asked. I nodded. She stuck her nose in her armpits and quickly jerked away, realizing that I wasn't lying.

"You know what?" she said. "The city sucks right now. There's no way to escape the heat. You have to go to work, which means you have to go outside, which means you have to go on the subway where there is little to no ventilation, and then you have to go up and down flights upon flights of stairs. All the movement creates even more heat, which then turns into even more sweat. You're doomed the minute you walk out of your apartment!"

"Come on, it's not that bad here," I said with some enthusiasm in my voice. That's all I needed, for Macie to be feeling bitter about the city during our renewal discussions. When Macie was in a cynical mood, she could make some pretty rash decisions. I jumped up and headed straight for the AC. Why hadn't I thought of this earlier? I switched it on to high and a steady stream of cool air burst forth like an arctic breeze. Macie ran over and stood with her arms out and legs spread out in front of it. A smile immediately radiated from her face. She was calming down and cooling down at the same time. I wanted to be sure her temperature was just right before I sprang the news on her.

"I just had drinks with this guy John after work," she said. "He was probably totally disgusted the whole time." She paused, letting the cool air blow over her. "Come to think of it, he never really got that close to me while we were sitting at the bar. Nuts! Blew that one, I guess. How can you be expected to date anyone during the summer?" She turned around and went to take a shower.

"He probably wasn't worth it anyway," I said as I followed her toward the bathroom. I still hadn't mentioned the lease renewal letter. Suddenly I decided that I'd wait till Syd and Tara came home too and tell everyone at once.

While Macie was in the shower, my mind began to race about what we and more importantly, I, wanted to do. Getting the letter prompted me to really think about the apartment arrangement for the first time. Was I happy in New York? Did I want to stay another year? The big question was would the other girls renew? Although living with Syd, Tara, and Macie had been quite an amazing adventure in and of itself, we had definitely encountered a couple of bumps along the way. Living with a bunch of cash-strapped women, and being one myself, wasn't easy. And trying to get four equally poor individuals to write a check, or should I say checks, for bills each month had been an extremely arduous task. From the beginning, I'd been given the unfortunate roommate role of bill collector. While I considered myself pretty responsible, the whole bill thing had been overwhelming. After two late charges on the Con Ed bill and a few fights over a couple of unaccounted-for Pay-Per-Views, I'd given up on being Ms. Tough Guy. I'd realized that in order for us to get along both fiscally and mentally, we would simply have to accept late charges and angry creditor letters.

So, to stay or not to stay? Sure we all wished for a bigger place, a backyard with a garden, a yellow Labrador to go running in the park with, a fireplace, and a cute boy by our sides at all times, but the likelihood of having all of those things at once was pretty slim. If the four of us had already survived NYC in an eight-hundred-square-foot, fifth-floor walk-up for almost 365 days . . . what was another year? Come to think of it, not one of the girls had ever mentioned moving. We even had a running list on our fridge of all the city secrets we had gleaned over the past eleven months—bread crumbs that would have made our transition from college grads to big-city gals that much easier had we found them in September:

Buy weekly unlimited Metro cards.

When the streetlight stops blinking its warning, DON'T WALK, you have exactly four seconds to make it to the other side, so don't break into a panicked sprint in those expensive heels.

Ask for the newest color/style of Louis Vuitton bags when shopping on Canal Street, and you will be brought into the inner depths of knockoff heaven.

Don't waste time looking for Seinfeld's famous apartment from his show. Its exterior is actually an apartment in Los Angeles's Koreatown. But Jerry's real home *is* on the Upper West Side.

When you get the political urge, go petition for a tax-free

shopping day. One of the blissful crowning achieve-
ments of former mayor Rudy Giuliani, now ensconced
only in our memories of days gone by.

There is a waterfall in Central Park. Go find it!

⌇

A couple of hours later, the rest of the girls were home. I
decided to wait until everyone had finished eating dinner and
nestled in for a little Must-See-TV before I sprang the news on
them.

"So we got a letter from Ludlow today," I said gently during
one of the commercials.

"It better not be a late payment thingamajig. I went out
with Stephen a few weeks ago to clear up last month's late fee,"
Tara said.

"Oh no, it wasn't a late payment letter."

"Shit, did we get an eviction notice?" Syd asked. "There's
no way they can do that. My dad's friend is a lawyer and—"

"No, it's not an eviction letter," I interrupted. "It's a
renewal notice. Ludlow wants to know if we are going to renew
the lease for next year." I looked around trying to read their
expressions. Syd's attention was directed back at the TV
screen and Macie was engrossed in some really thick novel.
Tara was focused on putting foam dividers between her toes to
touch up her nails.

"Oh that's it? Yeah sure, why not? I'm in!" Tara said non-
chalantly as she waddled toward her bedroom, toes up. That
was easy. One down, two more to go.

"Me too," Macie said, raising her hand in the air. "I'm not
going anywhere. Sure I'd like to live in Moscow or London
where it's not so fricking hot, but I think I'm here for the long

haul." She sighed like a true NYer in training. "Call me a romantic at heart."

Okay, two down, one more to go. This was going better than I had thought.

"I'm out," Syd said softly, her eyes never leaving Matt LeBlanc's face on the TV screen.

"*Whattttt?*" Tara came running out of her room, toe dividers left in the dust. "You're out? What the hell are you talking about, Syd? Where are you going?"

"Well, I've been meaning to tell you guys. It's just that I've been busy and all," she said alluding to her many hours spent hawking hair. I turned off the TV and stood smack dab in front of it in order to get her undivided attention.

"Is it something one of us did? Are you mad at us? Are you going to live with someone else? What's the deal, Syd? Come on." My mind was racing to pinpoint an exact moment this past year that would have prompted Syd to make such a drastic decision. She was kind of kooky, but after living with her, we had come to accept her off-center behavior.

"It's nothing to do with any of you guys. It's just that, well, I think Juan and I are going to make a go of it." She got up and flipped the TV back on. She was acting so cool and calm as if she was telling nothing new.

"Juan? Juan who?" Tara demanded, jumping into attack mode.

"We don't know any Juan, Syd," Macie chimed in with a perplexed look on her face.

"Yes you do," she replied. "You pass by him almost every day."

We all stood there with mouths open. It couldn't be. Could it? Did she mean Juan the doorman? Next-door Juan? We all stared at her waiting for an answer. She was grinning from ear-to-ear like the Cheshire cat. Then she burst out laughing like a giddy schoolgirl. It was clear that she had been keeping this secret for a long time and was relieved to let the cat out of the bag.

"Uh, okay, Syd," I ventured. "So where are you going and what are you and Juan going to do?" I was in complete shock. Partly because of Juan—but partly because the circle was being broken and one of our girls was leaving.

"Well, um, I've been dying to tell you guys," she said shyly. "Obviously you know how he and I met. White gloves and all. So one day I was walking by and I said hello as usual and he stopped me. He said that he'd been meaning to ask me something and I thought he was going to ask me if I sold guy hair extensions, which I do, or whether he should drink Coke or Diet Coke." Sydney had an obsession about which was healthier—calories or fake sugar. Random? Yes. Syd? Absolutely.

"But was I way off. He asked me if I liked to dance! Do I like to dance? Silly little boy, I thought. One word: Rico." Memories of her convulsing body bathed in the pink neon lights at the club flashed before my eyes.

"At first I was totally turned off. He is, or should I say was, a doorman. But seeing that there were no men knocking on my welcome mat, I said yes. And, oh my God, I'm so happy I did. He's fantastic! He's put the panache in my pooty!" She stood up and did a little salsa step and twirled around like a clumsy ballerina. "Oh and by the way, he's twenty-seven years old. Gotta love an older man." We all sat there silent and in shock, but one thing was for sure, we could tell that she was happy. Better yet, we could tell that she was in love.

Syd continued to dish about her romance with Juan, leaving no detail untold—from their salsa classes every Wednesday night in the East Village to going to his family's Sunday night dinners in the Bronx. They were moving out to Los Angeles to try to dance professionally. Looking back, in addition to her mail-order dance move videos, Syd had always been totally into those PBS dance competitions that came on from time to time. Personally, I was always freaked out by the dancers, who wore way too much makeup and strategically placed sequins. Their outfits were just a tad too tight for my taste. I hadn't taken Syd for a ballroom kind of gal.

"And I do love surfing," she added. "I have my old awards somewhere. Think of those LA beaches!" Syd? Surfing? I never knew there were any gnarly curls and riptides in Kansas.

"So we're heading out west next weekend. Road trip! Won't that be an adventure?"

"What, you're leaving next weekend?" Tears began to fill my eyes. And did she really think she could take a road trip without us? One of the baby chicks was leaving the nest and I couldn't handle it. Oh my God, I *was* turning into my mother. Countdown to Syd's departure: eight days—seven really if you subtracted today. Oh my God, I *was* turning into my father.

"LA? Whew . . ." I whistled.

"A true adventure. Think of the drama!" Tara was good at the glass-is-half-full stuff. "Think of the star sightings!"

"Don't forget that everyone drives convertibles," added Macie.

"And boas are acceptable at any occasion!" reminded Tara.

"You can skateboard to work . . . even at age forty," Macie offered.

"And those yummy fruit smoothies are just so dessert," Tara added with a Valley girl accent. She stood up and gave Syd a big hug and kiss.

"When can we come visit?" Macie added and jumped in on the hug.

"Don't go too tofu on us," I lamely commanded and wrapped my arms around the huddle.

❧

The next day at work turned out to be as tumultuous as my home life. The Diva was on a rampage because the Fourth of July was only two days away and she had nixed our piece on how the nation celebrates. We had sent producers all over the country to film the grandest, most lavish, most quaint displays of patriotism. We had footage of veterans gazing at fireworks cracking into brilliant colors over the Washington Monument (this pre–Fourth of July fireworks display was paid for by the Diva of course); a Texan grill-off complete with the state's top chefs vying for the number one BBQ sauce (the Diva provided all the savory spices to kick the event into high gear); and antique fire engines filled with flag-waving families parading down a Main Street on Cape Cod (our garden editor had a friend who had this antique collection; of course the Diva paid for the much needed mechanical work to get the old puppies rolling). But when the Diva saw the rough edit, she flipped! The heavens shook, and the ground opened up.

"What, I mean, *what* is this? Is this what I asked for?"

Everyone stood in stunned silence.

"I asked for Americana! This isn't Americana! Do you think my viewers can relate to this?" I wanted to point out that much of what she did on her shows was far beyond her viewers' means. The average American couldn't afford half of the stuff she whipped up.

"Yes, Jane. You're right, Jane," the horde of producers nodded.

"Do I have to do everything myself? I guess I do. Forget it. I'll deal with it!" she shouted. I couldn't imagine her manicured hands even pressing a rewind button, never mind redoing an entire piece.

"Yes, Jane. You're right, Jane," Margaret echoed.

"Stopping yessing me, you idiots! Of course I'm right!"

"Jane, we were told that you wanted Americana, but we figured that meant you wanted the most pleasing images of how this great country is celebrated," I began. She spun on me like a she-devil. When she realized that I was not one of her usual punching bags, she asked, "And you are?"

"Charlotte, Charlotte Brown," I replied.

"She's just a PA," Donna inserted. The Diva scowled in her direction.

"I know exactly who *this* PA is. Jennifer Lopez, flowers, right? Well, *this* PA has some gumption. Charlotte, this is not what I meant by Americana!" I could hear the anger begin to take her voice up another few octaves.

"What were you envisioning, Jane?" I asked. No one else had.

"I want Joe Six-pack who sets fire to his backyard on the Fourth of July with his homemade bombs. I want kissing cousins under the dock during dismal firework displays as a four instrument medley of patriotic songs blares from the broken speakers of an old boom box. I want the family mutt eating Nana's homemade pie (probably her last) as it cools on the windowsill. I want drooling retirees on their porch rockers. I want tipsy twenty-year-olds drinking boxed wine. I want trailer parks festooned with streamers. I want the true *Americana!*" For a woman known for her chair rails and precision picture hanging, this was a departure.

"Done," I answered. Donna's mouth hung open. Yes, I was feeling empowered. Maybe Syd's decisive mood had influenced me. I wanted to be in the mix, not just on the fringes taking notes.

"Charlie, you are going to head up this piece," the Diva replied.

"She's just a PA," Margaret interjected. I frowned.

"Well, now she's an AP. She is now your Associate Producer, got it?" The Diva glared. I grinned. A quick reversal of letters and I had a complete reversal of fortune. Plus, she had called me Charlie! I was in. I turned and left her office determined to find the most "pedestrian" Fourth of July celebrations ever. Tipsy twenty-something-year-olds? Boxed wine? Why, I could start in my own backyard . . . or should I say on my own rooftop?

�„⋄

*A*fter a few strategic phone calls to Ludlow, they relented and agreed to let *S&S* film a Fourth of July BBQ on our apartment's rooftop. The roof was flat and actually had old decking on it, but for some reason the management deemed it illegal for renters to enjoy the views. But mention the Diva's fine name, and add a payment for a location fee, and Ludlow was rolling over, bellies exposed. I shot out an Evite to everyone in my entire address book. We would make this celebration a grand ole event as well as a blowout farewell party for Syd. More bang for our nonexistent buck! You gotta love it.

We the People, of the United States, in order to form a more perfect Union, establish a Fourth of July party, ensure a good time, pro-

*vide plenty of drinks, promote joyous celebrating, and secure a rooftop
setting for ourselves and our friends, do send out this invite on behalf of
the United States of America.*

(*free steaks courtesy of S&S's own Jane Dough)

The response was overwhelming. Friends RSVP'd in droves.
A huge majority could attend—all but one: Dan the Man.
And to top it off, he gave no explanation as to why not.

"I don't get it!" I wailed. "This is the perfect opportunity for
us to get to know each other. Everyone will be having a fantabulous time, thanks in part to the Diva's food and drink
allowance, so there will be no one-on-one pressure! Happy,
happy, joy, joy! Right?"

"I don't know, Charlie. You two haven't been able to pull it
together to meet for a while now. He invited, you accepted,
but all you guys have been doing is talking on the phone and
exchanging e-mails here and there. Maybe he's just not that
into you?" suggested Macie.

"No!" I countered a little too forcefully. "We've just had
scheduling issues—he's been traveling a lot for work. It's just
that we've had such great conversations. Nothing too deep,
but they're just so easy. Come on, Mace. Why couldn't Tara
have hit the jackpot when she beelined for this guy in the middle of oncoming traffic? Why? Where is the universal law that
says this can't work out?"

"I do have the magic touch in the love connection department," Tara agreed.

As it turned out, there was a good reason why Dan the Man
couldn't come to my big July Fourth celebration. When I
arrived home from work that night, he had amended his e-mail

response to the Evite and explained in detail—to me as well as to the rest of the invitees—why he couldn't come.

Sorry that I can't make it girls. Would love to see all of you again and thank God it's not on a busy street. Big sis is getting married . . . and her little brother must attend. Have a fantastic Fourth, and Charlie, maybe we can see each other next week? Sorry to keep pushing back our "date." If you don't hate me for embarrassing you on a mass Evite . . . I will see you soon!

"So he *is* into you," Macie cheered after reading his response over my shoulder. "I take back everything I just said about Dan. He could be a total keeper."

"I agree," Tara said, nodding her head. "Looks like I haven't lost my touch."

"So I have to wait one more week to see him. Big deal," I said with a relieved grin on my face. "I think it could be worth the wait. And you have to admit that that is the most adorable response ever. No games with this guy." Plus, he was clearly a family guy—big points for that.

The rooftop setting meant the party would take place above the city's mugginess and within reach of the gentle breeze from the Hudson River that sent my star-spangled pinwheels spinning. It also kept rustling my hair in all directions—not good for the camera. When the cameramen arrived, Macie was busy repowdering while Tara was busy readjusting the keg pump. Immediately Tara abandoned the keg in favor of the key grip.

In true New York fashion, our guests arrived about half an hour late. The cameramen caught us all mingling and gossiping, but they didn't get their juice until Juan showed up with his boom box filled with salsa music. The keg flowed and the boxes of wine were poured as our friends laughed and danced the night away. As Syd and Juan took center stage, the New York fireworks display began overhead. Never a city to be out-done, the fireworks were garish, gaudy, just friggin' gorgeous. As they splintered into brilliant colors above, Juan and Syd swung in concentric circles below. They were doing some sort of tango or rumba: one, two, cha-cha-cha, boom, boom! Juan reached around Syd's back to dip her low. It was their final dip together in New York City. How romantic! And just as the camera man zoomed in closer and we all prepared to cheer "bravo," the two of them collided with the plastic table that held the red, white, and blue American flag cupcake display. They landed smack dab on top of the sweet, sticky mess. As the flag fell apart, my AP career begin to unravel before my eyes. But to my surprise, the entire S&S crew loved it. They were in fits of laughter behind the camera guys and were cheering wildly for the happy couple. I think even Donna was holding up ten fingers to symbolize their dance score. Snap!

"Booze is my friend," slurred Syd as we helped her to her feet.

"We're all your friends too," Sage reassured her.

"No, no. Booze is my friend. I feel no pain! Life is great!" Syd announced with a last pirouette.

All the independent women in attendance toasted to liv-ing in the moment. We all kept dancing as the cameramen moved to film another cute partygoer standing in a stiff salute with a suction cupped flag stuck to her forehead. (Note to self: Suction cup scars are B-A-D.) As the party wrapped up several hours later, the cameramen headed home, leaving the six of us cuddled together in the chilly night air and savoring the last morsels of our "Fourth of July Flank Steaks."

"Charlie, you have to let me know how to make this marinade," Tara gushed as she sucked on her fingers.

"Y'all? Do you realize what this means?" Wade asked, glowing like a proud mother hen. "Our Cooking Club has been a success! Charlie has cooked. Your mom would be sooo proud! I mean, this steak sauce is to die for. It has really marinated the meat. C, it's sooooo delicious."

"You know, it's all about the soy sauce and the lemons, oh and a smidge of Worches . . . oh my God! Listen to me. I sound just like my mother when she talks to her friends about recipes. Are you kidding me? Here's to my mom. And here's to me!" I cheered, raising my glass. "Happy Independence Day!" Laughing and crying, we realized that over the year, we had become some sort of younger, hipper version of domestic divas, or, better yet, delicious divas!

"You are ready now," concluded Wade. "Go get your man, honey! You've definitely got the burned kitchen mitts to prove it, girl!"

∽

The following Friday marked the big night—Dan the Man and I were finally going out on a date. Over the past week, we had traded voice mails, text messages, and e-mails several times while trying to finalize our plans. At last we had nailed them down.

Dan sounded like a better and better catch each time we had an exchange. He had an easygoing, unpretentious way of speaking, and he always called or e-mailed back within twenty-four hours—not your standard two-day dating-game bullshit. He and I had a connection, I could feel it in my bones, even though we had yet to meet face-to-face. He was the man of mystery, but that mystery intrigued me. And frankly, I had tired of the standard criteria checklist. So far I'd gleaned a couple of nibblets, all good: He had in fact attended and graduated from Yale. He spent his Tuesday nights in Harlem as a Big Brother. He had created some sort of antivirus software for computers. He lost one sock each time he did laundry. He had traveled in Tibet. He loved Mickey Mouse. He now worked for some nonprofit organization.

I'd been trying not to analyze every phone message or e-mail exchange we'd had that week, but it was hard not to. I was like all the poor heroines in those fluff novels: scarred, weighted down by soured dating experiences. I was determined that no matter what happened with Dan, I was going to transform from codependent zombie into independent woman. I knew that just going after "the one" couldn't be my *only* pursuit in New York City.

I had planned to meet Dan the Man on the corner outside of work. Originally he had planned to pick me up at home, but somehow *S&S* had become my real home these days and I e-mailed at the last minute to see if we could change it. Dan, ever the gentleman, cheerfully agreed. So accommodating! After setting up the shoot schedule, checking in with the floral department, and writing the last questions for the Diva's guest for tomorrow's beach show, I left the building five minutes late and darted past a gaggle of laughing teens taking over the sidewalk. Peering through the throngs of pedestrians, I caught a glimpse of Dan in profile, standing exactly where he said he would be. He was just like I remembered him. Light brown hair, about five-elevenish, tan, but not too tan. He was wearing nonpleated khaki pants (good call on his part), a blue and white buttondown shirt, and Reef canvas flip-flops. He looked casual, yet stylish. Oh, and might I add adorable. But the best part of his summer ensemble was the Nantucket–type belt he sported, you know the ones with the tiny little red lobsters stitched all around. I was melting and it wasn't because of the heat. I slowed my pace down a tad so as not to be too out of breath then I sprang inside the deli on the corner to do a quick once over in the mirror over the ATM (so handy). Hair straight? Check! Lipstick glossy? Check! Skirt smooth? Check! Okay Charlie, this is make it or break it time.

I sauntered up behind him and lightly tapped him on the shoulder.

"Hey you!" I said with my most inviting smile.

"Wow, you look great!" he said as he leaned in for a kiss on the cheek. I'll take it on the cheek. Not a bad sign! He had leaned in slightly awkwardly since his hands were holding two sizable ice cream cones. The ice cream was dripping all over his feet. He didn't seem to mind though.

"Chocolate chip or passion fruit swirl?" he asked. Was this some kind of first date test? I loved choices. Brunette or blond? Blue eyes or brown? Hopefully, before me stood the flavor of the year. As I pretended to ponder the ice cream choice, I let my eyes slide from his now-creamy wrists to the rest of him and felt the first sizzle of chemistry. I had only caught the most fleeting glimpse of him through the cab window back in May, but the first few weeks of summer had clearly been kind to him. Think Pierce Brosnan meets Matt Lauer with horn-rimmed glasses. Very good looking in a boy-next-door, I-could-actually-know-you kind of way. I noticed that he had a smattering of freckles across his nose with a ruddiness in his cheeks that indicated he'd been outdoors. I hid a smile as I noticed a white line near his ears indicating a very recent haircut. And he was tall; I had even worn my clunky heeled test sandals to assess the situation accurately. If I could wear these and not dwarf him, then stilettos were a go.

I reached for the passion fruit and faltered briefly when he locked his steely gray eyes with mine. They were a dusty gray—the gray of Tiffany's sterling silver anything. Stunning! Then I noticed that my passion fruit ice cream had inadvertently smooshed against his chocolate chip, and visa versa. His quick moves averted ice cream disaster, but the two scoops were now sharing flavors.

"Sorry!" he laughed.

"No, that's fine. I like both. Plus, I like to mix things up. You know, combine ingredients."

"Really?" he prompted.

"Sure. Last night I marinated a steak in this concoction I just happened upon—by mistake actually! And it turned out really well." Wait! Hold up. Was I, Charlotte Brown, actually bragging about my cooking skills? Was I talking about a recipe I'd invented? Snap!

"Some of the best things happen by chance or by mistake," he grinned.

"So what are we doing?" I asked, licking around the bottom of my cone.

"Now you mean?" The way he said it made me wonder if he was questioning the ludicrousness of our situation—meeting in a cab and now attempting to date? Or was he really saying that we were wasting time and should just elope? Mom and Dad would be pissed but they would get over it when they saw the goods.

"Yes," I laughed, "Now. What are we doing tonight?"

"It's a surprise."

"Drinks?"

"No," he scoffed. "I am going to feed you at least." His eyes danced as he reached for my hand. We chatted our way up Sixth Avenue toward the park.

The commitment of going to dinner was a big deal. Huge! If you asked any New Yorker, they'll tell you that getting drinks was pretty much status quo in the dating world, but going to an actual sit-down dinner (casual or formal) was a whole other ball game. If you had drinks, you basically fielded a couple of grounders, threw a few fly balls, and then decided whether your new opponent was worthy of a game or not. At most, these dates lasted thirty minutes, tops. There are some who will always start with drinks, but then offer up a full fledged game if they think they are ready to hit the field. Others, who are sure of a home run, will woo their opponent with a fancy dinner and some delish dessert mainly as a pregame warmup of sorts; then, the real playoffs take place in the bedroom later on. But after almost a year, I'd come to the harsh realization that most men are afraid of the big leagues. Dan seemed a formidable player though, not one to shy away from a challenge. At this point, it was promising—but the ball game could go either way.

Eight hundred and twenty-four acres of lush green foliage (and thousands of people and, once, a stray alligator) lay before us. As we walked into Central Park, the trees enveloped us, shutting out the city grime. Once in a while, you could glimpse the peaks of skyscrapers picturesquely rising from the treetops. We artfully dodged a runner (going against the flow), three baby carriages (a fierce front all in a row), and a wobbly bike rider (singing at the top of his lungs) with dog in tow.

We wound our way along the paths until Dan led me to a hidden, grassy knoll awash in late afternoon sunlight. There he proceeded to unpack a blanket and a bottle of wine from a backpack. I hadn't even noticed he was carrying a backpack (just didn't get past those broad shoulders, I guess). He laid out real utensils—not plastic—and tall wine glasses, which balanced precariously on the budding summer grass. My smile grew wider. Then from the bottom of the backpack, he pulled out several small cardboard boxes.

"Plain, pepperoni, veggie, meat lover's—" he grinned.

"What is all this?"

"Pizza! Come on, New Yorker, pick your passion!" He had brought me pizza. Not dead roses, but pizza. This guy was perfect!

"I wasn't sure what your favorite was. I figured you weren't a plain Jane girl, but I wasn't sure, and I knew I couldn't live with myself if you settled for second best." Was he for real? I shook my head to clear the violin music flooding my eardrums.

"Do you not want any?"

"Oh no, I mean, yes. I'd love meat lover's, please," I answered with the propriety of a schoolgirl.

"Next time I'll cook you a real meal," he said. Next time? There was going to be a next time? And . . . he could cook?

"Here are some napkins if you need to blot the grease," he offered. He'd thought of everything!

"Oh, I don't really mind the grease, actually," I said guiltily.

"My kind of woman!" he cheered.

∽

After some sips, slices, some great conversation, and a quick clean up (because he was all about keeping the park eco-friendly), Dan led me across the road and over to the famous

Boathouse. He sidled up to the boat master and slipped him a ten. At that moment, the boat master stepped back to reveal a dilapidated rowboat. Chipped blue paint covered the hull. Inside, two different-sized oars rested on weathered green boards. With an outstretched hand, Dan helped me into the waiting rowboat. I was going to be rowed! What a New York experience! As we pushed out onto the pond, the city fell strangely silent. I could *see* the pathway masseuses waving and calling to the runners, the drinkers reveling and laughing on the Boathouse porch, camera-happy tourists clicking and saying "cheese" by the fountain . . . but all I could *hear* were the pigeons cooing, the crickets singing, and our paddles dipping into the green waters as we pushed off.

At first we careened around in a circle. Dan blamed his overthrown college pitching arm for the uneven distribution of power. I dragged my finger lazily through the still waters until visions of mutant creatures lurking below the opaque surface got the better of me.

The water was a particularly odd shade of green. It wasn't the aquamarine color of the Caribbean or the sublime dark green of the East Coast's Atlantic. No, it was Emerald City green. Bright, strong, and unnatural. Unnatural yet fantastic! It was just so pretty, especially in those photos lined up along the sidewalk for tourists. I leaned to the side hoping that the green would reflect softly in my eyes. Everything around us seemed to pop in contrast.

And did I mention? I was being rowed! The butterflies in my stomach were on some ecstasy spree. Did I mention? I was being rowed! Was I supposed to lounge, recline, offer to grab an oar? I could hear Tara's sexually charged suggestion: "Stroke, stroke, stroke, and stroke!"

"Oh, I almost forgot—" He let the oars idle at his sides.

"There's more?"

"Yep." He bent down and reached inside his backpack, which was now seeming reminiscent of Mary Poppins's magic carpetbag, and pulled out an awkward object sheathed in plastic. Inside was a small delicate plant. And on one branch was perched a beautiful, solitairy, perfect gardenia bloom.

"Oh, my . . ." I said, holding my hand over my mouth in complete shock. Could someone please pinch me? Not only was he holding J. Lo's favorite flower, but it was mine as well. How the heck did he know?

"Is it too much for a first date?" he asked shyly. "Too cheesy? God, I don't want to be cheesy. But I got you a whole plant, pot and all, because I thought it would last longer than a bunch of flowers." I couldn't help but smile.

"I seem to ruin everything though," I murmured, not even sure of what I was saying. Was I referring to our tortured houseplants or to some deep-seated insecurity about relationships?

"Then I'll help you take care of it when I see you. Easier than a pet! You're going to love the scent. These things can last forever!" All I had caught out of his last few sentences were the words, "First date . . . last longer . . . help you . . . care . . . easier . . . love . . . forever."

It was too good to be true, but I wasn't going to question it. And before he could say another word, I leaned in closer to him. Little did he know that the gardenia was more than just a flower, it was a sign. It was a sign from up above, from the Goddess J. Lo herself.

I had come a long way over the past year and now another chapter in my life was waiting to be penned. New York City could have eaten me alive. I had lived in an apartment the size of my big toe and eaten nothing but canned soup until my paycheck went through. We had all cried over the boy that got away, the job that made us feel stupid, the cab driver who took us to the wrong part of town. We had all stood at the bar pretending to wait for someone or be someone. Yet, we, the Dirty Half-Dozen, had decided to combine all that drama with a splash of happiness and resourcefulness to turn the tables and serve it up with a cherry on top. And look at me now! I was being rowed, I had been given a nonpedestrian flower, I had received a promotion at work, I had come to admit that black was indeed a color (not the mere absence of), and I now knew how many ounces were in a quart. I looked up at the dusky sky and sighed. *New York* magazine was full of ideas just for me, a New Yorker; the *New York Times* Metro section was just for me, a New Yorker; the T-shirts and sweatshirts emblazoned with the city's fine name were just for me . . . and all the other 13,999,999 urbanites. I didn't just love NY, I was NY!

I am NY! I wanted to scream from the top of my lungs in the middle of Central Park. Instead I just let the high-wattage happiness beam from my smile.

The sun began to set as Dan the Man rowed, not showing any sign of slowing down. Even as the natural light escaped the city's skyline, I felt a warm glow radiate all around me. I felt bathed in sunshine despite the evening sky above us.

So ladies all around the world, listen up! We've all encountered burnt meals, wicked exes, bitchy bosses, and bad hangovers. But really, life is a dish to be savored. And no matter what your own personal recipe entails, you can't lose if you include three simple ingredients: good friends, sunshine, and orgasms.

Bon appétit!